# FIDDLERS THREE

## & OTHER STORIES

# FIDDLERS THREE

## & OTHER STORIES

ARTHUR RICE

BREWIN BOOKS

First published by
Brewin Books Ltd, 56 Alcester Road,
Studley, Warwickshire B80 7LG in 2011

www.brewinbooks.com



ISBN: 978-1-85858-448-5



A Cataloguing in Publication Record
for this title is available from the British Library.

Typeset in Baskerville
Printed in Great Britain by
Hobbs the Printers Ltd.

# CONTENTS

# *One*

# JOHN NOT JACK

The day after the murder everyone was talking about Jack the Ripper. This was nowhere more true than in Bedlam Asylum where John and Agnes Penman had been inmates since 1872. John Penman was upset, he remarked to his twin sister "I was christened John and always called John, I don't like being referred to as Jack".

Agnes replied "Everyone here knows you are a 'John' but I do know how it offends your sense of dignity. John the Ripper would sound much more dignified but of course no one knows we are the perpetrators. It must stay that way of course." John nodded vehemently.

* * * * *

The brother and sister twins had been inseparable since birth. They left Whitechapel Elementary School in 1850 three years after their father, a postman, had died of a severe mental disorder. John and Agnes Penman had lived in Bedlam Asylum since 1872 and had just passed their 50th birthday.

"Do you remember our first week at work?" Agnes continued. John was seriously ill, the same age as his father when he died in the same asylum three years after the young Queen ascended the throne in 1837. After many years at Bedlam John had been promoted to a small side room off a main ward of seventy people in Albert Ward. His twin sister had an identical room next to him. John nodded,

"The worst week of our lives".

"Yes, but you made up for it dear," she answered. Her brother smiled and said

"That detective James Munro never got anywhere near the truth. Look at all the suspects, an American doctor visiting from Ohio, the Duke of Clarence, that confidence trickster Michael Ostrog. They involved the Jewish community which you and I are not a part of. Yes, in retrospect we outwitted the police and the establishment. Remember, Agnes, when that chap Sherlock Holmes brought his doctor friend to examine Michael Ostrog, just in the ward opposite to us, we heard everything. They talked to him for two hours. It was obvious that they couldn't get anything out of Michael, the man was completely mad. Mr Holmes eventually appreciated the position and terminated the interview, but it caused us some merriment that the actual perpetrators were only four yards from the law at that stage."

Agnes wiped her brother's brow with a damp cloth; he was perspiring profusely, his temperature had risen to a hundred and four. "I'm cooling you down dear." John was now rambling. "Those six slags received everything they deserved. When they abused you and me little did they know they were playing with very dangerous fire. We thought we were lucky to get jobs at the Pennyfarthing Bicycle Company when we left school. In the paintshop," said Agnes, "I remember the manager taking us on and saying 'work hard and you'll be promoted'. On our first day that fat piece of feminine slobbiness, Martha Tabram, got hold of you and the other five held you down while she used the paint stripping gun on all your private parts after they'd stripped naked.

What a cheek she had only a few weeks ago demanding two shillings before she would sexually perform. Still, after you'd dealt with her I soon relieved her of that and the one and sixpence she had in her purse. I've always looked on that as a fine for how she abused us in the paintshop." John nodded "It was when they did it to you that it fired me, and then they pushed us out covered in striped paint all over our bodies and genitals into the main assembly area that was full of workers laughing and shouting at us, 'What a big one for a little chap!' the foreman said. It was humiliating. Those women didn't know what was going to hit them. We were fortunate the manager of the assembly shop was a man of mercy and he transferred us to the chain making department where they didn't have such sadistic creatures."

Agnes nodded, "It was a terrible tragedy when the bicycle manufacturing company went out of existence the following year. It's no good manufacturing a fine machine if the selling organisation is of a poor quality. When the sales manager and his team left to go to the Hercules Bicycle Works in Bow it was the beginning of the end for the Runwell. If you remember the Pennyfarthing Company was finally laid low when Hercules used the first blow up tyres with inner tubes instead of solid rubber. The directors at the Pennyfarthing said they would never catch on. What a huge mistake."

John replied "Yes, I didn't know what we were to do when the company closed, but I remember it was the first time I saw mother cry when we went home and announced we'd lost our jobs."

"Well," Agnes retorted "you gained that job at Smithfield Meat Market within a week of being unemployed. Then you obtained a position for me in the office, admittedly a year after, but a job that lasted nearly twenty years must have been right for us. Mother did magnificently well to provide for us on her tiny widow's pension due from Dad's old job at the Post Office and washing clothes for the gentry."

"The six women who worked in the paintshop were not so fortunate were they Agnes?" Agnes shook her head and John continued. "They hadn't got a trade in their fingers, none of them. They'd been taught with that paintgun, so when they were let go from Pennyfarthing they had problems making ends meet. They took any menial job they could, cleaners, washerwomen, hawking, and that meant opportunist thieving. Then they had to fence the stolen goods with the Shylocks of Cripplegate Alley who gave virtually nothing for them. I suppose the women's' main earnings were from selling their bodies. It was degrading, but that's the type of women they were. None of them had any decent male support, and they were perpetually drunk on 'mother's ruin'." Agnes nodded, "Yes you need a trade in the East End; it's all right for the toffs in the West End, they have money behind them, but down here extra ability makes the difference between life and death."

* * * * *

As evening progressed the perspiration was oozing from John's brow. His shirt was sodden, a progression of influenza germs were biting into his system and had been since the twins had galloped the half mile from Millers Yard in a thunderstorm. After dealing with Mary Kelly, their last victim, John had sweated excessively and then slept in his outside clothing. He had awoken with a chill in the damp November air. Agnes was cajoling him "Come on John smile, smile please, just for me." He shook himself and mumbled to his sister "Yes, I had a good teacher at Smithfield. Oliver Stanley was the best cutter of an animal in the whole of Smithfield Market. Taught me everything I know." His sister said "Yes, your experience was vital when we dished out our retribution to those abusers. I'll never forget the look on Martha Tabram's face when she thought you were a half-a-crown punter and the meat cleaver did its work." John nodded, "Yes you were a fine lookout, Agnes, I'm sure I would've been caught except for your vigilance." John whispered,

"We've been here nineteen years now and carrying out our activities from where we're sitting didn't give the police much hope of catching us. All I did was to go into the meat kitchen and borrow the tools of my trade, the type I always used at Smithfield. They carry a fine array of knives and cutting instruments here. It was quite easy to borrow a suitable knife and cleaver. When we caught Mary Kelly soliciting in Millers Yard I thought we were lucky. She didn't recognise us, of course. Being used to cutting up animals at Smithfield, especially sows, gave me a handier start; I even laid her innards out near her feet – you do that when pigs are killed. The public love pigs trotters and we had to lay them at the end of the carcass after cutting the dead animal into various set pieces. The gentry had the best cuts, the scrag ends were left for the people of the East End." His sister replied "She showed me no mercy in that paintshop, she jammed the paintstripper right between my legs and then let fly with the full load of red paint. It was a long time before I became myself again. You did a really fine job with her. It was then I was feeling a little envious, I thought perhaps I could do the next one and you be the lookout."

"Yes I know you had intentions that way but really it's a trained man's job."

"You were such a good lookout. I'd scarcely finished the cutting and chopping of Polly Nicholls when you whispered a nightwatchman was walking up Dutfield Alley. We were lucky it was still dark.

I read in the 'News Chronicle' that she'd been turned out of her lodgings and was looking for a punter to give her the four shillings she needed for a night's bed and breakfast." His sister answered "Yes dear, we could've put her up in the next room free and gratis." Her brother nodded but didn't interrupt. "It was that John which gave us the confidence to carry on and seek out the next two victims.

We were lucky to be able to walk the streets by locking our doors and slipping through the cavity after you painstakingly removed the window pane. When we were on the outside replacing it no-one ever knew of our absence. Moving back afterwards was never a problem, merely replacing the pane after we were back in our rooms, a very good wheeze."

"Yes, Agnes, I could never accept you doing one despite your protestations. You were an amateur, I had had a full apprenticeship of cutting up every animal; after all humans aren't too different. It's quite easy to cut and disembowel a human. I could've done the same had it've been men we were involved with. It was just a matter of replacing a pig for a sow in my mind when it came to the actual deed. But when you did it Agnes and I stood lookout, you went in and killed very quickly. This wasn't what I envisaged when we started the operation. The one you did was fortunate, she died quickly, the other five felt our retribution to the full. I let you have your way to kill Annie Chapman. You did a reasonable job considering you hadn't had the experience of mauling and killing animals at Smithfield. There's not much difference you know with a human, but whereas I knew what I was doing, where to cut, you slashed away in any direction. But the five I did had artistic merit. You surely remember reading the book 'Blood and Sand' about the bullfighters of Spain? Bullfighting in Spain is their national pastime, well more than a pastime it's a religious ritual. The book said the better bullfighters were the ones that killed slowly, artistically, and had the bull begging for the final coup de grace; the bull would stand there waiting, hoping, wanting to die and that was the high merit mark of the first division bullfighters. Those lower down the scale, the second division bullfighters who fought in the poorer and smaller arenas, usually killed far quicker. Anyone can kill a bull, I could, but it's the way it's done and I think I did an artistic job with the five women I dealt with, whereas yours was a quick job." Agnes answered his criticism "Yes, John, but I knew that woman had put the paintstripping machine into my body. Believe me, I wasn't thinking of artistic merit. It gave me great pleasure regardless of how quickly I did it to see her legs covered in not red paint but very red blood."

Her brother replied "Yes, dear, I appreciate what you mean but you do realise I couldn't let you loose on another one. You were too quick and they could have squealed and shrieked. They thought I was doing them a favour until it was too late."

Still it's now been two months since we finished the job. It completed the whole six who were involved with our humiliation. What strange stories the newspapers can come up with, I suppose they've got to print something but they were so far from the truth weren't they? The story about the Duke of Clarence being unstable, a throwback to his grandmother's insanity they said. It wasn't insanity with her she was just afraid of childbirth, only had one, told the old Queen she'd never have another unless she could buy it at Fortnum and Mason."

Agnes interrupted "Yes dear, but the piece in the newspaper that really hurt your feelings was the letter in the 'News Chronicle' signed 'Jack the Ripper' which stated he would mutilate many more women in a rough and crude way. To us it was an obvious hoax letter from a joker, but the newspaper and the police treated it seriously. No-one has ever called you Jack, you were John to Mother and myself and have always carried yourself with great dignity."

John's chest was heaving, he was now in an agony torment, he was coughing continually, lungs heaving. "I don't think I'm going to last the night, Agnes."

"Come on, John, you can do it, you can get through this, you've been through some terrible things in life, we both have, we've stuck by each other. Come on, pull yourself round."

"I'm trying Agnes," wheezed John, but his breathing was becoming slower and weaker. She cradled his head in her hands, there was nothing more she could do. His head fell back, he was breathing no longer. Agnes couldn't come to terms with the situation, "Come on, wake up, wake up John!" After a few minutes she realised it was a fruitless exercise, there was no more life, pneumonia had claimed yet another victim of the asylum. Agnes screamed at the top of her voice. An orderly from the general ward came in. Death in Bedlam Asylum was an everyday occurrence. It was treated without emotion. The nursing staff roughly lifted John Penman and carried him to the mortuary three flights below the main wards into the cellars.

* * * * *

John's funeral service was in the asylum's private church at St. Bartholomew's. There were few mourners. The Bursar represented the Master of the asylum and Mrs Ingram, the Master's wife, was also in attendance. Agnes was the only other mourner. The service, although highly religious, took only seven minutes.

With the accompaniment of the vicar, four inmates acted as pallbearers who carried John's coffin to the pauper's graveyard. After the internment Agnes walked from the graveside to the asylum with Mrs Ingram.

"I'm very sorry to see you alone now, my dear," the Master's wife remarked "what will you do?"

"Oh I'm content enough," said Agnes "I have my own room attached to Albert Ward, I shall get along all right. In fact my mind seems to have eased somewhat since John died it was very stressful caring for my brother who was more ill than I was throughout our formative years." Mrs Ingram looked at her. Agnes' face was cleanly scrubbed her hair brushed with a good clean parting, very different from the rag-tag appearance of many of the wretches in Albert Ward. She further noticed Agnes' shoes had been cleanly polished, her knee length stockings were black lisle and of smart appearance. Her loose fitting dress, again cleanly washed, put her considerably above the appearance and demeanour of an average patient who was filthy and unkempt.

"What did you do before you came here dear?" asked Mrs Ingram.

"Oh, John and myself worked for a wholesale butcher in Smithfield Market. John worked in the preparing room and slaughterhouse, I worked in the office keeping the books."

"Oh?" said a surprised Bursar who had joined them. "Yes, do you think you could report to my office tomorrow? At the moment our bookkeeper is away ill and it's probable she may not return but come down, have a look at us. If the job isn't suitable we could always keep you on as a cleaner if you're happy to do that?"

"Oh yes", said Agnes eagerly, work was virtually impossible to find for inmates.

Agnes presented herself at 9 o'clock sharp at the Bursar's office the following morning. She was shown the thick bound ledgers held together with a steel clasp at the back. It needed some considerable strength to manipulate these but Agnes had handled books very similar at Smithfield. She was presented with the expenses payments vouchers and was asked to make a list of the cheques that should be paid out at the month's end to companies and organisations that supplied the asylum with their services. Some were for food, cleaning materials and several sundry items.

There was a gas bill from the Robin Mantle Company. The Bursar remarked "It looks as though the Robin Mantle Company will shortly be out of business. They're refusing to acknowledge they have a rival in this new fangled electric bulb that Mr Edison, a Scotsman in America, has invented." Agnes' mind flashed back to the Pennyfarthing Company and the pneumatic tyre.

"Oh I do hope they learn their lesson and convert to an electric bulb."

It was only a short time before it became apparent that Agnes knew her way around the bookkeeping system. She could even use the double entry system and make the accounts balance. When the Bursar required a letter typing on the newly invented typewriting machine he found Agnes equal to the task. He was amazed when she told him that many years ago she had attended classes in Regent Street on the corner of Albemarie Street, run by Mr. Pitman who had invented a quick method of writing. The Bursar realised he had a little gem.

After six months' hard work Agnes' mind had improved; the deep stresses caused by placating and humouring John over the many years they had been together, had disappeared. Her new job had brought a light to her life, she had put on weight due to the extra food that she was now given as a staff member. The

Master noted the difference and the improvement in the Bursar's usefulness who was now free of menial tasks and able to devote more time to decision making.

The Master asked the doctor in charge of the medical side of the asylum to examine Agnes. The results were astounding.

"There's nothing the matter with this woman." the doctor informed the Master. "She's very alert, very sharp. I wish she had a medical knowledge instead of any accounting one, she'd soon be on my staff."

"Why has she been here for nineteen years then?" queried the Master. The Medical Officer replied "I saw an article in 'The Lancet' a few months ago which gave the psychiatric reason in the case known as the 'Corsican Brothers'. One brother, although on the island of Corsica, could feel the happenings to his twin brother in mainland France. If the brother in France suffered a pain it transmitted to his twin in Corsica, but not the other way round. It was not until the French twin was killed in a duel, he was a soldier in the King's household, that the Corsican brother had his mind freed. Although be suffered excruciatingly when the sword was lunged into his twin. I feel there was something similar with John and Agnes Penman. The umbilical cords entwined in their mother's womb and Agnes was under the domination of her psychiatrically ill brother. When he died this domination died with him. I have made a study of twins' behaviour together with my friend Sherlock Holmes and I concluded that this is the reason for the mind-freeing of Agnes."

"Thank you Doctor Watson" said the Asylum Master.

Agnes heard the explanation of the learned doctor and knew he was right. All her life had been dominated by her brother's psychiatric condition. The following week Agnes received her discharge papers. The Bursar immediately offered her a position on the permanent workforce of the asylum and the opportunity to live in the staff quarters which were situated a quarter of a mile outside the asylum building near Cheapside. The buildings were furnished. There was domestic staff to clean and provide meals. The job was joyful, Agnes was immersed in her work.

Agnes Penman had many years of happiness, dying in her sleep the same night that Queen Victoria passed away two years into the new Century.

# *Two*

# LUCAN – A CONCLUSION

FACT: Lord Lucan was last seen in Uckfield, Sussex, on 7th November 1974.
FICTION: What happened thereafter? See the script.

* * * * *

Lord Lucan swung his Jaguar XJ Sport into Berkeley Square at 2.30 a.m. He parked in a spot not metered at this time of the morning. The return journey from Uckfield in Sussex had taken a little over an hour. He walked the sixty yards to the entrance of the Rouge et Noir Casino and nodded to the doorman dressed in a costume that would have done credit to a marching soldier in a West End musical: three cornered black hat with gold braid, tunic with as much gold as black, trousers to match with highly polished black boots.

"Morning Jock," said Lucan. "Mild for this time of the year."

"Yes m'Lord, it's time we heard the nightingale sing," came the reply. An old chestnut Lucan had heard from him many times.

Ordering a large vodka and orange, he sat on a bar stool taking in the scene. There was a good crowd in tonight. Ten roulette wheels noisily chattered. The marker balls continuously spun. The wheel turners were women in low cut dresses, an attraction to the many tired men. Fresh croupiers were always more than a match for weary punters.

At 3 a.m. there was a change of staff. This shift made the house its biggest financial killing. Lucan was in no mood to gamble.

Hugh Pennington-Dyke tapped him on the shoulder, "You're daydreaming, old chap, your glass is nearly empty, time for another."

"Thank you, the usual please. See the Sultan of Sierra Grunn is in tonight," Lucan exclaimed. "He always has a following when he's in town. The Casino should charge a fee to watch him play. It's the high stakes he plays for, that's the attraction."

His friend replied, "Yes, I hear he lost three million pounds on Christmas Eve and made back over two million on Boxing Day. Where do they get that sort of money, John?"

"No idea, I think it must grow in oil barrels beneath the sand of Sierra Grunn," Lucan remarked.

"Your wife's not in tonight is she?"

Lucan shook his head. "No, not expecting her. How about Lucy?"

"No, she's let me have a night on my own. I wish she was with me, I wouldn't have gambled so much. She's a restraining influence. When she's here I say I'd have won more, but it's a certain fact that when she's not here I lose more."

Lucan replied, "This place makes the most money per square yard of anywhere in the West End. Even the nightclub in the cellars of this building at their extortionate prices is a minnow compared with this for profitability." Lucan called a Casino hostess who was squeezed into a bunny outfit two sizes too small, to bring a plate of sandwiches. "I like this Club, Hugh, I'd certainly miss it."

"Why, where are you going?" asked his friend. Lucan merely smiled and walked over to where the Sultan was playing. The Sultan knew Lucan of old.

"What's a lucky number tonight John?"

From the depths of Lucan's subconscious a number loomed as clear and sharp as the Sultan's eyes, "Seventeen...red," he said, and the Sultan placed three high value chips on that number which, by the grace of the oil gods, won twice consecutively. Lucan smiled grimly and walked on. The house wouldn't thank him for giving away that titbit of information. His six feet five inch frame, luxuriant moustache, brown piercing eyes and a demeanour that would have done credit to an Archbishop, he gave the impression of a Chairman of a top P.L.C.

In reality Lucan was a gambler, a waster of money, and deeply in debt to moneylenders.

* * * * *

After a further two hours and four more vodkas and orange he was anaesthetised enough to carry on with his plan. Lucan walked to the lift hall on the fourth floor. Coincidentally his wife's cousin, Jim Mortimer, was also leaving the casino. Lucan's lips parted in a humourless smile. He said, "Hello Jim, how are you?"

"Oh, not too bad, I won a few pounds tonight, enough to allow me back tomorrow night. It's sad we civil servants don't get the pay of a noble lord like yourself." He looked hard at Lucan and continued, "You're looking a bit down in the mouth, John, anything the matter?"

"I've had a bad night, I've had a bad time. It's weird, as if I've had a blackout or something like that I seem to have lost the last few hours, my mind's a complete blank. I heard on the car radio the police would like me to contact them."

Mortimer had heard the midnight news in the rest room at the casino. There had been a terrible murder in London's West End.

"Good lord John, so where are you off to now?"

Lucan hesitated. "I think I'll walk down to the police station at Piccadilly Circus. I feel something's not quite right, but I just can't put my finger on it."

Mortimer was suspicious, he must 'phone his cousin. He took Lucan by the arm and said, "Come round to the office."

The elevator, a long time arriving, opened its doors.

* * * * *

The 'office' was two hundred yards past the Washington Hotel in Curzon Street, opposite the archway to Shepherds Market. It was a large brick building, built in the early thirties to house MI6, the organisation dealing with government level external security matters. It was the headquarters to which overseas field agents reported. The seven floors above ground gave the innocent impression of a normal West End office block, but the five underground floors had a more sinister purpose.

The building was at the summit of its use during the Second World War, taking the overflow of enemy refugees from Traitors Gate at the Tower of London. Only organisation members, the Prime Minister of the day and his predecessors knew it existed.

Mortimer led the way to the lowest underground floor, opened a door and ushered Lucan through. When Lucan was clear of the swinging door, Mortimer crashed it into place, locked and bolted it from the outside. Cell Number 8 now contained one of the top peers of the day.

Lucan had to stoop, the cell was a six foot square box. A 2'6" wide bed from wall to wall meant reclining with bended knees. He spent twenty minutes hammering the door for Mortimer to return, before realising it was a hopeless operation. A toilet in one corner flushed directly into a sewer beneath Mayfair. It was the same with the wash basin in the far corner from the door. He cursed his great height and wished his parents had been titled circus dwarfs.

* * * * *

Dawn was breaking as Jim Mortimer telephoned his cousin, Veronica Lucan, in Belgravia, fearing the worst. He was shocked to hear her voice after only one ring.

"What's happened, dear?" he asked.

"The bastard's murdered Sandra. He must have thought it was me. We both have auburn hair."

"Have you reported it to the police?"

"Yes, hours ago. We've a couple of detectives in now, where he is I haven't a clue. He went off in the Jaguar and was last seen bolting out of the West End at about 11 o'clock this evening. I know he called at Uckfield, I've just had Lucy Pennington-Dyke on the 'phone. He called to see Hugh, gabbled on incoherently. She persuaded him to return to London."

"How are the children?"

"They're all right. He didn't touch them."

"Are you certain it was him?" Mortimer asked.

A badly shaken Veronica replied, "It was dark in the corridor and the nanny's screams were horrific. I'm certain he was the attacker. Who else could it have been, Jim?"

* * * * *

Lucan was left in his cell without any explanation. He ate and drank at normal mealtimes: jailers were seconded from the Tower for the express purpose. It needed three jailers to restrain Lucan each time his door was opened to allow him to exercise. At no time were his handcuffs removed outside the cell but on one occasion he threw himself down the stone stairs leading from the exercise court yard, not injuring himself badly but bruising and grazing his knees and hands. A first aid box was left in his cell which he constantly ignored. His constant abusive language made the jailers aware he would not accept his present position without a bitter struggle.

Mortimer was talking to his chief. "Sir, what can we do about Lucan? No-one outside the building knows his whereabouts. After locking him up, I drove his Jag. from Berkeley Square to Newhaven and left it in the docks, returning, on an early morning commuter train. The newspapers have picked up the story that he's crossed the Channel to Dieppe. There've been sightings all over Europe and even one from Rio; the public have vivid imaginations. Some busybodies report anyone over 6' 4" who has a bristling moustache as being the swine. Although it's only been a few days my cousin is a changed person from the morose creature she was. I think we should try him and if he's guilty take the appropriate action. We have the method available."

His chief replied "We can't just kill a peer of the realm. He has every right to be tried by the House of Lords. What little I know of Lucan he wouldn't do the honourable thing, he would exploit the whole situation and live in luxury whilst the trial was on. Certainly he'd plead 'not guilty', he wouldn't mind embarrassing his family and friends. No, he wouldn't do the decent thing. With friends in high places he could escape the full rigours of the law."

Mortimer replied, "Nobody in this building has any rights. You know of the summary executions that have happened. The spies that came over from Norway to Scotland were debriefed within these walls; British agents selling secrets to the Russians in the Cold War were sent to meet their Maker from here."

"You're being over-dramatic. Wartime was a very different kettle of fish to a peacetime environment."

Mortimer said, "The execution chamber is still functional, the hemp rope could be replaced by a silk one."

The chief of external security shook his head. "No, we must take this further through the Establishment."

* * * * *

The telephone line to 10 Downing Street was red hot. An appointment was made. The Prime Minister called the following morning; he was aghast at the facts related by Jim Mortimer, who had interrogated Lucan again for six hours the previous day. "I think he should hang," he remarked heatedly.

The Prime Minister nodded. "He's certainly let the side down, it's not what you expect from a noble lord. His great grandfather who led the Light Brigade at Sebastapol would have been devastated. A British hero a hundred and thirty years ago, and now his great grandson is a waster, living on gambling and borrowed money. The estates that the Crown bestowed on his family after the Peninsula Wars are mortgaged to the hilt. It's exactly this type of peer that gets members of my own party fired up. It fuels their reasons to abolish the House of Lords. The Home Secretary remarked to me only last week it's people like Lucan who show that peers of the realm are no different to commoners. Joe is on the extreme left of our party but it takes all sorts to make a decision."

"I'll talk to the Lord Chancellor for a legal opinion. The facts will need to be dressed up. No-one outside of this room must know the eventual decision, except Morrish of course."

The Prime Minister put on his white mackintosh and left puffing his pipe.

* * * * *

Lucan was a blubbering shell of a man. Mortimer had maliciously informed him he was likely to hang.

"Can I see my wife," Lucan requested, "and my children?"

"There's no way that's going to happen," he was told.

The building contained a labyrinth of tunnels and add-ons to the original construction. Escalators covered the twelve floors at great speed. Each security department had a floor to themselves, but the section dealing with the Eastern bloc and the Cold War had two complete floors with a staff of a hundred and ninety-five. All personnel had to be cleared at high security level. A large conference room was located on the first floor underground. This doubled as a courtroom. The interrogation unit, complete with instruments of persuasion, was on the lowest underground floor next to the cell block.

Lucan had recovered his composure and was demanding to be charged or let free. Every British citizen has the right of 'Habeas Corpus' going back to the Magna Carta, and he was demanding that this be implemented.

Jim Mortimer had deaf ears.

* * * * *

Mortimer's chief called at Downing Street. The Prime Minister said he had put a hypothetical ease to the Lord Chancellor, who informed him any peer accused of murder would be summoned to attend a court in the House of Lords. Their Lordships had full power to decide punishment if a guilty verdict were found.

The Prime Minister continued, "In the Honours List, which coincidentally is to be published tonight, you're to become Lord Jenkins of Mayfair. If you wish to try the man and move the courtroom from the House of Lords to an address in your jurisdiction, I shall have no objection."

* * * * *

In a small terraced house, one of a row of twelve only half a mile from Liverpool's Lime Street Station, a thick set, slim waisted man was answering the telephone. His broad shoulders were what had drawn him to his original work. A droopy moustache covered his upper lip, sharp, wiry eyes flashed with quick reflexes. His body and mind fitted his former work. He spoke in monosyllables.

"Yes, I could do that. Yes, I appreciate it's been six years since my last job but you don't lose the knack. You say it may or may not occur but I'd best be there, I appreciate the position. Yes, I'll bring my tools with me. Thank you for calling." Turning to his wife he said, "Sheila, at last they're bringing me out of redundancy. Only a one off, but with the prospect of a change of government you never know what might happen."

"Marvellous, darling. I'm delighted for you, Alfred, these last few years have been a terrible drag. It shows it was nothing personal when they let you go, to still think of you now."

Alfred nodded emotionally, "Yes, yes, it is satisfying."

Sheila telephoned her mother and asked her to pick up the two children from nursery school. This accomplished, Alfred took his wife on a celebratory lunch to the Italian restaurant they used on high days and holidays; red wine and pasta, a marvellous combination to concentrate the mind. "Happy days are here again," she murmured as they clinked their raised glasses.

The world had turned full circle, he was needed again. He packed a suitcase with two changes of clothing. He wasn't certain how long he would be away. A taxi took them to Lime Street. He was in plenty of time to board the 12.15 p.m. for the three hour journey to London Euston. Sheila gave her husband a loving last kiss.

"Do a good job Alfred, I want to hear all about it when you return."

He took the tube to Green Park, then walked the last half mile of his journey.

* * * * *

Lucan was having an increasingly uncomfortable time in a cell designed for a much smaller individual. He was exercised at gunpoint. Sometimes in these periods he merely gazed through the short grille window which overlooked Berkeley Square. By craning his neck he could see the flamboyantly dressed doorman at the

Rouge et Noir still smiling and telling the well-heeled patrons that he had heard the nightingale sing last evening. It shouldn't be too long before he heard those sonorous tones again. This scene had been an inherent part of his life.

The Square was a circle. The three feet high railings enclosed a three acre green sward. Couples courted there during the summer months. It was a first class dining carpet for the office staffs overlooking the square. Parking meters completely surrounded the perimeter. Traffic wardens buzzed in the most prolific profit-earning meter area the City of Westminster had under its jurisdiction. It was the heart of the 'Old Empire' that colonialists remembered with fondness and affection; the further their distance from Britain the greater their passion for the Square.

* * * * *

In blue denim prison uniform, navy blue shirt buttoned at the neck, shackled and handcuffed, Lucan hobbled up the steps to the courtroom. It seemed as though he had lost eight inches in height. His air of authority had completely vanished. Lucan was a far cry from the upstanding ex-guards officer of four weeks ago. He had allowed a beard to grow and his shoulders were hunched.

James Mortimer was to bring the case for the prosecution. Lucan had disdained the offer of a defence lord, saying he was capable of defending himself, vehemently shouting that a man who had not committed any crime could not be guilty.

In addition to the principals there were two armed jailers, one of whom Lucan vaguely recognised but couldn't give a name to. Lord Jenkins, as the presiding judge, hammered the gavel and said, "This Court is now in session." He addressed the prisoner, "Lord Lucan, on either side of myself you will observe Lords Robson and Dryden, both eminent members of the criminal Bar. The three of us constitute a quorum and are empowered by the Lords Criminal Act 1679, an Act promulgated by Oliver Cromwell after the Lords rebelled against his regime following the Battle of Monmouth."

Lucan replied "It's the first time I've heard of this."

Jenkins answered, "The Act has not been used since 1916 when the Irish peer Lord Tom Burke was tried for treason during World War One. He was found guilty by his peers and hanged at Pentonville Jail two months later. He did have the benefit of a silk rope to differentiate him from a commoner."

Lucan replied, "But that can't happen to me. The death penalty was abolished five years ago."

Lord Dryden interrupted. "It was indeed abolished for fifty six million commoners but the Lords Amendment Bill of 1679 was overlooked. An amendment to the Capital Punishment Abolition Act of 1969 is due to be voted on shortly to remove capital punishment to members of the House of Lords. It is likely to happen early next year, but as the Law now stands if you're found guilty the death penalty can be exercised by this Court."

Lucan's face turned a paler shade of white, "Surely I'll get a Royal Pardon?" he demanded.

Lord Robson commented, "You have not been found guilty yet, but I've heard it said the present monarch is in favour of restoration of capital punishment so don't place too much faith in that direction." Lucan looked around like a rat searching for a way out of a sinking ship.

Lord Jenkins hammered the gavel, "This Court is now in session. Do you, Lord Lucan, plead 'guilty' or 'not guilty' to the murder of Sandra Rivett on the seventh day of November 1974?"

Lucan replied in a scarcely audible whisper, "Not guilty."

The presiding Judge asked, "Did you intend to kill your wife?"

"I didn't kill my wife."

"No, but the nanny was killed."

"I don't remember doing it," Lucan replied. "I went to the house and let myself in so that I could tell the children a story before they went to sleep. My wife saw me and shouted at me to leave the premises. We had a stand-up row. I love my children and was desperate to see them. On the way out of the house my wife berated me for entering without her permission as the custody court had directed. I shouted at her that the verdict had only come about because of a crooked lawyer and a non-caring magistrate. It had been a set up. After the heated row she burst into tears and dashed down the dark passage to the front door. I was emotionally disturbed and my mind was fading. I vaguely saw a woman returning along the passage before I had a complete blackout. I have no recollection of what happened afterwards."

Lord Jenkins interjected, "There is an inference that you killed the woman coming towards you. You say you had a blackout and know nothing. Assuming you killed the woman coming towards you, after you blacked out but were still physically strong, does it seem like manslaughter to you?"

Lucan said, "I suppose it would if I'd done it, but there's this huge doubt. There were other people who had access to the house, not only me. Why did it have to be a man who killed Sandra?"

The prosecutor asked the Judge's permission to speak. "It was not your wife who returned, it was Sandra Rivett and you mistook her for Lady Lucan. The intention was clear you meant to kill your wife; the fact that it was another person makes no difference. You're guilty of first degree murder."

The Judge berated the prosecutor. "If you don't stop these accusations you will be removed from the court." Mortimer apologised. The Judge ordered the interjection to be struck from the court record.

Lord Dryden asked, "Why did you run to Sussex if you didn't commit the crime?"

"As I say, I had a complete blackout and had no coherent knowledge of events until I spoke to Lucy Pennington-Dyke in Uckfield. She snapped me out of the trance and advised me to return to London."

James Mortimer was asked if he had any further comments. "It's perfectly plain that the lady was murdered. The prisoner is talking of manslaughter but when a person is struck seventeen times, manslaughter, which is accidental death, went out of the window on the second blow. I ask the learned Judge to pass a murder verdict and look for a sentence that applies the full rigours of the law."

Lucan's eyes were now deeply embedded and red-rimmed, his shoulders even more hunched.

"No, no, it didn't happen," he insisted. "Even in my Army days I never killed anybody."

The Court was adjourned for the day.

* * * * *

The second day's hearing opened at 10 a.m. The Judge's summing up took over an hour. He reiterated the case fully and leaned heavily on the fact of multiple blows. When he considered the assumption of Lucan having a blackout he said,

"The accused's school and Army records contain no reference to a history of blackouts. The House of Lords annual medical examination details were also examined, again no reference to blackouts or emotional stress that would cause loss of memory. Harley Street was asked for an opinion as to whether amnesia or blackouts would apply to a person with the medical history I have outlined. Three eminent doctors gave separate opinions after examining the evidence that blackouts or amnesia are most unlikely to occur in the circumstances." He then addressed Lucan directly.

"Having heard your evidence and that of the prosecutor, and with our own knowledge of the case, the three judges empowered by the House of Lords give a unanimous verdict that you are guilty of murder."

Lucan cried out, "No! No! You know that can't be!"

The presiding judge asked Lucan if there were any mitigating circumstances before sentence was pronounced. Lucan, recovering slightly, stated, "My marriage had collapsed. There had been a well publicised court case regarding the custody of my children, all of whom I dearly love. I felt the divorce court should have given me custody. I'm much more rational than my wife. The decision went against me, I'll never know why. What matters is the upbringing of my children. Mortimer was about to interrupt but the presiding judge raised an arm that suggested silence.

Lord Robson placed a black cap on the presiding judge's head. Lucan was shaking visibly, grasping the rail in front of the prisoners' box.

"You have been found guilty of the murder of Sandra Rivett and you are sentenced to die by hanging. There is no appeal against a House of Lords verdict and the monarch of the day has given a pledge not to intervene. The sentence to be carried out immediately."

* * * * *

Lucan's ankles were unshackled but the handcuffs remained. The armed jailers turned him round and pushed him down some steps to a hidden exit. They ran him along a corridor to an open doorway and he was hustled to the top of more steps onto a platform. The ankle shackles were replaced. He was in the centre of the platform, the silk rope above his head.

The presiding judge instructed the hangman to place a blindfold around Lucan's eyes.

"Take that thing away!" barked Lucan in a final act of defiance.

The presiding judge asked, "Do you, Lord Lucan, born Richard John Bingham, have any last words?"

Lucan blurted, "I'm not the criminal, you are, you're murdering an innocent man!"

"I am not in a position to argue with you," was the reply.

A Church of England bishop was on hand to administer the last rites. "Have great faith, you will meet your Maker sooner then the rest of this assembly and I'm sure he will bring peace to you."

Lucan shouted, "I'm too young to meet him!"

"Calm yourself; my son," said the purple shirted bishop. Lucan was in mid-speech, blaspheming at the court, the officials, the bishop, when Alfred Morrish pushed a handkerchief into his mouth. Simultaneously, his left hand pushed a lever. Lord Lucan dropped through the hole. The loose silk rope stiffened with a distinct suddenness. A deafening crack resounded through the chamber. The grim operation had been concluded, the Court's verdict implemented.

The following morning, on the lowest floor of the building, London's oldest working incinerator completed a macabre task.

* * * * *

Beneath the grand crystal chandelier, which had cost the Washington Hotel more than they could afford, placed there to celebrate the second millennium that had occurred six months previously, an irate guest was berating Emma, the oversized, bubbly blonde receptionist.

"That Kanga hammer has ruined our stay and the dust has choked us. We only came yesterday. We're leaving now. I shall be suing the hotel for this."

"Sorry, sir, please don't. Several other guests felt the same and I've transferred them to our sister hotel in Bayswater. You won't be out of pocket. I told the manager not to let any rooms during the demolition period." Her plump figure shook with compassion.

"What demolition period are you talking about?"

"The building that's being knocked down was the former headquarters of MI6, the spy and security network. They say James Bond reported to M there," she continued, believing the gibes of the demolition workers. The guest's wife joined in.

"How spooky. What did they find? I'll bet that building hides a history of mystery."

Emma continued, "The building's being reduced to rubble, completely flattened. The underfloor rooms have been filled with ready mixed concrete and it's taken a hundred lorries three months to complete the operation. We're sending over breakfasts to all the workmen during the three year length of the operation and the foreman tells me the underground floors were a rabbit warren. Apparently when MI6 needed more space, another floor was built beneath London. They've dug deeper into the bowels of the earth than in any other excavation in the capital. The demolition workers took much more time to demolish the underground floors than the upper floors. They just couldn't get the Kanga hammer down there."

"Thank goodness for that, the noise would have been criminal," the woman spouted.

Emma replied, "In its heyday the building was used to debrief people who entered the country illegally during wartime. In 1990 over eight hundred people worked there, but since the Cold War with the Russians finished over ten years ago its use has been minimal and the building virtually unused. On the bottom floor there were even a prison cell block and an execution chamber." The complainants were agog but didn't interrupt the animated narrator, who continued, "As they were demolishing the prison block the foreman discovered an envelope buried in the grouting between some bricks. It was written by a prisoner and addressed to his parents in Germany. It said he was to be executed the following day as a spy even though he was innocent. He had been interrogated by security men who were going to find him guilty whatever the circumstances. He related his body was marked with torture scars and he had abandoned all hope. The letter also stated he had made the journey from Germany to Norway and then onward to Scotland in an open boat. He was a genuine refugee from the Nazis. The British Security Service had insisted the story was a cover for a spying operation. The letter was dated 2nd June 1942." The guests were fascinated, their anger now long gone.

"They shouldn't have knocked it down, they should've used it as tourist attraction," one remarked.

Emma ignored this. "Another point that perplexed the foreman was the scratching of initials on cell walls; there were lots of these made by prisoners who wouldn't see the outside of that building again. However, the demolition job is finished now. All the carved initials had almost faded into insignificance after all, they'd been done nearly sixty years ago. One puzzle the foreman couldn't find an answer to was a much more up-to-date carving than all of the others."

"What was that?" asked the curious guest, hanging on Emma's every word. The receptionist replied, "The most recently scratched initials were R.J.B."

## *Three*

# HERE TO-DAY

All manner of incidents occurred when Dick Dyson was in the vicinity. He was the type of man that incidents were talked about when he wasn't in the vicinity. He didn't suffer a painful death, it was very quick. Here when he went to bed late evening, gone when Gilly brought his usual early morning tea. But at aged 64 not a great consolation. He was a tall slim man in his latter years, I knew him firstly in our cricketing years three decades ago. He was much chunkier in those days, but still the impish smile that tempted a person to challenge his very definite statements. There were no grey areas of compromise.

His views were black or white, yes or no, very rarely a maybe – I know I never met one. His palid face coincided with an aortic heart valve murmur. This eventually did him. He never took the easier option, the more difficult the task the more it was food and drink, even though an available alternative would have been easier on body or mind. His face would light up at a view he disagreed with, rub his hands with glee. He'd show the other fellow. His waspish moustache and tiny goatee beard of very fine grey hairs seemed to have a life of their own, they bristled in league with a devilish smile that Dracula would be proud of.

My good lady and myself, on an Easter Bank holiday Monday lunchtime in a seaside village in Mid-Wales called into the lounge bar of the Penhelig Arms at Aberdovey. The village was a popular haunt of our own golf club members from back home in the West Midlands, so it was no great surprise to meet kindred spirits on a day when typical Welsh weather blew a fierce wind. In tandem with the gale the rain horizontally hammered the porthole shaped windows, sounding like the pair of woodpeckers giving full vent to the large decaying tree overlooking our eighteenth green at home. This clapping sound always seemed to start when I was bent over in full concentration on a putt that was to determine the result of the match. Those woodpeckers cost me dearly as a loser buying the first round in the nineteenth. Some golfers ignored the hammering noise – I never could it unnerved me and I paid the price.

In, the lounge bar I saw Dick standing with two friends overlooking their ladies who were sitting around a large oak round table. Instinctively I knew someone would pay a price. He was nursing a green bottle in his left hand holding it up to the light. He remarked "Only an inch left." On an adjacent table his half empty glass. "By jove here's Arthur hello old sport they let anybody in here these days. Not like it in Dad's day". Janet turned toward the other three ladies, joining in their animated chat. "Only an inch of what left" I asked. "Anyhow I bet you won't get all that in one glass, there's too much liquid in the green bottle to enter that glass you're holding". He looked hard at me "I'll get you a drink, the usual?" I nodded. He turned to the serving bar immediately behind our party to wait patiently in a crowded area for my 'usual'.

"No golf this afternoon" I remarked to cherubic Geoffrey, were you to play as a three ball?" "No our usual four, Jason's on his way here, just been on the mobile, he'll be here shortly but there's no fun golfing in this weather. A spot of lunch here and back to the house for a hand of bridge with the ladies." A tap on my shoulder, as I turned a large Guinness was thrust in my hand. Dick returned to the bar. Next time back he returned with a full green bottle which contained his favourite drink and the same glass as hitherto now thoroughly cleaned. "What's the bet then knowledgeable one?" We were now a group of four, Bingo an old school friend of Richard's sensing some sport joined us. "There's too much liquid in the green bottle to go into that glass." "No there isn't" said Richard "I asked the barman for the appropriate glass for this drink" I again looked hard at the bottle and then the glass. "Let's make it a nominal pound coin" I replied. "Not very confident Arthur, if you'll take me on as well I'll bet agin you" sad faced Bingo commented. "Accepted, but it's merely a token bet" I replied.

The effect on the crowded pub was akin to the Circus coming to town. An audience appeared as if by magic. Our ladies stood for a better view. A man in the crowded pub shouted Richard was right. Then another said "No he was wrong." I stood firmly shouted out "Only one bet and that's with the man holding the bottle and the glass, and Bingo here." Gilly shouted out "Spoil sport Arthur, I want to back Richard, he's rarely wrong in anything, although I don't let him know it. Hmph I've already said too much." "You have dear, put more water in the whisky next time." Janet answered quietly.

Richard stood alone in a space the crowd had parted on his behalf. Addressing the crowd he shouted "The moment of truth is to be revealed". Silence reigned. Richard held the glass high to give his audience a better view. Raising the bottle a little higher he began to pour. The liquid was without gas, a froth did not appear. The bar door burst open at this point, a short dumpy man appeared and slammed it shut with his shoulder against the gale and rain. He gazed at the assembly with astonishment and then to Richard "What do you think you're up to Dyson. You look as solemn as a judge about to give a life sentence." "Shut up Jason you've interrupted the moment of truth." The admonition had the required effect. The fourth member of the cancelled fourball knew his place and tightened his lips.

The liquid transferred to the glass as slowly as Richard could pour. The glass filled gradually to the brim. Richard willed more to enter even squeezing the glass bottle – but without avail. The liquid began to drip over the side of the glass. There was still an inch of green liquid remaining in the bottle. No amount of Dyson's urging could affect the issue. "Bugger it Arthur you've done me." The crowd applauded "Who'd have thought it" wife Gill remarked. The barman worked overtime to settle private wagers members of the audience had had with each other. Janet walked to Arthur and kissed him "I knew my hero would pull it off" the remark was in a loudish voice well in the hearing of Dick's wife. "Women are a funny lot" newcomer Jason said. "Not as funny as men" shapely Janet replied tartly.

Not much value in a pound these days but Arthur pocketed Dick's coin with more joy than a significant lottery prize. Gleefully biting it in mock query as to its authenticity.

Jason opened the bar room door to the elements, the rain and wind had marginally abated. It was time for "one for the road", rather than their three o'clock tee-time at the Golf Club. The weather is a two edged sword in holiday havens, especially in Welsh resorts where it is at its most variable. The pub was full to capacity, the new smoking ban probably keeping a few people away although it did attract several asthmatic alcoholics.

Dick's original group had grown to more than a dozen now sitting around the oak oval table. This table had seated patrons before the turn of the previous century. The matching dark oak chairs were a pleasing feature. An eight foot tall Grandfather clock chimed at half hour intervals. "The very recently replaced dark blue axminster with a pale blue diamond shaped pattern gave a more comforting feeling than when we were here last year Gilly remarked. "Yes there are far worse places in the world than here" Janet replied. "Like the Headmaster's study at Bromsgrove School when you've been caught absenting yourself from a cross-country run" chimed Jason Plummer. "Like I was, you had a very close-up view of his axminster for a few very uncomfortable minutes".

"Oh were both of you at Bromsgrove?" Arthur queried, continuing "I know Richard was, along with another good friend of mine". Gilly interrupted "I know Bromsgrove School was very popular among the boys I knew. The girls in general stayed at our sixth form colleges and lived at home but the boys went away. Who was your friend Arthur?" "Chap I used to work with name of Peter Collings. We became good friends during our time as student accountants. It's a few years ago now but we've stayed good friends and even now have the occasional business relationship". "Peter Collings was never a pupil at Bromsgrove School" Richard remarked stridently. "Oh yes he was" Arthur replied. Gilly interchimed "Shut up you two, you're sounding like a pantomime turn". Richard reached boiling point quickly, still smarting after his earlier loss of face. "Twenty quid says he wasn't at Bromsgrove". His wife rebuked him "Now you're being silly Richard. We came here for a quiet drink with friends".

Arthur was thinking hard. He knew Peter Collings had been away at boarding school, and had always imagined it was at Bromsgrove. He then remembered the photograph. "Done" he said in a loud voice. Both men shook hands.

Other patrons began to gather round the oval oak table, mostly had their drinks with them. "Is this the second Act gentlemen?" Peter the pub maitre d' asked. "It isn't, it's two silly overgrown schoolboys acting out their fantasies". Dick's wife replied, and addressing the emerging crowd said "and you lot go back to your own area, there's no more live theatre today".

Tokio Tony came in with his good lady Joan. "We've had a good journey from the Midlands, pleased to say the weather's improved in the last half hour. Pint of Guinness and a gin spritzer please". "You always arrive when it's my turn to buy." Jason Plummer replied. Two more chairs were squeezed round the oval oak table. "Where did Peter Collings go to school Tokio?" Arthur asked. "Not really sure, his brother went to Bromsgrove, I think Peter did but I'm not certain. It's an unusual request. Why do you ask and give me a hard look at the same time. It can't be that important". "Oh yes it is" Arthur answered. "Here they go again" Gilly answered.

* * * * *

"Great match and great results" John Ehrett said to the other four A level students. The England soccer team needs to beat the Germans tonight and our cup overfloweth with happiness. Great to be alive in the sixties. What say you Peter". "Terrific John, tremendous feeling of relief to feel our A levels are behind us. We can all look forward jostling in adult life, even girls are not out of bounds from tomorrow. Mind you from what Bruce tells me they haven't been for you and Nigel for some months now". "Enough of that now" John Ehrett replied "You know we wouldn't put a foot wrong". The five in the prefects' common room were dressed in their Sunday best suits having just returned from the after-match dinner in the Headmaster's dining room. Bromsgrove had played a hard fought drawn match with their archrivals Worksop. "Well that's the last rugby match that we will represent the school. But we all must make a supreme effort to play for the old boys next season. We must never let our camaraderie lapse or even falter. We must adhesive our deep friendship for all time." John Ehrett placed his right hand forward horizontally, rigid at the elbow. Peter Collings followed suit placing his hand firmly on top of John's. The other three followed in turn. "Together we will remain friendly companions throughout the remainder of our lives" John said. "Hear, Hear" chorused the other four in unison. Peter produced five plastic glasses and a bottle of champagne from the depths of his leather holdall of soiled rugby kit. The smell of my kit will add a flavour unique to us all" David Barnett remarked. The liquid didn't touch the sides of their throats on its way into their bloodstream and a feeling of exuberance. "Let's form a band of brothers" said John. His smile and sparkling eyes lit up the enthusiasm of the others. "What shall we call ourselves?". Many suggestions were considered. Cola was a poor substitute for champagne but a six-pack was found from beneath the square linen topped table which had been used for years of evening prep. The sparkling cola re-kindled the thought process of Nigel Brook "You've been the inspiration of us all John, ever since we started public school-life. You used to have a nick-name when we were fags years ago. I can't quite recall it. But it made people laugh". John smiled "I was quite small and skinny for my age in those days. I was called Ferret, rhymes with Ehrett but that would be totally inappropriate". "No, no" Nigel insisted. The cola-champagne was working well. The other three agreed with Nigel 'The Ferrets' were born.

Peter Collings said "Pity we can't have a memento of this evening. Need something permanent". John's eyes lit up "I have one of those new self-taking cameras. A present from Aunt Ellen on my eighteenth birthday, a couple of months ago now. Never even used it". John remarked. Nigel Brook happily chided "There's no time like the present to use a present". John departed to his own study, returning minutes later with a resplendent yellow camera firmly fixed to a tripod. "It has an in-built flash, light's neutralised, doesn't matter where we sit. How about under the school logo, all the better that has the year on it". The only three straight back chairs were placed in position. John sat in the middle one, flanked either side by Bruce Collings and his twin Peter. Nigel Brough and David Grant sat crossed legged in front on the floor. John shouted "Ready everyone, a nice smile when you think the camera will click". Bruce asked "How are we supposed to know that?" "It's about thirty seconds" was the reply. The group looked apprehensive for twenty-five seconds. "Now beam everyone. Remember I believe in castration". The roar of laughter was spontaneous. A copy of the resultant photograph occupied the first page in the eventual Ferret's written Constitution.

Peter Collings gazed through the study window, then called to his brother "My transport awaits Bruce. I'll give your love to Mum and Dad."

* * * * *

Arthur was in his office early the day after the cessation of the Easter break. A mountain of post awaited him placed by an even earlier attendee and devoted secretary. Since grateful clients of his taxation minimisation service pay their dues to him reasonably quickly, he had the wherewithal to luxurise his office. Eight paintings each by quality artists adorned the walls. The favourite was on the left side of the far wall immediately opposite to Arthur's red leather bound upright rocker, that gave luxurious comfort to the occupant. A seated twelve year old boy, his closed eyes resting on an open book opposite to where he sat. This relaxed Arthur during the very stressful moments of dealing with worried clients. Inland Revenue enquiries gave little peace to taxpayers they suspected of not playing by their rules. Arthur knew the rules and made sure his clients adopted them. Revenue officials assumed taxpayers who were ignorant of any rights they had stayed that way. Arthur and his elk gave succour to clients who thought they had committed a hanging offence, and were led along this path by ambitious Inland Revenue officials. But the boy picture gave Arthur much needed relief during such heated client meetings. The watercolour of a dreaming boy, his head buried between the middle pages of a thickly opened book, a tank, airplanes, Arab dervishes on horseback swirling swords around the dreamer. On Arthur's left in the centre of that wall a crayon picture of a green and black racing car of Jim Clarke winning the 1967 Grand Prix in the rain was always a source of enjoyment. The art work was superb Arthur imagined it was he performing the rare miracle of being first over the line at Silverstone.

His reverie was disturbed by the telephone blasting at his left elbow "Arthur, Jason Plummer here. Have you heard Dick Dyson died in the night?"

"What?" exploded Arthur visibly shaken. Jason Plummer continued "Gill took an early morning tea as usual. The alarm clock was still ringing, normally Dick's first move was to turn it off. She called the Doctor. Nothing he could do. A much worse heart attack than he had a few years back was diagnosed."

* * * * *

Wishaw Church had been the Dyson family worshipping place for several generations. Dick's Great Grandparents and Grandparents had been married and were buried there. The church was far too small for the numbers that would attend today's funeral ceremony. Dick had realised years earlier his life could be shortened suddenly. So made arrangements with the local vicar that whatever other circumstances existed he must be laid horizontally in this church on his day of judgment.

Janet and I arrived early. The overflow car park was jammed. The blazing sun from a cloudless blue sky was bathing the many mourners. Janet remarked of the weather's transformation from when we had last seen Dick alive walking along a stormy Welsh promenade only days ago. We spoke to friends who were content to take in the loudspeaker service in the churchyard surrounds. Old graves used as leaning posts. Janet found a single seat in a back row pew. I stood at the church entrance immediately behind her. The age old stained glass windows through which the sun sent brightly coloured rays sprayed the congregation with what I imagined was heavenly light. The church was full of friends, relations and colleagues from the old family firm. The maitre d' from the Penheig Arms in Wales had made the journey together with several drinking regulars. Dick was a constant attender when at his holiday home, but in latter years had to content himself with 'soft' drinks. His binge days behind him. "A nice day for a funeral" the man standing next to me remarked. "Hello Peter, nice to see you again although the circumstances could have been better."

"Did you know Dick well?" I asked. "Since schooldays and before, I played rugby for the Spartans with Dick and his bosom pal Jason Plummer. Who I see is speaking the main tribute today. He's the first speaker according to the order of service." "Tremendous turn out" I remarked, adding "Has your brother Bruce managed to make it for today?" "No Bruce has written to Gilly apologising. Had a long booked holiday in America. In fact had a card from him today postmarked Denver. Sad really, Bruce knew Dick far better than I did. They were at Bromsgrove in the same year y'know." This stopped me in my tracks "Well you are twins surely you were the same year as Dick" Peter smiled "Yes the same year but different schools, I was at Worksop. Our parents thought identical twins should be separated at least educationally, this is what they did."

A sudden buzz of activity in the church entrance stopped our conversation. The family and close friends had returned from the nearby Sutton Coldfield Crematorium. They made their way down the central aisle to the pews at the front of the church. Richard's three best friends, dumpy Jason, cherubic Geoffrey and florid faced Bingo were the last in line. It struck me all these were all old Bromsgrovians. I turned and looked at Peter Collings still nonplussed. "On your mantelshelf in your lounge there is a picture of five senior schoolboys, under a Bromsgrove school banner, a very jolly photo I recall, a truly happy scene." "Yes", chortled Peter. "That was the day England beat Germany in the World Soccer Cup and Bromsgrove and Worksop could only manage a drawn rugby match. I played for Worksop, Bruce played for Bromsgrove."

Our dialogue was silenced as the organ resounded to the opening bars of "Fight the Good Fight". Dick's family were hardened singers his old firm's male voice choir was renowned in musicals soirees throughout the Midlands in my father's working life at Dyson's. Often as a child I was serenaded by him on his return from an evening's choir practice. His voice embellished by the two pints of mild and bitter on his way home calling at the Wagon and Horses. My mother often remarked this was the main reason father attended choir practice. I know his voice impressed me in those early childhood years when the Dyson's dominated our lives from dawn to nightfall. My own family were so dependent on the success of Dyson & Sons Co Ltd. The firm had grown from a very tiny acorn before the First World War. By the time my parents purchased the Star Café within two hundred yards from the factory gate in Nineteen thirty three Dyson's employed over five hundred employees. My father was one of them, on many occasions being the last one to "clock in" during the two minutes allowance time after the 8 a.m. bell. Discipline was firm. On two minutes past eight the iron gates were slammed together and locked. Hurrying employees who didn't make the deadline had to return from whence they came without any pay for the day. My father never suffered this ignominy but was often so close.

After the playing and singing of the opening hymn had subsided, the Reverend Matthew Girton welcomed the full house congregation and the many mourners in the churchyard listening to the service through loudspeakers. The first prayers were spoken, the congregation following the vibrantly spoken words by the clergyman. He then introduced a tribute "From an old friend." Jason Plummer stood to his full height and made his way to the pulpit. Clearing his throat he said "We were all devastated by Richard's demise. He had been walking the tightrope of death for over twenty years, ever since his first bad heart attack.

Gilly and myself of course were ever ready for bad news, but when it came it shook us all to the core and beyond. Richard met Gill at the old family firm in Moorsom Street in Aston. Gill was Richard's father's secretary and as one thing leads to another, they married in this very church forty years ago this year. Their two sons and another son that Gilly brought to the marriage and whom Dick was as devoted to as his own flesh and blood are with us to mourn the death of their father.

"Richard and I met and boarded at Bromsgrove School so long ago and have been lifelong companions since. It is very pleasing to see so many Old Bromsgrovians here today. Old boys from other schools are also represented here in force."

Peter Collings acknowledged the mention with a nod and a smile. I grimaced. Jason Plummer continued;

"After recovery from his first heart attack Richard sought out his solicitor and included a codicil to his then Will. This provided funds for all who attends this funeral service to enjoy a celebration at the hospitality rooms at the Spartan's Rugby Club. All of us will have a drink on the man." Jason Plummer looked up towards the heavens and said "Richard we shan't let you down."

Returning his eyes to the congregation "Since his first heart problem Richard gave up alcoholic beverages. After all eighteen pills a day and whisky are not a healthy mixture. Prior to our respective marriages and after schooldays had ended Richard and myself purchased six acres of land on a never ending bank loan. This was the founding of the Spartan's Rugby Club. Richard did what be did best and became Club Secretary whilst I did what I did best and became first team Captain." Peter Collings looked at me with raised eyebrows. Jason then closed his notes and trundled back to his seat.

Psalm 23 seems obligatory to every self respecting funeral to be followed by Abide with Me. The singing for the latter was exceptionally fine. My father would have been so impressed. He knew Dick's father as an employer and provider of his lunch from mother's Café over many years. The directors had a private upstairs room with glistening silver service provided by Mrs Bensor, mother's finest and most devoted employee. But for this facility they paid fifty percent more than their employees on the café's ground floor. The cooking and quality of food was the same in all areas. People wearing suits and ties willingly pay extra for exclusivity.

Peter Collings and myself in the back row stood silently whilst the occupants of the front rows departed the church. Then the middle and back rows were vacated.

The lovely widow a touch of purple in a high crowned hat, full length black coat stood at the exit of the church as the mourners filed past her paying their respects and offering condolences. This was a lengthy process but very rewarding for mourners and the widow. Peter Collings slid away silently. I was the last mourner to walk to Gilly the final two people in the church. I kissed her cheek reverently and said how sorry I was at the tragedy. She looked and smiled wistfully, and said "Remember Arthur you owe him some money."

## *Four*

# THE FOUNDLING

"What's for dinner Ma?" the breathless twelve year old rushed into the living room at the rear of the street corner grocery shop.

"Now you're at high school, dinner is lunch to you Stanley. Anyhow it's boiled hock bone and your favourite parsley white sauce."

"Great", replied her son, "And who's cooked it, you or Rookie?"

"I heard you. Don't be cheeky young Stan," answered the short wiry handywoman-cum-cook.

"You burn the parsley sauce, tastes horrible it does."

His mother clips Stanley round the ear. "Rookie does her best so you eat it."

"What's bothering you Frances?" Stanley's mother asks of the young woman who comes out of the shop in a hurry.

"Policeman in there says he wants some bacon and he don't have his ration book with him, says you'd know Mrs Seaman."

Stanley's mother returns to the shop area, behind the counter. She says "Roger don't ask the new girl, she refused on instructions from me. Everybody wants extra and we just don't have enough to go round."

Mrs Seaman weighs out six ounces of bacon, wraps it in greaseproof paper and slides it furtively to the policeman who pockets it without offering to pay. Stanley's mother stays in the shop whilst Stanley and Frances sit down to their ham and parsley sauce.

"We've only fifteen minutes to finish our dinner," Stanley informed the new assistant "Dad comes from his factory job at 1 o'clock, then he and Ma sit down. It's the only bit of peace they get till the shop is closed just before ten tonight. Then Dad goes over to the pub for a quick pint before closing time." Frances nodded understandingly. "You were late coming in this lunchtime. Been playing football have you?"

Stanley replied that he had. "Got a real sweat on I did."

Frances smiled. Would the baby inside her play football immediately the school bell rang when he was old enough. It may be a girl, but no, Tom wants a boy. The sturdy chubby faced boy was inquisitive. "What do girls do when boys play football, Frances?"

"Oh a host of things. Sometimes they sew or help their mother with her work. Most Sundays when Tom's at home we go for walks, sometimes to Sutton Park although that's a long walk, takes two hours either way. Other times Tom takes me to the Lickey Hills on the tram. There are some arduous walks there. Sometimes we have to sit down in the bluebell woods on Tom's khaki greatcoat to get our breath back, if you know what I mean."

Stanley said that he did but secretly thought they could have been playing football, or something else useful. Frances, although only in her present job five weeks, was particularly liked by the customers who use Mrs Seaman's busy shop. Her moon face was constantly wreathed in smiles, eyebrows plucked with the merest hint of makeup. A couple of inches taller than the wiry Mrs Rooke, her mother, who had spoken for the vacant shop assistant's job when the previous incumbent left to join the Women's Land Army. Although Stanley was only five years her junior, she remarked to him in one of their lunch sessions that those five years was when a boy became a man and certainly a girl became a woman. Frances smiled to herself. The five years difference in age with her companion was the largest span in loving sex knowledge of any other like period in a normal lifetime. Stanley a hefty chunk was still a schoolboy whilst she had become a mature woman.

Yesterday, hand in hand with Tommy, they had made a quick dash for the noonday tram immediately after the Sabbath's morning mass. They sat upstairs on the open topped deck, facing a strong breeze sunning themselves during the five mile journey to the lovers' bluebell wood on the highs summit of Birmingham's Lickey Hills.

Looking up at a cloudless sky astride Tommy's khaki greatcoat was a feeling a twelve year old would know nothing about in the early 1940's. Frances wanted her Tom to return to the mud-filled trenches with memories to take his mind away from his horrific plight. Parting her thighs marginally wider allowed Tommy's rhythmic thrusts to reach that little further.

She knew from her church teachings that a Catholic boy would know when to withdraw, but Tommy was Church of England. She didn't care.

Before his leave expired Frances mentioned her trepidation. Tom smiled. An application for a special licence, doing away with the necessity of the wailing period when banns were read, was accepted by the Archbishop of Birmingham, who married the couple personally at the Cathedral on the morning of the evening that Tom Stephenson returned to France.

* * * * *

The first six months from war being declared in September 1939 was termed the phoney war, nothing happened militarily. Then the well prepared mighty German war machine moved into coherted action. The Maginot line, deemed impregnable by the French Government, was captured in a short number of days. The Hun over-ran Holland and Belgium, then careered into France. The British Expeditionary Force put up the stoutest defence of the European allies, the Horse Guards put up the must fierce resistance on the entire front, before being virtually annihilated by vastly superior numbers and advanced weaponry.

Frances Stephenson became a widow well before her eighteenth birthday, four months to the day she had been married.

* * * * *

"I'll keep your job open when you've had the bab," Mrs Seaman told Frances.

"What can I do?" Frances asked fearfully "I can't get any money from the Army, Mrs Seaman."

"Whyever not luvvie. Your husband died fighting for his country."

Tears were falling down Frances' chubby cheeks. "Army money for any child only starts if the marriage is at least nine months when the baby is born. My marriage will barely be five months when the little one first sees the light of day."

Mrs Seaman's arms cradled Frances. "I know your mother's not in a position to help you financially and that drunken father of yours should be horse whipped every day he don't turn up for work. You are in trouble dear, but I'll see what I can do."

Mrs Seaman's corner grocery store was as busy as ever. Black-market was rife; each customer officially receiving two ounces of bacon a week and one egg a fortnight, the traditional British breakfast now a distant memory. Chocolate and boiled sweets only for the very privileged or influential. Stanley Seaman was in the former category, his mother over indulged her son to the extent that he was obtaining an adult ration book due to a qualifying heavyweight schoolboy. Frances, still a minor, also qualified for an adult ration book, not because she was a heavy weight schoolgirl, but because she was pregnant.

* * * * *

The war on the Western Front finished in the Summer of 1940. A motley fleet of thousands of small, and in many cases tiny, boats rescued the remnant of the British Expeditionary Forces and their allies who had retreated to fight another day.

The war against Britain spread to the air. German bombers were unleashing load after devastating load of high explosives to the major cities. Royal Air Force fighter pilots put up a defensive force which brought daylight raiders to a halt in the Autumn of 1940. The German bombers then took to the cover of darkness to carry out their horrific missions. London Docks were largely annihilated as were those at Liverpool and Glasgow. Birmingham and Coventry ammunition works and strategic road and railway networks were tantalising targets.

A land-mine floated out of the sky harnessed to a giant parachute. Stanley's father shouted to the family taking cover in the cellars beneath the grocery store, "A German pilot's floating from the sky. Our anti-aircraft gunners have scored a direct hit" he shouted.

Stanley's father joined a crowd of friends led by Air Raid Wardens running towards the parachute. Mrs Seaman's fiery blood was bubbling as she ran closely behind her husband. Her father had been killed in the trenches at Ypres twenty five years previously. If a German parachutist was to land in their midst, she wanted a piece of him. Two minutes later Stanley Seaman became an orphan.

The devastating explosion rocked the district. The several thousand people sheltering in the underground railway tunnels had a miraculous escape as he parachuted land-mine plopped to its gentle fall seven hundred yards away in the middle of the vehicle parking lot of the Birmingham Post and Mail newspaper. The blast's havoc spread 180 degrees in every direction. This was a new phenomenon. Previously high explosive bombs penetrated the earth deeply, much of the havoc occurred beneath ground. Although horrific, it was slight compared to the damage caused by the new floating land-mines. The state of crowd panic was also much more widespread.

The blast completely demolished the grocery store and the living accommodation on the second floor crumbled with it, reducing the building to a pile of rubble.

Stanley, Frances and her mother were sheltering in the cellars for protection. The three of them were pulled to safety by sweating rescue workers eight hours after the explosion.

A much larger and older replica of Stanley's mother grabbed him by the hand, lifted him bodily from the rescue worker who had plucked him from his underground bolt hole. She shouted above the cacophony of noise, "Come here young Stan, your aunt Jane is your mother from now on." They left immediately by car threading its way through ambulances and fire engines strewn haphazardly across the street.

Frances and Mrs Rooke walked a few hundred yards in the opposite direction to the eye of the explosion to the comparative safety of a back house, bordering Summer Lane, the main thoroughfare separating the suburbs of Aston and Hockley.

* * * * *

It took Frances several days to come to terms with the fact that her protector was no longer available to help her through the darks days of a bastard pregnancy; at least that was how a khaki clad officer described her condition. We cannot, albeit will not, help a wanton woman who led on an unsuspecting army private so that he would have to marry her. "No pension for you my girl, don't even bother to ask."

Struggling to pay the two pounds reach each week, Rookie had taken a position as a cleaner at a rat infested greengrocer shop on Summer Lane. Since the land-mine, rodents ran freely. Frances' mother again came to her daughter's aid if only for a short period by securing a shop assistant's position at the same store. When customers began querying Frances' startling weight increase, she was asked to leave.

* * * * *

Father and daughter with nothing more to do than get under each other's feet, came to blows on three occasions and berated each other on an hourly basis. On the last occasion that her father punched Frances across her face, she slipped over a footstool, falling heavily. Her mother ran the hundred yards to the nearby medical surgery. An elderly Scottish doctor, his breath heavily scented with his native holy water, performed a premature child birth on the matted floor of Rookie's parlour Frances suffered a terrible hurtful birth.

The midwife arrived at the same time that baby Paul's head appeared. The terribly painful procedure continued, doctor and midwife perspiring profusely for a further hour before the birth was complete.

Frances was so weak she couldn't be moved for more than two weeks despite the excellent aftercare of Dr Macpherson and the midwife. Baby Paul had been moved to the maternity section of Birmingham's Women's Hospital where he made excellent progress doubling his five pound birth weight in the six weeks which coincided with his young mother's return to good health. Dr Macpherson remarked to Rookie it was only the grit and determination of the baby's mother that saved the day. He further reported Frances' father to the police for cruelly berating his pregnant daughter and causing her premature birth. Her father's absence in prison greatly helped Frances' convalescence. She began now walking properly and greatly looked forward to being reunited with her baby.

* * * * *

The only time Frances Stephenson saw baby Paul was a five minute viewing through the visitor's plate glass at Loveday Street maternity wing. She desperately wanted to hold and hug him but there were forbidding regulations. She looked hard at the circle shaped crimson birth mark on his right shoulder. She hadn't noticed this in the aftermath of the agonising birth. The intensive care ambulance had immediately whisked him to this safe haven.

Agreement to adoption was the most agonising decision she would ever have to make. Tears streaming dawn her waiflike moon face she was ushered to a bursary officer. No compassion was shown to a woman made pregnant out of wedlock.

"Sign there, there and there and then leave." Frances carried out the order then asked, "When will I see Paul, I must see him, soon." The curt reply hit her a mortal blow. "You will never seem him again, he's somebody else's now. Going to a comfortable home where the baby will receive an upbringing you could never give him."

Frances left the hospital with uncontrollable grief. "This is far worse than a funeral," her final words to an uncompromising Bursar.

* * * * *

Frances walked the one mile, having signed the adoption papers, to the slum she had lived in since birth. Her father, now out of prison, but still her worst enemy, with little to do with his time, was constantly complaining he was too old to join the army. When Frances pointed out that the authorities were taking from eighteen to forty-four year olds, both her eyes were discoloured by his clenched fist. "Calling me a coward are you?" The local priest was her only solace and made a point that she should walk into the town centre and look for a recruiting office. Both the Army and Navy recruiting officers turned down her application on the grounds of morality and being underage. Half an hour later, at the Royal Air Force recruiting centre in the former West End Ballroom, she was eighteen and unmarried.

The following day a letter bearing the King's Crest was delivered to Frances' address ordering her to present herself in three days time to the Royal Air Force Unit at London Bridge Underground Station. Henceforth known as Aircraftwoman Frances Rooke, she was to undertake training as a nursing orderly, but firstly to receive the harsh regime of eight weeks basic training "to improve her awareness to accept orders from a superior without question." Frances' mother was delighted, telling her daughter, "Anything's better than sitting around this house, wish the Army would take me, and don't think I haven't tried."

* * * * *

The leafy lanes were tranquil. Birmingham City dignitaries of the day made sure road signs placed in Aston never pointed in the direction of Handsworth Wood. Most large detached mansions built there was in upward of two acre plots. Immediately Frances had signed the adoption papers and left Loveday Street maternity wing for the last time, Mr and Mrs Leslie Cotton stepped from behind a screen in the Bursar's office for the signing of the Acceptees portion of the adoption papers that five minutes ago Frances' coerced signature had been plated on the Donor's section.

Mrs Cotton sped as fast as her legs could take her to baby Paul's cot, she swept him into her arms, cuddled him, loved him. Her face wreathed in smiles. Proudly showing young Paul to her husband who clasped his wife, "At last darling, now we'll see what a wonderful mother you'll make."

The livened chauffeur driving Leslie's chrome and black Rolls Royce didn't need signposts to guide him through the back streets of Aston to the foliage of Handsworth Wood.

* * * * *

Now in her second year of service, Aircraftwoman Frances Rooke constantly worked overtime, just not enough hours in the day or night. Australian Bomber Command's daily and night flights over Europe suffered severe casualties to the personnel in the Lancaster Bombers returning to home base after distributing their deadly message to the Hun. German Messershmitt and Junker fighters saw to that. The Spitfires and Hurricanes of Fighter Command could not wholly prevent their German counterparts from spitting bullets from their twin engine propellers into the bellies of some of the giant Lancasters. Injuries from returning aircrew were numerous and sometime horrific.

The almost raw recruit was involved in emergency surgery far beyond what her training prepared her for. In letters to her mother she described her RAAF station as "somewhere in England". The Australian air crew the bravest of all men.

Frances caressed Rear Gunner Miller's auburn tousled hair carefully into his pillow, she had a soft spot for Blue, who had been shot by a single bullet in the right shoulder which shattered his collar bone in a night raid over Hamburg. The boys in hospital had special food rations but there was never enough cigarettes to go around. Frances distributed her ration surreptitiously in the Emergency Ward. Blue Miller did better than most.

Eighteen hour shifts were normal, she never stinted, blood had become as natural a fluid to her as water. Frances was promoted to Corporal in the field whilst working on an amputation case in early 1942. The same day that Paul Cotton's first tooth appeared.

* * * * *

Church bells were still belting out their message of happiness and goodwill to the newly crowned Elizabeth four days after the event. Road traffic was halted for the weekend. Street parties were in full swing, following the London establishment's great ding dong in entertaining world celebrities. The twenty four stone Queen of Tonga was taken to the hearts of the nation with her version of the hippie shake televised live from Buckingham Palace.

On the ground floor at Handsworth Masonic Hall immediately after the solemnity of their nuptial vows and the usual obligatory photographs, Stanley and Lily Seaman greeted their ninety guests to a sumptuous feast; for the younger guests it was unique. It had taken many years to shed the austerity of post war Britain. The last ration book had been discarded with the abolition of sweet rationing. Marvellous happenings for the fourteen schoolboys celebrating passing their 11-plus examination in a small annexe on the second floor on the same day. Paul Cotton's parents had made the arrangements.

The Coronation celebrations were just as ardent in the newly crowned Queen's overseas colonies. Australia was agog. In Redfern, a suburb of Sydney, Frances Miller was viewing their street party through the bedroom window, with husband Blue gazing fondly at their first born, which had happened in the early hours. Frances remarked "This is our D-day exactly ten years after the real D-day in 1944, the day you asked me to come to Australia, marrying me two months later. The 6th of June always brings many pleasant memories."

She prayed they would not stay in the down-town slum area forever, remembering her upbringing in Birmingham, she had had more than a person's fair share. Subsequently Frances and Blue were to be parents to another boy and their youngest child followed two years later.

Blue's war wounded shoulder nagged through to his fingers. The spinning bite to turn the ball sharply just that bit more, painfully prevented him representing Australia at the highest level. He barely made the New South Wales State team, only Test Cricketers made it financially.

A day didn't pass without Frances wondering where Paul was and what he was doing. How was life treating him? What a sturdy boy he must now be.

* * * * *

Paul became involved in the activities of the University Conservative Club in his second year reading Economics. "An economic degree is indispensable to every aspiring Chancellor of the Exchequer." Student Union President Helen remarked as she and Paul, still perspiring in their squash gear, were relaxing in the union bar on a wet October Saturday afternoon.

"Chancellor," mused Paul. "That's heady heights for a little boy born twenty one years ago, just across the City from here." Helen answered firmly "You must have ambition from the outset. It saves a lot of time cutting corners as you rise the ladder in power politics, cut through the mundane, you know those people who are there just for the ride with nothing better to do or give the country. They'll support a man going places, a person prepared to put his head down and take chances. Look at that group from Liverpool they're changing the musical scene cutting out the old bringing in a new type of beat. You do the same in politics."

"Yeah, yeah, yeah" replied her amused boyfriend.

* * * * *

Barely two months later on Christmas morning, Paul's parents arranged a pre-lunch cocktail party for the good, the mighty and the wealthy of their Handsworth Wood mansion. Paul, Helen and a few university friends who lived locally were under orders to liven up proceedings with the older and more staid guests.

Paul welcomed their near neighbours with a dignified "How do you do Mrs Doulstridge. We haven't met before. Please have a drink."

The finely groomed lady had obviously taken time arranging her coiffeur and matching accoutrements. "A gin and dry martini young man, thank you. I understand you are graduating with an economics degree next year. Are you staying to take a doctorate?'

Paul replied, "No it's time I saw what the wide world is about I have offered a job lecturing at my present university if a first class degree is obtained, but I may train as a solicitor; that's what my parents want, but time will tell."

Helen brought over Mrs Doulstridge's drink "That's a lethal concoction ma'am" she said.

"I can handle it dear," was the quiet reply. Helen smiled before continuing "I overheard your question to Paul, Madame."

"Please call me Cynthia" the older woman interjected.

Helen carried on as if not interrupted, "I think Paul should enter politics. His vision of future events is remarkable with the power of a Member of Parliament, maybe even a Cabinet post, he could do untold good for the masses."

"I've promised Helen the job of being my agent if I ever decide that way."

"Please give it earnest consideration," came the unexpected reply "The Conservatives need good young blood. With your background an ideal candidate. If you do decide to make politics your first choice of career, take on the lecturer's job We are looking to find a suitable person to succeed Commander Prior in the Edgbaston constituency at the next general election. Old age has finally shot him down. A young man like you could be in line."

Paul Cotton's expression became very serious. "Cynthia you have a very confident attitude, can you deliver? A person's future is not a trifling matter."

"Yes young man, I hear what you say but I have the influence of being Chairwoman of the Edgbaston and Duddeston Conservative Candidates Selection Committee." She smiled "I wouldn't like trying to say that little mouthful after another gin and dry martini."

* * * * *

Bachelor Member of Parliament Commander Prior hadn't been informed that old age had "shot him down" He hadn't been shot down at Jutland in the fiercest naval battle in WW1, why should a young whippersnapper still wet behind the ears take over from a man still in the prime of life. Too old for WW2 but he'd kept himself fit, winning the British Veterans squash championship five years in a row. Hadn't the newly crowned George VI pinned the winners medal on his chest on the first occasion. This new boy would have to wait till the next election but one.

Despite the entreaties of Cynthia Doulstridge at the selection meeting Commander Prior won the day. Loyalty to any cause, is the Conservative Party's main weakness. It had been pointed out at the meeting that Commander Prior only attended the Commons to hear the annual March budget and his contribution to the seventeen times he attended the annual event, was to utter "hear hear" on Conservative budgets or dissenting "rubbish" using his knack of uncanny timing to considerable effect, when the opposition was in power.

But the young man in waiting had to earn a living. "Take a doctorate in Financial and Taxation Planning," the University bursar advised him "The State will provide." He knew his parents better than that. Lecturing in direct taxation after graduating with First Class Honours, took five years off his waiting period, "What a base for a Chancellor of the Exchequer often years hence" stated his thickly tummied wife Helen.

"We will definitely have our second before the next budget, hope It's a boy this time. It's a hot tip that Child Relief, as a deduction from tax, will be abolished. You can't trust these left wing bastards.

* * * * *

"Vintage champagne 1941 year", Aunt Jane retorted, "only the best for your fortieth Stanley."

"That is not really appropriate, Auntie dear. Think hard, the best champagne year was also the year you plucked me from the debris."

Aunt Jane's hands flew to her bosom. "Sorry boy that wound is still open. But let's have the same venue as your wedding, Lily would love that."

"So would the kids, they've heard so much about early June 1953," Stanley replied, adding "the Queen's put a little weight on since she was crowned?"

"Well she's had two more kids," answered his aunt defensively.

* * * * *

New Economics graduates at Birmingham University heard at their first interviews that Paul Cotton had become a young legend, not only lecturing but also his annual Westminster parties were not to be missed. His friend and seat protector made a special effort to make a second annual visit. Now well over his allotted three score and ten, still playing regular squash matches Commander Prior depressed Paul by remarking, "The next election will be my last, eighty is a good-year to retire from politics."

Paul could not restrain. "Don't you think your constituents deserve somewhat more than two visits to Parliament each year? You are a little leech clinging to the backs of the eager and ambitious."

"Not at all my boy, experience is a valuable commodity. I have that in abundance, your time will come soon enough."

Paul conceded to his pupils at the 1973 Westminster visit "At least the old boy throws a good luncheon party." This was the last luncheon party Commander Prior was to mastermind whilst his party was in office. His Prime Minister sought to teach the country a lesson a month afterwards. The coal miners were threatening strike actions, the Conservative Party's stock was high. Edward Heath let industry have electricity power to enable production on three working days in each week. When the unions decided on further industrial action to stop the Government's meagre action. It was time the unions were put in their place. A General Election was called later that year, which the Tories were a racing certainty to win. Commander Prior safely held Edgbaston and Duddeston but the remainder of the country was not as generous. Labour was returned to power and Harold Wilson became a reluctant Prime Minister. "Oh no Mary", he remarked "just when I was enjoying politics. Why did the bloody Tories throw the towel in?"

* * * * *

Paul and Helen were lucky to have procured a wet nurse as a babysitter for the Christmas morning cocktail patty held at the Doulstridge's grand house. Commander Prior, his grey moustache finely coiffured, was the soul of the party. The ladies cringed a little over a risque story he first told at Jutland, then his junior officers roared dutifully, but it was out of place in Handsworth Wood. The event was a carbon copy of the event held annually in one of the area's grand homes. Commander Prior made his apologies exactly at midday. "Have to dash Cynthia, Jimmy Macallum and myself have arranged our usual Christmas squash game before we sit down to your sumptuous lunch, just after the Queen's speech, of course. See you later then."

Cynthia tested the hot turkey sauce nodding to her cooks. "Very tasty Anne, up to your best standard." Anne curtsied her thanks. Neither paying attention to the sirens of the passing emergency services

"The Commander's late dear, he's invariably back from the Squash Club in time for an aperitif well before Her Majesty's broadcast," Cynthia addressed her luncheon party ensemble,

Paul Cotton answered, "Probably partaking a whisky mac – he likes those, but I can imagine him sleeping into the early evening, waking in tune to listen to the Annual Commonwealth review"

He then switched to BBC1. As an unsmiling newscaster related "Commander Prior had a majority approaching 20,000 at the general election two months ago. It will be the first by-election of the new parliament, and is certain to test Labour's popularity. Now to Buckingham Palace for the Queen's Speech."

Paul Cotton fumbled the remote to newstext. The three inch headline "M.P. dies playing squash" Commander Prior's dying words were, "What a wonderful way to go. All the best to Paul Cotton."

* * * * *

New apartments and homes were rising at a rapid rate throughout the transforming early seventies. The recently completed Rotunda dominated Birmingham's skyline. Lloyds Bank took most of its available office space. Paul's taxation lectures to their senior staff were always well attended in the Conference Room on the Penthouse floor.

"Hope you will still speak at our meetings when you're Chancellor of the Exchequer" a Branch Manager remarked at one of their sessions.

"Getting into Parliament is enough. I don't even think what happens afterwards. Any office I am offered will be a bonus."

* * * * *

Grammar School had been an excellent springboard to University for Stanley Seaman. He qualified as a solicitor two days after his twenty fifth birthday. Already married to Lily three years before, their twins appeared after a further month. A delighted Stanley told Lily, "Let them be the first of many, I can manage the financial part."

Lily cradled the little girl saying, "Your part is easy dear, I say very pleasurable, but the word 'many' brings a tremor of anguish. Two babies at one go is enough to think about for a very considerable time. Let's take things in easy and long distant stages." But memory dims pain, a baby boy was born shortly after Stanley became the youngest partner in his firm's history two years later.

However another six pleasurable years ensued before the good natured Lily produced the sweetest little girl. Stanley insisted she was called Frances. Stanley often spoke to Lily about Frances and the good old days in his mother's shop. Lily spoke sharply, "You're wasting valuable thinking time moping on about Frances. Take some action, your business often takes you to Broad Street's Registry of Births and Deaths. Do some research, or forget it all, you're getting to be an old bore." Suitably chastened, on his next professional assignment to the white mausoleum building, after collecting evidence on behalf of a client contesting a paternity case, Stanley Seaman browsed the 'births' list of May 1942 for servicemen fathers. There weren't many to peruse, most red blooded men were fighting in the numerous spheres throughout the Globe. Only two sailors, seven airmen and twenty soldiers were registered as fathers in the whole month of May 1942. None of the army men were named as Rooke or Stephenson. Stanley perused further, were there any uncharacteristic listings? Frustration goaded him, perhaps Lily was correct. This his right index finger abruptly halted on 25th May, a birth without a mother. 'Impossible' he thought. The father was listed as Alfred John Cotton, White Gates, Friary Road, Handsworth Wood, Birmingham 16. Occupations Steel Stockholder and City Alderman. Stanley spoke to the lady librarian. "Everybody has a mother, how about the little fellow listed as Paul Cotton, only a father?"

"People were a little coy in those days" she answered. "Invariably the baby would be illegitimate and then adopted, his natural mother losing all legal claims to the child."

Stanley had never met Alfred Cotton but knew of him through the news media as a client of his firm's senior partner. Only five years previously he was hailed as a Dick Whittington figure, when he became the new Lord Mayor of Birmingham. As a destitute boy he had travelled the South Staffs canal route to Birmingham's

Gas Street Basin in time to hear Big Brum's twelve doleful chimes commiserating the Titanic disaster in April 1912. He was now a living legend.

Stanley murmured to Lily as they nestled cosily on their two-seater plush red settee, "I know he has a youngish son. His twenty-first was announced in 'The Times' recently. He also has a considerably younger wife, the old man must be in his mid-sixties, but no mother listed, how extraordinary."

* * * * *

The previously absent Tory voters came out of hibernation in droves. Not bringing themselves to vote for another party prior to Paul's candidature they were delighted to have a young enthusiastic, eager and keen person to represent Edgbaston and Duddeston. The well-breached highly coiffured ladies took Helen to their hearts, canvassing all hours of every day till the booths closed on polling day. "When women have a cause," as the visiting Tory leader in the Commons said in a by-election speech at the Edgbaston County Ground, "they espouse it, cling like a leech" The Labour candidate of the last three General Elections heckled in a broad Brummie accent, "Ow do'you knew, yo'er a bloody bachelor." The leader guffawed with his well known shoulder shake laughing action, then retorted "The onlooker sees most of the game sir, and you just wait to see the result of these ladies. You won't like it one little bit." With false bravado the reply of "I can 'ardly wait, mate. I still think our next meeting with be in the House of Commons when I address the House as a new member." The Tory leader smiled ruefully "We can only wait and see."

* * * * *

The Edgbaston Duddeston constituency was the first result of the General Election to be announced. Television crews of the major broadcasters were out in force. The Labour candidate peeked at a piece of paper the Returning Officer was carelessly resting on his coat sleeve. A brief glance was enough to know his congratulationary speech to the Conservative candidate would need to be made in his 'Oxford' accent, rather than the 'Brummie' he had cultivated. The Returning Officer, after giving thanks to the administrators for their speedy work in ensuring the constituency maintained the record of being the first result to be announced, gave the peoples' verdict:-

Paul Cotton 39,079

Bernie Greene 13,786

A Conservative majority of 25,293. I duly confirm Paul Cotton will represent this constituency in the forthcoming Parliament.

Paul Cotton took the hand microphone, thanked the constituents who had voted for him and commiserated with the Labour candidate who had put up such a good show and added "In an area where far left wing politics are not acceptable, a Tory victory was really the only result ever likely to be!"

Bernie Greene with the resigned smile of the defeated, replied that his opponent would do the constituents proud and added "The fact that the increased majority of more than 12,000 indicated the electors felt that my friend Paul Cotton would serve them well in the years to come. Although from results that have come in since ours was announced, it will not be as a Government representative but in a Shadow Cabinet role. This pleases me of course." Adding, after giving the matter deep thought, "I am sure we have with us tonight a man who will attain high office, if not the very highest I wish him every piece of good fortune." The defeated candidate's words were prophetic. Paul Cotton became Shadow Financial Second Secretary to the Treasury three months after his maiden speech.

* * * * *

Helen fitted into Parliamentary life exceptionally well, nursing the constituency from their Edgbaston Park Road home whilst Paul was making life very difficult for the Chancellor of the Exchequer's team in the Commons. Early in the new Parliament he caused red faced embarrassment by predicting devaluation within six months. He was asked to withdraw this highly dangerous slander or meet his counterpart in the House of Commons gymnasium. Paul Cotton did neither, and when America called in its Loan Notes, the value of the pound against the dollar plunged violently downwards. He made a speech which did not contain the words "I told you so" but the inference was blatant. "This man is going places," the Opposition Leader suggested to his deputy, the Shadow Minister of Education. "I'm sure you're right leader", she added unenthusiastically. But Paul Cotton was made Deputy to the Shadow Chancellor in the shake up after the following year's budget.

Apart from Edgbaston's massive by-election result the Tories in opposition were not making headway. In the City and County elections of the following two years the Tories trailed. Labour leadership was weak, with corruption and sex for favours, the flavour of the period. The Government were there for the taking, but it did not happen. The bachelor Leader's policies were too close to the Government's own. The difference between the right and the left, red and blue, was blurred. A Mark Anthony figure in a skirt was gathering support. Paul Cotton felt if the trend continued his own position would be jeopardised. In a televised interview she referred to the 'wets' in the party, whose very presence she found difficult to tolerate. Sharing a bottle of red wine during their evening meal, Helen remarked, "If that lady becomes Party Leader, you should look for another job outside politics. You're far too left of her politics. The country has had a left wing Government since Douglas-Hume lost in sixty four, and that was twelve years ago. Four years of the period they called themselves a Tory Government but they were as left as the Opposition and you still have the same Leader. I think you should cover your tail Paul, deep down you favour the peasants rather than the rich and mighty. To continue with that woman you would have to live a lie. I know you, I breathe as you do. The country is ready for right wing policies, even I think the Unions need a sound spanking. Should a job outside politics appear don't disdain it without very serious consideration." These were words he did not want to hear, but would be perilous to ignore.

Tradition demands the Finance Bill is published three weeks after the Chancellor of the Exchequer stands in the Commons to deliver his Annual Budget Statement. This year the furore of the media with its publication was overshadowed by the resignation of the Prime Minister on the same day. The country's lack of direction had suffered as he had spent more time in close company with Constance his parliamentary private secretary than he had directing Great Britain Limited.

Pressure had been brought; a strong left winger direct from the repressive regime of Inland Revenue Fraud Squad had replaced the easy going pipe smoking white gannex-mac wearer.

With Labour moving far left to the borders of communism, the Tories were swinging to the far right; but they were a divided party. The Leader and his chosen team were moderate. Paul Cotton was content, but many other colleagues were smouldering for change. The Tories annual election to confirm its leader was in the offing. Unity to the leadership, a Conservative stung point, following incumbent went without saying. Deep down many Tories would like to vote against the incumbent, but if they did and the Leader was re-elected, they were yesterday's people. The Shadow Minister of Education knew she had nothing to lose. Since her 'wet' interview, the Tory Leader had moved her from "Education" to "Commonwealth", known in politics as an 'Irishman's rise.' She knew it was now or never.

* * * * *

An interview request at his House of Commons office had been accepted from a University friend he hadn't seen since graduation. The auburn haired, long legged, sweet smiling youngest director of programming on the BBC employment roll opened his office door. Without a preliminary, she walked forward to Paul planting a full lips kiss and hugging him. The MP only stopped walking forward on impact. "It's been a long long time since that happened," he said, adding "and its heart musing." She replied; "Far too long, but Helen had that tender caring touch that a long couldn't match, but I'm not complaining, You're looking well how about me?" she said twirling a complete circle.

"Good," he replied "the fuller figure suits you fine."

She pulled a face, "And bugger you too, still I didn't come seeking compliments, there are other doors I could knock if I had to."

Eye to eye across an expensive civil servant's desk she opened, "Our political editor says you might be seeking an insurance policy."

Paul thought deeply. "I thought you worked for the BBC not the Scottish Widows fund."

She smiled, "You're acting naïve Paul and I know you're not. You're unlikely, no very unlikely to become Shadow Chancellor now that your mentor has lost the leadership. There are more types of insurance policies than those written by the Scottish Widows fund and of course their competitors. With more time on your hands why not host an early morning television programme?"

Helen's words of a few days ago were prophetic. "I'm all ears Yvonne but why me? No experience at that sort of thing."

She replied, "Since you became an MP? I've followed your rise and rise at the dispatch box. You'd come across very well on TV. You enter peoples souls, bring out the interesting bits."

Paul Cotton replied, "Complete flattery, but I like it. However politics is my lifeblood. There must be a General Election during the next two years, certainly before nineteen eighty, probably a year earlier. With a Winter of discontent, dustbins not emptied for weeks generating disease, I can see this Government falling badly."

"So can I," she answered quickly "but will you be part of the Phoenix that rises?" She was cut short by the ringing of Paul's mobile.

Paul Cotton listened expressionlessly before speaking. "Terribly disappointing you appreciate my years of devotion and self denial. Evidently the last years count for nothing?' He listened further before replying "Well you won't mind me taking a job outside politics?"

Yvonne strained her ears and heard a woman's voice "No I think that would be a very good idea."

Paul Cotton looked about him. An original painting of "The Snowstorm Derby of 1821" by LF. Herring the Chippendale bookcase with five first editions. His thick pile Axminster wall to wall. The George IV antique desk he was sitting at. Very soon every one a thing of the past.

Paul Cotton looked at Yvonne Ashmore and asked, "When do rehearsals start?"

* * * * *

Paul Cotton cancelled his morning TV shows for the month immediately preceding Polling Day on 3rd May 1979. Despite the national leader desperately trying to guide a right winger into Edgbaston, the local constituency party remained loyal. Cynthia Doulstridge remarked, "You are a wonderful constituency MP. Your Saturday morning clinic's always packed, she doesn't know what she's missing. This new leader obviously has her own set but we'll raise heaven and earth to keep you as our own."

On the second morning after Polling Day, "Cotton" returned to its early morning spot A bleary eyed chat host sat among his invited audience, the morning's show entitled "Defeated, what happens now". Paul Cotton held the loud volume mike, speaking to the now ex-MP for Cannock in Staffordshire, "You held high office at the Overseas Ministry until two days ago, Barbara. Now out of work, What now? It's an arrow embedded in your heart." She replied, "Paul I haven't recovered by a long way. The polls said I couldn't lose Cannock, a traditional mining town. Miners and their families are our base. Miners just don't vote Tory. Yet here I am on my way to sign the unemployment register."

The plumpish elder stateswoman's tears welled. Recently widowed from the then incumbent Minister of Labour and Employment, she was in despair. Paul Cotton sympathised. "It's even worse than my own position and that's bad enough, twenty seven years a Member, now on the scrapheap. Although my majority increased by twenty per cent, I was told not to expect any office. Certainly the new Prime Minister has been true to her prior word. My 'phone number hasn't changed, it didn't ring yesterday, I will sit on the back benches in the House with the largest Conservative majority in the country, and no political job."

Barbara Lee replied, "You joined the wrong party Paul."

He answered, "I don't think so, I joined a mainstream Conservative party. It's not Mohammed moving from the mountain. It's the mountain that's moved from Mohammed."

The auditorium held fifty former MPs on packed benches, most raising a hand to speak. Paul and his microphone moved two rows down, "What's the future for you Jack? Your large majority into reverse mode."

"I'm luckier than most, the carpet firm I left seven years ago still had retained my phone number. It rang yesterday, the old boss wants me back. With my new debating skills honed in the House of Commons, and the mixture of loom colouring I used to do he offered a good job in Marketing and Sales. So if any viewers want a high quality, very reasonably priced rug ring me at Jenkins on Kidderminster 479 3412."

Paul Cotton with mock horror, "That's free advertising my masters will send you a bill! I'm being serious now, we can't let the talent on show here today go to waste." He paused, "Don't go away, we'll be back after the commercials." Paul twinkled a smile at the cameras before fading out.

"So far so good Paul" Yvonne remarked during the break. "We've had six communications from companies interested in the talent on view, also a 'phone call from the Prime Minister of two days ago, now your Leader in Opposition." He said "Tell the defeated on your programme they are not being deserted, ask them to show some true grit and have faith."

"Have faith in what?" Paul Cotton asked.

Yvonne shrugged her shoulders and said, "Whilst they're having faith they still have food and rent to pay for."

Paul interrupted, "What's on the programme tomorrow?"

Yvonne replied, "We've the defeated MP's spouses having their say. You will have to do some research later today. We've filled each morning show quite easily with a political theme for the next three weeks. After that I think the country will be fed up with Politics. We'll have a look at sex and travel after that, always adds spice to the show and gives the ratings a boost."

Paul Cotton replied, "I leave you to arrange the sex side of the show, but like the idea of travel. Have a hankering to do shows for homecoming ex-pats who are still based in the old colonies."

"You'll have to double your ratings before that luxury," Yvonne answered.

Paul Cotton then took his applause to host part two.

The ratings for "Cotton" continued to surprise Yvonne Ashmore, she was fast running out of time for other work. In the Commons Paul Cotton had become a Commander Prior figure.

His appearance at the House was highdays and Budget days. He made an occasional speech when television was a topic on the day's green paper. On those occasions the Prime Minister sought his services as an 'expert' but never a 'political expert'. The Conservatives again swamped the county at the 1983 election, a war had been fought and won, she was invincible. Again Paul Cotton was not mentioned when high political posts were handed out the day after the Election. He still had the same telephone number.

* * * * *

The following year, Cynthia Doulstridge, Paul Cotton and three members of the Prime Minister's staff were clustered in a group at a "fringe" drinks party at the September conference in Blackpool. The PM's Parliamentary Private Secretary again congratulated Paul on increasing his majority at last year's election.

The Parliamentary Private Secretary continued, "It must be something to do with that TV show you host. It's very popular with the common people" Paul restrained his feeling of anger. The Parliamentary Private Secretary flicked the dagger deeper "But we would like to put a more enthusiastic person into your constituency."

Bejewelled Cynthia, now hair completely grey but still showing the old fighting spirit, "If the leader took an interest in Paul his abilities and enthusiasm would return, Just as they used to. Exactly the same as it goes in "Cotton?"

The Parliamentary Private Secretary over-shouted her, "We want Edgbaston for a younger man who's probably the Foreign Secretary ten years hence. Be a good chap don't block progress."

Paul was crestfallen, Cynthia Doulstridge fumed, "Paul's the best constituency MP in the country, and if the bloody Leader considered ability rather than mates she knew at Uni, he'd be the best Chancellor since Lord Grey".

The Parliamentary Private Secretary looked her in the eye. "He's too wet for us" he answered.

Paul's equilibrium had returned, he was deeply hurt but knew they had the whip-hand his centre stage policies had no place in the PM's far right dogma.

With acute timing to retain his dignity he resigned his seat in January of the following year.

* * * * *

Stanley Seaman read of Paul Cotton's resignation as Edgbaston's Member of Parliament ensconced with Lily on their new bouncy crimson settee. "Sorry to see that chap go, the most vicious example of skulduggery politics I've ever come across".

Lily answered, "He's far too nice a person to serve under the Iron Lady. However with the success of his chat show he'll never want for a crust"

Stanley interceded, "And with the inheritance from old Sir Alfred he's become a multi-rich man. Speaking of inheritance, before my old senior partner retired he passed Paul Cotton to me as a client I had my first business meeting with him last week. His wife seems very conscientious and loyal. They've three lovely children. He didn't show his political disappointment, but Helen inferred, when her husband took an outside 'phone call, that the wound is still wide open."

Lily smiled and jolted, "Oh Mike called today, said Sydney was blistering hot. 'It's the time of the year,' I heard Petra shout 'And the bush fires have become too dangerous for comfort. Two firemen already burned to death'."

"Why don't they come back home. With partner retirements, an opening could be found at my firm."

"They're established in Australia. Now our first granddaughter's born. Can't see them returning to the old country."

Stanley retorted, "Took all my persuading for him to follow my profession, then to throw it away moving to Australia" Lily raises her hackles. "Throw it away rubbish, he's working for the State Insurance Service in a very high position." Stanley and Lily had been down this route many times. "Did he say when the family's returning for a holiday?"

Lily answered quickly, "He wants us to go there, and it's about time we did before we become decrepit."

"We'll see, but unlikely this year. There's just too much on at the office."

* * * * *

Paul Cotton's early morning chat show finished, closely followed by the priming for the following day's arrangements. The news media of the past few days covered the death of a premature born baby to the wife of the British Foreign Secretary. Yvonne had targeted this. She had little difficulty in arranging a studio audience of similar sufferers. "There are many more premature deaths than a normal person ever envisages," Paul nodded a reply. He knew he had a long evening of arduous preparation. His usual end of show glass of fine red wine was placed before him. "Sip it slowly and enjoy," she said. Paul lifted the glass towards her as a token of thanks and drank it at one gulp.

As he left by the rear staff entrance a cheer greeted him. A crowd of devotees to his show slapped him on the back, he signed autograph books placed in front of him. Smiling to one young woman, I'm trusting you not to have a cheque and carbon paper under the next page."

He then commenced his usual two mile walk from the studio in Pebble Mill, the most peaceful part of his day. It cleared his mind from the hurly burly surrounding the show. Reading, then interpreting the minds of his victims in the audience was excruciatingly mind wearing. He walked through a small estate of new houses, mainly an Asian enclave. Turning left onto the traffic congested Bristol Road, he passed several sports grounds. Tennis courts were prevalent, pitches for team sports, rugby, hockey, soccer and cricket. Many were used by local schools in the area. Arms pumping high, he strode manfully, he really should find more recreational time. He turned right at Birmingham University Medical Research Centre into Edgbaston Park Road, walked past the two King Edwards Schools for both boys and girls. His journey ended at number 27, Helen was waiting in the lounge. "My handkerchief was soaking wet watching your show this morning thought you were terrific. Let's have a dry sherry before lunch, then onto the Beef Wellington with a blob of paté on the top as a special reward."

Paul felt better than for some time, murmuring 'Perhaps there is life after politics."

* * * * *

The Iron Lady began to falter from the day following her third successive General Election victory. Ignoring the advice of Dick Black, her most influential adviser and the communicating cord between her backbenchers right up to the top of the stairs in her ivory tower, she appointed discredited party member Derrick Ashley as Chancellor of the Exchequer.

The disquieting silence when she chaired the first full party meeting after their election victory was ignored. "Am I not impregnable," she demanded her audience. "Three in a row, no other politician has completed this feat" The usual unrestrained twenty minutes rapturous applause was replaced by a three minute restrained polite response from the floor. The exception being the appointees to high office on the raised platform, Derrick Ashley took her hand kissing it passionately. The new member for Edgbaston was unrestrained giving a standing ovation from the far left of the platform reserved for junior ministers. When silence had been restored the member from Portsmouth South asked, "Why did Dick Black resign as Chairman of the Conservative Party?" Without awaiting an answer, he continued, "The news media coverage stated he wished to spend more time with his family, this seems strange. He said nothing about this prior to our election result of two days ago... Then as soon as he had taken soundings on high office appointments, he resigns."

The Prime Minister replied, "We don't wish to sully our great election victory with the idiosyncrasies of a former member of the Cabinet."

Dick Black's slight figure stood up from the back row of the auditorium, "All of you must realise that my wife has not yet recovered from the horrific injuries she suffered from the I.R.A. bombings at Brighton and is still confined to a wheelchair. I am taking time out to attend to her needs, please let matters rest I would add that unity of the party is more important than the personal feelings of its constituent members.

The PM had lost considerable credence also the guiding influence of her most able statesman; headstrong she didn't recognise it.

* * * * *

Yvonne Ashmore wasted no time in the days following the General Election. The Prime Minister disdained an invitation to attend a Paul Cotton morning show but that was the only refusal. A two week session of ten weekday morning shows brought the Government little succour Paul's own position as a reluctant resigner came over loud and clear, viewers 'phone calls made this an important Government error. However the most keenly debated issue was the appointment of the now Chancellor of the Exchequer, who four years previously had made his secretary pregnant on a promise he would divorce his wife and many her. He reneged on this promise and was forced to resign high office due to the huge public outcry. Now the Prime Minister had restored him as an important Government minister, a position denied to others who had retained their dignity and sobriety, Chatshow host Cotton was constantly quoted. The viewers had not forgotten his tremendous promise in the Shadow Chancellor role before the advent of the Iron Lady.

The heat generated from "Cotton" as well as severely hurting the Government greatly increased the daily viewers of the morning chatshow. This didn't go unrecognised by the world media, especially Kerry Packer of Channel 9, Australia's most popular TV channel, which in four months time would be at the forefront of the media coverage celebrating the two hundredth Anniversary of the arrival of the first convict ship to enter Botany Bay on the 26th January 1788.

In a telecon Kerry Packer reminded Paul Cotton they had played cricket together, although on opposite sides, when Packer toured the United Kingdom with the Australian University Select team. Paul Cotton had represented the Combined British Universities as a very promising all-rounder. Paul and Yvonne were freshmen at Birmingham at the time "All those many years ago," she smiled. "I remember it well. It was before you met Helen, and you and I were an item. This invitation is an opportunity we can't pass over." She immediately rang International Directory Enquiries. "People like Kerry Packer sometimes have second thoughts," she added.

* * * * *

"Young Frances was three last Tuesday, we've missed the best years of her growing into a little girl. If you won't go and see them, then I shall go alone."

Lily was heated. She and Paul were sitting much deeper into the plush bouncy crimson settee, they were slightly heavier themselves, and in the intervening years the springs had eased somewhat. Stanley was on the defensive. "I'm not quite as busy at work since George Moore, my new assistant started work. Perhaps we can emulate Paul Cotton, he was telling me last week his TV show "Cotton" is doing a one-off spectacular in Sydney to coincide with the Two Hundredth Anniversary celebrations early in the new year. Perhaps have Christmas here in the UK, have our usual family festive, then off to Mike's in Sydney. Probably spend two or three days in Hong Kong on the way. Lily breathed a sigh and paused before saying, "I don't suppose we shall be on the same 'plane as the Prince and Princess of Wales even if we travel first class," Stanley agreed, "No the Queen's flight is a little beyond our means and influence."

Lily replied, "It's going to be very exciting, royalty and all that, I can hardly wait." Stanley warming to his subject added "Paul Cotton told me to look him up, he gave me his room number at the Hilton on Circular Quay."

Lily now beaming with enthusiasm, said, "It's beginning to sound the adventure of a lifetime."

* * * * *

Blue Miller stepped onto the 16a all yellow bus followed by four colleagues. The bus left the terminus in Redfern town centre two stops earlier commencing the early morning run to Sydney City centre. Six other colleagues were already seated. Further in its journey another eight employees joined the group. The sole topic of conversation was the Test Match against England to start in five hours time. Blue remarked heatedly to the companion on the other side of the bench. "We must beat the bloody Poms on our two hundredth anniversary as a country." His friend nodded and equally passionately, replied, "They sent our ancestors over here. Very, very few ever went back. We've just got to show them Jack is as good as his master."

Blue nodded, "I've been to the old country, served with the Australian Air Force during the war. I met the sweetest girl in the world over there, then brought her back. We've lived happily for thirty-three years as man and wife. Couldn't give her life's luxuries that I promised her, a damn war wound stopped me playing cricket at the highest level. It was the only career that ever mattered to me. All history now, but Frances stood by me from day one."

"Next stop the Sydney Cricket Ground," shouted the conductor. "You lot make every Brit pay double," he laughed.

The nineteen colleagues from the Redfern district walked directly to the Don Bradman stand. Blue often remarked to Frances how well he knew the great man. Australia's best ever batsman, I even played with him several times in England before I was wounded.

There was already a large crowd of their colleagues awaiting allocation. Immediately at 8.30 am the foreman in charge directed two gatemen to each turnstile. Blue, together with another former cricketer who had fallen on hard times, were sent to an entrance immediately on the roadside outside the Clem Hill Stand. The foreman's parting words ringing in Blue's ears. "Stamp on all bastards trying to enter the ground illegally. Get them or I'll get you, especially you Blue Miller, you ain't caught one in twenty years. The old bosses have all gone, so watch it."

* * * * *

After close of play cashing up, the gateman's sole topic on the return journey to Redfern was the indiscipline of England's opening batsman, Chris Small, who had flung his bat at the stumps, physically breaking two of them, when given out leg before wicket by a "cheating Australian Umpire", as he described the incident in a television interview at the close of play Blue was incensed. "Should never be picked to play for his country again, the Don would have had an apoplectic fit at that kind of behaviour."

The gatemen's conversation continued to dominate the bus' upper deck "Turned over to the police five illegals trying to crawl under my turnstile," stated a colleague guarding the Victor Trumper Stand. Another said "I only got four, two less than the one day match against New Zealand last year. I think our zero tolerance approach is getting through."

Blue Miller looked embarrassed, he had been far too busy watching the Cricket. During their evening meal Frances was agog to hear Blue's experience of the first day. She heard far more about the playing side, who did this, who didn't do that and how Blue himself would have improved the scoring, "if only he could get his war wound repaired" Frances waited patiently before asking "Did you spot any illegals today?" she knew the answer before he spoke. The sheepish look was enough "Try to do better tomorrow dear," she said.

Blue and Frances liked strong coffee. It was his contribution to the meal to make the brew. Now re-seated, he asked "How did your day go dear, how are the grandkids?" Frances smiled "I only got to see Roger and Jean's two, but every time I see them they're two inches higher!" Blue smiled, "Perhaps that's a bit of exaggeration, but it's nice to hear. Anything lined up for tomorrow?" Nothing definite, but I may have a day at the coast. Manley Beach isn't too far away and there's a good bus service."

* * * * *

The tide currents off Manley were some of the strongest in Australia. Red flags warning sun bathers not to swim were three times more in evidence than the OK green flag periods.

Stanley Seaman, on a hot but windy morning, was walking the promenade with his three Australian grandchildren immediately in front of the Manley International Hotel. The two boys were kicking a football to each other. Stanley was holding his granddaughter's hand, listening intently to her jabbering excitedly about her new school friends.

Daniel kicked the ball towards the handrail guarding the raging torrents. Frances had been trained by her elder brothers to chase the ball, she tore her hand from her grandfather's and ran to save the ball. Stanley panicked, at the top of his voice, he shouted "Frances stop!" The little girl halted two inches before the handrail as the ball rolled into the sea.

The abruptness of the action caused the only onlooker, who had been gazing at the sun now clear of the horizon, to turn suddenly. She moved much more swiftly than her advancing years seemed possible, bodily lifted the little girl cradling her in her arms. "There there, dear, you did well to obey your Grandpa," pausing briefly. "You have a lowly name. I know because it's the name my mother gave to me all those many years ago." The baby began to cry, and said, "Grandpa was horrid, he shouted at me, my other Grandpa in England never does that."

"It was for your own good dear," the old lady replied. Stanley and his grandsons were now beside the baby and the old lady, who continued, "That's how accidents happen dear. Then turning to Stanley the lady continued. "You're a lucky grandpa to have such a lovely granddaughter, and two strapping grandsons."

Stanley still panting after his sudden run forward said, "Thank you for comforting her madam, it was a close run thing" his voice tailed off. The older woman returned his incredulous look 'We've met before haven't we" she said. Stanley nodded and kissed the lady. "I've never forgotten you," he replied.

"Nor me you", she answered, adding, "you must have children to have such charming grandchildren." Stanley nodded, "Very lucky. How about yourself?" Frances smiled, "I have three children and six grandchildren'.

Stanley added, "We have so much to catch up on. Come and meet my wife and my eldest son Michael and his wife. They arrived an hour ago to join us for breakfast."

* * * * *

Lily was intrigued and astounded when Stanley introduced Frances at the breakfast table, "A shot in a million," she said, continuing; "I have heard so much about you, the impression you made on a twelve year old boy was enormous. I think you were the first person to treat him as an adult and a youngster never forgets that."

Breakfast rolled into lunchtime. Mike, Anne and the kids had long departed for their normal work and school days.

After two hours and three jugs of coffee, nothing had been mentioned of Frances' first baby. Lily was not going to miss this opportunity, she had heard so much of the circumstances surrounding the event. "The last time you met Stanley would be when the land mine floated into the Birmingham slums, and that must have been nearly fifty years ago."

Frances agreed, "That explosion altered all our lives forever, Not for better or for worse, but nothing was ever the same. My baby, by Tom my first husband, had to be adopted. I joined the Women's Air Force, met my second husband in an RAF hospital and eventually came here to Australia with him. If the land mine hadn't dropped how different my life would have been, very different to how it's turned out, I'm sure."

Lily ordered more coffee, then on Frances' recommendation, succumbed to a bottle of dry white Chardonnay fermented in the nearby Hunter Valley. The wine loosened tongues even further. A persuasive maitre d' obtained agreement to move them into an alcove in the adjoining room with a wonderful view of the sea which was still battering the protective walls and lashing the promenade decks more fiercely than earlier in the day.

Whilst digesting the hors-d'oeuvres and awaiting the main course, Lily enquired in a quiet voice "Tell us more about your first-born, Frances? Are you in contact? It's always intrigued Stanley".

Possibly the wine, the company or the suddenness of acquaintances from the old country, Frances' eyes filled, the lump in her throat choked any words she had ready. She excused herself for nearly fifteen minutes. During which time Stanley had rebuked Lily for being so insensitive. "Don't mention it on her return" Lily was informed in no uncertain manner. But on return Frances felt there was a burden to be rid of. "I haven't seen my baby since I left the maternity hospital, forty six years ago, scarcely a day passes that I don't think of him. I just don't know what happened to him, what he's made of his life, even whether he bears my name."

Stanley had adopted the role of listener, leaving the ladies with their natural inquisitiveness to satisfy their emotions. After an interminable time and no opportunity to intervene, he was abrupt "I have a theory as to who your baby is Frances, even what he's doing now, but I may be wrong" Frances looked startled and shaken from her reverie, but Lily answered, "I think you are wrong, dear. You just have a very vivid imagination, and those short stories you keep catering in competitions and never winning I may add, just fires your creative inventiveness. The tales you wrote about where Lord Lucan is and who Jack the Ripper really was, is just the stuff children's fairy stories are made of and the one about who is baby Paul is in that league" Lily's trade was interrupted by the maitre 'd's polite cough. The main course was ready.

Stanley's version of what happened to Paul as a baby and his progress through adolescence to manhood, his subsequent career to the present day, left Frances awestruck. A wonderful story. "I would like to believe my baby achieving such dizzy heights, but no Stanley I agree with Lily, you always did have a creative streak in your make-up. Even so, I'm looking forward to meeting Paul Cotton. His fame has not reached this country, so I have no preconception of the format of his TV show, or even what he looks like."

The main course of baked kangaroo steak was a first for the British couple. Frances had recommended this delicacy although apologising for herself, choosing cooked ham from the hock bone and white sauce embedded with parsley. She looked at Stanley coyly. "Remember how my mother used to burn the sauce. I'll let you know what this tastes like." Stanley replied "Let me have a spoonful, the taste will revive such memories of when you were sweet seventeen and made an adolescent boy swoon." Frances smiled and replied "As I did when Sinatra's first film ever reached the local fleapit. Tom and I had seats in the back row of the circle. Servicemen were treated preferentially in 1941, and not only by the cinema management" she added with a wistful smile.

Frances had to run to catch the 4.30 bus for the return trip to Redfern, but not before Stanley had made her promise to attend a noonday show at Sydney Opera House on the day the tall Ships were sailing into Sydney Harbour. Frances pardoned the absence of her husband. He was one of the very few people who had to work on this unique day.

* * * * *

The end of the race of ancient tall sailing ships from Hobart in Tasmania to Sydney Opera House ended in splendour. Vast crowds had begun to assemble in every nook and cranny vantage point since early dawn. Sydney City centre contained hundreds of thousands of local inhabitants bolstered by half as many tourists. Stanley and Lily Seaman had joined Mike and Anne's family and their friends, picnicking on surrounding hills overlooking the harbour, with an excellent binoculars view of the winning post. The editorial in that morning's Herald encouraged onlookers to stretch their imagination to a time exactly two hundred years before when their forefathers entered the same route, but not so luxuriously appointed as the crew and passengers travelling on the tall ships sailing in such grandeur today. Their forefathers were chained to every conceivable part of the sailing vessel that had brought them in seriously terrible conditions from England. Many had not survived the voyage, hundreds of human carcasses had been consigned to an ocean burial. One of the survivors to step ashore on the first ship was a nineteen year old woman who had been awarded seven years hard labour, with transportation to Australia, for stealing four yards of silk dress material concealed beneath her skirts. Paul Cotton had set two members of his team to try to discover the whereabouts of her dependants. The team members had the benefit of access to the pubic records, as every convict who had landed in the colonies had been carefully documented.

* * * * *

A one hour television show with a live audience could only chat to about seven or eight persons of one hundred or so people who made up the audience, but Stanley Seaman was a determined man. Each possible interviewee could bring a friend to sit with. Stanley sat next to Frances Miller in the centre of the third row. Yvonne Ashmore and her team had researched the fifty possible interviewees and had placed written details of each person alphabetically in a pile in front of Paul Cotton's desk for immediate reference should he require memory jogging data. At precisely midday she was "on live" introducing "Themes from our past", which is a reference to the Australians whose forbears had landed on the original Tall Ships that arrived at Botany Bay on 26th January 1788. To make up our numbers, but staying with our theme, we are including war brides who had met Australian servicemen during two world wars." Her final words before vacating the podium were "And here is Paul Cotton."

Tumultuous applause greeted his appearance, his wide brown eyes lit up the smile that fluttered millions of female hearts. The quiff in his brillianteened light brown hair combed to perfection. Frances visibly jolted. Stanley turned. "Are you alright dear?" An ashen faced Frances shook herself "Yes, fine thank you." Now hoping ardently it would not be long before the show host sat in the empty seat beside her. Her chances were only seven out of twenty but?

Paul Cotton moved to the sixth row from the dais. "You are?" he enquired "Norman Kelly" replied the old wizened faced man who had a gaping hole where his two front teeth should have been. "I believe you had a famous grandfather, or perhaps infamous would be nearer the mark" The mouth surrounding the gaping holt lit up with a smile. "Yes, Grandfather Ned's grandfather came in on the first convict ships. You see, he came from the stock that villains are made of Ned's old granddad was a pickpocket and burglar who worked for the first organised crime godfather Jonathan Wilde in London's Whitechapel area. He was lucky not to have been hanged at Tyburn but a softhearted judge at the Old Bailey gave him 14 years hard labour with transportation to Australia in which to serve it. Every inmate on the first fleet came from villainous stock, thieves could only steal from thieves – no wonder they all became honest men, they had to so something different, you see." Cotton laughed out loud "So your great-great-grandfather arrived in irons, our grandfather a leader of the most notorious gang of outlaws in Australia has seen its two hundred years' history did the curse of villains ever transfer to you "Oh I am almost honest" replied the old man "I've never succumbed to the Eleventh Commandment, although I must have broken most of the others. I am seventy-seven you see and living in a rough tough neighbourhood."

Paul Cotton asked "What's the Eleventh Commandment and where do you live?" The old man was getting attention and he liked it "The Eleventh Commandment is "Thou shalt not get caught" Before he could continue Frances called "And he lives in Redfern in the next street to where I live. How he keeps out of jail, and I have known him for nearly thirty years, I will never know." The audience broke into happy laughter. The toothless one replied "Don't pay to be honest in Redfern, madam, your husband hasn't improved himself since I've known him. Arrived as a State cricketer now he is a gateman, that's what honesty does for you." Frances was about to retort but Paul Cotton's loud hailer over-rode any voice that may embarrass the show. "Thank you Norman, I may come back later if time permits." Stanley Seaman whispered to Frances "That's one way of saying don't ring us." Frances turned as Cotton took the seat next to her "Ah, Frances, you obviously know our friend two rows back, how about yourself from my notes you came to this country over forty years ago. How's it been for you?" "Very hard work, especially raising three children in a deprived area. Now I have six grandchildren and a lowly sweet natured husband, despite what old Kelly up there says. Blue would make ten out of that Kelly man, I'm sure he would." Consoled Cotton. "You were a war bride, met your husband when he was serving in the Australian Air Force and came back here with him over forty years ago." Frances replied, "Forty two years precisely. My childhood and early years were in Birmingham, where I went to school in Aston, an area not dissimilar to where I live now." Cotton interrupted "I was brought up not far from where you describe, my father was a businessman and indeed a civic dignitary." Frances smiled, "I did hear of him in my early years. Australia is a tougher environment than the old country, here what you earn you keep but you have to earn it, nothing's given for nothing, unlike what I read of State benefits in the old country. I arrived as a new bride. My mother-in-law was a widow living on a meagre war pension, her man died of wounds suffered in Gallipoli shortly after returning from the 1918 war" Cotton nodded "Have you been back to the United Kingdom for a visit since you left in Nineteen Forty-Six?" Frances replied "Both my parents died before I'd been here three years and of course it's very expensive to return to the United Kingdom for a worthwhile holiday. On a more encouraging note I recently discovered the man sitting next to me. He's a very old acquaintance from the Aston area. Cotton nodded "I understand the vast majority of immigrants from the United Kingdom have never been back for financial reasons. I do know the part of the City where the three of us were born. I am looking forward to an in-depth chat after the programme. Thank you." Paul Cotton moved and sat in the aisle. "Thank you Your Royal Highness for attending our show." Diana acknowledged with a nod and her sweetest smile. Cotton continued. "Have you been in Australia long enough to express a view on Australia and whether, like most of our audience, you could settle in this part of the world?" The smiling countenance lit up to a hearty laugh, the Princess replied "I do not think that's a fair question. I prepared myself, as did my husband, with a close study of Australia.

With only that knowledge and having been here a mere few days, I would be in a better position to answer you at the end of our visit, but the situation I am, the job I do must always be based in the United Kingdom, so I must answer in the negative with regard to settling in Australia. From what little I have seen it makes me think the people who moved here have not regretted their decision, but I shall be interested to hear other speakers. I was very interested in the lady born in Birmingham, which I have visited frequently." Paul Cotton's loudhailer answered "It is a coincidence that Stanley Seaman, Frances Miller and myself were all born in the town you mention. Only Frances got away. Before Paul Cotton could continue a man's voice shouted "Two hundred years, that's nothing except it was the marker date of the white man stealing the land and heritage of my people." Paul turned to the fourth row of the right hand aisle to see a black faced man dressed in the dark blue uniform of the Australian Navy. Three wide bands of gold braid on the lower section of each sleeve showed that he held the rank of Lieutenant Commander. Cotton's microphone was switched off immediately and he whispered an excuse to the Royal personage. Her face switching from radiance to anxiety. Although Paul Cotton gave a show of annoyance, the interruption was – television. Confrontation held viewers' attention more than any other emotion. An usher asked the man next to the sailor to move seats, Paul Cotton took his place. "Who are your people sire? You wear the uniform of the Australian Navy. Aren't you proud of that?" The man's appearance of a jet black face, deep sunken eyes and squashed nose embedded into his face, left nothing to the imagination of his origin. The man ignored Cotton's question. "Two hundred years is nothing to the 11,000 years ago when my people migrated here. We are the true owners of this Continent, not the usurpers who came in chains in 1788". Controversy was one thing but this from an officer of the armed forces sounded like treason to Cotton: An important representative of the Queen was seated a few rows away. "How can you tie your allegiance to the Government of Australia and the Queen of Great Britain and refer to their ancestors as land robbers. The situation as we have it, has evolved over the last two hundred years. The position in situ" Cotton stated. The Naval Commander interrupted "My father is King of the remaining few thousand aborigines. My forefathers had been ensconced in Australia 11,000 years when the white people came here. If that is not ownership by possession. I do not know what is." Norman Kelly's voice was distinctly heard "Well what are you doing in the uniform of a naval officer?" The Naval Commander replied "My father could see the trend. The lessening of authority and the non-involvement in politics of Aboriginal leaders. He had me educated in a white man's school and used his influence to obtain entry for me as a naval cadet. After that it depended on myself. Never has a cadet been so determined to succeed but that does not excuse the plight and suffering of my race. Cotton said "You have used your influence as a senior naval officer to obtain entry to this show to advertise the plight of the aborigines." The black man was incensed. "Today you are celebrating the coining of the white man to these shores a mere two hundred years ago, that's a pittance in time, as I have already said. It was guns and explosive against spears, we did not have a chance." Princess Diana was shocked at the outburst. "Could we meet afterwards, the Queen in the United Kingdom must hear your views." Norman Kelly shouted from his seat at the rear of the auditorium "These black men never give us a moment's peace with their constant moaning about the treatment they infer the white man has done to them. Where would they have been without us." The veins on the naval officer's neck bulged "In the first instance there would be a million of us without the white man's guns. Whisky and gin have killed and reduced considerable numbers of my forefathers to a stupor state." Cotton felt distinctly a comfortable, his loudhailer said "This is a good time to take a short break. When we come back we will take listeners' phone calls. My assistant, Yvonne, has signalled that the content of the programme has sparked off a furore." Cotton's smooth smile faded the programme to let commercial advertising take over the channel.

In the interval Yvonne Ashmore confronted Paul Cotton "On this day of all days the Aborigine problem has been raised. Paul, how could you have been so naïve? A fax from the Prime Minister's Office says "Change the subject". He is with Prince Charles, hosting a lunch at Government House for the Captains and crews of the Tall Ships, but his aides consulted him. His wife is in our audience with Her Royal Highness. Our show was meant to be a background show to the main event, mainly for the Australian ladies, not a political hornets' nest. In the second half of the show return to emigration from the old country after two World Wars. Forget convicts, penal colonies and aborigines." Paul Cotton, suitably chastened, prepared himself for the second part of the live show.

Addressing the audience "The phone lines to this Channel have been inundated. My staff, under the direction of Yvonne Ashmore," he smiled her a sheepish acknowledgment to where she sat on the podium, still looking daggers drawn "will edit these and time permitting, we will have a debate." Cotton then walked to the fifth row in the auditorium and sat by a middle aged man with greying hair but had a huge salesman's smile. Cotton opened. "You've lived in Australia about 16 years I understand." "Brought my wife and two kids here in 1972 and never regretted it. We ran a sub post-office in Boxall, a small village near Manchester, but the tax rates soared in England eighty three percent. On my level of income, thought it time to bugger off, if you know what I mean." Paul grimaced and said he knew the feeling, it had hit him too. "Well why didn't you get out and come here?" shouted ex-Postmistress Ivy. "Thought I'd stop and fight my corner from inside the House of Commons. I was an Opposition Member of Parliament at the time you mention." Tom looked shocked "So, you was one of the buggers who forced us out." Paul smiled "No no, I was on your side. Tried for lower tax rates. With the top rates now only forty percent why don't you both go back?" "Never, not with this wonderful climate" answered Ivy. Paul smiled and returned to the empty seat next to Frances.

* * * * *

Controversial programmes drew larger audiences, the TV controllers became anxious when Paul Cotton ignored his pre-break victims for a more sedate climate. The Director of Programming whispered to Yvonne Ashmore to let Paul Cotton know. 'Get back to the black naval man and Norman Kelly' was the gist of the communication. Yvonne watered down the message, prepared to accept a few thousand viewers switching off to save an international incident. Australians were controversial and generally loved a fight. She remembers her father telling her of 'bodyline bowling' and how the Governments of England and Australia had become so incensed with each other that diplomatic relations between the two countries were almost severed. The Government of Australia accused the England fast bowlers of aiming at the body rather than at the wicket and this was merely a game of cricket. What would happen if Paul Cotton took sides in the Aboriginal dispute.

A gold braided arm was constantly raised showing a black wrist below the white naval shirt. Norman Kelly shouted "It's my turn, bring the mike over here." But Paul Cotton's had had a steady grasp of the situation. "Sorry gentlemen both of you had a good part of the first half of the show and in fairness we must move on." Which he did, to a tall very slim woman in her late fifties, her very pale face was unusual during this fine Australian Summer. "I came here from Coventry in the Summer of fifty two. Paid a one way fare of ten pounds and travelled steerage. I would like to travel to Georgia in the USA rather than go back to the old country. But husband Billy here, who I met on the boat coming over, is a very homely bird, but I am still working on him" Lily Seaman's eyes lift up, then interrupted the speaker, "I know why you want to go to Georgia, Edith." The pale faced woman was astounded by the English accent, when went on "When we worked together in the offices of the button factory, your hobby was reading 'Gone with the Wind'. You must have read it eighteen times in the five years I knew you. You could recite a complete page without a mistake." Paul Cotton interjected "Have we brought together another set of old friends?" This programme is beginning to sound like 'Where are you now?' Doubtless you two ladies will not be short of topics when we meet at lunch after the programme."

Whilst Paul Cotton was speaking, Edith Bletchly rushed from her seat moved four rows forward to the left side aisle seat and threw her arms around Lily Seaman. "What a marvellous surprise, Lil, it seems an eternity since I was your bridesmaid. The two ladies still in an embrace were now off camera. Paul Cotton was in deep conversation with a new entrant to the programme, discussing whether Britain would have a commitment if a foreign aggressor attacked Australia Paul Cotton drawing on his political experience as a former Shadow Minister gave the view that Britain would leave no stone unturned to help that sort of situation. Cotton reported "I'd don my old National Service uniform and fly out here with the first troops." Tom Sambrook interjected "You don't look old enough to have done National Service, conscription finished in '56. I was one of the last to be called." Cotton replied "So was I, joined the Royal Air Force in 6 January 1956." "Ah, I was in the army at the same time." Sambrook answered. Kerry Packer walked on stage, hailed host Cotton "Don't you think the modern youth of Britain, and that includes the new masters in the present Government, would be too young to remember the bonds that held the two countries together before and immediately after two World Wars." Cotton's view was the bonding between the two countries was as close as ever. Kerry Packer seemed doubtful. "Looking at the cricket scene for example, the present English team includes five players who were the sons of immigrants from the West Indies and the Indian Continent. I can't see why they should have such an affinity to the Antipodes. The Naval Officer did not wait for an invitation to speak. "The New Zealanders would be better thought of by Britain's new immigrants and their children. They treated the Maoris much more humanely than the Aborigines were treated by the whites here. Kerry Packer nodded to Paul Cotton, programme time was ebbing away. The host acknowledging his cue, flicked the microphone switch whilst walking to the centre of the podium to face the audience.

"Ah, I see Edith has returned to her seat. Norman referred to not saying it again but Frances must have further thoughts on that staying in Australia has benefits beyond returning to the UK, even for a short visit. We have heard Tom and Ivy went back, then returned here, what does that signify?" Before he could answer his own question Frances interjected "The only reason I would have returned home, and it is home whatever anyone says, is to determine a happening in my earlier life. This programme has opened my eyes to events that happened when I was little more than a slip of a girl and the Birmingham I knew was being showered with German high velocity bombs and land mines. The forerunners, it grieves me to say, of the millions of land mines laid in the present day in places such as Moscovo, the Middle East and other parts of the globe to this day. It doesn't seem man has become more friendly to his foreign and national brothers than when my first husband was killed in France forty seven years ago. Programmes such as this highlight the problems, but no improvement ever happens. One can only hope that man will improve his attitude to his brother, but as wars have been going on since eternity, I deeply doubt it. There would only be a massive advance if women ruled the world."

"Thank you very much, that was a fine epitaph to my programme, Frances." replied Paul Cotton. "I do not think anything further need be added, especially as the programme has overstretched itself timewise, and the Queen's Speech, which is live by the way direct from London, simply cannot be delayed. Thank you to my audience, especially for the contributors. Also particular thanks to Her Royal Highness the Princess of Wales for her contribution." Diana smiled her acknowledgement. The red light of live programming prevailed.

Paul Cotton sat back on the podium, mentally strained. This happened on a daily basis in the UK, but today's programme had plumbed the depths more than any other.

Yvonne Ashmore knew the symptoms, his walk from Pebble Mill to his Edgbaston home being denied him, she called for a larger than usual glass of red wine.

* * * * *

The podium was full of people milling around. Norman Kelly was jabbering about Australia being too good for the Abo's. Yvonne was trying to guide him elsewhere. The black naval Commander was addressing an audience leaving the auditorium. When his entreaties were ignored, he buttonholed Kerry Packer, who suggested they defer any conversation until the Celebration Lunch. "Plenty of time to talk then, I'm sure the Prime Minister's team that will be in attendance will have something to say to you." The Naval Commander replied "All they suggest is that my people should retreat further into the bush. Away from the coast line to that inferior mass of the country that nobody wants to know."

* * * * *

Stanley Seaman had moved to the aisle seat a few feet from the podium, speaking with Frances on his left. A waiter descended the steps on Stanley's right carrying a large glass on a silver salver, he was walking slowly but deliberately. Near the bottom he gained more confidence and moved a little faster. On the last step, about to present the salve to Paul Cotton, his left foot was gently nudged against his right foot. The full glass shot off the salver, hitting Paul Cotton's right shoulder, the contents staining his gleaming white tuxedo. The hubbub ceased. Yvonne Ashmore glared at the waiter as she rushed past him to comfort Paul, who was shaking himself. "Accidents will happen, no harm done, the glass missed me." Yvonne answered "The contents didn't. I'll get your spare shirt" and hurried away. The unfortunate waiter was full of apologies "I must have tripped over someone's feet I'm dreadfully sorry."

Frances walked forward towards Paul Cotton, "Son, you do look in a sorry state." Paul smiled and was about to reply but Yvonne Ashmore appeared with the replacement shirt and a white towel.

Paul slipped his shirt off, towelled the red liquid from his body – pulled the replacement shirt over his head. "No bother, people" he smiled, "perhaps we can proceed to the ante room. I understand lunch will be served in fifteen minutes, just in time for me to shower."

The crowd broke up, mostly heading towards the ante room, but Frances beckoned Stanley Seaman "follow me please." They walked tough a warren of corridors, arriving at an unmarked door. Frances stopped, turned toward Stanley and said "You didn't have to go through the charade of tripping that unfortunate waiter. I knew who Paul Cotton's natural father was the moment he stepped on the podium to open the show. He is a replica, older of course, of the nineteen year old Tommy Stephenson I married in 1941. My maternal chords tugged oh so sharply. I'm really pleased I came here today." Stanley was nonplussed. "What's this nonsense, you will be sitting next to Paul at lunch, that's already arranged. Ask him if the red circle on his right shoulder came from the wine. See his reaction. Come on Frances, see the funny side of it" She stared hard "Stanley, if I wasn't a lady I'd hit you full in the face." She paused momentarily before continuing. "Never tell Paul of my connection with him, write to me about him, I must know what he's doing." She smiled and whispered "All is forgiven then" and kissed him gently on the cheek. Turning she lifted the bar on the emergency door onto the Opera House Gardens.

The bright afternoon sunshine startled her, she'd completely forgotten it was daytime. She walked smartly down the stone steps through the rose garden. There were still many tourists and town residents enjoying what little remained of the Bank Holiday.

Frances knew the journey very well from the time she worked as an usherette at the Opera House when it first opened. She hastened her step, only five minutes left, almost at a run she completed her journey.

Passengers had started to load the 4 o'clock fast bus to Redfern. She half expected to see Norman Kelly, but then remembered he would never miss a free lunch.

She relaxed on the front upstairs window seat. On the journey the wind blew through her hair reminding her forcibly of the journeys she and Tommy had enjoyed to the English Lickey Hills all those many years ago.

* * * * *

At the Sydney Cricket Ground bus stop a crowd of the gatemen boarded wreathed in smiles. Australia had beaten the Poms in the Bi-centenary Test Match. Blue was particularly boisterous, emulating to his mates the attacking cover drive to the boundary fence completed several times by the Australian captain during his double century. Blue sat next to Frances and continued his joyous banter. When he simmered down she asked the dreaded question "Had he caught his first illegal entrant?" Joy turned to embarrassment "Almost, but he ran faster through the gates than my old legs could travel."

Frances was wreathed in smiles, they held hands tenderly till journey's end.

THE END

*Five*

# CAN MONEY BUY ME LOVE?

Main Character Outline

1st. Lady Daphne Greey (pronounced Grey) a member of the aristocracy. Recently widowed. Has the responsibility to find a suitable marriage to a top business executive or a "title" for her youngest daughter, Vanessa, who has recently completed a three year course at a finishing school in Switzerland.

2nd. The Hon. Vanessa Greey – youngest child of the late Sir Harry and Lady Daphne Greey. A voluptuous, slim waisted but heavily breasted natural blonde, a real eye turner. Loves people around her. Is popular with both sexes. Concerns her mother as she spends her time with people she likes rather than eyeing the half chance of a liaison with a suitable potential husband. Very popular on both the playing and social side of the golf club. On the social side she helps the club secretary in an honorary position.

3rd. Peter Porterson – jolly chap recently out of university. Had spent most of his university life on the golf courses of Oxfordshire gaining a golfing blue but a very weak 2:2 pass in Modern Art. 'Can bluff most people with that subject', he confided to his father with a nod and a wink. His father smiled knowingly. 'Bullshit baffles brains, son, keep up the good work'. Teddy Porterson – Peter's father's wealth came from a catering company formed many years earlier aimed at rich and famous customers. From meagre beginnings the company prospered splendidly. Sadly he discovered a taste for the high life himself. Since then the business struggled.

4th. Berkshire Heath Golf Club – situated near Henley-on-Thames. Membership of the golf club is still a much sought after prize. It is still a bastion of the Victorian age and male chauvinism. The bar is the congregating area and meeting place of members, a great thirst quencher after a four hours round. Socially the members create a happy environment. This is added to by "Old Arthur and young Daisy", the steward and his assistant. The Clubhouse includes a large baronial type dining room on the first floor overlooking the golf course. The professional shop on the ground floor is at the rear of the converted country house.

5th. Andrew Dutton-Clough – tall gangling fellow with affectations of a fop, brought up at the family seat, educated at Eton. Heir to 3500 acres spread over the borders of Oxfordshire and Berkshire. Family wealth connected to the "Establishment" of England. Has entry into all the domains of aristocracy. Member of the exclusive Pall Mall and Carlton Clubs. Doesn't work as 99½% of the UK population defines work. Administers the family seat and collection of rents from the innumerable tenants in the farms and villages owned by the family estate. Had as much time as he needed in his formative years to become an excellent golfer.

6th. Arthur – the golf club steward. Formerly a piano player in a famous jazz band, now on hard times but still retains the twinkle in his eye. Invariably wears a McGregor tartan blazer, white shirt and matching tie, balding, popular with the golf club members. A darling with the ladies who seek his advice and wit. Will accept a gratuity from members he likes, refusing the others with a "Thank you but your need seems greater than mine sir".

7th. Young Daisy –Arthur's niece, expert at providing drinks quickly. Wears a tartan shortish skirt tightly pulled around the thighs (this matches her uncle's jacket) and a white blouse with tartan epaulettes. A popular woman with male members, most of whom include a drink for her when buying a round.

8th. Golf Professional – Jack Greaves – tall willowy Welshman. Employed at the golf club since returning from the Falklands as a demobbed soldier.

9th. Club Secretary – short and pompous, clipped moustache, wears navy blue blazer with a club badge on the pocket. Grey flannel trousers. Very shiny black shoes.

10th. Cynthia Jones – excellent golf player. Came from working class folk in the Welsh Coal Mining area. Boyfriends come a poor second to her golf aspirations.

11th. Geoff McBeath – A good enthusiastic golfer. Member at downmarket Moor Hamlet Golf Club. Playing partner of Cynthia Jones.

12th. Spencer Dutton-Clough – top aristocrat. Andrew's father.

13th. Teddy Porterson – Peter's father. A Captain of Industry.

14th. Madeline Dutton-Clough – Andrew's mother – streetwise aristocrat in the mould of Lady Daphne Greey, but without Daphne's financial burdens.

**Can Money Buy Me Love?**

Lady Daphne and her daughter Vanessa seated on bar stools both drinking vodka and lime juice in tall glasses. Arthur was holding back on the change.

Lady Daphne: "Have one yourself Arthur".

Arthur: "Thank you your ladyship, I'll have a small beer".

Arthur popped a pound coin into a pint size glass near the till.

Vanessa: "Mummy, both Peter Porterson and Andrew Dutton-Clough have shown more than a passing interest in my welfare".

Lady Daphne: "I should think so dear, you are far too good for both of them of course, but I suppose these days we have to consider every option".

Vanessa: "I hadn't gone as far as thinking as either of them as a husband dearest. I'm far too young for that".

Lady Daphne: (tartly) "At twenty-two you are not 'far too young for that', your dearly departed father's Estate won't last much longer at the rate of knots we're spending. Thank goodness your Swiss finishing school fees have ended. The drain on the bank balance was haemorrhaging our reserves".

Vanessa: "Yes, when it was necessary Daddy did have the knack of pulling large wads of cash out of his top hat. Like a magician with a rabbit".

Lady Daphne: "I certainly miss him for that, almost as much as keeping a smile on my face in the bedroom".

Vanessa: (thoughtfully) "Unusual you should say that Mummsy, I never imagined you and Dad doing that sort of thing, if you know what I mean".

Lady Daphne: "Where do you think you and your brothers came from, if we didn't do that sort of thing. Sexy loving isn't only the prerogative of the working class you-know. The aristocracy love to do it and we're better at it. More control and passion dear".

Andrew Dutton-Clough enters and walks over. His face a fixed smile. Kisses both ladies.

Andrew Dutton-Clough: "Hello D and V, bit of poetry there you know. D and V see what I mean eh. Can I get you a drink?"

Lady Daphne: "Thank you but no, our glasses are full: We're discussing Vanessa's business future. She's had a good theoretical background in business studies at that Swiss place. (she pauses) I don't suppose you need a secretary that can't spell well do you?"

Andrew Dutton-Clough: "No thanks Lady D. I already have one".

Vanessa: "Mummy please don't go on. I want more from life than being a shorthand-typist. I want a job with adventure, excitement and a spice of danger".

Andrew Dutton-Clough: "Why not train as a Chartered Accountant. You know Vanessa we must have another practise round in the near future. You could be my partner in the next foursomes competition. With your beauty and my skill we're bound to win".

A booming voice is heard before its owner appears walking in.

Peter Porterson: "Don't consider that offer Vanessa, I've been practising avidly in the last two weeks. Win with me, Andrew's not serious enough with his game now'days. Far too serious amassing wealth".

Andrew Dutton-Clough: "Peter, you certainly don't diminish in size. You obviously enjoy the pleasures of your father's business too much to take golf seriously".

Peter Porterson: "Yes the dear old Dad provides victuals for the rich and famous. Does all the catering at Royal Ascot you know. Next Tuesday does the Royal Academy Summer Exhibition opening night. Can't keep a good chap down".

Lady Daphne: "Peter you are a boastful peasant. I was at Ladies Day last month. Didn't notice whether the food was exceptional or not. The champagne was but your father didn't ferment it with his own hands. If your bottom line matches your arrogance your firm's profits must be having a bumper year".

Peter Porterson: "Well of course m'lady quality and profitability are not necessarily close bedfellows. We are seeking a little more capital to finance our increasing turnover".

Lady Daphne: "If you ate a little less of your own products it would help".

Intervening diplomatically.

Vanessa: "Mummy's exceptionally bright at knowing her quality food. Didn't you attend a whole week's cordon bleu course at the Pans Ritz in the early sixties dear?"

Lady Daphne: "Yes, I did. Cesar Ritz himself asked me to advise the kitchen staff after the course. Couldn't help him though, I was having trouble with that Flossie Beaumont-Sharpe. She was flirting outrageously with Vanessa's father, the late Sir Harry. (Lady Daphne paused and bowed slightly in memory of her late husband). Took a few weeks to repel the raider. Even after we were married the vixen didn't give up, but with the wart on the top of her nose, she never had a real chance. But it did stop me advising at the Ritz. You never know, I could have been a master chef earning a mint per annum. Still, never mind".

Andrew Dutton-Clough: "I hope you don't mind me saying this Lady D, but the number of times you say 'never mind' in quite an apologetic way, it would make an excellent nickname for you".

Vanessa (directly to her mother). "I think I will still call you 'Mummy'. 'Never Mind' seems a little over the top".

Arthur (mischievously) "What shall we call you, 'M'lady' or 'Never Mind'?"

Lady Daphne: (insulted) "You steward will call me Lady Daphne. Anything else will be an insult. The late Sir Harry would have had you horsewhipped for even thinking about such familiarity".

Arthur withdraws from the bar touching his forelock.

Peter Porterson: "Certainly put him in his place, Lady Daphne, (pausing). You must excuse me all, I'm having a golf lesson from Jack the professional in a few minutes". (He gulped his glass empty and departed at speed).

Vanessa (To the remaining two) "Peter's certainly taking his golf seriously, I'm going to face a very difficult decision, both of you asking me to play in the foursomes".

Andrew Dutton-Clough: "The golf decision may only be a small matter-compared with a decision on life's future. You must know how much I fancy you, Vanessa. I suspect the fellow that just left our company may have similar designs but I'm sure you will be guided by Lady Daphne, who knows about these things". (He departs the bar).

Lady Daphne: "That sounds very much like a marriage proposal to me deaf. I like the idea of being a mother-in-law to the landed gentry, a country seat, a London house in Eaton Square. Grandchildren riding ponies, attending the best prep schools. Just my cup of tea".

Vanessa: "Don't get carried away, dear. I'm not certain I quite see it the way you obviously do".

Arthur (appears) "A message from the maitre d' ladies. Your table for the luncheon you reserved is now ready".

End Of Scene

Lady Daphne and The Hon. Vanessa now seated at a table for two in the opulent dining room in an alcove reserved for members requesting privacy.

Lady Daphne: "The soup-du-jour is usually excellent, I'll go for that, dear. How about yourself?"

Vanessa: "Perhaps the hors-d'oeuvre followed by steamed mackerel. After a hard round of golf this morning, I'm feeling peckish. Both Andrew and Peter are keen to further our relationship. When we last played they almost came to blows over who should rake the bunker at the last hole after I walked out of the sand".

Lady Daphne: "You really have made a deep impression: I could take either of them as a son-in-law. But you realise you must not let your heart, or whatever other part of your anatomy has a craving for male attention, rule your head. You only satisfy your sexual desires for a small part of a week. The rest of the time, you must administer a wealthy estate or in Peter's case, a high class catering business. We know from his boasting that the Queen eats their products. It's also show on their company headquarters emblem 'By Royal Appointment'.

Vanessa: "I understand what you mean Mummy. I must be highly sexed as I enjoy that side of their relationship much more than a round of golf.

Lady Daphne: "Don't be a silly girl, loving sex is a by-product of selecting a good man".

Vanessa: "Well if I don't make the choice by selecting the more virulent and satisfying sex partner, how do I make it? I simply can't see any alternative. The girls at finishing school all agreed a well hung man is the first requirement for happiness".

Lady Daphne: "You silly soppy girl, haven't you heard of the key test?"

At this point they are interrupted by Steward Arthur.

Arthur: "Can I get you any drinks, ladies?"

Lady Daphne: "Yes, Arthur, we'll have our usual. Two dry martinis, pinked by angusduras, please".

Arthur (pausing) "Sorry, madam, we have run out of angusduras bitters".

Lady Daphne (looking saddened) "Never mind".

Arthur breaks out into an involuntary chuckle.

Lady Daphne: "Enough of that Arthur".

Vanessa: "Use gin instead of the angusduras Arthur, and take that smile off your face".

Arthur: "Yes, madam". (His face changing from hilarity to severity as he retreats bowing).

Now alone – Vanessa eyeballing her mother.

Vanessa: "What is a key test mother? Is it something to do with unlocking the heart of a man?"

Lady Daphne: "No, dear, it is something more to do with unlocking the wallet of a man".

Vanessa: "I'm intrigued".

Lady Daphne: "It's surprising that you know nothing of the key test. When I was your age it was part of a normal gal's upbringing. (Pause). Every man no matter his social standing carries a bunch of keys in his pocket. Many ladies do but that has nothing to do with the moral of my tale".

Vanessa (impatiently) "Carry on mum cut out the foreplay".

Lady Daphne looks shocked.

Lady Daphne: "You will have to use quite a lot of foreplay to get the best out of the key test, dear. When you are in a compromising situation, maybe on a chaise lounge and he is thoroughly relaxed, you somehow procure his bunch of keys. Select any key and casually ask 'What door does this open, darling?' Depending on what he says, you mark the answer from one to ten".

Vanessa: "A bit like a cricket scoreboard. The batsman with the most runs wins the fair damsel for the evening".

Lady Daphne: "You're getting the drift dear".

Vanessa: "I'm probably being a little stupid mummsy, but how do I determine what number of points are earned by a particular key? Keys come in all shapes and sizes don't they? There are thick steel ones for the front door of a mansion and tiny ones for your luggage case".

Lady Daphne (interrupts): "If you ask about a certain key that you have selected, he may answer, 'that is for the front door of my London apartment. I use the flat some times when I find it bally inconvenient to get home to my country house in Berkshire'. You mark that ten out often. However, if he says 'it's for the outside lavatory in my terraced house in Whitechapel that would only score one (pausing thinking about it further) it wouldn't even merit one point".

Vanessa: "I see that is an extreme example I presume. Neither Peter or Andrew are likely to have an outside loo in a terraced house in the East End. Otherwise they wouldn't belong to this club".

Lady Daphne: "Precisely, dear. Both of your young men have the trappings of wealth but I think the key test is most important. Some men may have millions of pounds worth of debts and living on a bank overdraft. You can't be too careful".

Vanessa: "Well that was a splendid lunch darling mum thank you for the advice on how a well brought up gal should select a husband. I wonder if I will act on your words of wisdom".

Lady Daphne: "You'd better. Since Sir Harry's death the family income has virtually dried up, please don't let the title down by marrying an impecunious drifter".

Scene Ends

Vanessa is behind the counter in the professional shop. As a favour to Jack Greaves, (the professional) she has agreed to 'look after' the shop for a few hours whilst he is playing golf with three club members. One of whom is Andrew Dutton-Clough. Peter Porterson enters the shop.

Peter Porterson: "Hello, Vanessa, starting a new career in retailing".

Vanessa: "Only very temporary, Peter. Just two or three hours whilst the pro is away on official duties. It makes a change from sitting behind a desk. Don't need to wear my specs for this job".

Peter Porterson: "Oh, I fancy you in specs, Vanessa, in fact I fancy you without specs as well".

Vanessa (teasingly): "I hear it said men don't make passes at women who wear glasses".

Peter Porterson: "That was in your mother's time, with modern frames it heightens the sex adrenaline, especially those scarlet red ones you're wearing".

Vanessa is a little flustered by the compliment and thanks Peter.

Vanessa: "Shouldn't you be slaving over a hot desk on a weekday afternoon earning an honest crust or even baking a crust in your line of business?"

Peter Porterson: "I suppose so but I can work overtime tomorrow, much rather spend some time with you. We could even go into the club workshop through the back there. They have three golf clubs of mine to put new grips on the shafts. Nothing like looking for yourself".

Vanessa: "Well you know where it is, I'll wait here. Serve the vast crowd of customers I'm sure will charge through the door at any minute. Ah, here's one now".

Enters Arthur the Steward.

Arthur: "Hello madam, I'm usually on that side of the counter and you on this. I only want some cough drops, Jack the pro keeps some for me. Oh, hello Mr Porterson, it may be bold to say it but you seem to be attracted to Lady Vanessa like a moth to a flame. I suppose it's something to do with being young. Also Lady Vanessa has the type of figure that does cause some men to skip work for an afternoon and hope for the best, if you see what I mean".

Peter Porterson: "You old fraud, I understand perfectly well what you mean but Lady Vanessa and myself are particularly keen to produce the perfect golf swing.

Spend hours working on the theory and we will finish by using the practice mat in Jack's absence".

Vanessa looks over her specs with wide enquiring eyes.

Arthur (replies): "Oh a mat finish eh, mat finishes are a speciality with my decorator sir. Good luck". (He hurries out of the shop, touching his forelock as he retreats in his usual backward motion).

Peter Porterson (irately): "That old bugger only pays lip service to the members, takes the piss out of us something awful and its our subscriptions that pay him".

Vanessa suddenly remembers the key test.

Vanessa: "Peter are the men's lockers built the same as ours? Not enough room in mine for my overloaded handbag. When there's a club function I have to go home and change. No space to store anything really".

Peter Porterson: "Oh, ours are quite large, they were constructed when the clubhouse was new in the early twenties. The ladies lockers came after world war two, then utility furniture had to be used".

Vanessa: "Just look at my small key, what size is yours Peter? The keys of course".

Peter bursts out laughing.

Peter Porterson: "What else, Vanessa dear? Here's my locker key".

Vanessa's perusing the key intently. The pompous prig Club Secretary bangs the door behind him.

Description of Secretary – Navy blue blazer, club's coat of arms on pocket; grey flannels sharply creased. Club tie, moustache tightly clipped, hair parted down middle heavily gelled. Clipped speech, humourless.

Club Secretary: "Where's Jack? It's pay day and I need some change".

Vanessa (replying discourteously): "I'm in charge, we don't have any spare change".

Club Secretary: "Well, that's a good enough reason not to pay the staff. They will have to wait till tomorrow".

Vanessa: “Now I know why the staff love you so much. You could have arranged change at the bank yesterday. I know young Daisy must have her wages today. Her mother relies on her to pay the rent”.

Club Secretary suitably chastened raises his nose in the air, opens the door to leave.

Club Secretary: “Answering back to a superior club official, in my young days at the club that would have meant an instant visit to the Lady Captain’s room”.

He departs banging the door.

Vanessa: “Oh, forget that old busybody, (her attention returning to the key test). By the size of my small key (she now had hold of his complete bunch). It’s the usual situation of the ladies having the rough end of the arrangement and having to settle for less. What’s this long one for? It’s bent at the end. Should imagine it’s for a very unusual lock”.

Peter Porterson: “It’s for the safe in the Board Room. It’s a two key safe. Dad keeps the other one. The safe can’t be opened unless the two of us are together”.

Vanessa: “Very ingenious. I suppose you keep oodles of cash in there. Black money from the tax man”.

Peter Porterson: “No, no, nothing like that, we have to spend any ‘black money’ as you call it on the necessities of life. Like beer, ciggies, wine, also wild women”.

Vanessa: “Oh, so you are interested in the firm side of a woman’s wrath, are you?”

Peter Porterson: “Hardly dear, that was a weak attempt at a joke. The office number cruncher keeps the Register of Members, Minute Books, lists of shareholders, that sort of thing. Oh, we also keep the petty cash box in there. But it’s full of IOU’s rather than hard cash. Dad’s like that, they don’t call him ‘On the tick Billy’ because he’s interested in clocks. You do seem bloody interested in my keys Vanessa”.

Vanessa (a little flustered): “Not really, Pete, only morbid curiosity”. (She looks at another key and raises a quizzical eye to Peter.)

Peter Porterson: “That’s only my car key, you can see the beast from here”. (He points to a Jaguar on the car park).

Vanessa: “Beautiful motor that one, all highly polished and smart, probably extremely valuable. Is it a vintage or whatever they call it?”

Peter Porterson: "Well, you can see it is an 'L' reg, keep asking Dad to get me a personalised number plate to hide the shame of a seven year old car".

Vanessa "You could ask him to buy you a new car at only a fraction of the price of one of those flashy number plates. EAT 1 would suit you in the catering game".

The door bell rings again, before Peter can reply Lady Daphne walks in.

Lady Daphne: "Hello dears, (addressing the couple) thought I'd pop in to see that no one is ravishing Vanessa".

Vanessa: "No Mummy, I can but hope".

Lady Daphne (irately): "The modern miss is getting too big for her boots, don't you think, Peter?"

Peter Porterson: "Well, they are very nice boots, Lady Daphne. We have just had a few words about the way of the world".

Before he could continue Lady Daphne sees Vanessa holding a bunch of keys.

Lady Daphne: "Whose keys are you holding, dear?" she says with a knowing wink.

Vanessa: "Oh, they're Peter's he's giving me a lecture on what each one opens. This long straight one with a bent end is something to do with petty cash. It looks like a phallic symbol to me".

Peter Porterson: "Not as much as the next one to it, which opens the firm's London apartment. It was acquired when the firm took over a competitor twenty odd years ago. I can use the flat on the last Wednesday in each month. It's like a time share with the rest of the senior staff. Saves an enormous amount of money on hotels despite it having to be re-mortgaged two years ago. The old man keeps it out of sentimental value it can never pay its way nowadays".

Lady Daphne appears disappointed at this reply. Looks at Vanessa whilst Peter is practising a golf swing with a new club taken from a rack. Mouths silently. "How's the key test going, dear?"

Vanessa grimaces and shakes her head with disappointment.

Lady Daphne: "Well I must go about my business. Have to make a call at the bank. The manager wants to see me. Just can't imagine what for?"

Peter Porterson: "I don't like answering those calls from above. It's usually 'when are you going to be paying-in a substantial sum, Mr Porterson?' Hope you have better luck, Lady Daphne".

Lady Daphne leaves the shop, turns and smiles as she closes the door. Vanessa detects Peter is unhappy with business.

Vanessa: "Isn't the business bustling Pete? Lots of new customers, that sort of thing?"

Peter Porterson: "We're very busy but record turnover doesn't necessarily mean record profits. Competition is intense. Dad had to return early from a millennium cruise to sort out a banking problem. He has the Midas Touch. Eats bank managers up before breakfast".

Vanessa: "Aren't you empowered to do that, dear boy?"

Peter Porterson: "Not in my Dad's league. He's premiership class, I'm only second division. I do have my moments though, dealing with the new businesses seeking managers. Only recently I started a good system that should circumvent some of our problems and help the old bottom line".

Vanessa (all agog): "Oh, what's that, Pete love? You are not into women's underwear now?"

Peter Porterson: "No, Vanessa, only yours of course. No, no the bottom line in business refers to the last line on a Profit and Loss Account which is the net profit a company makes in a year".

Vanessa: "Sounds might important to a little girl like myself. Have you a large bottom line like your father? They say like father like son, don't they?"

She smiles at Peter, he ogles back. The shop door opens sharply. Jack Greaves the club professional moves swiftly through it.

Jack Greaves: "Nipped off the course at halfway stage. How are you coping Vanessa?"

Vanessa: "Quite well Jack, seems to be selling masses of sweets but not many new golf balls".

Jack Greaves: "No it's upsetting. The head greenkeeper is flogging balls to members that his staff find when they cut the fairways. I keep meaning to talk to the club secretary to do something about it".

Eyeing Peter Porterson who has a new golf club in his hand.

Jack Greaves: "Like the feel of it, sir?"

Peter Porterson:"Yes Jack. I could hit the ball a mile with this fine iron".

Jack Greaves: "Well don't wear it out while you keep my new assistant company, she may entice more sales if you were on the course practising".

Jack looks through the window.

Jack Greaves: "Ah, my playing partners have moved to the next tee. Must dash".

Vanessa: "What's this gold coloured key for dear?"

Peter Porterson: "You do ask a lot of questions, Vanessa. Is this the start of a new game show?"

Vanessa: "I like to have an idea about the lifestyle of my boyfriends".

Peter Porterson: "Boyfriends in the plural I hear. You have more than one?"

Vanessa: "Well, there are boyfriends and special boyfriends. But come on Peter, what's the gold one for? Shouldn't be surprised if it's for the firm's Monte Carlo apartment?"

Peter Porterson: "Well it isn't. If you must know, it's the locker key to my London club. Keep a change of clothing in there, the old school tie, a few quid in cash, a squash racquet, my swimming trunks. Very useful key is that gold one. Saves the need for London accommodation when I can't get my hands on the company's flat. Come on, Vanessa, let's go into the workshop for a little snog".

Vanessa: "Peter, you're insatiable, you heard what Jack said. You shouldn't be here disturbing me from selling all of those beastly golf balls". (She pouts). "How about this tiny, tiny key? That sort of key could open a bank safety deposit box that holds the family jewels".

Peter. Porterson: "It is not for a safety deposit box. That key unlocks the wheels of my car when I have a punctured tyre. Without it the wheels can't be removed".

Vanessa: "Sounds like a safety device to ward off thieves".

Peter Porterson: "It does have a slight deterring effect, but they usually open the driver's door and nick the car in its entirety rather than just pinch the wheels".

Both look radiantly at each other.

Peter Porterson: "I wouldn't mind a thief nicking my car. It's seven years old. No new cars to be bought in this year's company budget. That even includes the old man himself".

He walks to the door, puts the lock in closed position. Turns over the card which reads 'Back in thirty Minutes'.

Vanessa: "What are you doing, Peter?" Emphasising 'are'.

Peter Porterson: "I'm not wasting further time. Come on".

They walk arm in arm through the door to the unoccupied workshop area.

End of Scene

AUTHOR'S NOTE
To get a golf game onto a stage would need a green carpet on a moving track. The golfers with body movement and following the flight of the ball with eyes and voice would give the audience the action, along with the narrative.

Vanessa and Andrew Dutton-Clough are about to start in an annual golf match representing Berkshire Heath Golf Club against nearby rivals Moor Hamlet Golf Club. Their two opponents are Geoff Macbeath and Cynthia Jones noted for her down to earth approach.

Lady President of Moor Hamlet (To Lady Daphne): "These days winning is everything. Social graces don't seem to count. Not the jolly good fun it used to be when it was an honour to lose. As long as it was done with good grace, of course".

Lady Daphne (With a microphone addressing a small cluster of spectators at the first tee): "We now come to match number four. The players for Moor Hamlet Golf Club are Geoffrey Macbeath". (Geoffrey Macbeath interrupts). "Call me Geoff and I'll call you Daph".

Lady Daphne: "At this club we like to maintain standards of speech, as well as dress". (She looks pointedly at his denim trousers). "At some clubs you would be asked to change into more appropriate pants, but we are liberal in our views to visitors".

Cynthia: "Which interpreted into common English means 'Watch it or you'll be shown the door mate".

Lady Daphne: "Before I was quaintly interrupted, Miss Cynthia Jones is the playing partner of Geoffrey Macbeath. Their opponents from our host club is Andrew Dutton-Clough, a particular favourite of mine, who is playing with my daughter, Vanessa.

Geoff Macbeath: "Will he be playing with her tonight, Lady D?"

Lady Daphne: "We can do without smutty observations, thank you. Geoffrey Macbeath will take the first shot followed by Andrew Dutton-Clough. May the best foursome win the day".

She steps from the microphone. Geoff Macbeath takes his position on the tee. Gives two practise swings, flexes his knees. Places a ball on the tee and whacks it forward.

Cynthia: "Good shot. Straight down the middle".

Andrew replaces Geoff on the tee. Places his club on the floor stands behind it and bends, touching his toes, then stands up, repeats the touch toes again two more times before picking up his club, walks to the ball and gives it a deafening crack.

Lady Daphne: "Oh, good shot, Andrew, fifty yards past the man wearing jeans".

Vanessa (A little embarrassed): "Mummy must have her little joke".

The four golfers walk forward fifty yards to the ladies tee. Six spectators move forward to follow them.

Vanessa: "Take the first shot Cynthia, guests always have that honour".

Cynthia: "Thank you, Vanessa. It's nice to be considered honourable".

Cynthia walks to the ball, practises the swinging shot without hitting the ball, then stands to the ball. With a classic swing follows through the ball to hit a straight drive, almost as far as the men had driven. The six spectators applaud.

Cynthia smirks.

Cynthia: "Let's see you put a ball past that one, Honourable Vanessa".

The Moor Hamlet spectators guffaw.

Vanessa smiles grimly, realising Cynthia Jones is an exceptional player.

Vanessa: 'I'll try my best, Miss Jones".

She then shows a more feminine attitude to the game, swaying her bottom provocatively as she saunters onto the tee. Bending places a ball on a tee-peg.

Vanessa: "Wish you could do that Miss Jones?"

Cynthia grimaces. Vanessa then plays a good shot, but without Cynthia's power, her ball is some sixty yards shorter.

Vanessa: "Looks as if I shall have to makeup what I lack in length of shot, by my crisp short game and accurate putting".

Cynthia: "My short game isn't too bad darling".

The four golfers walk forward to their balls. They arrive at Vanessa's first. Cynthia places her right hand on her forehead in a distance viewing position.

In a loud voice meant for the spectators.

Cynthia: "The other three balls are rather a long way from here".

Geoff Macbeath: "Have a heart Cyn dearest, Vanessa just doesn't have your broad shoulders".

Andrew Dutton-Clough: "Thank goodness she doesn't. I know many a man who would be proud to be possessed of Cynthia's upper torso".

Vanessa chuckles together with the spectators. Cynthia looks daggers drawn.

Cynthia: "Thank you for those unkind words. Jealousy will get you nowhere".

The company walk forward to the other three balls, which are in a small cluster in the centre of the fairway, Vanessa walking with Andrew.

Vanessa: "Our lady opponent is a very good player. We can be flippant about her hitting the ball like a man, which she does. But we must devise a strategy if we are not going to get our noses rubbed in it".

Andrew: "How do you mean, Van, dearest, rubbed in what?"

Vanessa: "If you'd have been at my finishing school you would have known what your nose had been rubbed in. And it didn't smell of roses".

The two male golfers and Cynthia take their shots. Again Cynthia's length of shot keeps up with the men. Vanessa walked beyond her own ball to the three balls some way past her own. Recognising Cynthia's ball, she looks back to the others who were engrossed in conversation. Vanessa's shoe sole walks on Cynthia's ball 'accidentally' pushing it half an inch into the earth. Vanessa stands aside awaiting the other three to reach her.

Geoff Macbeath: "Oh, what a rotten lie. Your ball's in a hole, bad luck Cynth".

Cynthia grunts as she takes a club from her bag.

Cynthia: "The head groundsman should be hung, drawn and quartered and that would be too good for him. Fancy allowing deep holes in the fairway".

Vanessa: "Oh what bad luck dear, I shall certainly mention that hole to the chairman of the greens. He'll have it sorted by tomorrow".

Cynthia: "Doesn't help me today does it? What happens now, I can't play a bloody ball embedded in the ground".

The other three look nonplussed.

Andrew Dutton-Clough: "The rules of golf say it's the rub of the green. Just bad luck really, but I'd be happy to let it be removed without a penalty. What do you say Vanessa?"

Vanessa: "Not really dear, rules are rules. It is bad luck on Cynthia of course but she will have to play the ball as it lies in the hole".

Cynthia stamps her foot. In a wicked temper she grabs a club from her golf bag.

Cynthia: "It just isn't bloody fair".

She walks to the ball. Without any preamble hurls the clubhead at the embedded ball. The ball shot at a right angle into deep bushes and undergrowth.

Andrew Dutton-Clough: "That's a lost ball, you'll be very lucky to find it in that undergrowth".

Cynthia: "Damn, bloody damn!"

She walks over to the undergrowth to look for her ball, whilst the others play their shots to the green. Cynthia takes an interminable time searching the undergrowth.

Vanessa (Shouting from the green): "Hurry up dear, you have five minutes to find it otherwise you're out of this hole. Rules of golf you know".

Cynthia stamps from the undergrowth, shoulders slunk. Marches to where the others have putted out and finished the hole.

Geoff Macbeath: "The buggers have won the hole. Vanessa had a long putt to go into the hole for a par".

Cynthia: "Lucky old Vanessa. So we are one hole down. It won't be for long".

The six spectators had returned to see the start of the following match, Andrew steps onto the tee at the second hole, carefully selecting a golf club from his bag.

Andrew Dutton-Clough: "Think I now have the honour of going first, having won the last hole. It's only a short distance, which suits my accuracy".

He swings his club at the ball, there's a pause as the ball is in the air.

Andrew Dutton-Clough: "Damn, it's gone into the bunker on the right, never do that normally".

Geoff Macbeath: "You can't be perfect all the time".

Vanessa: "If we were perfect we'd be playing for England".

Cynthia: "In my case it would be for Wales. In fact I have represented my country at this game".

Geoff Macbeath: "With me it would be for Scotland".

Andrew Dutton-Clough: "Well, with Vanessa and myself it would be for England. But with all the good players in this country, it will only be in our dreams".

Geoff plays his shot.

Cynthia: "Good shot partner, tight onto the green. Should win this hole, you only need a good putt".

Andrew Dutton-Clough: "Hey, hold on a minute. Vanessa hasn't played yet, let's see if she can get close to the hole.

Geoff smirks at the others.

Geoff Macbeath: "Thanks, Cyn, putting is my strong suit of course".

Vanessa to Andrew: "What a big headed loudmouth. Makes my blood boil. That's the trouble with these brash peasants from a public course".

Andrew Dutton-Clough: "No proper breeding Van, that's what it is y'know".

Again the ensemble walk forward twenty yards to the ladies tee. Vanessa walks forward and bends, her designer pants showing the full shape of a tempting rear, provocatively placing a tee peg in the ground. Turns and smiles, knowing the men will appreciate her little cameo.

Cynthia: "You do nothing for me in that bending posture", she snaps.

The absence of a smile and a clenching of teeth denotes a touch of jealousy.

Andrew Dutton-Clough: "I dunno, I rather like seeing Van teeing her ball. Makes me feel younger than my twenty nine years".

Cynthia: "There's no answer that I can think of. What are you grinning at Geoffrey?"

Geoff Macbeath: "You old scout".

Cynthia: "Don't call me an old scout. Old scouts are men who blow whistles and wear funny pointed hats".

Vanessa: "I think a funny pointed hat would suit you, Cynthia dear. Most self respecting witches wear them".

Andrew Dutton-Clough: "Now, please ladies, we are only on the second hole and falling out already. Please, Vanessa, play your ball otherwise we will not get round the course till after dark. I don't want to miss dinner".

Vanessa plays her shot exaggerating her swing by bringing her club high over her left shoulder at the finish. Presenting a good view of the contents of her tight fitting sweater.

Andrew Dutton-Clough: "Oh, you've saved the day, Vanessa. Ball's on the green only a few feet from the flag. Good shot".

Cynthia in a foul temper puts the ball on the tee with venom. No thought for careful consideration and swings at the ball. The ball, on its way to the woods on the right of the green smashes into the trunk of an oak tree then ricochets onto the putting surface a mere 12 inches from the hole.

Cynthia: "That's the best way to shut some people up, especially exhibitionist sexpots".

Vanessa throws her hands to her head, stamps around the tee.

Vanessa: "You fortunate person, you lucky sod. You couldn't do that again if you had a thousand hits".

Cynthia: "I don't need a thousand hits when one has done the trick. This hole is between you and me, dear. My putt's far easier than my partner's and yours is a good five feet away from the hole".

Vanessa (with venom): "Except for that tree your ball would be buried in the deep woods".

Cynthia: "If you don't stop whinging you will be buried in the deep woods. Let's go".

They walk forward in their respective pairs, reaching the putting surface at the same time. With Cynthia's ball two inches from the flag and Vanessa's about five feet.

Andrew Dutton-Clough: "You're furthest from the hole, Geoff, so it's you to play first".

Cynthia (interrupts): "To save time should I go first, mine is a mere tap in. As a gentlemanly gesture you might even deem my ball is in the hole, it's an insult to make me putt it".

Andrew Dutton-Clough: "Yes of course, I'm sorry. Take the ball away".

Vanessa: "I have seen such putts missed. Just put a marker nearer your ball and let me go first".

This remark rouses Cynthia's anger. She places a coin behind her ball and snatches it away. Vanessa then looks at her putt, raises her putter to line up the ball and the hole.

Vanessa: "This is a wicked looking five footer".

Cynthia (sarcastically): "Quite like the person about to play it".

Vanessa: "Thank you for those kind words. I hope to ram them down your throat by holing this".

Vanessa walks to the address position and plays the putt. The ball going straight for the hole deviates in the last few inches of its journey, moves around the hole but stays on the rim.

Geoff Macbeath: "Very bad luck Vanessa, deserved a better fate".

Vanessa smiles, picks up her ball. Cynthia has re-placed her ball. Vanessa knocks it away with a wry smile.

Vanessa: "Your hole dear. Makes the match even going to the third tee.

Geoff to Andrew: "I can't take much more of this needle between the ladies. We came out for a pleasant game of golf, not a bloody war".

Andrew nods his agreement.

The third hole is the longest on the course. The marker notice on the third tee said it to be 527 metres long. Good players should take five shots to do it.

The ladies were in no mood to bury the hatchet. They expected their male partners to support their cause. On the third hole after the teams had driven off they kept to themselves, walking in pairs. This gave Vanessa the opportunity to further the key test theory. She and Andrew sauntered down the fairway towards their golf balls some two hundred yards away. The opposition pair were some forty yards in front.

Vanessa (coyly): "What's that bulge in the front of your golf bag, Andrew?"

Andrew Dutton-Clough: "Oh that is where I keep my keys. Like to keep them with me then nobody can raid my locker when I'm on the course. Always keep a bit of cash in there.

Vanessa: "Good thing to keep your keys with you, then nobody can steal your car can they? Makes sense but it is rather a large bunch to carry".

Andrew Dutton-Clough: "I do the same with my bifocals, I don't need them to play golf. As a security measure I always carry them with me".

Vanessa: "Could I have a feel of the bulge – in the front of your golf bag of course".

Andrew Dutton-Clough: "Oh, bad luck, I thought it was my lucky day".

He opens the zip of his golf bag pocket. Vanessa puts a hand in the pouch.

Vanessa: "My, you have a lot of keys here. Must weigh you down".

Andrew Dutton-Clough: "Yes, old Peter Porterson thought I had a hiatus hernia when I had the keys in my left hand trouser pocket. Not so of course".

Vanessa was walking pushing her mechanised trolley in her left hand. She suddenly stopped.

Vanessa: "What is this short gold key for, Andrew dear? It looks like proper 22 carat at that I bet.

Andrew Dutton-Clough: "That's the spare key for mother's Lamborghini, an Italian job you know and the key next to it is for a double lock on the garage in the stable block at Grey Gables, Our country house. Mother keeps a key but leaves it on top of the garage door, not much security there. It means I have virtual free use of the beastly car.

Vanessa: "I don't think I have ever seen you in it. They are about £170,000 aren't they?"

Andrew Dutton-Clough: "Something like that. I'll take you for a spin in it one day. They say it's an excellent bird puller, bright red – you might like it. It does nothing for me".

They had reached Vanessa's ball at this point, she was smiling.

Vanessa (to herself): "Maybe there's something in this key test".

Andrew picked up the sound.

Andrew Dutton-Dough: "What did you say dear?"

Vanessa: "Oh nothing darling (cursing under her breath). Look what a rotten lie my ball has come to rest in".

Andrew Dutton-Clough: "A bit like Cynthia's lie when you accidentally trod on her ball".

Vanessa (guiltily): "Did the others see, it was an accident you know".

Andrew Dutton-Clough: "They were gloating over his shot close to the flag to give a thought to you. Ah, here we are, my ball's okay, standing up on the fairway gives me a clean hit".

Andrew selects a club carefully, changing his mind twice before being, certain he has the correct club. Takes two practise swings, exaggerates the swaying leg movements, walks to the ball, takes a careful aim, crashes the ball high into the air.

Andrew Dutton-Clough: "At least two hundred and fifty metres Van dear. A flick with my wedge it'll be on the green. A couple of putts will give us a par".

Vanessa (nods, murmurs): "Good shot partner".

Then she calls to the opposition who are forty metres to their left.

Vanessa: "My partner's having a lucky day".

Cynthia smiles mirthlessly.

Geoff Macbeath (standing over his ball) to Cynthia: "This shot must travel good. That bugger can certainly play the game".

Cynthia: "Comes from not having to work for a living, idling his time at Cambridge whilst you and I were working to earn an honest crust. Damn unfair the way wealth is shared out in this country. Bloody death duties should be a hundred percent, that would make all people equal".

Geoff Macbeath: "You are a bit hard. Somebody in Andrew's family must have worked hard to put him in the position of a landowner. I have little objection as long as I have good health and nobody stands in my way of playing this game a couple of times a week".

Cynthia: "Really Geoff you'd make two men of that charmless wonder, she seems interested in him because of his wealth, it's obvious the way she's sucking up to him".

Geoff Macbeath: "Now now, jealousy will get you nowhere".

Cynthia: "Jealous of that stuck up trollop, give me a break".

The four contestants now on the green, stand in pairs either side of the flag. Cynthia through clenched teeth addressing Vanessa.

Cynthia: "You are furthest from the flag dear, you are to putt first".

Vanessa seemingly not letting an opportunity pass for a confrontation.

Vanessa: "I rather think my ball is a shade nearer to the flag than yours Cynthia".

Geoff Macbeath: "Not much in it really. It doesn't matter a tinkers cuss who goes first".

Andrew nods his agreement.

Vanessa: "It matters to me, rules are rules. Rule one in the golfers manual states that players in a match cannot collude to override the laws of the game. The person furthest from the flag putts first".

Geoff Macbeath (whispers to Cynthia): "She's deliberately provoking you, don't bite".

But Cynthia's look of rate, her face a puce red, remarks.

Cynthia: "I never thought I would need a tape measure as part of my golfing gear".

She then begins to measure the distance by walking in calculated steps from her ball to the flag, being very deliberate that each pace should be exactly the same as the other.

Cynthia: "I make that four and a half paces, now I'll measure from your ball".

Ignoring Vanessa's protestations that it wasn't necessary, Cynthia walks from Vanessa's ball straight to the flag deliberately firming her foot into the turf on each step.

Cynthia: "I make that four and three quarter paces. I stand to be corrected but you are the furthest from the ball, Vanessa darling. You to go".

Vanessa (almost in tears): "You beastly horrid cow. You've deliberately made marks and ridges in the line that my ball will travel. That's unfair and I shall report you to the Captain when we get in".

Cynthia: "Stop moaning you spoilt brat. If we were men we'd be squaring up to each other by now".

Andrew: "Men wouldn't get into your type of tantrum over such a trifle as to who's nearer the hole. Never heard anything like it in my life. Both of you deserve a three week suspension from the game or better still a stiff fine".

Geoff: "Those punishments together would be about right".

He then looks at Andrew and says:

Geoff: "Accept a half old chap".

Andrew nods and picks up Vanessa's ball. Geoff picks up Cynthia's ball, puts it in his pocket, walks over to their golf bags and together steps sprightly towards the next hole. The ladies follow, walking behind each other to the fourth tee.

Now on the tee.

Geoff: "Amateurs are supposed to enjoy the sport they play, let's carry on the game in the manner our Royal and Ancient founders meant the game to be played. In any dispute the spirit of compromise to be accepted by all of us, especially you two", (forcing a smile to the ladies).

They both nod and smile weakly. The game continues in the new spirit of Compromise for the next four holes during which time Vanessa picks her moments to query Andrew on certain keys on his bunch, especially.

Vanessa: "This rusty cast iron key looks very ordinary compared to those special ones you've already mentioned, Andrew dear".

Andrew: "Thank goodness you've moved way from that fracas with Cynthia. We can now talk in a more friendly manner. Yes, that key is to a shed in field No. 7 where we keep the pride of my father's eye. The herd of pedigree Herefords. Specially bought from a cousin of Dad's, whose grandparents emigrated to the States at the turn of the Century. Very valuable those cattle, so the old chap tells me. Think he loves them more than his own kith and kin. That includes myself". (Vanessa nods knowingly).

Having driven off from the ninth tee, the match still all square. Andrew and Vanessa walk up the fairway together. Not content with her now valuable information Vanessa shows Andrew a silver key with a green holding part.

Vanessa: "Looks highly decorative, is this for the new estate wagon I saw you driving yesterday, darling Andrew".

Andrew: "No Van, that particular key is only used once a year. It's usual for a member of my family to switch on the village Christmas illuminations. Been a tradition for some sixty odd years. After Dad retired he passed the squireship to myself. I don't broadcast the fact of course. Don't want snide remarks from golf club talkabouts, but once a year I have to use that key to open the meter box and hit the switches. Causes an instant blaze of light at six o'clock on the 14th December of each year".

Vanessa: "What's so special about the 14th December dear?"

Andrew: "It coincides with the first squire's birthday long long ago. In our village old traditions die hard".

Vanessa: "So they should. You must be well thought of in the village, Andrew".

Andrew: "Well we do own the freeholds of all of it, except the Inland Revenue's office block. The villagers pay rents in perpetuity for the buildings they occupy".

Vanessa: "Except the Inland Revenue I suppose".

Andrew: "Yes, blood suckers like them insist they owe no allegiance to the aristocracy. All a lot of damn left wing socialists. They'll get their comeuppance when the Countryside lobby get a few members into parliament to bolster up the Tories".

The four players, now in a much more friendly ambience walk from the ninth green in a bunch.

Andrew: "All square at halfway point, quite satisfactory Geoff old chap. Let's have a G and T in the hospitality marquee. Always think this is the most important part of a golf match. Cements friendships".

Cynthia: "Geoff and me will stick to orange juice if you don't mind. Alcohol disturbs the concentration. I can see we can't give you an inch, or you'll take over".

Geoff: "You talk for yourself old dear, don't want to be thought an old stick in the mud who can't take his drink".

Cynthia: "What does that remark make me then?"

Vanessa: "Sounds like an old stick in the mud, eh. Ah, ah joke you know".

Cynthia glowers.

Geoff: "Now ladies I assumed we'd got over little fracas of a few holes ago".

Arthur and young Daisy are manning the makeshift bar dressed in their traditional tartan (described in the 'main character outline').

The golfers observe a round table to seat eight persons, four chairs are occupied by the fourball immediately in front of Andrew Dutton-Clough's group.

Andrew: "Mind if we join you?"

Peter Porterson: "Course not Andy, nice to see you. Flow's your match going, enjoying it are we?"

Andrew's group move to the four vacant chairs nodding acquaintance to the other four.

Andrew: "Oh yes Peter, our game is certainly something different. We're even-stevens at the moment, how about you?"

Peter Porterson: "Oh our opponents have their noses in front, they lead by one hold but the way Jane's playing and her determination is legendary. It won't stay that way for long".

Jane: "You are putting pressure on me Peter. You are always doing it. When this happens I go out and try to play better than I am, and make a bally mess of it all. Just keep your mouth shut and get on with your G and T'.

Vanessa: "Keep your cool dear, Pete's only trying to encourage you. You are lucky to have him as a partner you know. He's most accurate around the greens".

Jane: "We all know you have a shine on the sod".

Cynthia: "Now now you aristocrats, don't ever let a man see you're falling out over him. Swells his already massive ego".

Vanessa: "Who asked you to interfere? Keep to making your own partner happy".

Andrew: "Why does mixed golf bring out the worst in ladies".

Peter: "Probably justifying their luck in having a man to play with".

Sarah (Peter's playing partner): "You stuck up male chauvinistic pig".

Cynthia: "Did you say prig or pig dear? As none of our male partners have the courtesy to introduce us, my name is Cynthia Jones, and before she says it, (pointing to Vanessa) I hit the ball like a man".

Vanessa (interjecting) "It's those broad masculine shoulders that does it".

Geoff: "Don't you start again or I will ask the Lady Captain to whip you both".

Jane: "Must have had one hell of a match so far".

Geoff: "Let's not talk about the war".

Before anyone could reply a man with a jockey hat and Berkshire golf club tie waved a starting flag. Calling over to the round table, "The tenth tee is now clear, would you start your second half now please".

Peter Porterson acknowledges the summons with a wave and said "Just going". The four hastily consume their drinks, and move sharply to the door.

Andrew: (to the remaining three) "This place doubles as a dance marquee when a club member needs it for a wedding function or something like that".

Vanessa: "Something like a wedding function – the only thing like a wedding function is a funeral function and that's not quite so jolly. That's until the widow leaves of course. Had some really impressive funeral do's here. One old member left a couple of grand for us to give him a right royal send off. We didn't let him down".

Geoff: “Same at our club, a departed friend of mine left five hundred quid to give his mourners a good time after he had been reduced to ashes. A wonderful do. Think I'll do the same myself. Trust it won't be for many years yet”.

Vanessa: “You've a lot more soul than I took you for Geoff, coming from the golf club you do. Why don't you apply for membership here. You could spread the gospel about a ‘bit of a do’ on a funeral. The modern funerals are excellent. Daddy's was. I miss him terribly now, he had such a profound influence on me. I think daddies and daughters get on well. I'm sure I miss him a lot more than my brothers do”.

Geoff: “You're speaking from the heart Vanessa, you will make some lucky sod a good wife. I think he will have to be rich though, for you look as though you have expensive tastes, but you will certainly give good value”.

Cynthia (tartly): “Pardon me interrupting your reveries but we came to play golf. How about getting re-started”.

Andrew: “Fascinating listening to Van, reminiscing about her father. I knew him very well. Dear old Sir Harry he was a real charmer. Not so good at golf but you can't be a businessman extraordinaire and a top player. One or the other but not both. I've tried and feel very fortunate to be a recipient of a long line of wealthy forebears, saves a lot of time immersing myself in business matters. Leaves me far more time to practise”.

Cynthia (with bitter feelings): ‘That's the trouble with inherited wealth. Only a few people have it, and I'm not one of them. Perhaps that's why I am so bitter about the time sacrifices I have to make to this game”.

Vanessa: “I don't know how lucky I am but mummsy says it is my want. I was born to it, but the manner I was treated by the nuns at my old finishing school makes my bottom wince at the thought of it, even now. They certainly took it out of my hide when I went wrong. I think it's for the best, knocks a lot of the starch and pomp out of a spoilt brat like I was before I went. More humbling you know”. Makes someone with my family upbringing accept the purgatones of people who've not been so fortunate in life as having a daddy who takes life's severe knocks on behalf of his kids and still comes up smiling with bundles of notes in his mouth. Oh I do miss the old sod”.

Cynthia: “Never thought I'd have heard sentiments like those coming from your finely shaped lips: Wasn't your father Sir Harry Westwood? Received his gong for being an honorary chairman of the Oxfordshire and Berkshire National Health

Trust? Gave his time unflinchingly to provide the most expensive dialysis machine imported to this country from the States. I met him personally when I had a hysterectomy at the Oxford General. Tried to pay a bit back while recuperating, did some secretarial work in the admin office. Quite impressed by his dedication to his fund raising. That machine alone has given a much better quality of life to hundreds of people in this area".

Vanessa: "Yes that's my father. He put more into his charity work than in his business interests in his latter years. Charity work doesn't earn the pennies a family seems to need".

Before she could continue the marker's voice again penetrated the marquee. "Next four down your drinks in one, you're on the tee".

The four did as they were told, draining their glasses as they hurried through the flap. Passing Arthur and Daisy at a fast pace, Arthur smiled and asked, "Take a drink on the course ladies, sooth your nerves when you play a bad shot".

No one stopped but Lady Greey retorted, "I'll take you up on that Arthur, I'll have the freebie instead of my daughter. She seems keen to get on the course".

Lady Greey was joined by the club secretary and the club professional. Both nodded to Arthur for a refill by brandishing an empty glass.

Club Secretary: "There's a little tension in that group, I've heard I may have to referee their match. I understand cheating has been mentioned, always hate that kind of behaviour. Rumour of it spreads like wildfire in a dry climate. What can you expect when they let people into the club just because they are good at the game. The first requisite of membership at this club should be quality breeding even if they continue to miss hitting the ball when trying to hit it".

Jack Greaves: "Making air shots you mean, sir".

Club Secretary (nodded): "Bloody do, Greaves, bloody do".

Arthur (whispering to Daisy): "Silly sod is living in a bygone age".

The professional turned and winked with a smile.

The four golfers marched sprightly to the tenth tee, the ladies walking together. Now a more friendly spirit Peter Porterson's four were still waiting their turn to commence play when Andrew's four arrived.

Andrew: "What's the hold-up old chap? Thought you'd gone off a few minutes ago. We had to finish our drinks at double quick speed, could have taken our time".

Peter: "The lot in front have lost a bloody ball, have spent an awful lot of time looking for it. They must know they have only a five minute searching time. Should have invited us through. That is the key to good manners".

Andrew (pricking his ears): "That word you have just used, key. Vanessa seems to have a fixation on keys, seems to want the full story on each one on my ring. Weird I call it".

Peter: "Funny you should say that, she's been giving me some jip on the same subject. Is she up to something Andy? I don't want to tell her outright that it's none of her business, but it isn't is it? Had to make up a cock and bull story when she had her mind set on one of the smallest in my bunch. It wasn't to the office petty cash box but to the committee members private lavatory at the Army and Navy club. What can she be up to? Seems to be more than normal curiosity don't you think?"

Meanwhile Vanessa walks away from Cynthia.

Vanessa: "What are you two mumbling about, worse than a couple of girls discussing last night's date".

Andrew: "No Van dear, just discussing our game so far. It's the most unusual match I've ever played in. Anyhow I think the second half will prove to be much better. The drinks interval's given us a better rapport with our playing partners than we had in the first nine holes".

There was a noise from the tee, one of Peter's four shouted. "They've found their ball and are now out of range. I think it is my first off'. The four then played and moved forward off stage.

Vanessa's four moved onto the tee.

AUTHOR'S NOTE: More of the same to complete the round of golf if needed.

Penultimate Scene

Lady Daphne and Hon. Vanessa Greey were seated in the alcove of the bar three weeks after their original conversation in the same place when they first spoke of the 'key' situation. Arthur and young Daisy were on duty whilst the titled pair sat drinking vodka and limejuice in tall glasses. Awaiting being called to lunch.

Lady Daphne: "Not too much vodka in the glass is there dear?"

Vanessa: "Rather the reverse mummsy. I think the dissolving ice has weakened the drink somewhat. Still a more diluted drink is required this lunchtime. I'm playing with Peter this afternoon. I do wish to retain some semblance of sobriety".

Lady Daphne: "Oh Peter is it? I thought when the key situation was discussed last week it was Andrew who was winning on points, and by a considerable margin. Now you are playing with 'Peter' (accentuating the word Peter). I though Wednesday's had been devoted to Andrew.

Vanessa smiles distantly as her mother continued.

Lady Daphne: "Vanessa listen carefully. The bank manager rang this morning. He said "I know you've been out the district the last few days", which of course I haven't, as you only know. He then went on "Presumably that's prevented you from calling at the branch with your paying-in book. He was sure I would like to know that the overdraft has exceeded the limit the late Sir Harry arranged some eighteen months ago. If by any chance, but I'm sure I couldn't be of course, that your finances require remedial action. You would have been in touch".

Vanessa: "What did you say to that? We're not in real financial trouble are we? No of course we're not. Money grows on trees in our family".

Lady Daphne: "No it does not Vanessa. We have been giving the overdraft one hell of a bending in the last few weeks. The Hunt Ball we gave at the manor cost a fortune. To fly strawberries in from the Canary isles in November is not cheap, not to mention orchids on every table. Little things cost a lot".

Vanessa: "That sounds like a song title mummsy".

Lady Daphne: "Silly girl, that was 'Little things mean a lot'. I just hope the Dutton-Cloughs were suitably impressed enough to let Andrew take you to the altar in holy matrimony".

Vanessa: "Not a problem in that respect, Andrew is charm itself and is keen to name the day".

Lady Daphne (with intent determination): "How about the last Saturday of this month, I should be able to shy off that leering bank manager till then. Although it would hardly give me enough time for the wedding dress and six bridesmaids dresses to be made, but we would cope. Cash-wise time is of the essence".

Vanessa: "I think I will have another drink please, and make it a double this time Arthur, and no ice please".

Her mother raises her eyebrows.

Arthur (eyes twinkling, replied): "In my army days madam it was a well know fact that large vodkas put hair on a soldier's chest".

Lady Daphne: "Arthur sometimes you go over the top, I don't mind a slight chuckle now and then but please know your place".

Arthur retreats touching his forelock.

Vanessa: "He means well mummsy. He does make me laugh sometimes".

Lady Daphne: "There are limits to what members will take even from that old reprobate. Anyhow why did you need a double and just before lunch as well".

Vanessa: "Changed my mind it's when you talk about marriage so vehemently it makes me apprehensive. I don't want to get married yet, I want to enjoy myself, play the field a bit if you know what I mean. There's plenty of time to settle down and raise children later on in life".

Lady Daphne (in exasperation, her patience finally exhausted): "The family's reputation depends on you making a financially secure marriage, (as an afterthought), and producing children quickly. After you've had your feet under the Dutton-Clough's dining table for a few years you can then think about enjoying yourself".

Vanessa: "But by then Peter will have married somebody else".

Lady Daphne: "Oh so that's it, you can't let your heart rule this financial situation. That Peter Porterson hasn't got two halfpennies to rub together. His family might have plenty of goodwill with the Royals, feeding them with their precious victuals, but cash on the table the Porterson's ain't got".

Vanessa: "Don't be vulgar mum. It doesn't suit you".

Lady Daphne (rising on her stool): "I am not being vulgar, I am being practical and it's time you took a leaf out of my book. Stars in your eyes never won the respect of a bank manager especially a callous one like we have. Anyhow what's the final verdict on the key test? I know Andrew Dutton-Clough was miles in front and if it had been the Derby he would have won by twenty five lengths. I know the Portersons have been touting the catering company for sale around the city without any success at all".

Vanessa: "How do you know that? You're not in a 'knowing position' like you were when daddy was alive. He knew everything financial, I do wish he was still with us".

Lady Daphne: "So do I, deeply I do, but life goes on (and as an afterthought) and of course death also". (She wipes a tear from her eye).

Vanessa knowing she is on the losing end of this conversation. Smiles at Arthur in the background craning an ear to obtain the gist of their animated conversation.

Vanessa: "Peter is such a darling, he'll take me anywhere I want to go, funnily enough I want to go where he wants to go, there's something about him I pine for. I don't get the same vibes from Andrew even allowing for his massive key test superiority".

Lady Daphne: "I wish you could see life from my age whilst retaining your youth and vitality, but the good Lord does not let youth and experience go together, (she sighed and paused) when you've lost your youth, what's left is experience and you have to be very lucky to land a big fish with experience alone. Please dear, marry Andrew before it's too late".

Vanessa: "You know I love you and the family, but it is my life after all".

Arthur returns to the bar alcove and smiles an invitation to follow him to their table.

Arthur: "Your starters await, ladies".

The two ladies followed Arthur towards the dining room. On their way they bump into Cynthia Jones.

Vanessa: "Congratulations Cynthia on having your membership application accepted. How does it feel to be a fully paid up member of the Berkshire Heath Golf Club, quite a change from that flea pit you used to belong to, eh?"

Cynthia: "You never give up do you. Thank you for the congrats, answering the first part of your question, it is super to belong to this golf club. There are not as many outrageous snobby members as I imagine there would be, present company excepted of course. The playing facilities are a vast improvement on my previous club, but no improvement on the friendliness of the members, I shall certainly miss playing with Geoff Macbeath my mixed partner at the Moor Hamlet Club.

Vanessa: "I played against him with Andrew when I first met you didn't I?"

Cynthia: "Of course you did".

Vanessa: "A charming man, he'd be a good member here, I tried without success but couldn't you talk to him?"

Cynthia: "He can't do it, with a wife and three kids he can't run to the expense of moving here".

Lady Daphne (peeved at being left out of the conversation): "Perhaps you would introduce me Vanessa".

Vanessa: "Oh sorry mother, (pausing) this is Cynthia Jones, I played in a mixed fourball with her recently, (as an afterthought) there were two men involved as well".

Lady Daphne (tartly): "Obviously, otherwise it wouldn't be mixed would it? Sometimes I wonder whether the cost of private education is worth it".

Cynthia: "Pleased to meet you Lady Daphne, should I shake hands or curtsey to your title?"

Lady Daphne: "You'd do well to button your lip or remove the sarcasm from your voice dear. After all you are a new member and doubtless want to be socially accepted".

Cynthia (subdued): "Sorry Lady Daphne, it won't happen again".

Peter Porterson (walks in the bar): "Good afternoon what a bevy of beauty all under one roof especially you Lady Daphne you look more desirable every time I see you. Being the beginning of the month must have something to do with it".

Lady Daphne (haughtily): "I don't see what the beginning of the month as to do with my desirability, I would rather think that's down to the pink gin I saw you drinking with your father. How is the old rascal, still horsing it with the princes. Hoping to flog them champagne and strawberries?"

Peter: "He hasn't played much polo lately. Been chained to his office desk trying to drum up orders for our new range of patés and caviar. How many dozen jars can we send to your country pad, Lady D?"

Lady Daphne: "The way to sell is to get off your backside and knock doors, not to tout business in the golf club, most infra dig".

Cynthia: "You don't pull your punches m'lady, well done I do think men who take unfair advantages deserve pegging down on every conceivable occasion".

Peter (looking askew – addressing Cynthia): "Diplomacy isn't your strong suit Cynthia is it dear. Well I've come to take Vanessa on the links this afternoon. It's sad but we must make an early start. I've a business appointment back at the ranch at 4.30 this afternoon. Our accountant says he's got some nasty queries on my expenses he'd like answers to".

Lady Daphne: "Vanessa and myself are just taking our places for our usual weekly lunch. Chef's prepared crown of lamb, new potatoes and mint sauce from the mint grown in the secretary's garden. We can't let that go to waste can we".

Peter: "I am afraid we must and I'm extremely sorry but business comes before pleasure, dear lady".

Lady Daphne: "Vanessa and I are to talk business, serious business and you are part of it".

Vanessa: "Mummsy, lunch will have to wait but we could have a mountainous evening meal. I have just taken a telephone call from Andrew. He is bringing his parents to a private dinner party here at the golf club and we are invited".

Lady Daphne (her eyes light a large smile appears): "Lunch doesn't matter of course, I always prefer dinner especially those with a theme to them". (She then hums the wedding march quite loudly).

Vanessa (sidles to her mother): "The Portersons have also been invited, both Peter and his father, so it will be quite chummy mummy. There I go again with my natural poetry".

The happy demeanour of Lady Daphne disappeared more quickly than it came.

Lady Daphne: "A nice dinner party of Andrew, his parents, you and I Vanessa, would make a nice occasion. Why involve the Portersons. After all it would merely be Peter and his father.

Vanessa: "Father and son Porterson have accepted, coming after some boring business meeting with their accountant", (as an afterthought she turned to Cynthia): "Why don't you come Miss Jones. It would even up the sexes, we don't want to be bullied by the men do we?"

Cynthia: "If that is a serious invitation, I would be happy to be available".

Vanessa: "That's it then, a happy eightsome".

Lady Daphne was looking more unhappy by the second. Peter Porterson takes Vanessa's arm: "Come on, let's get changed, it looks like we will only have time for twelve holes".

End of Scene

AUTHOR'S NOTE: If needed more of the same as the last 37 pages can be written but I am now going on to the last scene.

Table Plan

Lady Daphne Greey
Spencer Dutton-Clough  Teddy Porterson
Andrew's Father
Cynthia Jones  Madeline Dutton-Clough
Andrew Dutton-Clough  Peter Porterson
Vanessa Greey

Madeline: "Kindly observe, from the seating plan where you're sitting. I've been a bit strategic, especially as this little private alcove gives us the privacy we need".

Teddy: "Quite right m'dear. You never know what saucy stories your Spencer relates when he's had a few bevies".

Spencer: "I beg your pardon. I'm quite the soul of discretion and politeness".

Vanessa: "Some inconsiderate persons would equate that with boredom Spencer dear".

Madeline: "No, no. Teddy I was thinking more of statements of intent. What the future may bring especially to the younger members of this little gathering".
Peter: "Who America might bomb next, or whereto build the Olympic Village, that's if London gets them in 2012.

Arthur appears with a tray of aperitifs. Whilst serving.

Arthur: "London will not get those Games. We've not got graft and bribery down to the fine art form that 'Johnny Foreigner' has. We'll have to be content holding the international sex convention in Soho. Good at that we are".

Lady Daphne: "You're at it again Arthur. Won't you ever learn not to speak until you are spoken to".

Arthur's smile of bonhomie disappears, he retreats touching the space where a forelock would be if were not bald in that spot.

Teddy: "You are right to chide him Daffy dear, but he shakes the meanest rusty nail cocktail this side of heaven".

Lady Daphne: "Don't call me Daffy, sounds like a duck from Walt Disney, and as you'll never see the other side of heaven, it must be the best cocktail anywhere".

Teddy (nodding): "I stand corrected".

Vanessa: "Oh Mummy Teddy was trying to be funny. It's what life's about Making ladies laugh is the first lead into the bedroom. When she laughs she relaxes".

Madeline: "Vanessa, you are incorrigible. I thought you were too young and innocent to make a remark like that".

To the assembly she continues. "Please drain your glasses whilst young Daisy serves the duck paté".

A short silence as they drain their glasses and Daisy serves and bends. The men smile and nod their appreciation. The ladies turn their faces.

Spencer: "Jolly excellent dining nook this, and so cheaply priced when compared to Claridges y'know".

Cynthia: "Never been to Claridges your Honour. I accept this place takes a bit of beating. Far superior to my Public Park Golf Club where I've just come from".

Spencer looks down his nose with closed lips. The others look pityingly to a person who was a member of a Public Park Golf Club.

Lady Daphne (speaking to Andrew): "Did Vanessa partner you in last weekend's foursomes my dear?"

Andrew: "Vanessa's short game is exquisite, she chips and putts excellently, helped me enormously I would very much like her to play a more permanent role in my life's partnership. (As an afterthought). But she does have a fixation playing with my bunch of keys especially when we stroll the golf links, it's become almost a habit".

Peter (interrupting): "Funny you should say that old toff. She plays with mine While walking the fairways. (Hastily adding) The keys of course.(Addressing Vanessa) What fixation do you find with keys – is it some sort of fetish?"

Vanessa flustered and embarrassed.

Lady Daphne (addressing Madeline): "I'm sure you know the answer to that Madeline, I'm referring back to our younger days of course".

Madeline (nodding): "I do see where you are coming from my dear. Obviously our boys do not. Young men are so naïve. But streetwise old birds know that quality keys gives a girl comfort and wealth. Diamonds are not a girl's best friend when compared with the keys of the door, or of a strongroom or two".

Cynthia: "Appears I'm at the centre of a love-match. Sounds more like tennis than golf; but it's intriguing. Who you gonna take V?"

The congregation quietens as Arthur and Daisy serve the main course.

Arthur: "No need to stop your conversation because of us. You all know we are the souls of discretion".

Lady Daphne: "Hmph. You get your kicks from tittle-tattle. Anything you hear to-night is public knowledge in the morning. Announcements are history when members read them in The Times".

Arthur: "Never mind Lady D".

Lady Daphne: "Don't call me Lady D. It's above your station and you know it".

Arthur retreats into his mock servile mode. His niece flaunts her charms to the men. Bending forward serving the vegetables.

Madeline (nodding towards Daisy): "Provoking the men. That would be stamped on at Claridges. Something to say for paying that little bit extra".

Teddy: "Yes Mad, but it keeps us young and warms us for late evening action. You should be pleased for us".

Madeline averts her eyes and coughs disapproval. Arthur and his niece retreats towards the kitchens. At the door he turns to the assembled group.

Arthur: "Now you can carry on talking with what you don't want spreading around the Club".

The men smile, the elder ladies exasperate.

Cynthia: "Come on Vanessa, whose taking you down the aisle then? I can't take the suspense".

Vanessa: "This key thing seems so clinical. It doesn't leave much to the emotions. So cut and dried it is".

Lady Daphne: "You stay on course Vanessa".

Andrew: "Do you mean a golf course. Mother-in-law to be?"

Lady Daphne: "Mother-in-law", to be I do like the ring of that phrase Andrew. (A slight pause). Speaking of rings you don't have one with you, do you?"

Peter: "Don't forget me. I'm the other contender in the blue corner (he adopts a boxing pose). Vanessa laughs with me much more than with that fuddy duddy over there". (Nodding at Andrew).

Lady Daphne (hackles apparent): "Andrew would make a girl laugh all the way to the bank. (She pauses). Sorry I should not have said that, makes me sound commercial, and of course we Greeys are not that way inclined at all".

Spencer: "I thought I'd come to a congenial evening gathering. Not a mating contest. Can't trust women to let a fellow relax even at the dinner table".

Cynthia: "Especially at a dinner table Spencer. It's one of the few occasions a woman can make points in her own time especially at the soup stage, before a fellow can make his excuses to move away. But I'm still agog. Come on Vanessa put us out of our misery".

Vanessa: "This key thing that Mother and Mrs Dutton-Clough put so much faith in was acceptable in their day. A woman did not have much of a say in her future life. If she became awkward by putting her own views she'd be kept quiet for a few years by a rampant husband making her pregnant. Most likely on instructions from his parents. Nowadays by regularly sucking a pill we can have more of a say in matters without the worry. Make a choice closer to the heart we can".

Spencer: "I don't like the trend this conversation's lurched into. It's the duty of all young wives to provide children for future posterity. If they all took your view Vanessa, the world would come to an end in about sixty years".

Lady Daphne: "I couldn't keep my bank manager at bay for that long".

Vanessa (ignoring her mother's intervention): "Women being the adorable creatures we are would make sure the world would not end in sixty years. Merely delay the baby bits till a later date and participate in real life for a longer period of time than our mothers did. They poor things didn't have the option".

Madeline: "There's a lot of truth in that. Andrew was born nine months to the day from our wedding, and our daughter a further year on. You know, in retrospect, I'm glad I didn't have the option".

Lady Daphne: "What about the key test. We can't completely ignore it. Andrew wins hands down. Peter's polite, pleasant but impecunious. It's no contest".

Vanessa: "Mother's right it is no contest but the winner is not as she would like. Besides making me laugh and relax more in his company, Peter is the proud owner of the strongest firmest penis I've ever been pleasured by".

Lady Daphne faints in her chair.

Vanessa (shouting to the wings): "Arthur bring the smelling salts".

Arthur appears and places a large green bottle beneath the nose of Lady Daphne.

CURTAIN

(THE END)

# *Six*

# THE HAPPY WAKE

## *Chapter 1*

"Next client please" Charlie Griffiths' voice rang through to his dining-cum-waiting room. Alan Hartwell walked into his study, speaking as he sat down. "Your boss has upset Iris. She called to see him this morning. When she left the Revenue offices she took a taxi home. Too upset to drive her own car."

Griffiths replied, "In her file was a letter from her Bank, noting a figure of £18 interest for last year. This didn't go on her tax return. It's like doing forty-one miles an hour in a forty mile limit" remarked the illicit tax advisor.

"He's threatened to send her to gaol, and me as well. Says he's going to investigate me since I left the Army all those many years ago. Where does that man live? He's not going to upset Iris like this. She's never cried in public until today. She begged that bastard not to send to gaol."

Griffiths replied "I'll lose your file. It will stop the investigation temporarily. Hopefully he will soon be transferred. He's already past his sell by date at Lichfield."

"It won't work" Hartwell answered. "She's arranged another appointment for next Monday. Agreed to take me with her."

"You have too much to hide. Keep away" Griffiths responded.

"I couldn't care less. I'll kill him" an angry Hartwell retorted.

Griffiths eagerly pocketed the forty pounds consultation fee.

* * * * *

David Elwell was gazing through the window of his penthouse office, which overlooked Lichfield Cathedral and its grounds. He was looking through his twenty four hour vision field glasses.

A funeral procession was in a solemn march. Probably an important man, he thought. Most of the men were dressed in expensive suits. The ladies in fashionable black designer outfits.

Elwell lifted his Polaroid. He took twelve exposures, aiming at the apparently more wealthy mourners.

He instructed his secretary to discover the name of the deceased. Also, obtain a list of the mourners. Maybe some future business for him? It's no use investigating paupers. People with money were those that attracted him, however honest they may be. The could be made to cringe and pay.

Elwell rang to an office five floors below and asked the officer in charge of personal taxation to come upstairs. An alarm bell rang. It was rare for him to receive a direct call from the Chief Inspector.

He breathed a sigh of relief. A colleague of the same rank was seated in front of the Chief's desk. Charlie Griffiths filled the vacant chair.

Elwell waited before speaking "Both of you live in the district. I do not. Head Office rules that District Inspectors must reside outside the area he controls. This has an obvious disadvantage of not being able to mix socially. I play bowls, but it must be fifteen miles away. You, Dennis, are a member of the Lichfield Bowling Club."

"That's correct, sir, but other members shut up business talk when I join them. Conversation switches to the weather or football."

"Same with me" said Griffiths. The District Inspector nodded.

"I hope their attitude doesn't stop you from trying to obtain data that will help our enquiries."

His junior colleagues vigorously shook their heads.

"Dennis, what have you discovered recently?" Elwell asked.

"I visited the premises of Jack Shaw. On tiptoe I peeped through his rear lounge window. There was a massive Wurlitzer Organ complete with huge expensive speakers. In the next room a white baby grand piano. He lives on a very small wage from his newspaper shop. Tells us he has no personal assets. I suggest we throw the book at him."

"How about his wife?" Elwell queried.

"Yes, she attended the Bowling Club centenary party with Jack. She dripped with jewels, even wore a diamond tiara."

"Well done, Dennis. I have a meeting with Shaw next Thursday. He'll sweat blood. Any other local knowledge? I'm interviewing Eric Wilkins soon."

Dennis Crossley answered "He has the largest fish and chip takeaway this side of London. He again seems to live on fresh air. Says he doesn't smoke or drink."

Elwell raised his eyebrows "Is that true?" he queried.

"No, it's a deliberate lie," Crossley continued. "He calls into the Conservative Club each night after the business closes. Always has at least a couple of pints of bitter when he's playing snooker. From his wife's cough in the shop, I would think she's a thirty dayer."

"How are the villains of Chalk Hay, Charlie?" Elwell queried.

"My mother's an invalid, sir. Just do not get into the community as Dennis does."

"It would help you if you did" was the curt reply. Was this a reference to the annual staff assessment? After a pause for effect, Elwell went on "What do you know about Alan and Iris Hartwell? They live near you."

"They seem respectable people. I see them in church occasionally." Griffiths was back pedalling.

"Iris is bringing her husband to see me next Monday. I would like some background information. He hasn't completed a tax form since he left the Army after the Falklands War. He doesn't draw unemployment pay. It may only be a trivial case but Farrows Bank sent a slip showing Mrs Hartwell has a small deposit account with them. Till recently they lived with her husband's parents who provided funds for them to live on. Think hard man. You were in the same regiment. Didn't you come across Hartwell?"

"No, sir" lied the underling.

Elwell turned to Dennis Crossley. "Fill in a report on the cases mentioned and let me have it by tomorrow."

Griffiths also rose to leave. The District Inspector motioned him to stay seated. When they were alone the Head said "I am disappointed you do not supply information. Especially as I have reason to believe you are in a position to help us more than anyone else here." Griffiths looked askance.

Elwell threw a letter across his table. "Read that" be commanded.

Griffiths picked it up. He noticed the letter was not signed. Neither was there an address.

"To Head Inspector.

"There is an evil man employed by you. If you can pay enough money he will destroy official mail or doctor it to give a false impression. That man is Charles Griffiths."

## *Chapter 2*
*Three days later*

The lunchtime edition of the Evening Standard blazed a headline "Headless corpse found on luxury Blackoaks Park."

"At 7 this morning a head severed from its body was found in a footpath off treelined Pottah Avenue. The torso was discovered lying against a hedge fifty yards further on.

"A buckled and bent motor cycle was lying in the driveway of a mansion owned by Sir George Rothstein, a City Banker.

"Our reporter learned the deceased was a Chief Inspector of Taxes, based at Lichfield, fifteen miles from the scene."

D.I. Ablett, the police officer at the scene was mystified. The severance was so cleanly cut? Usually in a road accident "It's a bloody mess" to quote the officer, who added "This had the neatness of a French guillotine. Merely a tiny trickle of blood."

* * * * *

"That can only be Derrick Elwell", Chris Small read aloud to Anne Kirby; his chief clerk.

She replied "That man's been courting disaster since be moved here. I can think of a hundred and fifty of our clients who won't grieve."

Small answered "That's in this firm, adding our competitors, it would be nearer five times your figure."

She nodded. "His District employs over two hundred and fifty people. None of them liked him. Even his Number Two had to make an appointment to see him."

* * * * *

Jane Kerr arrived late and breathless for a meeting with the Head of Inland Revenue at Somerset House. She apologised, her train was late. After a few moments to recover she opened the discussion "There's little doubt the District Inspector works very hard and long hours. But he's still bottom of the national league table, both in terms of money collected from errant taxpayers and finishing off cases. He has four times the national average of open cases still under investigation.

"Are you recommending we remove him from the District?" Jane's Chief asked.

She replied "It's not the Government's wish to stress innocent people. Elwell isn't giving a damn. He seems to get a private kick out of using his authority to terrorise taxpayers. He has no compassion in his soul. I've seen women leaving his office sobbing uncontrollably. He shows them to the exit with a glowing grin. This is his result. No amount of money he extricates equals the pleasure of the terror he instils. The more a person begs the longer he continues the investigation."

"There was a suicide of a Sub-Postmaster. Elwell put it down to poor health and financial problems. I am not so sure." Her chief was listening intently and let her continue. "Elwell had called on him when the man was ill in bed. What threats occurred I don't know. The following morning the man staggered to his garage and turned on a pipe from the exhaust to the car interior. The rest is history. As you appreciate, death completes a case. Elwell made great play that he had finished this case within schedule."

"You've been very thorough Ms Kerr. I assume the man covers his tracks?"

She answered "His files show no reference to his gratifying antics. The interview reports are on a par to those I see in other tax districts."

"Does the man have any hobbies?" he interjected.

Jane Kerr replied "Work is his life, but I understand he plays an occasional game of bowls. You already know Elwell and I met in the Army. I suspected his motives there. My best friend said I was misguided. She had the naivety to marry the man."

"When I was inspecting at his offices I tried to arrange a social dinner with his wife and himself. It didn't get off the ground.

"Elwell rides a motor cycle. This is parked in the car park before 7.15 each morning. He has a few sandwiches and a ten minute lunch break. He rarely leaves the office during a working day until he departs for home, promptly at four in the afternoon, his panniers loaded with business files."

"Any substance in the complaint from Chris J. Small & Co?" her Chief asked.

"They have a point, in fact, several points. I was meticulous in my examination of George Dolman, a client of theirs. For the past four years Dolman has been receiving only seventy per cent of his wages. Elwell has refused authority to his employer to pay him the full amount."

The Head interrupted "He's refused to issue a Form 714?" Jane Kerr nodded.

"He's asked irrelevant questions by letter. On receiving a reply he has waited several months before asking more irrelevant questions.

The Chief was assimilating the data. Some action had to be taken. He said "Let's go to lunch. We've had a depressing morning."

* * * * *

Jane Kerr returned from lunch with the same edition of the Evening Standard that Chris Small had been discussing with his chief clerk. "It seems our troubles are over, Sir" she said.

## *Chapter 3*

A week later the tax advisory firm received a visit from Det. Insp. Ablett. He asked Small & Kirby if they could think of a motive. Both spoke simultaneously "Yes."

Small answered first. "He was the most unpopular taxman I can recall. I have seen twelve District Inspectors come and go. Derrick Elwell led the field by many lengths as being the most despised. He instilled his own methods into his subordinates. The Lichfield tax district is notoriously feared."

Ablett replied "That picture came through from the other three firms I visited. Will you give me the names of clients who will benefit. Also, those who have reason to fear him."

White replied "It was a favourite ploy of Elwell to investigate a wealthy businessman. Usually he selects one with a longstanding marriage. He would bring the wife into the investigation, ask her to call, attack their honesty and integrity. He would threaten her with veiled innuendos, how easy it would be to prosecute her husband. Tax offences usually carry a long prison sentence. Women have come directly here from such a meeting, deeply in distress. It's easy for a man in his position to terrify."

Ablett replied "If a police officer did this he would be in serious trouble."

Small answered "Business people don't report him. Most have a small tax skeleton in the cupboard. It gives a guilt complex. Invariably it's a small blemish, but Elwell gives the impression it's a hanging crime. He is quite merciless."

Ablett nodded, "Thank you. Here's a large envelope for your list of suspects. Send it to me at Police HQ."

Chris Small replied "Sorry. I can't help. It is a breach of professional confidence to supply client information to third parties."

Ablett looked askance "When I subpoena you as a witness you will have to disclose."

"By then you would have charged someone. I would be immune from a civil action."

Ablett sighed "I'm up against it. Can you give me a lead?"

"Why not make a thorough examination of the cases that Elwell and his team have under investigation" Small replied.

## *Chapter 4*
### *Time – Spring 1982*

The Canberra cruise liner sailed on the fine Spring morning of 9th April; destination the Falkland Islands.

Privates Charlie Griffiths and Alan Hartwell were part of 3 Commando Brigade. During the voyage Charlie was constantly sea-sick. The two soldiers who started Infant School together, were lifelong companions.

The hour after hour deck exercise and training in only shorts and plimsolls were making a hardy breed even tougher. Training in the art of guerrilla warfare was a priority. All soldiers needed to kill an enemy, silently, without using a weapon.

Lieutenant Derrick Elwell was keeping a lonely vigil. He was the task force's Chief Security Officer. Recruited quickly from Inland Revenue Training School the day following the Argentinean invasion. A week later he was a member of the Task Force. Basic training in Public School Army Cadet Corp had been implemented with service in a Territorial defence unit. At the rear of the fighting line he was to head a solitary unit.

He viewed the rigorous exercises of the fighting force from the Officers' deck. What a wonderful sight. All of them acting in unison. In battle some would be brave, a few very brave to foolhardy. The majority would act as ordered, no more, no less. He was to make examples of the tiny minority who actions failed to match up.

Two women Non Commissioned Officers saluted him. Jane Kerr said "After five weeks, boredom is setting in, sir. Have you any work lined up?"

Elwell shook his head. Said their real work would start after a beachhead had been established. Meanwhile, keep fit, play some deck games.

The whistling wind became more fierce as the Canberra ploughed a relentless course. After a further six days a treeless land mass came into sight.

* * * * *

"Why didn't you jump?" Elwell quietly asked a shackled Private Moran of 3 Paras.

"I can't swim, sir. When I saw the mountainous waves I knew I would have died" was the reply.

Elwell countered "Scores of soldiers who did jump can't swim. You were issued with an inflatable floater."

"Sorry, sir. Can I join my mates ashore? I want battle action" said the eighteen year old.

"I think you would run backwards from a battle line. We can't have that, can we?"

The soldier didn't reply. The eighteen soldiers who were drowned were not mentioned.

At midnight Private Moran was told a landing craft was to move in three hours. He would have a second chance. Elwell gave him a mug of very strong coffee and instructed him to "down it in one."

Still in shackles, an ankle ball and chain, Elwell manipulated the drugged soldier to an open porthole. With a tremendous heave Moran plunged into the open sea.

The following morning Elwell informed the Adjutant's office of an error by Administration. There were nineteen personnel who failed to reach the landing crafts.

## *Chapter 5*

Security Organisation HQ was established at Port San Carlos after 3 Paras landed on 21st May.

An advance force surprised four sleeping Argentinean guerrillas. No P.O.W. compound existed. Elwell obtained handcuffs from the Canberra stores. Sick quarters had been raided for its supply of straight jackets.

Jane Kerr mentioned her concern to her colleague. "I don't like the look in his eye. At University he kicked the head of a Harlequin forward in a scrum. The player died. My boyfriend who was playing said it was malicious, no provocation."

Maureen Bullock retorted "You are constantly criticising him, making him sound a monster. No, he is doing a soul destroying job in difficult circumstances. I'm sure his heart is in the right place."

Jane Kerr shook her head. "The man has no heart. I am sure there was foul play the night before we came ashore. You're sweet on him, aren't you?"

Maureen replied "He's nice to me. He wants to meet me when we are home. I'll have nothing bad said against him."

Jane shrugged her shoulders. "Sorry," she replied.

Both Non Commissioned Officers had been trained to kill. They were the only female members of the S.A.S. included in the task force. They made perfect guards.

Jane Kerr rode pillion as the two colleagues visited the Canberra to request food provisions. Now even more would be needed. At gunpoint the prisoners had constructed a makeshift barbed wire compound.

Elwell's first class degree in Spanish was invaluable in his interrogations. The Argentineans had by chance been on a hillside position and viewed the British landings at San Carlos.

The most junior informed Elwell he had observed a soldier climbing from a porthole the night after the landings.

"You can see in the dark?" queried the British Officer.

"We have twenty four hour vision field glasses" the Argentinean answered proudly. The British Officer demanded to see them.

The same afternoon Elwell sat in intense thought on a rock overlooking the compound. He was nursing a heckler sub-machine gun. The N.C.O.s arrived to take the prisoners on a one hour exercise march whilst Elwell made a thorough inspection of the vacant compound.

In the afternoon Argentinean aircraft were heavily engaged over San Carlos bay. Each time a plane was shot down the two N.C.O.s gave a hearty cheer. Elwell's continual frown relaxed. When HMS Argent received direct hits and sank, it was the prisoners turn to cheer. The youngster was uncontrollably joyful. Elwell looked hard at him.

Warrant Officer Jane Kerr was fast asleep in their stone hut. Her colleague and Elwell made love silently and fully clothed at the far end. Daylight had given way to a bitterly cold night. The prisoners were calling to their captors to show mercy and give them shelter. Elwell's ears were deaf to their pleas.

Two hours before midnight the cries ceased. Elwell immediately moved into the open air. He was armed with his Heckler, his newly acquired binoculars hanging loosely around his neck.

The prisoners compound was silent. Raising his binoculars he viewed it was empty. He thought they can't be far, and moved faster towards the main track leading to the beach. Taking a more sheer route he arrived as the first prisoner came from the undergrowth onto the beach. His binoculars were again useful. The ex-prisoners walking abreast headed towards Middle Bay.

When they were ten metres past, Elwell stepped from the undergrowth. Raising his heckler he sprayed the four. He heard groaning from only two and finished his gruesome job from close range.

## *Chapter 6*

"Shot whilst attempting to escape" was the heading on From 256. The two S.A.S. women read Elwell's spidery handwriting. The report extended to cover a thousand words. They were asked to sign as witnesses. Maureen Bullock signed immediately. Jane Kerr was reluctant.

"It was my turn to sleep" W.O. Kerr retorted.

"Think of your future career. War is war. My duty was clear" Elwell answered.

The Warrant Office replied "Why was the compound wire cut so cleanly?"

Elwell thought before replying "They must have hidden a cutting tool, which we didn't find. It only needed a sharp knife."

Jane Kerr said "I searched the dead bodies and found nothing."

Elwell continued "We are splitting hairs, now sign."

She authoritatively shook her head. He marched away and mustered "You'll regret this."

*Chapter 7*

"Goose Green" said Charlie, "That's a funny name. I wonder who thought it up." The march from San Carlos to Goose Green was past Sussex Mountain. The cold and wet was far more fierce than on the shoreline.

Their three year Army stint was expiring as the Falklands crisis loomed. Service in Northern Ireland was easy compared to the encounters in the South Atlantic. There was little chance of foot soldiers distinguishing themselves at Goose Green. It was an officers battle. Diplomacy and iron nerve outwitted the Argentineans. More foul weather and fierce fighting occurred through the mountain passes en route to the Island's Capital Town.

A sigh of relief from all ranks was audible on the 14th June 1982. The Argentineans had surrendered at Port Stanley.

"Thank God for that" said Charlie. "I need a good night's sleep. Let's get back to that cruise liner."

Elwell's return journey included events that would fashion his future life. He had found a woman who admired him. Usually his attentions to the opposite sex were spurned after the first date. His was not a normal sense of humour; being the only man to laugh out loud when a soldier was hurled into the sea by a freak wave.

* * * * *

Time was taken on the return voyage by the Personnel Section to discuss future career moves with the men and women whose contracts with the Service had expired.

The S.A.S. women were interviewed jointly. The Education Officer questioned Jane Kerr what her future plans were?

"I am destined for the Civil Service."

"I think that's a wise decision" he remarked, glancing at her service record.

"How about you, Corporal Bullock? You are too invaluable to let go."

She asked "Is a Royal Commission available, sir?"

The interviewing officer replied "I can't promise that, but you can stay at your present rank. A Corporal's life is extremely pleasant."

Maureen smiled ruefully. "I am considering a proposal of marriage. Thank you all the same."

The interviewing officer sighed "We are losing two N.C.Os, both of you trained to kill. You'll be costly to replace. It must have been a bitter occurrence killing four heavily armed Argentineans who were attacking your billet. You are to be congratulated almost as much as your Commanding Officer."

In Maureen's cabin, Jane queried what he meant. "He seemed to infer we had killed somebody. I could cheerfully strangle our immediate boss" she laughed. "However, we are getting to the time when we can lose him forever." Her colleague frowned but remained silent.

Privates Hartwell and Griffiths were summoned. "We can't lose valuable battle hardened campaigners to leave the Commandos" remarked the Officer. "Give us another three years, you'll never regret it."

Hartwell remarked "Sir, you sound like Lord Kitchener all those many years ago. No, I am returning to the family butchering business. My parents were heartbroken when I joined the Army. There's no-one to kill the beasts. My only brother emigrated to Australia years ago. Now my father is too old to operate the guillotine."

The interviewing Captain replied "From your records you did your share of killing in the recent conflict. There'll be good opportunities for you."

Hartwell was resolute in his refusal.

"What say you, Private Griffiths?"

Charlie replied "My parents are three years older than when I enlisted. My mother's become incapacitated. She can't look after my father."

He was then asked "What sort of career prospects have you?"

Charlie continued "I had four years as a counter clerk with the Inland Revenue before I joined the Army. Think I'll try there first."

At Captain Elwell's meeting he was congratulated at being promoted in the field of action. "You are quite unique, considering the short time hostilities lasted. You must have impressed a red star General."

Elwell gave a smile which inferred "if you have it, it will show." He didn't inform the interviewer with his one finger typing he amended his record file by forging telexes deemed to emanate from the United Kingdom.

"If your speedy promotion to this level is maintained you could be a full Colonel by the time you're thirty" Elwell was informed.

"Thank you, but my future is mapped out. I qualified with honours at the Inland Revenue Training College. The present conflict prevented me accepting a posting to Somerset House. I can now give the time to sifting out errant taxpayers."

The interviewing officer replied "I understand that area of tax law contains the fastest career moves."

*Chapter 8*
*Time – The present*

At Lichfield Police Station Chris Small was having a gruelling meeting. The tall figure of Jock Ablett was sitting eye balling him.

"I took your advice. My staff have been examining the Tax Office files, day and night for the last four weeks. Elwell's file on your tax practice was the thickest. Your firm's clients filled an entire cupboard. It seems a vendetta has been in operation for five years."

Small agreed "Yes, since Elwell came to Lichfield. I wouldn't let him use bullying tactics. There are over one hundred and fifty investigation cases still open. Only a handful have been settled. That's where clients have instructed me to settle at a much larger cost to themselves than my firm recommended."

Ablett asked "Why should they have issued such instructions?"

Small answered "Clients want to continue their business and personal life free from stress and worry. Some people will pay heavily for the privilege."

Ablett listened attentively. "You have a strong motive for seeing Elwell dead."

Chris Small was vehement. "I didn't murder the man."

"Who said he was murdered?" the policeman replied.

"The newspapers inferred he was", Small replied.

"Elwell blacklisted your firm with every other tax district in the United Kingdom. Did you know this?"

"I guessed as much. In the last two years we have been having a harder time. You will also be aware that we have complained about his conduct in strong terms to Somerset House."

"There was no reference to this in his files" Ablett countered. He then went on "But I did see a reference to him complaining to the Institute of the Tax Faculty, your governing body."

Small replied "Yes. I am attending a disciplinary meeting in London next week. Elwell had been asked to attend."

Ablett interrupted "He won't be there now, will he?"

*Chapter 9*

Ablett took the train from Lichfield to London the following morning. He arrived by taxi at Somerset House in time for his 10.30 appointment with Jane Kerr.

Ablett opened the discussion. "You must have confidential files on each individual Inspector within the United Kingdom?"

"I've become boggle-eyed searching files at Lichfield. Spent four weeks looking for motives."

"Did you find any?" Jane Kerr asked.

Ablett replied "Far too many. Thankfully he has two fine paintings in his office which gave me some relief. Depressing subjects, but wonderfully painted."

She brightened. "Aren't they nice? I admired them on my recent audit visit. Both are of older men. The one gazing intently at his late mother; the other, the man eagerly looking through a window in anticipation, entitled 'Waiting for her to visit'. A table in the background laid for tea for two. I wouldn't want it because of the sadness it portrays, but the fine quality of the painting is unique. There's one by the same artist in the Courtauld Galleries next door."

Ablett's face shone. "Could I see it?"

They silently paced Gallery Four to view the painting. "That's how the money goes," A working man, his money spread on the kitchen table, looking appealingly at a wall portrait of a dominant Queen Victoria in her later years.

Jane Kerr gave an aside "When Elwell calls at our office, he always pops in here."

Ablett walked to the security guard and showed her a photograph. "Ever seen this man?" he asked.

"Oh, yes. He's a regular visitor. He's nice. Spends at least fifteen minutes in front of the old Queen's painting."

Jane Kerr was admiring other pictures. Ablett spoke at what sounded like an aside "I've been examining your Army records. You seemed to have a chequered time in the Falklands."

"Never even mentioned in despatches. Most disappointing" she replied.

"Did you see much action, other than in a bedroom?" he queried.

"Sorry you have the advantage," She reddened with anger, but continued "I was in the 3 Commando advance on Port Stanley. There were only two women in the squad of three hundred paras when Mendendez surrendered. It was only after this that I enjoyed the luxury of a bedroom. What are you driving at?"

"A note by your C.O. left no doubt you used your rank to order the other woman para to bed. Ordered her bring a carrot shaped sex toy and very little else" Ablett replied.

"This is outrageous. We had a womanly affection. Nothing more than that," Ablett answered "Now you know why the British Empire Medal didn't come your way. From memory the final remarks on your record sheet read something like this:

"I am pleased this W.O. is to leave the Army by her own choice. Due to her undoubted bravery in the field I suggested if she resigned voluntarily no disciplinary action would be taken. I informed her homosexuality is a Court Martial offence."

Jane Kerr retorted "The fiend, he's insanely jealous. He said nothing about homosexuality." Ablett nodded to her outburst.

The nearness of Somerset House to Scotland Yard gave Ablett the opportunity to flit between both. At Scotland Yard, amidst a mountain of paper, he thought on motive alone the second favourite suspect must be Chris Small. His Taxation advisory practice was in grave jeopardy. All he had worked for in twenty five years blown away. Every Revenue office he dealt with were giving him a hard time; based on a biased report. Dealing with the Tax districts were now more expensive because of the additional time taken. He couldn't charge the additional costs to his clients. His practice was now in financial difficulties. If he lost his licence to practice he couldn't work. Bankruptcy loomed.

The main charge was that his firm was a refuge for illegal taxpayers. He was defending Clients without being true and fair.

Elwell didn't care how much of his department's time was wasted. The Government was paying for that. His sole object was to destroy the firm of Chris J. Small & Co.

Ablett concluded third on the suspect list must he Charlie Griffiths. With Elwell dead his illegal tax service could continue unabated.

Alan Hartwell would benefit by the Inspector's death. No more harassment for his wife. His illegal liaison with Charlie Griffiths could continue.

Hartwell had telephoned a Maureen Elwell, a name he discovered in the Stafford Telephone book. Discreet enquiries made him believe he had the address he was looking for. Hartwell's phone had been tapped. Ablett had a voice transcript of the innocuous conversation.

## *Chapter 10*

Ablett read the invitation on the back page of the Funeral Service at Lichfield Crematorium.

"Maureen wishes to express her thanks for your prayers and tokens of sympathy at this sad time. She would be pleased to welcome you to her home following this service."

After the congregation of six had prayed and rendered the hymn 'Abide with me', the curtains closed as the shortened coffin slid forward on its rollers. The vicar gave an appreciation of the deceased. He trusted the persons present would make use of the offertory trays. He also reminded them of the invitation.

* * * * *

Jane Kerr poured and served the wine.

Ablett was the only person to stay with orange juice. People were trying to think of nice things to say, but the more wine consumed, this thin line of conversation petered out.

Ablett asked Small how the meeting with his Institute had concluded.

He replied "I produced three Tax Inspectors from other districts as witnesses. All gave my firm excellent references. I was given reason to think the case against us will collapse."

"Lucky you, no doubt the absence of the main witness helped your case?" the Detective replied. Small looked grimly at the policeman, but said nothing.

Ablett moved on and admired three pencil sketches on the lounge walls. "These are quite well constructed. Who painted them?" he remarked to the new widow.

She replied "I did, I had a lot of spare time. Derrick wouldn't let me work. He demanded I paint mature authoritative women."

"Why was this?" Ablett asked.

"He couldn't control the way he was created. I didn't fall into the category" she answered.

"Were you happy in married life?" Ablett asked.

"No, he didn't turn out to be the man I hoped he was. I don't know how I've survived so many years with him. His constant vendettas against colleagues and taxpayers have been overbearing. I had to agree they were all wrong and he was correct. I was little short of insane. Another few months and I would have completed flipped my lid. He refused to consider children or even adoption. I've forgotten how to laugh. Jane's changed all that. I'm happier now."

Ablett's mind was working overtime.

"Surprised to see you here, Ms Kerr" Ablett remarked.

Jane replied "Why? Maureen and I have been good friends for many years. In a death a woman needs her friends."

He changed the subject. "The pictures on the walls seem to have a common subject. Just like those in Elwell's office and at Courtaulds."

"The man had a mother fixation, ignored his wife totally. Maureen's led a miserable existence since leaving the Army."

Ablett moved into the library. He sat alone still sipping orange juice. The rest of the party were now into the fifth bottle of wine, peals of laughter were emanating. Ablett picked up a slim volume 'Commando warfare behind enemy lines'. A chapter on 'Seven ways to maim without weapons' fascinated him. The use of trigonometry in sizing up a victim was prominent. He mused "Never thought of maths being any use to a Commando."

Looking through the library window he observed washing hanging to dry in a small orchard. The objects seemed to have no visible means of defying gravity. Curiosity killed a cat, it was dusk as he re-entered the house.

Charlie Griffiths was the life and soul of a swinging party.

Hartwell remarked "Never seen him so happy since demob night in Portsmouth." Ablett's smile was without humour.

"You seem to be in fine shape for a man with a serious tax problem" Ablett said.

A startled Hartwell asked "How did you know that?"

"I examined your file" was the reply. After a pause he continued "Did you kill Elwell?"

"No, Sir, definitely not" and moved away.

Only the vicar had left the wake. Ablett listened at a cloakroom door. "You must return to London with me" he heard Jane Kerr demand. "We can take up where we left off on the Canberra."

The widow replied "If only we could. It sounds like heaven."

Jane Kerr changed the topic. "You'll have to stop heavy drinking. It's destroying you."

Maureen answered "When you're stuck with an ogre drink was my only escape. His beatings were endurable under alcohol."

* * * * *

The following evening Ablett called into a detached freehold on Chalk Kay's Jubilee Estate. Charlie Griffiths' weekly surgery was in progress. Four people were awaiting the tax guru.

"Next, please" Ablett heard from the ceiling speaker. Conversation was minimal. Each taxpayer had sterling notes in their pockets. In recent weeks the cost of a consultancy had taken a steep rise.

Ablett entered the main office as the fourth person left.

"I wasn't expecting you" said a shaken Griffiths.

Ablett replied "You knew where Elwell lived?"

"No, it was a close secret, not recorded in the office files. I knew he came down on the A59 highway. On occasions I followed him the last two miles into the town centre. We were both early birds."

Ablett interrupted "Did Elwell know about this illegal business?"

"It is not illegal for people to come here for advice" commented Charlie.

The policeman ranted "It's what you are doing at your workplace that's illegal – destroying and tampering with Royal Mail was a hanging offence two hundred years ago. You'd get ten years today. Help me and I'll make it easier for you."

## *Chapter 11*

"The meeting of 4th July is now re-convened" Chris Small continued. "Since we last met, a kind person has completed the reason for our original meeting. We all attended the funeral service. I quite enjoyed the party afterwards."

Jane Kerr nodded agreement. "I think Maureen took it quite well. Fourteen years is a long time to suffer such cruelty."

"The manner of his death is a classic example of page seven of the Commandos Manual. Three of us were trained by that publication. It only leaves Mr. Small incapable of the killing."

"Be careful what you say" Charlie Griffiths interrupted. "The Landlord's serving the next room." The meeting quietened as a waitress brought four more drinks.

Chris Small spoke again "As you all agree, I couldn't have done it. Who did it is of no concern. Let us quietly finish our drinks. Then we can go about our business as though this organisation never existed."

Alan Hartwell replied "I would like it placed on record I didn't kill the bastard. Given a clearer opportunity I would have. So whichever of you pair did it, congratulations."

The annex bar door opened. Ablett walked in and nodded a greeting. "I thought you'd be here. I've been considering charges against the four of you. Conspiring to murder is the one most likely. You are one short of a quorum. It's understandable as I have her locked up." Jane Kerr visibly stiffened. "I am now looking for an accomplice."

The policeman continued "I interviewed Sir George Rothstein. He is an early riser. Saw Elwell on a number of occasions riding past his house in the last few years. Said he wondered what the man did for a living – a market trader he guessed. A few days before the accident he observed a man and woman waiting on the pathway of the next house. After the mysterious driver rode by, they disappeared into the mist."

Charlie Griffiths stubbed his cigarette and asked the significance of Ablett's remarks.

"Curiosity killed a cat, Mr. Griffiths. Sir George figured there was an early morning romantic assignation. Thought the man had a military carriage. Walking smartly and upright."

"I again called for the service records. Those of Mrs. Elwell were missing. On loan to Lichfield Recruiting Shop. She was trying to re-enlist."

Jane Kerr remarked "That's tommy rot. They don't take women of 38."

"She didn't know that, did she?" Ablett mocked. "You seem upset Miss Kerr? Is it because Maureen refused your advances?"

"I'm going home. Lunch will be ready" interrupted Hartwell.

"You're going nowhere" replied the Inspector. "I have warrants for all of you. I'm hoping for a confession."

He turned to Jane Kerr "Mrs. Elwell refuses to name her accomplice, the man Sir George saw from his bathroom window. We both know Ms Kerr that man was you in drag."

She replied "You'll have one hell of a job proving that lie."

The annex door opened. Maureen Elwell was pushed through followed by a policewoman. She ran straight to Jane Kerr "Whatever are we to do dear?" Maureen asked. "You make all the decisions."

*Chapter 12*

Anne Kirby was perusing the Situations Vacant column of the late night's Evening Standard. She was disappointed and returned to page 1. The banner headline and report was the guilty verdict in the case of the Headless Corpse. Sentence was to be passed after psychiatric reports.

The incriminating piece of evidence that Defence Counsel couldn't successfully counter, came during a long session with Inspector Ablett in the witness box. The policeman was asked how he first suspected the defendants were involved.

He replied he had met Jane Kerr in another context of the case. He had noted her strength of character and authoritative manner. Throughout the investigations it became obvious Elwell had a fetish for this type of woman. A thread began to run through my mind. From her Service records he noted Jane Kerr's refusal to sign what had now proved to be a false report of an abortive escape by four Argentinean prisoners of war during the Falklands conflict. Partly out of revenge the deceased married the weaker personality. This added power to the conflict between Elwell and Jane Kerr, who were on a collision path even before the marriage ceremony. Jealousy seeped through, Jane Kerr longed for a permanent liaison with Maureen.

At a reception after the funeral I noticed female clothing apparently without visible means of support hanging to dry in an orchard attached to the Elwells' house. I made a cursory inspection at the time but later returned when I knew the house was unoccupied. I exchanged the makeshift washing line for a new one issued as main kit to recruit commandos.

Defence Counsel prompted "How relevant was your discovery?"

"Very. I sent the razor wire to Forensic."

On further prompting, "with what results?"

The Inspector continued "Despite being thoroughly cleansed, there were still minute particles of blood attached to a five inch portion of the wire, mid-way between its stretched length. The blood group matched that of the deceased."

Defence Counsel replied. "It must have been an amazing coincidence that the stretch of wire at the scene of the crime, if indeed it was a crime, was exactly the height to decapitate a man. Surely some other explanation is necessary for the freak accident!"

The detective replied "This was a worrying concern until I noticed that promotion to Warrant Officer necessitated an '0' level in Mathematics. This included the use of trigonometry. Knowing the height of a man and measuring the height of his motorcycle, the exact position of the wire from the ground could be ascertained."

Defence Counsel had no further questions.

On page 5 of the same edition Anne Kirby read a report of a related case which concluded earlier in the week.

Three defendants were found guilty of conspiracy to murder. They were Charles Claude Griffiths, former Inland Revenue employee, Alan Hartwell, self-employed butcher, and Christopher James Small, proprietor of a taxation advisory service. They were each sentenced to two years imprisonment.

The same charge was not proceeded with against the two other members of the conspiring group, who were today convicted of murder.

Anne Kirby sighed. Who would employ her now? In the morning she would call on Slater and Hawkins, Taxation Recruitment specialists.

# *Seven*

# THE BANK STATEMENT

I was gazing with acquisitive eyes on First Viewing Day, my target was lot 261.

The catalogue referred to it as 'The Bank Statement' by Charles Wagstaff. My hands were trembling with excitement. I had been chasing this author's work for over four years without any real success. I had secured a preliminary drawing for a paltry sum. This had been used for a major picture bought by the late Queen Mary from the 1950 Summer Exhibition at The Royal Academy. I wanted a major work but the prices had spiralled since royalty had acquired one.

A bearded man in the picture was looking worried. How the artist brushed the anxious lines in his brow I shall never know, nor how he included the lifelike grimace at reading the bad news. Obviously exceeded his overdraft limit, I thought. An antique barometer placed on the wall behind the elderly Victorian dealer. Three antique chairs to his left. They looked expensive. The picture was overflowing with the paraphernalia of a well stocked dealer. This picture I must have.

On the last of the three Viewing Days – I had attended each day – a tall overweight man elbowed me away from 'my' picture. "Delia" he boomed to his slim dark haired companion "The best example of this artist's work I have ever seen. The fine brush strokes make the painting 'vibrate'. I really must follow the old man in the painting's example and see how much our Gallery has in the Bank." His loud voice carried through to anyone vaguely interested in the Wagstaff. She nodded a timid affirmative.

"I'm sure you're right, Mr. Gray."

I had done my homework. Consulted my own bank statement, adopting the same pose as the old man in 'my' picture. £125,000 I noted gleefully. The Solicitors had certainly hastened to convert my old aunt's assets into cash. My only cousin had received the other half.

With that amount of cash burning a hole in my bank statement, I felt the Wagstaff was just within my grasp. Especially now that the owner of the leading Gallery in Mayfair had given his stamp of approval.

* * * * *

There had been few gasps of surprise from the audience in the first 260 lots. Several didn't sell but a similar amount exceeded the reserve price.

The loudspeaker crackled. "Lot 261. We have a fine example by this well known Victorian painter which he called 'The Bank Statement'. I hope all of you aren't as worried as the man in the picture when you open your bank statement. No, I'm sure you don't, otherwise you wouldn't be at today's auction." He laughed at his own joke. My mouth and lips were too dry to join the general merriment.

The overweight dealer made his first appearance of the morning, moving to the left aisle seat in the row in front of mine. 'Good' I thought. 'I can see him bidding.'

A porter held the smallish picture above his head. The auctioneer opened. "80,000". The audience remained silent, as did the bank of telephones to my right. "Alright, perhaps I was a little ambitious, £60,000." I raised my hand.

"Thank you, sir" said the BBC voiced auctioneer. With my help the price doubled with a series of bids at £10,000 each. The stout man hadn't moved a muscle.

The auctioneer retorted "We haven't reached the reserve price yet. Please someone put another £10,000 on the price." He seemed a nice man. I nodded.

"Well done again, sir. Now I will sell the picture." His sales patter continued "Notice the several framed landscapes and portraits painted into this picture. You are getting more pictures for your money – quite an extraordinary painting." I thought with his enthusiasm why isn't he bidding himself?

The blonde on the third telephone raised her hand. "Tony, I have a bid of £150,000." The auctioneer flashed pearly white teeth.

"Thank you Beth, keep up the good work." The price had reached a record for the artist. But I must have this picture. I nodded again, as did Beth, then myself; then Beth, then myself. Beth shook her head. The auctioneer looked hard at Beth, and in a stage whisper said "Surely you can sweet-talk your client."

Beth gave a resigned smile but I heard her quieter stage whisper "My client is a lady."

Mine at £200,000, I thought. Then the stout man discreetly twitched his catalogue. Oh hell, still if all else fails I can re-sell the picture, get my money back with a bit to spare probably. I held up my hand, he twitched, then my hand. The twitching stopped.

"Sold to the gentleman with the very pale face." I heard the auctioneer's voice through the mist of fear. The audience broke into spontaneous applause. One man clapped me soundly on the shoulder. "What theatre" he chanted. The auctioneer called for an encore. I was in a fearful sweat, my bank balance and the loan from Bothebies totally dissipated.

* * * * *

The address on the back of the envelope resting on the 'Welcome Mat' of my apartment was from the same firm of Solicitors that my late aunt had used. Perhaps a bit of interest on the monies they had held on my behalf; I thought optimistically. There was not a cheque enclosed. The contents will remain embedded in my mind as long as I live.

"Dear Sir,

"Referring to the legacy cheque which you recently encashed, your late aunt's Will has been contested. We have received a communication from a firm of Solicitors in Melbourne, Australia, acting on behalf of seven clients who purport to be the children of your aunt's deceased younger brother, who emigrated as a Ten Pound tourist fifty years ago. The Will referred to 'all of my nieces and nephews living at the time of my death'.

Please retain the funds of the cheque taken from our office on the first day of last month in accordance with our instructions to retain the funds in gilt-edged assets for a twelve month period.

Yours sincerely,

L. Jacobi-Brown, Partner"

The picture was in the boot of my car. My bank had wired the funds to Bothebies within an hour of the sale finishing. Bothebies own finance facility had provided the 50% balance which I was to repay over three years. I now had to sweat out the period to see if my legacy was to be decimated.

It was back to the office the following day, meeting clients, administering my section. Throwing my energies at my job would take my mind away from my financial predicament.

At lunchtime I passed and re-passed the two Mayfair Galleries of Dennis Gray and Associates. The larger of the two was situated between the two major auction houses in Old Clasp Street.

Having spent the price of a good lunch for two on renovating the frame for my picture, it now stood resplendently over the fireplace. Must have a christening party, I thought.

The bombshell arrived by a telephone call from the senior partner. "Sorry about this, Mr. Hannon, but the Australian claims against your aunt's estate have proved to be genuine."

I replied "But I have spent every penny of it. Haven't you a claim fund you Solicitors can go to when this sort of thing happens?"

"Sorry, sir" was the reply. "You were warned by letter that acceptance by you of the legacy was subject to ourselves not receiving further claims against the estate within a period of one year. Our Indemnity Insurers insist this clause is placed in every cash receipt signed by a client when he takes a cheque from us. You will remember signing such clause."

I replied "You must agree, sir, that you gave me the impression that it was only a formality and there would not be a problem."

The senior partner took offence. "We do not issue statements of mere formalities. Any clause we ask a client to sign is taken very seriously."

I gazed at my Wagstaff as I replaced the receiver. "Sorry, old chap, but you'll have to go."

I took a day's holiday from work and called to see Dennis Gray. I told him of my misfortune but received scant sympathy. Most plump men have this antipathy to thinner humans, probably jealousy at not being able to control the weight factor, I consoled myself. The dark haired P.A., still looking gravely anxious, remembered an urgent 'phone call. I came clean, told the full story to Dennis Gray and asked him to buy the picture at the price he bid, prior to my final overbid.

"Sorry, sir, we do not transact business in that manner. We didn't want the bloody thing in the first place. I already have twenty Wagstaff. Our aim was to raise the price for the artist. In you we saw an opportunity."

I looked hard at the man. He had a triumphal gleam in his eye. Surely he'd had more gin than tonic in his early morning 'livener'.

He continued "We must have a mark up of at least three times the price we buy a picture for. How else do you think we can afford such luxurious exhibition rooms in the most expensive area in the British Isles?"

My stomach was making rumbling noises. "Surely you will take it from me at a fair price?" The gleam was still with him.

"With all the publicity of the sale you have succeeded in raising a considerable amount of public interest in Wagstaff. We have sold two paintings since the auction and the telephone is constantly ringing from potential buyers. We have reduced the mark up we want so that we can be out of this artist. You see, sir, my Gallery makes the market price in Wagstaff. If we are absent at an auction a picture can go for a very low price. To protect our extensive stocks of this artist we never miss attending an auction. We look for potential buyers looking for a cheap picture, then my staff target him. Nowadays we would rather use your money than our own. Who do you think the telephone bidder was?" he boasted.

Past caring, I shook my head.

"It was smooth tongued Delia, my Personal Assistant."

Then Dennis Gray had a further thought. "Does the picture belong to you? I noticed you at the Loan Counter at Bothebies."

I replied defensively, "I had a small loan facility from the auction house."

"In that case, Bothebies have the title. In default of an instalment they will reclaim the picture. Go across the street and see their Finance Manager, and as our American cousins say Have a nice day." These last few words were spoken with heavy sarcasm.

I slunk slowly towards the door but was stopped by dark haired Delia on my march to the gallows. What a radiant smile she now had. "I overheard your conversation with Dennis. You really shouldn't listen to loud voiced dealers on Viewing Days."

## *Eight*

# PARCHED JOURNEY

Bank Holiday on a sweltering August evening is a rotten time to travel North. Everyone wants to escape London.

Euston concourse was crammed with people. The earlier train from York had failed to show in the Capital. Two lots of travellers, now aiming at my train. Seats would be at a premium. 'Move quickly'. I thought.

The barriers opened, six hundred people moved as one. I was at the rear. The Charge of the Light Brigade must have started this way. A gentle trundle became a trot. I galloped on the outside. Dressed in a city suit, completed with bow tie and bowler hat. My umbrella at the charge. A formidable sight to women and children.

Arriving at the carriage next to the engine, I flopped into the last available seat. Minutes later the doors closed. The aisles were full of people standing, the hallways between carriages heaving with passengers who failed to find a seat.

The speaker system opened for the first time. "This is your conductor. A failed engine gasket caused the delay. However there is a train standing on Platform 7 travelling to the same destination. If standing passengers would like to transfer, there is only a 45-minute waiting time with plenty of seats available." No-one moved a muscle. Beware of Greeks bearing gifts.

Ten minutes into the journey a female voice came over the sound system. "The buffet is now open for the sale of food, coffee and tea. We also carry a fully licensed bar. Today's cheap priced speciality is a four-pack of cold beer. Please make your way to the centre of the train."

I drooled. Dare I leave my seat with so many standing passengers? The decision was made for me. Looking across the table that divided me from a sallow-faced man with a drooping moustache and thin drawn features. Also sporting a navy blue flat cap. Not a glimmer of recognition or a smile in answer to my greeting. He merely pulled the loop of a beer can in front of him. That can had three companions. Printed on each "15% extra for the month of August."

The speaker system blared again. "The air conditioning is not working due to a faulty valve in the cooling tower system. Sorry to cause you any inconvenience."

The sun was beating relentlessly through the curtainless plate glass window. I had already loosened my shirt buttons and removed my tie. I immersed myself in the Evening Standard watching sallow-face sip at his first can. A particular long belly draught finished it.

With thumb and forefinger he squeezed the centre of the can to convey its emptiness, at the same time smacking his lips with satisfaction. I couldn't take this.

I had to reach the buffet bar and take the chance that my seat would remain vacant.

My jacket and the copy of the Evening Standard remained to guard my seat. The buffet car was six carriages towards the centre of the train. Not only passengers but their belongings were crammed in the aisles. I stumbled. Why did someone want to take a dartboard to the North, darts is a Winter game! Trampling over people and their chattels. I tripped over a fat lady in a red-spotted dress who refused to budge from the centre aisle. Turning sharply my bottom hit a seated man in the face. He jumped and barked: "Watch your bloody step, mate!" Oh for a first class ticket!

The junction hall that joined the two carriages was the most tightly packed area. It was impossible. I would never make the buffet car. I made a slow and careful retreat.

Luckily my seat was still vacant. The humidity caused by a mass of bodies, a relentless sun and no air conditioning made me think of the Black Hole of Calcutta.

Having passed Watford on the journey to Rugby, sallow-face was deeply into his second can, the empty one placed to his left. I buried my face in the Evening Standard. The only items that forcibly struck me were advertisements for drinks. I was urged to take Courage, a beer I often drank. Guinness is good for you was a blaring headline. Lemonade for the masses at only 30p a large bottle but nowhere, just nowhere did the ads say where they could be conveniently purchased on a sweltering hot train travelling at over a hundred miles an hour. What had I done to deserve such treatment? All my shirt buttons were now unfastened. Coat and waistcoat discarded. Could I do a deal with this man? The Evening Standard for a can of beer? How about the offer of an extortionate price?

I said "Very hot and humid in here old chap."

The 'old chap' did not reply. He merely raised his can and swigged the contents from the punctured hole at the top. He then gave it the thumb and finger treatment.

Sweat was streaming from my brow. I made a three-cornered hat from two sheets of my newspaper. At least origami lessons as a child at school showed a benefit this evening. The hat, firmly in place, provided some relief but the streaky black lines from the print falling down my face gave me an eerie appearance. Other passengers were engaged in various ways to alleviate the oppressiveness. Most of them seemed to have brought some liquid relief. Perhaps it was my plumpness that distressed me more than most passengers. I really must diet.

The train had passed Rugby and was well on the way to Coventry when my travelling companion pulled the loop on the third beer can. I thought about his personal comfort. The man must have hollow legs. He had made no attempt to rise from his seat for over an hour and a half. He had now consumed three pints of liquid, plus the additional 15%. Taking a larger than usual swig, he placed the almost empty can in front of me. He gave a glimmer of a smile before his face reverted to its expressionless look. He had not discarded one item of clothing, but perhaps his thin build did not cause heat distress? The third can was squeezed. Three empties in a row.

The speaker system blared again. "Due to a small technical problem, the train is travelling more slowly than our normal speed. People progressing to Shrewsbury will miss their connection at Birmingham International. There is only a two-hour wait. Sorry about this. I must also mention that the train is four carriages short. When this replacement train left the depot this afternoon, the carriages were left uncoupled. It arrived at Euston without them. Very sorry to the standing passengers." Not much consolation, I thought.

I heard a passenger across the aisle grumbling. "When this line is privatised, the service must improve."

His friend nodded and said: 'Yes, Stagecoach plc are taking over the service. If there was a bust gasket with them, they'd get a herd of horses to pull the train.'

Both passengers laughed. Sallow-face didn't think the remark was funny. Not a muscle moved.

Would I have a problem? My ticket was operative from the evening 6.15 train. I had caught the 5.45 late. The ticket collector arrived. I smiled. He punched my invalid ticket without a second thought. Sallow face passed his ticket "Both you gentlemen departing from us at Birmingham International I see. At least you haven't too far to rid yourselves of this heat oppressed oven. Unlike most of the others who are journeying non-stop to our final destination at York. Poor sods."

We went through Coventry and were only fifteen minutes from Birmingham International.

My mind was now rambling with thoughts of my car waiting in the station car park. It was a beautiful car, all that fresh air blowing through an air conditioning system, an electrically operated sun roof, a large interior with sweet air.

I couldn't take this Chinese torture any longer. I rose from my seat, destroyed the temporary hat, stomped past my travelling companions, and waited near the exit doorway. All windows were sealed. People in the next carnage had adopted a war-time attitude, songs were being sung loudly: 'We'll meet again.' Not if I can help it.

The speaker system opened again. "To all travellers leaving the train at Birmingham International, I hope you had a pleasant journey. I look forward to welcoming you again." Words failed me.

Looking back sallow face was sound asleep. Chest heaving rhythmically. Four empty indented cans in a uniform row resting as a souvenir to his thirst buds. A pity to wake him.

The train stopped. I leaped through the open door. Gulping fresh air as I jumped. Heaven must be like this on the first step through St Peter's Gate. Doors locked the train edged forward. It startled sallow face from his reverie.

He threw himself at the window, his face pressed against the glass a horrific expression. Hammering the window. I stage mouthed "Give my regards to Dick Turpin, borrow Black Bess for your ride back." I gestured with my fingers that he had a two hours journey to York. A further like gesture but finishing in a higher sweep "And a further two hour return."

*Nine*

# GREASE SPOTS

'She was a bit of alright, was Doreen' remarked Jock to his best friend. 'She'd have made a good wife for you.'

Stanley Spenser was in Glasgow for the christening ceremony of the second son of Jock and Enid Dodds. Stanley was also godfather to their first son.

'Why she didn't reply to our letters we shall never know' continued Jock.

'Never is a long time, maybe one day' remarked Stanley.

Stanley was still playing professional soccer at the highest level. He had to miss the Sunday clash with United to attend the christening. It was a small price to pay to see his friend again. Six months had elapsed since their last meeting.

Jock had chided his friend on this, but added 'We can also celebrate the tenth anniversary of D-Day'.

Stanley nodded thinking Jock should have known better to touch on such a sensitive topic.

D-Day was still four months from fruition. Professional soccer players posted to the same camp, stuck together, hunted as a pack.

Stanley Spenser and Jock Dodds were vying for the attentions of the 'Sweetest Angel in Blackpool' as Stanley described Doreen in a letter to his mother. Doreen was a corporal in the Women's Auxiliary Air Force, who made the most of fashioning her best Air Force blue uniform. Skirt an inch above the knee, King's regulations decreed an inch below the knee. The breast filling part of her tunic a shade tighter than regulations allowed. The cobbler on Central Pier had been persuaded to add a half-inch to the length of he heels of her official 'sensible shoes'.

Both airmen were smitten.

Mrs Spenser prayed her son would make the fifty-mile journey from Blackpool before being transferred to the battle zone. Hopefully bringing Doreen for their first meeting. Perhaps after Saturday's football match? She thought.

Doreen's mother secretly thought her daughter's charm and good looks could spell trouble. Where did Doreen's enigmatic smile come from? Certainly not herself or husband, Bill. Her own elder sister had a way with men, the careless disregard, the disdain; a certain type of man couldn't resist this treatment. A natural asset her eldest daughter possessed and with some to spare. Doreen accepted it was only a matter of time before her two handsome swains were transferred to the south coast. All that I will have to remind me of our wonderful friendship will be the two patches of Brylcream grease on the lounge wall at the back of the sofa, where you rested your heads and drank cups of tea.

England was due to play Scotland in the fifth annual wartime fixture of the Calcutta Cup at Old Trafford, Manchester. Stanley Spenser was England's most lethal weapon playing on the extreme right; he would be used prolifically. Without Jock Dodds, Scotland's strike force would be a handgun to England's advanced armoury. Even in wartime, government authorities gave the annual fixture top billing. The nation needed some deviation from the never-ending hostilities in every part of the world.

The players representing both countries were sent away to a Lancashire base for two days extensive training, prior to their private battle.

After a hectic tussle the nations drew their match, two goals each, both Spenser and Dodds featured amongst the scorers. Sunday was a rest day prior to the participants returning to their base the following day. All the talk was of the forthcoming invasion of Europe. How would each individual participate? The South coast of England was heavily tilted with a million personnel under military orders. The Royal Air Force still had to add to this number.

The following Monday both players called at Doreen's parents' boarding house. A twelve-year old boy from the Midlands on a week's holiday with his mother gazed at them in awe. International soccer players were a rare event. What a tale to tell his schoolmates.

Doreen's younger sister was also impressed with the two men in RAF uniform, both sporting three stripes with a white flash in their side caps denoting their trade as Physical Training Instructors. Audrey advised both airmen not to rest their heads on the wall behind the settee. 'Mummy gets upset. The grease simply refused to budge' she said in an excellent imitation of her mother's chastisement to the elder sister.

The lounge door opened. Both men looked eagerly. Disappointment was covered by their smile and greeting to Doreen's father, a tidy sincere man who worked as a zookeeper at Blackpool Tower.

'Sorry to inform you chaps. Doreen's unit has been posted to somewhere in England. That's the official description, bound to be on the South coast. Must be something to with the invasion' he confided as though Winston Churchill had given him a personal telephone call.

Both men were chagrined. Stanley had summoned up courage during his playing leave to propose marriage to his fair-haired angel and Jock was very near to making a similar commitment.

Jock answered the old soldier. 'A bit sudden? She was here last Wednesday and, without embarkation leave or notice, she's left the district.'

The reply came quickly. 'She was one of fifteen hundred WAAFs who moved. They were all taken by special train last Saturday afternoon. You two were playing football of course, otherwise she would have called'.

As an afterthought he added 'Perhaps she wouldn't have called. The squadron was under orders of strict secrecy.'

Fifty-four years on, Lord Spenser of Cleveley's, honoured for his service to British football after playing a record number of times for his country, received an Email from Savannah in South Carolina. 'Coming to UK for a visit. Love to see you. Doreen.' His heart leaped.

They met on 6 June at London's Savoy Hotel.

'Very appropriate, it's the fifty-fourth anniversary of D-Day' were Stanley's first words after fondly kissing his love of so long ago. Her figure still trim, her eyes had not lost their sparkle. The warmth of her greeting made Stanley grimace, how much he had missed her. He had never married; throwing all his energies into the sport that had made him internationally famous. The world's top footballer for more than two decades, a legend in his lifetime.

'I followed your progress through letters from home' Doreen told Stanley. 'The media in the United States is very short on soccer. Baseball is another thing of course, but my late husband and I saw you play in an exhibition match in New York. We came up for the occasion' she smiled.

Stanley said 'You should have made yourselves known. I have missed you terribly.' She gave him the enigmatic look he knew so well.

'I missed you but whilst Frank was alive I couldn't face the ordeal of meeting you, but I did persuade my two sons to join your fan club. They both followed soccer from afar. I have made them honorary Blackpool supporters.' The couple drank in silence for some minutes. It was broken when Doreen asked 'Do you see anything of Jock?'

Stanley answered 'Alas, he is no longer with us. His funeral was in Glasgow over five years ago. A massive turnout. The cathedral was packed to the rafters. Thousands of his old fans filled the cathedral close taking in the service from radio speakers. He was a well-respected father of five children. I am godfather to two of them, you know.'

Doreen gave a little squeal of delight. 'No, I didn't know. I wished I had. It was difficult for me having two such handsome swains. If I had had to choose, you would have won the contest, but only just.'

'Why didn't you keep in touch. At least invite me to the wedding?' Stanley asked.

Doreen took two deep breaths before replying. 'It was wartime. You acted on the spur of the moment. Death was an acceptable way of life. Please forgive the sick joke. The WAAFs were sent over the water three weeks after the men landed on D-Day. We were to provide administrative duties. For four months I worked in the American hospital at Caen, mostly helping in the canteen, but took on any duty. I even helped as an orderly on emergency surgical operations.

'My first specifically allocated job, and incidentally it was also my last in the forces, was chauffeuse to Colonel Frank Daniels. His parents were long ago Irish people. From this appointment in 1944 to the end of the war some fifteen months later, Frank and I were inseparable. In the thick of battle one day, the following day back at Headquarters. The job was not a nine to five operation, we virtually lived together. It was not surprising that we married. Dwight Eisenhower was best man. Frank himself was by now a one star General. He left the Army shortly after the war in Japan abruptly finished. We settled down in his hometown in South Carolina. The rest is history, as they say.'

Stanley replied 'I understand now,' then changed the subject abruptly.

'How's your younger sister, the one who played gooseberry when we finally managed to be alone in the sitting room?'

'She's fine' smiled Doreen. 'It's her that I'm staying with. She married that snotty nosed kid from the Midlands who wheedled many, many autographs from you and Jock. I'm sure he had a ready market for them at his school. A clever boy was Leslie.'

Stanley was relaxed, the way he always was with Doreen. He was at his most vulnerable.

She said 'I'm thinking about returning to live in Blackpool. Without Frank, there's nothing to keep me in the States. My eldest son and daughter-in-law live and work in Germany. I haven't seen my grandchildren for three years now. My second son hasn't married but his job has taken him to Canada. The distance is too great for frequent visits. My sons can fly to England just as easily as South Carolina.'

Stanley's head jerked a little. Was his bachelor-hood being threatened? He looked directly into Doreen's eyes.

'Your memory has been the sunshine of my life. I prayed things could have been different but we play out life the way the cards are dealt.

'I was honoured in the Queen's Birthday list eight years ago, and became a baron.' He laughed. 'And that was for doing things closest to my heart.'

Doreen said cheekily 'I thought I was the closest thing to your heart'.

Stanley gave a resigned smile. 'That was then, now is now. A baronetcy commits a person's time to the obliteration of all other interruptions of life. Constantly attending the House of Lords makes tremendous inroads into my time'.

Doreen realised Stanley's sentiments. 'It's been great meeting you. Don't let it be another fifty-four years.'

The couple embraced at the hotel entrance whilst waiting for their separate taxis.

*Ten*

# EYE EYE

CAST IN ORDER OF APPEARANCE

1. Murcott
2. Lady Receptionist: June
3. Turbanned Asian
4. Mr Ashley: Optical Consultant
5. Store Manager
6. Store Manager's Assistant: Jennifer p.8
7. Young Frame Adjuster: Jeannie

* * * * *

Opening Title EYE EYE
(Duration half-an-hour)

1. STREET

Murcott walks down the railway station ramp into the town centre.
Immediately recognises his goal, Hammond & Topekas – Opticians to Royalty.

Murcott: 'Bit bloody damp out there Miss'.

Receptionist: 'You'll be alright in here sir. It doesn't rain in'.

Murcott throws his wet mack on a coat stand.

Murcott: 'Very funny madam but its no joke when your trousers are wet to the bone, if you get my drift'.

Receptionist: 'I do appreciate your discomfort sir, but what time is your appointment?'

Murcott: '3.15 dear. Made it by two minutes. Punctuality is the prerogative of the Murcott's as well as royalty. Notice your firm has a Royal Charter'.

Receptionist: 'Young Prince Harry uses our Mayfair branch. How did you hear of us sir. We do place discreet advertisements in local newspapers'.

Murcott: 'I'm a very old customer'.

Receptionist interrupts curtly: 'We do have one or two older than you'. She adds thoughtfully 'but not much'.

Murcott: 'You have a sharp sense of humour miss. The type of wit you see in lonely hearts columns. Blondie from Bermondsey W.L.T.M. tall gent who can walk, talk and chew gum at the same time'.

Receptionist: 'We're straying sir. Shall I tick recommended by a friend?'

Murcott: 'No, you wrote to me saying it was five years since I saw that nice Mr Blake. He was from Turkey I remember'.

Receptionist: 'Oh Mr Blake a very handsome man, I remember him very well. He left us two years ago to set up his own business in Torquay'.

Murcott (grimaces): Turkey or Torquay, yes quite a geographical difference. I shouldn't think they wear the fez in Torquay'.

Receptionist (into the spirit of things): 'I wore a fez in Torquay, had "Kiss me quick" on the crown'.

Murcott: 'Didn't have much success did you dear. Oh sorry, I meant with your looks. No must shut up'.

Receptionist (clearly annoyed, accentuated the word "Sir"): 'Take a seat at the far end of the store Sir. On the empty bench Sir. A consultant will be with you shortly'.

Murcott (walks as instructed whilst speaking over his shoulder): 'Tell the consultant I'm in a bit of a hurry, trains are few and far between to Lichfield'.

A turbaned Asian enters the store. Engages the receptionist in whispered conversation. They ignore Murcott who eye stretches them to no avail. He rises to inspect the spectacle display stand. Lifts a pair in the air bends the arms, places them over the bridge of his nose, then puts a finger through the empty left aperture.

Murcott (shouting to the receptionist, still in deep animated conversation): 'Be more practical with lenses in'. She raises her eyebrows but carries on the conversation with the new customer. Murcott now inspecting his bespectacled face through a mirror'.

Passing male consultant: 'Very handsome indeed sir'.

Murcott: 'Yes'. (sighs) 'Why do some men have all the charm'.

He replaces the spectacles walks to the sunglasses display, flexes the arms of a gold framed pair. The lenses almost jet black.

Murcott (stage whispering to the receptionist): 'Things are looking dark dear'.

She nods appreciatively.

Receptionist: 'Very masculine sir. You'd cut a fine figure on Torquay beach. Give the ladies a deep glowing thrill'.

Murcott: 'Back to Torquay are we'.

He then borrows a black trilby hat from a hanging peg, dark sunglasses still in place. Twirling around he adopts the manner of firing a rifle.

Murcott: 'Godfather two dear'.

Receptionist: 'With my Torquay fez I could be Godmother two, too. Get it Mr Murcott?'

Murcott: 'A very weak attempt Miss. Stick to your day job, leave the funny stuff to me. I make Ben Elton seem as funny as a newsreader'.

Receptionist (relaxing): 'Indeed you are a breath of fresh air sir. Be careful of the store manager though. His jocularity is as stale as last week's burnt toast'.

Murcott returns to the bench, merely to find the turbaned Asian seated at its head. With annoyance be walks to remonstrate, only to be interrupted by a dispensing optician opening a suite door and addresses the Asian.

Optician: 'First in the queue sir. This way'.

Murcott: 'But I'm first. I'm a 3.15er, he's a 3.30er'.

The other two ignore him. The consultancy door is slammed shut. Murcott shows his annoyance by aiming a kick at a fire hydrant. It starts to wobble. He bends hurriedly to grab it. A tearing split appears from the back crotch to the belt of his trousers.

Receptionist: 'Sky blue thongs Mr Murcott. All the rage in Torquay this Summer'.

Murcott snorts at her, grabs his mackintosh from the stand. Sits heavily at the head of the bench. Staring threateningly at anyone who appears. The consultancy room door opens.

Turbanned Asian to receptionist: 'I've passed. I can go home at no cost.

Receptionist (Shocked): Surely you require new spectacles sir? I've never known Mr Ashley not prescribe new lenses'.

Turbanned Asian: 'No a clean bill of health, I can hear as clear as a bell'.

Receptionist: 'But people come here for eye testing sir. I should go quickly before Mr Ashley discovers your little secret. The hospital for impaired hearing is to turn right at our front door then first left.

Turbanned Asian: 'Sorry what did you say' (turning his ear to her).

## 2. IN THE CONSULTING ROOM

Murcott and Ashley shake hands. Murcott is guided to a padded chair. Nervously he clenches the chair arms still wearing his protective raincoat, ignores the optician's offer to place it on a coat rack, The screen he's facing is about eight feet from his chair, it is equally divided between a red sides and a green side. In each half there are three rounded targets similar to archery targets. Above this screen is a large board with five, lines of letters of diminishing size. The top and largest letters being an 'L'.

Murcott: 'The bottom line looks like a row of ants on the march'.

Consultant: Can you identify the letters on the last line but one'.

Murcott: 'No I can't but I can make out the top letter which is. 'L''.

Consultant: 'Even a blind donkey could read that sir. Now try the third line down most people can read that line'.

Murcott then whistles the tune "I wish I was in Dixie".

Consultant: 'Very droll sire but we're here for an eye test. Not a whistling competition'.

Murcott: 'Should be bloody obvious D.Y.X.I.E. stands out a mile it does, just like Wigan pier'.

Consultant (challengingly): 'Try singing the answer to the fifth line down sir'.

Murcott (screwing his eyes): 'R.N. no no that's an M, next is an 8, no I'm wrong there it must be S then U for Uncle, B for bunny rabbit'.

Consultant (prompting): 'And the last letter sir'.

Murcott: 'I thought that was a question mark. If it isn't I'll guess at Q'.

Consultant: 'You mustn't guess sir. If you guess right I could end up giving you the wrong prescription, and you, walking off the end of Wigan Pier'.

Murcott: 'Sorry, I do see your point. By the way never been to Wigan'.

Consultant: 'Look at the lit up screen immediately below the letter screen. One half is red the other half to the right is green'.

Murcott (testily): 'Yes I can see that. My mother had the best eyesight in the district. Being a boy I inherited her good vision'.

Consultant (interrupting): 'and girls inherit the paternal line'.

Murcott: 'Yes Nellie my sister's very short-sighted, as was the dear old Dad until he forgot his glasses and came to grief'.

Consultant: 'Had an accident eh'.

Murcott: 'Yes drank a glass of black ink with one swallow instead of his usual Guinness'.

The Consultant places a heavy copper pair of frames over Murcott's ears. The frames contained four slits around each aperture, so lenses could be changed intermittently to arrive at a satisfactory end product. He removes Murcott's spectacles. Turns up his nose disapprovingly.

Consultant: 'These need a good cleaning, not surprisingly if you fall off kerbstones or bump into lamp-posts'.

Murcott: 'Quite true, I do suffer those surprises. Used to clean my glasses with the end of my tie. But since my divorce I don't get new ties bought me. Must keep up the fashion trend, wouldn't be seen dead in an old tie'.

Consultant: 'Try pulling out the front tail of your shirt and using that, quite effective. Now grasp the arms of your chair. Stare intently at the colour screen. What are your thoughts Mr Murcott'.

Murcott: 'Having my head fried in the electric chair'.

Consultant (laughing): 'Oh you are a one'.

Murcott: 'Oh, oh, I trust you are not a one. Not with this split in my trousers. No no, you come round the front where I can see you. I've been a bit suspicious of you from the outset'.

The Consultant shades Murcott's left eye with a postcard.

Consultant: 'Clearer green or clearer red'.

Murcott: 'Red, although there's not much in it'.

The Consultant then slots an additional lens into the frame.

Consultant: 'How about now?'

Murcott: 'The other way now, green is much clearer. What is this a game show for the tele'.

Consultant: 'No it's to give you a better vision than with these' (brandishing the old ones).

Murcott: 'Nothing wrong with those, had them five years'.

Consultant: 'But you screw your eyes when you look at me, just like Harold Steptoe'.

Murcott: 'Nothing to do with the lenses. I had them from that nice Mr Blake when he was here. I think I'll go to Torquay. He didn't upset me with unusual gestures. No I trusted him to walk behind me. You come round to the front where I can see you'.

The Consultant walks in front of Murcott pushing a two wheeled contraption. Midway between the wheels was a rod 4 feet high, on top a binocular shaped object was fixed. Attached was a rubber tube leading to an ancient motor horn.

Consultant: 'This is my puff machine. It only needs two sharp honks to work it'.

Murcott: 'Don't start that again. All I came for was an eye test. That looks a Heath Robinson invention'.

Consultant: 'It seeks out eye infections, maybe a little painful but all in a good cause'.

Murcott still not sure, grimacing with doubt. The door bursts open. No warning knock. A bald six foot tall, plump man marches in. His striped business suit facing a battle to restrain an ever increasing frame. He's closely followed by his secretary sporting a short mini-skirt and a cleavage revealing red blouse, carrying a clip-board in one hand, a pencil in the other. Wearing a pair of dark blue spectacles.

Store Manager: 'Merely making a random audit check. Do one a week to ensure client satisfaction. Trust you don't mind Mr. Murcott'.

Murcott: 'Does it matter if I do? It is appreciated you have a job to do and frankly I'm a little suspect of this optician. I should give him a few more surprise visits. The ladies will be quite safe I'm sure'.

The lady receptionist scribbles on her pad at a quick rate.

Lady Assistant: 'Must let Head Office hear of this little gem'.

Store Manager: 'A nice comfortable chair you're sitting in sir'.

Murcott nods agreement.

Store Manager: 'Maybe even more comfortable if you removed your mackintosh. Our central heating system's very efficient'.

Murcott: 'I'm sure it is, but I'm quite content as I am thank you'.

Lady Assistant addressing the Manager: 'Shall I make a note that some patients prefer to wear a mackintosh during eye tests sir?' Remember we have a psychoanalyst at Head Office who has theories on strange happenings in branches. I am sure he would come up with an answer'.

Store Manager: 'I agree Jennifer there must be an underlying reason for it which is not readily apparent to you or I'.

Murcott: 'The deep underlying reason is that I split my trousers accidentally about twenty minutes ago. You can tell your Head Office I am worried about this puff machine. This chap. says it could be painful. I hope you're insured against injuring patients. I don't like being hurt by optical sadists'.

Lady Assistant: 'Are you long or short sighted, Mr Murcott?'

Murcott: 'Long sighted Miss, I can see the destination of a No. 11 bus two hundred metres away, but when it comes to reading the latest Jeffrey Archer. I must have glasses'.

Lady Assistant: 'Much the same as myself. Although it's John Grisham that troubles me'.

Murcott: 'It's not surprising, you wearing that see through blouse'.

Store Manager (intervening): 'Well I think we can safely mark you off as a satisfied customer. One that will use our store for evermore'.

Murcott: 'If I live that long, but I do miss that Mr Blake who tested my eyes on the last few visits here'.

Steng: 'Oh he left to start his own business in Torquay'.

Murcott (warming to his task): 'Not Istanbul then'.

Store Manager: 'That's in Turkey, I said Torquay'.

Murcott: 'Yes I know we've already covered that ground with your Receptionist'.

Murcott (continues): 'I'm glad you're here miss. I need a red blooded woman to take my mind away from having a sharp arrow of wind squirted into my eye like this sadist was about to do before you came through the door without knocking'.

Store Manager: 'I did say our visits are a surprise. We must ensure our consultants remain diligent at all times'.

With this he raises his eyes looks to the ceiling, turns and slowly marches out of the consultancy suite, Closely followed by the Lady Assistant marching in tandem.

Consultant: 'Thank heaven thought they'd never go, let's get on with the test. Place your right eye through the aperture, and don't blink. Blinking at the wrong time spoils the effect'.

Murcott did as he was bid, opened his mouth to speak, before he could do so a sharp pain hit the pupil of his right eye.

Murcott (jumping bolt upright): 'Hell that hurt. I don't like pain at any time, especially my own'.

Murcott dances up and down rubbing his eye.

Consultant: 'Don't be a baby. This treatment is given to children. They don't make this noisy fuss'.

Murcott: 'They're younger than me, got stronger eyes'.

Consultant: 'Come on you fat sissy, let's have a look at the other eye'.

Murcott: 'Don't you call me a sissy. The boots on the other foot. It's alright for you you're on the squeezing end of that bloody pump'.

Consultant: 'Place your chin on the cup with a non-blinking left eye'.

Murcott did as he was bid.

Consultant: 'You've both eyes shut tightly. I can't do my job unless you co-operate'.

The consultant picks up a newspaper rolls it into a tube. Murcott's eyes are still closed. The newspaper is banged on Murcott's head. He opens his eyes in shock. The pump is squeezed. Murcott jumps in the air, holding both eyes.

Murcott (stamping around the room): 'I'll never be the same again. I'll sue you, see if I don't'.

Consultant: 'In five minutes you'll wonder why you've been making such a noise'.

Murcott is given a glass of water to sip.

Murcott: 'Water is all you give me. In the Navy they'd give me a large tot of rum to deaden the pain I've been through. I wasn't joking when I said I'll sue you'.

Consultant (cajoling): 'Come now sir, we're nearly there. The prelims show your eyesight has only changed marginally in the last five years'.

Murcott: 'I said that the young Mr Blake was a good man'.

Consultant: 'It's nothing to do with the young Mr Blake. It's how the good Lord has looked after you'.

Murcott: 'Don't bring religion into this. I look after myself I do. So I don't need new spectacles. These Buddy Hollies will do for a few years yet'.

Consultant: 'Oh there are a few minor changes in the prescription I shall write out for you. Yes new lenses are a must. These frames have also seen much better days'.

The Consultant was holding Murcott's old spectacles in the air, sniffing with disdain.

Murcott: 'Has there ever been anyone in this chair whose left here without a prescription for new glasses'.

Consultant: 'Only my father sir'.

Murcott: 'Well why did he come? If his eyesight's that good'.

Consultant: 'He's a senior citizen. The State pays us you see, and of course your immediate predecessor in that chair didn't need glasses'.

Murcott: 'He told me, thought you did ear testing. Came for a hearing aid he did'.

Consultant: 'Had the finest eyesight I've ever encountered. Still you can't win them all. Ah, time for the store finance meeting'.

Whilst he had been talking, he had been scribbling out Murcott's new prescription. Murcott was still rubbing his eyes. Shaking his head from side to side. The Consultant hands him a new prescription.

Consultant (continuing): 'Take this to the lady at the desk. She'll advise on a pair of frames suitable for a man of your age'.

Murcott: 'What do you mean my age. Still a spring chicken. I'll bet she's trained to guide me to the most expensive frames in the shop'.

Consultant: 'Sir, you only get what you pay for, but please note buy two pairs get the second frames free. You only pay for the lenses'.

Murcott: 'But it's the lenses that have an eight hundred percent mark-up you rascal'.

Murcott marches out of the consulting room. His mack still in place. His parting shot:

Murcott: 'No such thing as a free lunch'.

As he walks past the Manager's Office, he cranes his ear to discern the conversation without success.

3. MANAGER'S OFFICE

The manager and the lady Secretary, still dressed in an alluring business suit and revealing blouse, are joined by the consultant who had given Murcott a hard time.

Manager (with an air of superiority): 'See we had record takings last week. I know we had intermittent showers in the last few days and that brings in the customers. But we must be doing something right to obtain such excellent results'.

Consultant: 'Wish there was something extra in it for us. All this work and we're on a basic. We also have to deal with weirdos like the one that's just left my consulting suite. A few more like him and I'd retrain as an airline pilot'.

Lady Assistant: 'I imagine airline pilots have their problems. Think of Murcott on a plane to Majorca with some drink in him. No just consider yourself lucky to meet his type infrequently'.

There's a knock on the door, Murcott walks in.

Murcott (with a disarming smile): 'My ears are burning, weren't talking about me, were you?'

Manager: 'Have better things to occupy us than to discuss you'.

Murcott: 'Well you'd better get someone out here to tend the store. I've already seen two shoplifters walk out with smiles on their faces and pockets stuffed with sunglasses'.

Lady Assistant: 'Oh dear I've been here far too long, promised to cover for June's lunch break. But the weekly report to Head Office always worries me stiff. They want to know every minute detail. At least this week, we can report on you Mr Murcott. We don't get many patients like you'.

Murcott: 'What's special about me then. Just a normal law abiding citizen. Helping my country at every conceivable opportunity'.

Lady Assistant: 'But you are different. Not too many Murcott's in town'.

Manager: 'Thank heaven, one's too many in my book'.

Murcott: 'Now now no cheek from you plump one. So this is where it all happens, the counting house and you are King'.

Manager (nods): 'I have that privilege, yes'.

Lady Receptionist (doomsday worried addresses the manager): 'If you can finish the weekly report without me I'll go out and look after the store'.

(then addressing Murcott): 'you scoff about shoplifters Mr Murcott, but we have grabbed three already this week'.

Murcott: 'It must make a change from shirtlifters'.

Murcott casts a glance at the consultant who grins as if the remark was complimentary.

Manager: 'Have you selected a pair of frames Mr Murcott?'

Murcott: 'I'm not sure I want to at the prices marked on them. But I will see your Jeannie and let her try her luck with me'.

Consultant: 'Don't forget buy one pair get another pair free'.

Murcott: 'There's a catch somewhere. By the way do you sell aspirin?'

Manager: 'What do you want aspirin for?'

Murcott: 'Deaden the pain in my eyes from Puffing Billy here'.

Manager: 'We only sell items relevant to the ophthalmic profession'.

Murcott: 'Other goods don't give the 800% mark-up you look for. Doesn't it embarrass you stealing money from the general public, most of them not knowing where their next penny is coming from?'

Lady Assistant (feeling the discussion's too heated): 'Sir I really must take over the Receptionist's duties'. (she leaves)

Murcott (following her out): 'Mr Manager, young assistants never catch shoplifters. Too scared to confront them'.

Manager: 'Never short of a word are you sir, using three when one will do'.

Murcott: 'Do I detect a little venom Mr Manager'.

Murcott completes his departure from the office.

4. BACK IN THE STORE

A number of customers milling around mostly perusing spectacle frames. Some waiting on benches to see consultants. The lady assistant editing the report of the morning surprise visits.

Murcott (bending down her neck): 'Giving me a good word eh? You lot stick together like marmalade to a blanket'.

Lady Assistant: 'When matters are not in accord with company procedures they have to be reported to Head Office. Sometimes they take disciplinary action'.

The manager noticing the discussion, walks over.

Manager (giving the Lady Assistant a hard look, addresses Murcott): 'My staff shouldn't be discussing company policy with third parties sir'.

She circles her hands in a motion of apology. Then turns to Murcott.

Lady Assistant: 'Have you selected your new frames sir?'

Murcott (brandishing his old frames): Not yet. I don't think there's much wrong with these. Could save me a few bob putting the new lenses in these'.

Lady Assistant: 'Five years hard wear and tear is a long time for any frames sir. Time for a new pair'.

Murcott (still wearing mack as protection from split trousers): 'Yes but you haven't to pay for them, like I have'.

Lady Assistant (grimaces): 'Time to see a lense consultant and frame adjuster'.

Murcott: 'Two more people. This is costing an arm and a leg, not even mentioning two sore eyes'.

Lady Assistant: 'One expert will do both jobs. We keep our costs low, sir'.

Murcott: 'That's better, bring on the dancing girls'.

She picks up the internal phone.

Lady Assistant (whispering): 'Jeannie time for you to see another victim'.

Murcott (browsing the store, addresses a fellow customer viewing new spectacles through a mirror): 'Still raining "cats and dogs" better off in side today. I'm staying, not another train for an hour'.

New Customer: 'Yes far better inside. Do these frames do anything for me?'

Murcott: 'Well as I didn't know you before sir I'm not in a position to judge'.

New Customer: 'I was addressing the lady receptionist not you. I need an expert opinion'.

Lady Receptionist: 'Oh those frames are you sir. Machoman oozes. Well worth that little bit extra'.

Murcott: 'And of course, a second pair goes free'.

Lady Receptionist: 'Not with the gold frames I'm sorry. The extra gilt costs us you know. But how affirmative you look sir'.

Murcott: 'There are so many conditions on the price tabs. You just don't obtain what you think you are getting. Need to be a barrister to break-down the price structure. I'll persuade my niece to become an optician. If Al Capone had only known this trade, he could have dispensed with drugs, murder and prostitution'.

The Manager overhears Murcott's outburst.

Manager (whispering to the Lady Receptionist): 'Can't you get rid of this moron. He's bad for business'.

Lady Receptionist (answering with a stage whisper): 'He's on a short fuse from buying two pairs of tri-focals, big money for us. Have a little more patience. Ah here's Jeannie'.

A young woman walks to the open plan area Complete in company uniform. Sits at an unoccupied desk in an alcove.

Jeannie: 'Mr Murcott please'.

Murcott appears from behind a frame stand, and sits facing her.

Jeannie: 'Have you selected a pair of frames that you like sir. That patient talking to the Manager has chosen a nice gold pair. Seems quite happy'.

Murcott: 'Quite a bit lighter in the pocket though'.

Jeannie: 'You only buy frames every few years. You must go for it. Let the ladies in your life have a treat. They'll love you more, I know I would'.

Murcott: 'Oh you fancy me then'.

Jeannie: 'I do go for the older man'.

Murcott: 'Eh eh not that much older, still in my prime I haven't made a final choice takes time to be certain, but I am working on it'

Jeannie: 'Yes my colleagues commented on your progress, or lack of it in your particular case'.

Murcott pulls a face at the admonition.

Jeannie (continuing): 'Looking at the results of your eye test, I think vari-focals would suit your eyes better. Tri-focals are much more costly and in many cases not good for the patient's eyes'.

Murcott : 'Tri-focals are good for me. The middle section gives a perfect view four feet away. With my upside-down vision, I can read the nasty remarks you have on that report in front of you. A troublesome customer indeed. Your former colleague Mr Blake introduced me to tri-focals a few years ago. Do you remember him?'

Jeannie: 'I've only been with the company four months I joined directly from University Mr Blake is a long way in the past'.

Murcott: 'Oh what did you study at Uni Jeannie? I can call you Jeannie can't I'.

Jeannie: 'Of course you can Stanley'.

Murcott: 'How did you know my name dear?'

Jeannie: 'I didn't say you could call me dear. No too familiar on a first meeting. Mummy warned me about men like you'.

Murcott: 'Oh sorry about that'.

Jeannie (rising): 'Let's peruse the frame board. We have a nice selection, ideal for a moon-faced patient'.

Murcott (upset): 'I didn't think my face is a complete circle, quite hurt about that. My Mother said the Murcott side of the family had long faces. It was her side that had a more rounded "bit and brace".

Jeannie (puzzled): 'Bit and brace ah of course. Your Mother was a cockney? But spectacles do hang better on a horse face rather than a moon face'.

Murcott: 'Tell me about my free spec's Jeannie'.

Jeannie (becoming irritated): 'Not free but freeish'.

Murcott: 'Freeish seems a double-entendre. It is an expression that says "Beware Stanley"'.

Jeannie rises and walks to the frame board. Murcott follows. He tries on two pairs before selecting a silver-coloured pair. Poking his little finger through an aperture.

Murcott: 'These frames are a little lightweight but I do like the shape and colour'. They return to the desk'.

Jeannie: 'My computer tells me those frames can't take the weight of In-focal lenses'.

Murcott: 'You've only been in this game four months. Not long enough to form your own opinion. What did you do before you entered this hall of frame'.

Jeannie: 'As I said before I was at York Uni studying Greek Mythology. Why this sudden interest in my past life?'

Murcott: 'You're not telling me from personal experience. The message from that computer is the same for everyone. I want an individual opinion, for me alone. Not just a phrase from a P.C. that only marginally differentiates between every client in the Queendom'.

Jeannie (agitated): 'Stanley, don't go on so. The other customers are more interested in us than conducting their own business'.

Murcott: 'Sorry it's a hobby horse Computers rule because people let them. Its an easy way out. But patients don't get best satisfaction and good results. It seems a conveyor belt system. But it shouldn't be. Each customer is different'.

Jeannie: 'Now you've put the world to right, but I was trained at the company HQ in London on a full two week course'.

Murcott: 'Then they let you loose on us poor souls. I had a five year apprenticeship in Engineering before being allowed to service a motor car'.

Jeannie: 'You do go on a bit. I bet you have an understanding wife'.

Murcott: 'No never married. How much are frames I rather like'.

Jeannie again pounds the keys on her computer.

Jeannie: 'If the frames were strong enough to take tri-focals, which they are not. The cost would be £275.00'.

Murcott: 'Almost as much as David Beckham's haircut. Still with a second pair free it would halve the price'.

Jeannie: 'Not so Stanley. The frames on the second set are free. The lenses are £195.00'.

Murcott: 'I'll go to the Bank next door and top-up my mortgage'.

She dials the Store Manager. Telling Murcott she needs senior assistance.

Jeannie (whispers to Manager): 'Can you send in the cavalry sir'.

Manager joins them at Jeannie's desk.

Murcott: 'Ah you're the cavalry. My eyes may be a bit dodgy but there's nothing wrong with my ears, Miss Stage Whisper'.

Jeannie stiffens up, glowers.

Manager: 'My staff can't give of their best with your constant criticism. I may add it's totally inappropriate for you to wear a mackintosh throughout your visit'.

Murcott: 'I will reiterate. I have my reasons; I've been in this blooming store nearly two hours and I'm no further forward but it has kept me out of the rain. Also your prices are incompatible with my budget'.

Manager: 'The eye test was free, you can't get less than that'.

Murcott: 'That's the sop, that's the con. A free eye test and God knows how much for the rest of the service. The rent and rates here must be astronomical. Heating bills going through the roof. All the staff wear these silky nylon uniforms. Everyone on a high remuneration package I assume, company pension and all that from the likes of me. I'll bet you have a top of the range Jaguar car?'

Manager: 'Wrong there I have to get by on a bottom of the range Rolls Royce'.

Murcott: 'My heart bleeds. By the size of your frame, you don't exactly stint on company meals'.

Manager: 'Sir you have become too objectionable. It seems obvious we will not satisfy you with our products and service'.

Murcott: 'That's one thing we can agree on'.

Murcott turns and peers through the window.

Murcott: 'Ah the sun's shining and that bloody rain has stopped. Makes a man glad to be alive'.

Whilst striding to the door he further exclaims.

Murcott: 'Please send my free prescription through the post. I'll try a cheaper optician nearer home'.

Murcott opens the shop door takes a deep breath.

Murcott (in a loud voice): 'Glad to be alive now that April's here. Except that it's January. I think that's what Shakespeare wrote, and if he didn't he should have'....

He slips off his mackintosh, places it over his arm and strides through the front door.

The assembled staff gaze after him now striding along the main city thoroughfare. His trousers flapping in the breeze. His moon face buttocks bared for all to see.

# *Eleven*

# WHAT'S IN A NAME

We had reached the coffee stage of a celebratory dinner. I was to marry Angela at the end of the following month. We were having a last relaxing meal prior to the hurly burly of the run up to the wedding.

Angela wondered if she should send a late invitation to a distant aunt. "Who is she?" I asked out of politeness. "She's a Mrs. Barratt, widowed years ago."

"Barratt", I replied incredulously. "That name seems to have dominated my life!

"My form master was called Harold Barratt, a real sadist who ruled our class with a rod of iron, or bamboo in his case."

"Tell me more", said a more interested Angela.

"He was tall and balding, with a face like a skull nobody liked him. The nearest I ever saw to a smile, was a sadistic grin when he was about to cane a boy."

"Not you, surely", she prompted.

"Twice in one week!"

"I can't imagine you being punished, your father's always saying you were such a gentle boy."

"I wrote the title of an essay "The Milkman", then crossed out the first 'a'. Harold Barratt ordered me to the front of the class and raise my left hand. I was only ten. You always remember the first time. Something very similar happened a week later, when I spelt Thomas à Beckett with a small 'b'".

"I can see why the mention of the name Barratt gives you bad vibes", commented Angela. "Were there any more Barratts?"

"Yes, several. My first job after University was with a firm of Solicitors, Messrs. H.F. Barratt & Co."

Angela replied "Yes, I remember you telling me about them. You had just changed jobs when we first met."

"I was interviewed by Martin William Barratt, a white haired bachelor in his early fifties. He was surprised when be observed my birth date. Stating what a coincidence that I was born the exact day his father died.

"I couldn't stop him talking about his family. His elder brother had been killed flying a Spitfire in the Battle of Britain."

"What other family had he? What happened to his late father's wife?" Angela asked.

"She was the second wife of the firm's founder, but much younger than him. She gave birth to a boy within a year of the marriage, a half brother to my principal."

"Fascinating, both these Barratts seem pillars of society, he being a family solicitor, she seemingly a good mother" Angela answered.

"Yes, I was able to meet Rose Laura on social occasions during my ten years with the firm. Although I didn't know her well, she certainly had a twinkle in her eye and knew her way around the male partners."

The waiter arrived and asked if we would like more coffee or a liqueur. Angela was quick to answer, "Why not? Now, tell me more about Martin."

"Without him, I don't think I would ever have qualified as a Solicitor. His young half-brother, Frank, and myself were on the same study path. He spent time with both of us.

"Towards the end of our studies Martin had to sack Frank. He was caught with his trousers down, forcing his attentions on a senior secretary. She complained to the partners, and Frank had to go."

"Poor Frank" my beloved replied. "What is he doing now?"

"Last thing I heard, he was a car park attendant at the Grand Hotel. Martin had already had to bail him out financially. He ran up huge debts in a business venture. Fancied himself as a theatrical impresario.

"Funny lot these Barratts", Angela commented. "Was that your last brush with that name?"

"Far from it. Only last month I joined a Gentlemen's Club in the city centre. It was my first visit as a new member. I called in after work on a Friday evening. The twin brothers Charles and Jimmy Barratt hailed me to enter an ante room. "Have a drink?" Said Jimmy. I must have appeared uncomfortable. As you know I am only a social drinker."

"Well, I wouldn't want to know you, if you drank like a fish", said my partner.

"Try a double gin topped to the rim of the glass with French Vermouth", said Charlie with a heavy "You will" in his voice resonant. I agreed, never having heard of the concoction. The drink was like nectar.

"Try another", said his brother. After two in a short time, relaxation was complete. Jimmy went to the bar. He came back with three drinks. "Same amount of gin but topped with a mixture of both Vermouths", he said. "I could hardly wait for the next which Charlie procured a few minutes later."

Angela, sipping her coffee, said "Drink like that after we're married and I'll get Harold Barratt out of retirement."

"No, dear. It's not what it seems. I was involved in a new members initiation ceremony, happens to everyone who joins. However, after two further rounds of gin and mixed vermouth the world had passed me by."

"The Chief Steward drove me home. My mother thought I'd been sent home from work violently ill. I knew nothing about Saturday other than visits to the bathroom."

"Have you seen those brothers since?" Angela queried.

"Oh yes, I play snooker with them regularly. The initiation taught me to know when to stop."

She was angry now. I'll be keeping a weather eye on you!"

* * * * *

The great day came. I walked down the aisle with my brother who was the best man. We took our seats. The organ rang out the Wedding March. An angel in white attached to her father's arm smiled as she passed.

"Do you, Derek John Simpson, take this woman, Angela Jennifer to be your lawful wedded wife?"

"I do", was my prompt reply.

Kneeling at the vicar's feet, I observed he had not cleaned his brown shoes for weeks. He then spoke to my dearest, "Do you, Angela Jennifer Barratt, take this man Derek John Simpson to be your lawful wedded husband?" "I do", said my beloved.

There was a mistake. Surely Angela's surname was Dale.

The main wedding party retired to the vestry to sign the Register of Marriages. Both mothers were crying with joy.

Angela smiled at me mischievously, then lovingly kissed me.

"What's this Barratt nonsense?" I thundered.

Angela replied "I asked my adopted parents if I should marry in my name at birth. My adoptive parents took me from my natural mother at hospital when I was only three days old and brought me up as their own daughter. They are my parents. They never changed the name on the Birth Certificate. When the banns were read in the three weeks prior to our wedding, which you hadn't the time to attend on those Sunday mornings, prioritising playing football. The Vicar said there was not enough time to alter the official forms before today's ceremony. So I thought I'd surprise you dearest."

"Who is your natural mother and why were you given away at birth?" I demanded.

"One question at a time, darling husband."

"It was only six months ago when my parents told me I was adopted. That was when I told them we were to marry. A few days later I met my natural mother for the first time.

She told me a year after her husband died she had a liaison late in life with a professional man. She didn't realise she had not passed the age of child bearing. I was the product of that liaison."

"You should have told me this before we were married", I said furiously.

"Would it have made any difference to ourselves becoming man and wife? If so, we will not sign the Register," Angela answered.

"Of course it wouldn't have made the slightest difference but I feel annoyed."

She answered "I suppose I should have told you. But I thought it would be nice to surprise you."

I shook my head. "You've done that alright. Shaken me to the core. Where is your natural mother now?"

Angela opened the vestry door and a much older than I remember Rose Laura gave me a mischievous smile and a gentle wave of good luck.

## *Twelve*

# DOUBLE CROSS

Jonathan Wild's world had fallen apart. The previous Saturday his elder half-sister Hannah, who had brought him up as her own son, had become the second wife of William Penn, the widowed Quaker colonialist. Fate, had destined Hannah Callowhill, to be foster mother to Charles Wild's children, but Penn's swoop on the young spinster changed her life. She left Bristol in the Spring of 1683 on the "Light of Christ", accompanying her husband on the long voyage to the New World.

* * * * *

There was nothing left for Jonathan Wild in Bristol. Hannah had taught him all she could about sums, reading and writing; he had been a keen pupil and an avid learner. Now aged twelve something had to change.

The day after Hannah sailed to the New World, Jonathan ran away from home with the one shilling and threepence that he had stolen from his father's trouser pocket earlier that morning. He felt no tinge of conscience; what totally consumed his thoughts was how to get to London. Hannah's new husband had advised him to go there. Were the streets really paved with gold?

It was warm and the sun was rising, a fine June day in prospect. As he walked the three miles from the centre of Bristol to the London Road, passing moored sailing ships, the chandlery, the splendid offices of the New World trading companies, the brightly painted shops selling their produce, Jonathan's thoughts wandered – was he leaving too early? After all, Bristol was the hub of transport to the New World. Dismissing this intrusion into his thoughts, he wallowed in his newfound self. As he approached the George Inn, the staging post at Bristol, a fine sight met Jonathan's eyes. A piebald, a light grey, and two chestnuts made up the coaching four, the brasses on their harness glistening brightly in the sun. The Stagecoach's wheels and doors were painted a bright red, the remainder was shiny black except for the gold lettering of the Adam Coach Company. What would it be like to ride in such a carriage? The travellers were yet to board, they were waiting on the coachman who was tending to the girth straps of the frisky piebald.

Jonathan asked the coach driver how far he would be able to travel for one and threepence. Noting the youthful appearance, the man laughed and said

"The price's a hundred times what you're offering and then you'll need lodging money for the six coaching stations we stop at on the way. It takes over a week to get to London." Jonathan explained how desperate he was to get away.

"All right, I'll let you travel alongside me as lookout; you can bed down with the horses in the stables," the coachman told him. "There's not much danger on this trip; the highwaymen tend to plague the northern roads to York." Jonathan clambered eagerly into the rickety seat beside the driver.

To make full use of the daylight the coach started straight away. After nine hours without a break, the first part of the journey was over. Reaching the staging post at Pucklechurch, the horses were fed, watered and settled down in the stables. The weary team deserved their rest. The following morning a fresh coachman and new horses would be hitched to the now muddy coach. An exchange between coachmen allowed Jonathan to continue his journey. The eight travellers spent the night in comfort at the Inn; the rooms although sparsely furnished, were cosy each with a small log fire. Jonathan slept with the horses.

At daybreak, the travellers moved on to the next staging post at Sutton Benger. The journey was uneventful, but Jonathan was getting a taste for travel, not realising his good fortune in meeting such a kindly coachman at Bristol. On the final stretch from Reading to London, Jonathan elbowed the driver who, with whip in hand, was berating the horses to get a move on. The driver was anxious to be at St. Paul's stage in time to enjoy the charms of the coach company's hostesses at the Wig and Pen. Jonathan had seen something ahead.

"Look over there in the bushes; I can see a horse", he said. The coachman grimaced. From out of the hedgerow rode a masked figure mounted on a jet black steed; both barrels of the pistols he held were pointed at the coachman's chest.

"Stand and deliver". The highwayman had picked his spot carefully. A sharp bend had caused the travelling coach to slow down to a minimum. The coachman, his hands high in the air, kicked the brake with his foot. As the highwayman dismounted he shouted to the passengers to get down from the coach. He tossed an empty black wooden chest to the ground and ordered all the travellers to strip naked. There were mixed reactions; the gentlemen found it amusing, the ladies did not. Blue Skin Blake looked at the unkempt Jonathan Wild and said,

"You can help me. Play your cards right and you'll be rewarded. Try anything though and you'll be in the next world without a head." Jonathan was bewildered but noticing both barrels were still aimed straight at the coachman his decision was easy.

Lady Prisch-Fairbrother, slim and well-shaped, had been debutante of the year two decades previously. She had succeeded to the title on the death of her father-in-law, Lord Prisch-Fairbrother, three years earlier. With an imperious wave of her hand she disdainfully refused the highwayman's demand.

"Never will I lower myself to undress in public!" The coach driver, extremely alarmed, begged her to co-operate.

"Please, my lady, do as he says. Just three months ago he shot dead a colleague of mine when a passenger refused," Blake interjected,

"Yes, but I won't be shooting the driver this time!" Realising the inference, Lady Prisch-Fairbrother removed her clothes more speedily than on her wedding night.

In a few minutes passengers and coachman had removed all their clothes. The highwayman called to Jonathan,

"Go through the pockets. Place everything you find into the wooden chest. If you steal anything or get up to any tricks I'll blow your brains out."

The coachman pleaded with Blue Skin Blake not to harm anyone.

"We'll all do what you say: just don't hurt any of us." The highwayman was complete master of the situation. Jonathan did as he was bid and placed the valuables, money and jewellery in the chest.

"What commercial goods are you carrying?" the highwayman asked the coachman.

"Mariners' equipment. We're taking it to the Port of London for a boat tied up at Greenwich." The equipment was no good for selling so it was left behind but the haul was nonetheless considerable. The chest laden with gold coin and valuables sparkled in the midday sun.

Blue Skin Blake ordered the whole party to walk in the direction they had come, do nothing for half an hour and then return. Lady Prisch-Fairbrother shrieked in indignation.

"I'll see you hanged!"

"You may well do that m'lady," replied the highwayman, "but not today, and if you don't hurry you'll not be able to walk with your companions." Standing on ceremony was gaining nothing, so she moved. The entire party began walking, hands on their heads as instructed. Blue Skin Blake, smiling beneath his mask at the retreating group, turned to Jonathan,

"What a pretty sight. Stay here, young man. You can help me with the chest. It's heavier than usual".

Jonathan was excited by the events. Was it really this easy to obtain money near London? The highwayman immediately became a cult figure in his eyes.

"Do you ever shoot anyone?" he asked.

"Only when necessary, but it's happened."

"Aren't you scared for your life?" was the second question.

Blue Skin Blake answered, "You ask too many questions for a youngster, you just stay out of trouble. I do it for excitement and gain. This way I don't have to work every day of the year; a good haul like this once every few weeks is enough for my needs, even with the low prices the fences pay."

Jonathan looked curiously at the highwayman and asked, "What's a fence?"

Blue Skin answered, "It's a person who pays money to a thief for goods he knows have been stolen. The fence makes a larger profit than the thief when he sells the things on", he continued. "The travellers should be well on their way by now, we've plenty of time. Where are you lodging in London?" Jonathan was asked.

"I don't know yet. I've only got one and threepence. I'm on a free trip as lookout; I certainly saw you a long time before the driver. I told him to whip the horses up but he just laughed at me for being a callow youth." The highwayman had taken a liking to Jonathan and gave him a half-sovereign.

"You should do well in London, lad. I could possibly be at the inn in Cock Alley, Cripplegate, tomorrow night – about eight o'clock. If you're passing we can sup together."

Jonathan asked, "How will I know you – your face is hidden by that mask." Blue Skin answered, "I'll know you."

* * * * *

Jonathan slept the night rough in the coach stables near St. Paul's. The authorities had interrogated him at length since he had spent more time with the highwayman than the other travellers. Jonathan felt more protective of his masked acquaintance than wishing him harm. No-one had seen the man's face, but from the coachman's description and the audacity of the crime there was little doubt it had been the notorious Blue Skin Blake.

* * * * *

Jonathan found Cock Alley and waited outside the inn. Inside the public bar he could just catch a glimpse of the bawdy activities of the print workers, the penny blood newspaperman, and the drunken hags who lived in the vicinity begging a glass of gin. Prostitution was rife; for a large cup of gin any service was available. Pickpockets were plying their trade with any customer who looked faintly like a businessman. The authorities rarely came by this way.

By now Jonathan had already spent sixpence on lodgings and food. A large hand was placed on his shoulder.

"Come inside". Two tankards of mead were ordered. "It was a good haul yesterday", his companion said. Seated opposite was an overweight, blue-jowled face with heavy eyebrows and protruding ears. It was obvious where the nickname came from. Jonathan would never have recognised this man as the highwayman of the previous day, now dressed so elegantly in a dark red jacket with gold buttons and full lace cravat.

"I like it here", said Blake. "I feel at home."

Jonathan's mouth opened, the activities in the inn left him google-eyed; the place pulsated with criminal activity. The highwayman seemed to know everyone.

"You'd a good haul yesterday Blue Skin, any chance of a guinea or two?"

"Nothing doing: it wasn't that good," lied Blue Skin, turning to Jonathan and saying, "Never lend or borrow money: always let people be in your debt, that way you'll always have a hold over them. Nearly everyone here is living beyond their means: they're all looking for an easy living without working. Look around you. This is the sort of place where crime flourishes; I enjoy it, but you my lad must be industrious." A sudden thought struck him. "There's a moneylender over there. He was looking for a clerk last week". The highwayman shouted,

"Jim Cripps, over here!" The moneylender walked across to them and sat down, "I've a young man here, he can read and write and seems to have been well educated" Jonathan interrupted,

"My sister Hannah taught me everything. I know geography, all about the New World, America..." The moneylender interrupted,

"I'm not interested in your geography, can you add up and take away, can you write the King's English?"

"I can indeed," said Jonathan.

"Come with me."

It was the last time Jonathan saw the highwayman for many months.

* * * * *

Jonathan went to work for Jim Cripps at the place where he both lived and worked near Moorgate. He was given a tiny attic room, three floors above the shop front. Cripps was a stern taskmaster, his wife even harsher. If Jonathan didn't do as they bid, be was beaten with a broomstick. He soon learned to please.

When the poor of the City needed money they brought their valued goods as security for a loan. They were given only one quarter of the true valuation Cripps put upon them. Whenever they couldn't afford to repay the loan and the high rate of interest charged goods were impounded. Jonathan Wild was aghast at the treasure trove contained in that small house in Coleman Street, his home for six years. He served his apprenticeship well. He knew the villains of the day and the ladies of the night and on behalf of his master would frequently place a job their way in return for an excellent commission.

It was time to leave Jim Cripps and his wife. By siphoning off cash entrusted to him, he had managed to amass a cache which he had kept under the floorboards until he could buy premises of his own nearby.

Jonathan Wild was soon in business. His main accumulation of wealth was from fencing goods; burglars, pickpockets, highwaymen would bring their booty to him. He gave a varying proportion in cash to the criminal. Often he approached the original victim who in many cases would be prepared to pay a good ransom to ensure the return of their own goods.

* * * * *

Wild, now aged 21, kept a ledger sheet for each criminal he controlled. Over the years the ledger grew to include more than seven thousand villains of both sexes. One entrant was Bess McGuinness, a notorious highwaywoman. She struck a harder bargain than most of the other criminals as she supplied Jonathan with his feminine needs, playing relentlessly on his weakness for sadomasochism, a legacy from Mrs Cripps' broomstick. Bess lived at his house when lying low, but refused to be involved with fencing operations. Cuddling on their flock mattress, she amused him.

"Jono I'm a good clean thief, nothing else, but if I had to, I'd blow your balls off!"

Bess was short and stocky, no more than four feet ten inches. She needed powerful limbs to carry out her trade. Jonathan liked to see her unpin her long black hair and watch it snake down the length of her back, touching her buttocks. Jonathan's other particular joy was her cheerful countenance. In different circumstances he would have married her. Dressed in the clothes of her trade, with full face mask and ugly looking musket, she terrified travellers approaching London. Her pickings were invariably made without violence but she had a vicious streak for any traveller not eager to part with their money.

* * * * *

William Penn treated his new bride gently on their first night as a married couple. She was his second wife, but for Hannah it was her first experience. After a long Quaker wedding ceremony the guests finally departed and William and Hannah boarded the "Light of Christ", renamed in tribute to the large fellowship of Quakers who were making the journey to the new lands across the Atlantic. The journey was a hard one, but through constant prayer it had been made bearable.

Her new husband and his friends helped to strengthen Hannah's knowledge of Quaker beliefs, even though her father and his father before him, had been originators of the cult. She implored William to let her take an active part in the movement when they arrived in Pennsylvania. To her constant entreaties he had finally replied,

"Although the Indians are comparatively gentle in attitude, constant watch must be kept. I'd like you to use your energies to help foster goodwill between them and the white man for I believe if they are treated properly they will respond well to our teachings. It is in this area you could be involved, possibly form a school and teach English."

Hannah answered, "That would be something to look forward to," She added, "Maybe I could involve my brother Jonathan, he's bright and hardworking. The Americas need such enterprising people."

* * * * *

Jonathan Wild was now in his mid twenties. His reputation for fencing goods and arranging crime targets had become notorious. He was becoming a rich man. The Authorities gave him full license, they were content to apprehend criminals they targeted with a minimum of trouble from under cover information supplied by Wild.

In return they gave him full license from the law to continue his nefarious trade. They wanted Blue Skin Blake, he'd been too boastful and scathing to travellers of his ease of detection from the Authorities. The official reward of £20 was doubled in a private arrangement with Wild. Jonathan took the money.

On his journey from Fleet Prison to Newgate in a trumbel Blue Skin denounced Jonathan Wild as an informer, shouting at the top of his voice to press borne the accusation. Pausing for breath, be glanced upwards. On the second storey in an office overlooking the execution route a crowd of aristocrats were showing disdainful interest in his fate. One aristocratic lady only twenty feet from Blake raised her arm and, with a particularly wicked sneer, shouted,

"I told you I'd see you hanged one day!" Blue Skin immediately recognised her even though she was now fully clothed, and raised his hat. With a wide body sweep and a bow the journey continued.

That night Jonathan Wild put two crosses in his six inch thick ledger beneath the folio marked 'Blake'.

Wild never removed a page from his ledger. When a client died of natural cause he placed a cross to signify no further transactions would take place on that sheet. There were many completed sheets where the signature at cessation had two crosses; the second cross signified that Wild had informed the authorities of the whereabouts of a client, and in some cases an easy way to pick him up. Such clients invariably completed the short journey to the scaffold at Newgate. This being the origin of the saying "Double Cross".

* * * * *

Bess McGuinness became more than a little worried. If Jonathan could inform on Blue Skin, his mentor, what were her chances? A forty pound reward was a good deal of money and Wild had become a compulsive miser. 'Saving for me old age m'dear,' he told Bess. Money was his God. She could no longer trust him. She must find another fence. The Cock Inn had its share, maybe not so generous but infinitely more reliable. Wild didn't know it was to be their last night together. She was minded to murder him in his bed but his notoriety with the authorities made him of high importance to them. She would be targeted with no consideration given to cost.

As things were she could slip in the City and out again with her business clothes in a cloth bag. A nod and a wink from the authorities and the occasional gratuity to a gate guard gave her a safe passage. Without the protection of Jonathan Wild she would have to be more careful. This did not prevent her from dealing painfully with him on their last night together. His bruises would take a long time to heal.

* * * * *

Some stolen goods were well known and their legal owners refused to deal with the crooked fence. On one occasion two outraged owners tried to lead the authorities to Wild in an elaborate trap, but the wily Jonathan with a foot in both camps was warned in time.

Any unsold valuables were returned to Jonathan's vast warehouse in Whitechapel. He had acquired a sloop and moored it on the Middlesex side of the river in Battersea to be used to sell such valuables in Continental Europe.

The sailing ship and a full crew journeyed to Antwerp with its cargo and from there a Dutch agent disposed of the booty to the highly profitable antique area of Amsterdam. There was usually a ready market when the sloop sailed into port.

Jonathan was becoming a wealthy businessman. He dressed as a dandy with a gold knobbed walking cane, three-cornered hat and powdered wig, pleasing his ego by showering coins on the begging poor of Moorgate and Fleet Street.

Now in his early thirties be became a member of the Worshipful Masters of the Grocers' Guild, a highly respectable brotherhood of trade.

* * * * *

Of the three trips Hannah Penn made from the Americas to the Old Country during her lifetime, the last one was the hardest. William, some years older than her, had been ill long enough for his wife to have taken a proxy on the Governor's reins from him in Pennsylvania. Acting as Chairman of the Senate she made peace with the Delaware Indians, banned the sale and barter of whisky to them and dealt ruthlessly with any white liquor trader who defied the ban. In 1723 William Penn died; elections for the new Governor to be held two years later. In the meantime Hannah was invited to be temporary Governor.

She made her final journey back to the Old Country to bury her husband in Bristol, his home town. On the return journey to America Hannah had arranged to meet Jonathan in Antwerp. She begged him to return with her, telling him about her life in a peaceful, law-abiding Quaker community in Pennsylvania.

"I want you to be part of this. Come and work on a tobacco plantation. I'd arrange a good position for you".

"How much time would I have for my own activities?" he asked her.

"Well, Quakers are rigid in the hours they devote to work and prayer and to the time they spend helping others".

"Will I have time to sleep?" he asked.

"Don't be facetious!"

"How about my sexual needs?" he asked.

"Well, eventually you'd meet and marry a good Quaker woman, have children and help in the growth of the colony. We all work for each other, helping the less fortunate and the sick".

"I don't like the sound of this", he told Hannah. "In the City of London I am king in my own domain; I can do anything I want".

"Your egoism will be your downfall", his sister said. "I've heard of your reputation and I'm appalled".

"And there's so much more you don't know", he boasted.

"So you won't come to America with me?"

"I fear not, dear sister".

"You'll walk to the scaffold in a very short time I fear", Hannah told him.

Jonathan laughed, "I'm far too important for that!" He kissed Hannah on the cheek. She went back to the faithful ship 'Light of Christ' to continue the journey back to the New World.

* * * * *

Wilbur Johnson, the captain of Wild's sloop, had been arrested at the Port of Antwerp and entombed in the Castle Prison. The Dutch customs authorities had boarded his ship on a routine inspection and been amazed at the valuable treasure that was entering their country illegally.

On a prison visit Johnson made it clear to Jonathan that he must be freed, leaving his master in no doubt as to the meaning of the word 'must'.

With the aid of thirty crewmen Wild engendered a riot during Johnson's courtroom hearing. The judge was shot and the Courtroom thrown into chaos. In the confusion the captain made his escape.

Rum was flowing freely aboard the sloop 'S.S. Dark Wild' during its return visit to London. In happier vein Johnson told Wild he had known he wouldn't be let down. His master smiled grimly; although loyal to his men he was ruthless in disposing of persons who threatened his safety.

Returning to the Port of London, Johnson fell victim to Wild's double cross. A minor villain turned King's evidence against the sloop Captain to obtain a lesser sentence. Wilbur Johnson was arrested, tried and hanged for treason. Wild made no move to intervene.

* * * * *

Two days out of Antwerp and sailing back to the New World, Hannah was holding court and helping to plan the future of the State of Pennsylvania with other leading Quakers, following William Penn's funeral. The Elders suggested Hannah as the next Governor, realising her strength of character and knowing she would make good use of the men around her. With Hannah's integrity and honesty she would make an ideal choice.

She was flattered by the suggestion of the elders but concerned that her six children may not be cared for in the manner her late husband would have wished.

He had been several years older than Hannah and had seen her as a homemaker and protector of their children. Being a natural born leader himself, he had not been aware of Hannah's own leadership qualities. But if provision could be made for the upbringing of her children she would throw her hat into the ring. William Penn had had nine children by his first wife and four of the sons were on the sailing ship. They were wholly behind their stepmother as a future Governor. Their wives would succour Hannah's children.

The long journey home was ending. A green and pleasant land was sighted. The 'Light of Christ' moored in Philadelphia harbour.

At the wharfside Hannah noticed several Indians nearby smoking the new weed tobacco and drinking the raw liquor that was distilled locally; the combination of these two evils had left a large section of the Red Indians dissipated men. Doubtless white people also abused themselves in this way but the Indians had the innocence of children and needed to be protected.

It was not all despair however. Three hundred yards further down towards the government buildings a group of six Indians were examining cloths for sale by the settlers that had been woven in the Old Country. The leader of the Indians, with red parrot feathers fixed to his head, was proudly showing his squaw a piece of yellow cotton material proffered by a green-coated trader who was kneeling in front of the Indians, the material spread across his outstretched arms. The squaw was delighted with the texture and made noises which clearly showed she would like to acquire it. The bargaining group were considering how payment should be made and the happy bonhomie between all parties gave Hannah great encouragement; it should be possible for the differing peoples to accept one government. She felt strongly there should be a delegation of Indians in the legislature, indeed Parliament should include representatives of all groups which made up the diverse cultures of Pennsylvania.

* * * * *

A meeting of the Quaker elders confirmed Hannah Penn as their choice as Governor.

There was only one other contender, the owner of one hundred and forty slaves to the North of the Delaware river. His tobacco plantation covered several thousand acres and the black slaves, mainly born on the plantation, were treated unmercifully in the endeavour to obtain the tobacco leaf cheaply. It was normal practise in the area and like-minded tobacco growers supported Jeremy Cox as their candidate for governorship. Hannah accepted she must contest the election with such an inhumane opponent. Slavery was what the Quakers were fighting so firmly against.

* * * * *

Although Quaker in name, Hannah's fellow members of the legislature were the forerunners of the Democratic Party. Benjamin Franklin, later to frame the American Constitution, gave Hannah his wholehearted support; he took time away from advancing his own career to mount a campaign on her behalf from his printworks in Philadelphia. "The hideous evil of slavery must be abolished," he said, "and I call on all liberal minded persons in positions of power to aid our cause. If a slave owner is allowed to become Governor, slavery will flourish: more and more pitiable souls will be pressganged from Africa to perpetuate this inhuman and despicable practice. We must campaign relentlessly to ensure this cannot happen."

The franchise was white male only. This appalled Hannah's innate sense of justice and she vowed she would fight to her last breath to alter things. Why shouldn't women and native Indians be included?

Jeremy Cox's campaign was forceful and direct. Rather than use persuasion, his aim was to instil fear into the voting settlers. Two black slaves and a white plantation worker were publicly branded on each shoulder two days before the election took place. Their alleged crime was not working hard enough. Such undisguised brutality had the reverse effect to that anticipated by Cox's supporters. The following day Franklin made the most of the situation by circulating an illustrated drawing of the atrocity. It was headed '*If Cox is elected this could be you*'. The leaflet persuaded any voters who had been wavering. The result was an overwhelming majority for Hannah Penn.

Her opponent took defeat badly. Ranting and raving defiantly from the results platform he swore it would take a strong sheriff to maintain law and order from his group in future.

* * * * *

Jonathan Wild's 'help' to the authorities was wearing thin. The use of the double cross had sent several criminals to the gallows, even more to long-term imprisonment and transportation. But he had undoubtedly upset the Guild leaders: his aspirations to become one of them had become all embracing. It was becoming unsafe for them to walk the City streets unless they had committed allegiance to Jonathan's Lord mayoral ambitions.

* * * * *

The Lord Mayor was elected from five City Guilds. It was the turn of the Grocers' Guild to provide a nominee for the following year and Jonathan Wild was determined it would be himself.

His reputation for fencing stolen goods directly back to their original owners augured badly against him. The house of the Grocers' Guild Chairman had recently been burgled and expensive jewellery and paintings stolen. Jonathan immediately offered to assist in their recovery. No reward was sought for the favour: it was made obvious, however, that to allay further thefts or possible harm to close relatives, supporting votes from both the Chairman and his friends were expected. Wild had overstepped the mark Blackmail was not a welcome trait in a future Lord Mayor.

At the Annual General Meeting in the Spring of 1725 the election for the nominee was held in the Grocers' Guild headquarters. Wild was certain his nomination as Lord Mayor was already secured. He reckoned without the integrity of the Guild's voting members. By an almost unanimous vote, Ian Wells Hancock was declared nominee of the Grocers Guild for the following year's Lord Mayor of London.

Jonathan Wild, dressed resplendently in finest livery and with powered wig and gold walking cane, drew himself up to his full height and swore vengeance on the Grocers' Guild.

The Guild's Chairman was now even more certain they had a rogue in their midst. Jonathan's crimes were a hundredfold. He would not change. In fact he could not change; he was a compulsive criminal. In earlier days Wild had shown him his personal ledger and there had been numerous double crosses. The Chairman knew it was time to take action. A word to the authorities about the burglary at his house, together with information concerning the murder of a competing moneylender, were sufficient to secure Wild's arrest.

Wild was not a stranger to prison: he had spent some of his early years in the Debtors Prison at Newgate. For a time he managed to continue his business whilst incarcerated but when his well-stocked warehouse was looted and set on fire by former workers he lost any remaining goodwill he had with the authorities.

Brought to trial, he pleaded. 'Not Guilty' but had given no thought to a planned defence. He was convinced his own status and personality would be sufficient to obtain an acquittal. Wild, nevertheless, proved no match for a ruthless state prosecutor who had given careful consideration to his brief. The dispassionate Judge sentenced Wild to hang at Tyburn: the King refused his appeal for clemency.

* * * * *

Friday 24th May 1725

Hannah Penn's inauguration as Governor of Pennsylvania took place in regal splendour in Philadelphia. All white settlers and native Indians had been invited to the ceremony at the newly consecrated cathedral. Only a small proportion had accepted, a blessing since there was seating for a mere fifteen hundred people.

Dressed in velvet and ermine robes, Hannah mounted the steps majestically. As she glided effortlessly down the aisle, music from the Quaker orchestra swelled to the roof of the cathedral and the congregation raised their voices to sing the hymn that had been composed in her honour. King George sent his representative. During the service Hannah gave a dedication speech: she committed the rest of her life to work unstintingly for the advancement of the State of Pennsylvania, affirming she would do everything in her power to enhance the living standards of all people who lived there. It was a day she would never forget.

At midday she curtsied and stretched her neck forward: His Majesty's Representative placed the gold chain of office around it.

After the ceremony Hannah was speaking to His Majesty's Representative. Accepting his plaudits of a splendid occasion. She replied,

"The one sad point is the absence of my young brother Jonathan. We were so close in his childhood. I do so wonder why he didn't reply to my invitation."

* * * * *

At dawn in London the same day his sister was inaugurated, the condemned man, dressed in full Lord Mayor's regalia, was hustled into an open cart pulled by a donkey: two soldiers rode as escort, one ahead and one behind.

An eminent member of the wealthy classes had transgressed. Egotistically he had issued finely printed invitations to friends and acquaintances, renting first floor rooms at vantage points for the occasion. Since daybreak those who had accepted had been occupying these rooms, supping the fine wine and gorging on the rich fare his executors would pay for after the event.

On his journey to Tyburn the condemned man was jeered unmercilessly. The common folk of London were not going to miss such a wonderful opportunity. Rotten fruit was finding its target with unerring accuracy. His innate spirit undaunted, the man raised his hat in mock bravado, bowing slightly from the hips to acknowledge a particular insult. Head held proudly high, he mounted the scaffold steps with ease.

His Majesty's representative was busy adjusting the noose to the required length. The condemned man slipped behind, picked his pocket and threw the coins flamboyantly to the cheering crowd below. It was the only genuine cheer of the day. Still smiling, he stretched his neck forward. The noose was placed over his head. His Majesty's Representative pulled the hemp rope until it was taught. The man's legs left the ground, his body danced a macabre swirl. It wasn't until midday that his suffering was brought to an end.

As he left the grisly scene the Chairman of the Grocers' Guild smiled grimly. He walked the short distance to his private office. He took down the subscription ledger from a high shelf, opened it at the 'W' section and thumbed through to the account of 'Wild – J' An additional cross was inked in at the foot of the page beside the cross penned in two months earlier.

## *Thirteen*

# GHOSTRIDER

Three lines of bookmakers were desperately trying to attract customers at Epsom Racecourse for the last race on Derby Day. The race was the Aboyeur Memorial Stakes, an annual fixture named after the only horse to be disqualified in the history of the Premier Classic after passing the winning post in first position.

Although fifteen runners, Fancy Table the red hot favourite, was not attracting any business at 4 to 1 on. Punters were wary of risking money for such a negligible reward – an outlay of £40 to win £10 caused little interest among the crowds of punters standing back from the bookmakers' easels.

Captain Niblett III, a respected bookmaker who barely eeked out a living from his trade, usually did well at this particular meeting. His clerk, pen poised, waited for an end to the inactivity, but still virtually nothing. Then a tic-tac man 'armed' a message to his principal. Niblett wet his finger and halved the chalk mark odds to 2 to 1 on. The punters moved as one to besiege his easel. An unruly crowd were thrusting money at Niblett; his clerk's pen was scribbling as fast as a fiddler's elbow playing an Irish jig.

Some neighbouring bookmakers reduced their odds, attracting a few punters from Niblett's crowd.

Niblett's tictac man 'armed' another message to amend the odds still further in favour of the punter. Niblett's easel was again inundated, allowing him no time to lay any of the money off, this greatly concerned his clerk. His boss stood to lose £500,000 if the favourite won.

* * * * *

The starter called the jockeys to order "Get ready, get ready." The horses entered the stalls for the six furlong flyer. The favourite was last in. The starter pulled the lever, the front gate flashed into the air. The horses were running.

None of the morning paper tipsters opposed Fancy Table. She was the class filly in the race. It surprised the racing fraternity that she should go for such a low first prize, instead of contesting the Premier Classic settled two races earlier.

Fancy Table moved into a three length lead at the two furlong marker. It was a one horse race, the Clerk clenched his eyelids in anguish. At the half way stage the filly had a commanding four length lead. Crowds of punters jostled around Niblett's easel. All wanting to be the first to be paid.

Niblett was gravely anxious. Why had his tictac man caused the odds to be shortened so dramatically. His mind flew back to the suicide of his grandfather.

At the four furlong marker the field had arrested the flight of the runaway favourite. The second favourite, Long Memory, had shortened the distance between them to three lengths by the end of the fourth furlong.

With a furlong to go, Fancy Table was still commanding, but Long Memory was moving strongly. Long Memory was cutting the distance between the two horses with every stride. What had happened to the favourite's dynamic finish?

With fifty yards to go the horses were almost level. The favourite then violently lurched to the left losing half a length. Long Memory raced passed the filly and won the race by a neck. The groans of the punters around Niblett's easel were audible all over the bookmaker's enclosure. Niblett and his clerk were hugging each other. The line of bookmakers were beaming – a great result.

* * * * *

Their exultation was short lived. Within a few seconds of the race finishing the loudspeakers blared "There's been an objection to the horse passing the post in first position. The owners, trainers and jockeys of the two leading horses past the post are to report to the Stewards Room immediately."

The chairman of the stewards sat in central position behind the carved antique table that had served "objections" for over two hundred years, flanked by a junior colleague on either side.

The owner of Fancy Table couldn't be restrained "That bloody horse should be thrown out of the race, a damned disgrace to the sport of kings," The Chairman hammered his gavel before harshly retorting "This meeting will be governed by the normal procedures, so Sir Norman you will be quiet until I ask you to speak".

Sir Norman was having none of it "I bloody put fifty grand on Fancy Table. I don't intend to lose that because of some stupid jockey 'taking the ground' of my filly, preventing a true and just result. Now I will shut up."

The Chairman turned his attention to Long Memory's jockey. "Why did you lurch across the favourite as you were passing her near to the winning post?" The Chairman tweaked his right shoulder as he spoke.

The jockey replied "if that happened, but I don't remember it, my horse moved without my guidance. I did feel my horse and myself take a slight movement to the left but took it to be a strong cross wind."

The Chairman again tweaked his right shoulder before replying "Yes, the conditions were inclement today, a very strong gale blew immediately the race started."

The ghost of Captain Niblett the First was enjoying himself, sitting comfortably from his perch on the Chairman's right shoulder giving it the occasional tug.

Both trainers could not add anything of value to the enquiry despite both making long speeches putting the blame on the other. The Chairman's gavel concluded the meeting. The participants were ushered to an outer sanctum whilst the stewards considered their verdict.

* * * * *

Punters were tightly packed surrounding the bookmakers' easels, this time in anticipation of Long Memory being disqualified and the race being awarded to the odds-on favourite. Captain Niblett was a picture of dejection. "Like grandfather, like grandson" he murmured to his clerk.

"They'll lynch you" was the reply.

The neighbouring bookmaker to Niblett shouted across angrily "Why did you improve the odds you stupid idiot?"

The only reply was a bland forced smile from a thoroughly beaten man.

* * * * *

The stewards had started their deliberations. The most junior, this being his first "objection" stated the case 'cut and dried'. "It seems sir, we should disqualify Long Memory and award the race to Fancy Table."

The second steward was nodding in anticipation of a unanimous verdict.

The Chairman's right shoulder twitched violently "I'm not so sure. I accept that Long Memory lurched a tiny bit, but the video showed nothing deliberate. To me, it was either Fancy Table's jockey making a mistake or the horse taking a slight stumble. It is the latter of these points I think to be correct."

The Chairman was retiring at the end of the present season, his junior colleagues were contenders for his position. Both had a change of heart.

"He may go even sooner" the newcomer whispered to his colleague. "Look at that violently twitching shoulder, probably the oncoming of a nervous breakdown."

* * * * *

The loudspeakers crackled "This is the result of the objection in the Aboyeur Memorial Stakes. Merely as an aside there has been a coincidence today. Exactly one hundred years ago the horse Aboyeur was disqualified in the Derby for 'taking the ground' of the red hot favourite. Today's race was inaugurated the following year and has been run each year since that date. Let us all hope it goes on for many years yet."

One impatient punter shouted loudly "Cut the small talk, I want my money."

Almost as an aside the loudspeaker continued. "After very careful consideration the Stewards have unanimously decided the placings in the race remain as the horses passed the post. Long Memory is confirmed as the winner."

The roar of disapproval that followed the announcement was the loudest ever heard at Epsom. The clerk to the course had caused the announcement to be delayed until he had extra police reinforcements in place.

* * * * *

The Sun Chariot bar was still open. Captain Niblett III, his clerk and their tictac man found a quiet table. "Good result for you Niblett" the ticky said.

Captain Niblett nodded and said "Thank God the favourite didn't win. Memories of my grandfather were flashing before my eyes half way through that race."

He changed the topic "Where did you get the new odds from?"

The tic-tac man replied "I don't know, something came over me. I felt I had little control and when I lengthened the odds eight minutes before the off, I had no firm information from the national bookmakers that that was the correct odds. I would have been mortified if the favourite had been given the verdict."

Captain Niblett replied "You say you would have been mortified. Indeed I would have been crucified."

His clerk said "Boss, I think with the money you have won you should retire. You're getting too old to take the enormous risk that happened today."

Niblett looked astonished and said "I only do what I have been doing all my bookmaking career, and that is following the information given to me by a reliable tic-tac man."

The jockey who rode Fancy Table was one of a cluster of his contemporaries sipping fruit juice at the bar. Niblett called him over.

"What happened to your horse? Fell away badly didn't it?"

The jockey said "She seemed to running backwards after the initial four furlongs. To that point I could see little chance of any of the other horses passing me, but then I felt as though my shadow was riding with me. It was weird. A feeling I never experienced before, nor do I want to again."

The ghost of Captain Niblett was smiling contentedly in the remaining empty seat around the bar table. He had given his grandson some recompensation for the dreadful time the stewards had given him in the Derby of so long ago.

The present Captain Niblett said to the jockey "I don't know what would have happened if your horse had won. I had that much money floating on it that I thought I must emigrate on the first plane out of Heathrow. I just didn't have time to lay any of it off and even if I had I would have got terrible odds, much worse than I had given to the punters who backed it with me."

His clerk said "I'll wager your grandfather's predicament of 1908 flashed before your eyes."

The jockey who was little more than a boy looked enquiringly. The tic-tac man continued "Captain Niblett's grandfather had his first stand at the Derby meeting here at Epsom 100 years ago this week. It was his first venture since leaving the Army from his last posting in India. A first class Cavalry Officer who had put on more weight than British Army orders allowed. His pension alone would not sustain a wife and son in the grand manner that officers enjoy in the Punjab.

Niblett took a crash course at the London School of Bookmakers. His Army connections gave his application an advantage in the sought after pitches at Epsom Racecourse. However he only stood once as a bookmaker.

No-one backed a horse called Aboyeur in the Premier Classic of that year. It was a rank outsider and considered little more than cannon fodder to the finest thoroughbreds of the day. The red hot favourite was placed second, Aboyeur came from nowhere to win by a short head. The bookmakers were chuckling – a long odds horse had won the Derby. There was a Stewards Enquiry. The result of this said that Aboyeur had bumped and barged and "taken the ground" of the favourite, impeding him and preventing him from winning the race."

The ghost in the empty chair grimaced, thinking there was nothing wrong with Aboyeur's running of that race. With the disqualification of Aboyeur he was ruined. He couldn't pay everybody and made a run for the exit after promising to pay out at the end of the last race. Jumping off Putney Bridge was his way out.

The ghost chuckled inwardly. Utilising his one-day-a-year powers he always made certain that Captain Niblett II and Captain Niblett III did well in their bookmaking stands in the Aboyeur Memorial Stakes. Today was the big one. His grandson had made more money than he had ever seen and the obvious course was to retire in peace.

This course would be in tandem with the ghost himself, his one hundred year tenure was expiring at midnight. His shroud was being hung up for the last time to soar to the great mystical cemetery in the sky. He still had time to give the jockey who rode the favourite a hard slap on the shoulder as he passed, causing him to spill his drink. "There it is again" the jockey remarked to Niblett III. "I'd better go home before I start believing in ghosts."

* * * * *

The ghost lastly used his powers in the Steward's Room, which had that evening withstood the siege of riotous punters. The Chairman was still ghastly white and badly shaken but the police assured him that all was now under control and he could leave his hideaway from beneath the antique table.

He was seated comfortably in his chair for only a few seconds before he crashed to the floor. The ghost had again sat on the Chairman's shoulders but this time was using his human weight, exactly as he had done whilst riding pillion on Fancy Table from the half way mark in the race.

## *Fourteen*

# WHERE THERE'S SMOKE THERE'S FIRE

This is my lucky day. An invitation had been received to play my Bank Manager at his Golf Club, he was a newly elected member and without much playing experience at the game.

"All work and no play, since joining the Salisbury branch of the bank on leaving school. It has been work, work, work. I am now going to make up for lost time" he told me on the first tee.

"Any relevance in asking me to play on the 5th November?" I asked him.

"No, no" he assured me. "Merely a coincidence. I am not going to give you an explosive time" he laughed. "Not like the time, three years ago now, when my head office ordered me to chop your feet from under you. You just could not keep within your overdraft limit. However, it must have done you good, been a first rate customer since then. Look on today as a little reward."

All went well with the two of us for the first three holes, with Eric hacking large lumps of turf out of the fairway.

On the fourth tee, he removed his jacket and tie, rolled up his sleeves, placed a new Titleist golf ball on the tee and told me he was going to hit this one the proverbial mile. It will soar across the gorse, onto the far away fairway, and leave an easy second shot. He swung his driving club backwards and gave a mighty heave at the ball which rolled forward all of ten yards and sat up theoretically mocking him, sitting between two large gorse bushes. An un-bank manager curse rented the air. I smiled inwardly but not so silent chuckles made themselves heard. Three older members of the Committee, including the Club Chairman, who had stood watching, taking time off from building a massive bonfire, could not help breaking into laughter at the new member's ferocity and lack of success. Eric shrugged his shoulders but glowered in their direction.

He then took a new Top Flight ball from his golf bag, this time saying nothing but with grim determination was about to swing again when I asked "Should you not be playing that ball sitting between the gorse bushes?" He was a devil without horns.

"Move out of the way Charlie and watch this shot." With precisely the same effect, the second white ball hurtled along the ground and struck the first one a meaty blow. Both balls then moved forward along the ground, the first ball burying itself deeply in the right-hand gorse bush and the second ball ricocheting equally deeply into the gorse bush on the left.

Eric Langley opened his arms above his head, gazing skywards and queried "Oh, Lord, what did I do to displease you?"

I certainly did not hear a direct reply to Eric's question. Whether he did, as a silent response to his prayer, he never confided in me. What I did hear was the unrestrained laughter of the Club Chairman and his two Committee colleagues. Eric was clearly upset at their reaction and muttered to me "I'll get those bastards one way or another."

It is the only time in my life I have ever seen two balls lost with one golf shot. As I had played first, Eric picked up his golf clubs and marched forward without even a cursory glance at either gorse bush, and apparently left the balls for lost.

The round of golf continued with Eric's strike rate marginally improving. Within another two hours we had reached the sanctuary of the Clubhouse. Our wives met us in the Clubhouse for a meal and a drink before we were to sally forth to light the bonfire. Eric as a new member had 'volunteered' when the Club Captain asked him to help out with the bonfire proceedings. I gave him a hand throwing pallets of wood onto the fire in the spirit of the evening. The now massive inferno was reaching high into the sky over the South Downs. Eric was congratulated by the Captain, but added "Isn't the fire getting a bit too much out of hand? Its edges are getting quite close to the gorse trees."

In the evening darkness, the Club Captain could not see the maniacal look in Eric's eyes. Instead of toning the flames down he encouraged their spread by placing the more inflammable plywood strips near the outside edges of the fire. The two large gorse bushes where Eric had his ball losing episode only a few hours before were clearly endangered. Sparks from the edge of the fire floated onto the left-hand gorse bush and inflamed the centre. A few minutes more and the entire bush was in conflagration, a short while later by a petrol soaked plywood path between the trees, the right-hand gorse was aflame.

Eric was looking on with grim satisfaction and instructed me not to add further wooden pallets to the fire. "I think it would be best to let the fire dwindle to embers."

The fire and the surrounding trees reached a safety level after another two hours. The Club Captain bellowed over the microphone "Time to slake our thirsts, I'll buy the first round of drinks at the bar." To a person, the now dwindled crowd of onlookers left the embers to benefit from the Captain's invitation.

We had been drinking in the bar for almost an hour when Eric made an excuse that he had left his torch near the bonfire.

In a quarter of an hour he was back to finish his beer. With our wives we went home after a different but enjoyable day and evening.

My business partner, Geoff Forest, was on the Committee of the Golf Club where Eric Langley and myself had played on bonfire night. Some days later we were discussing the events of that day and he remarked "Our bank manager is showing signs of becoming an interesting member. He wrote a letter to the Captain and suggested we inaugurate a new annual competition to be played each 5th November starting next year for Committee members only. Importantly he sent a trophy to be presented to the winner which would be held for one year."

"What was the trophy?" I enquired innocently.

"Well, it is shaped in silver plate, some three inches high like the Roman V. I suppose it means 5th for the day it is to be played, but I am not sure. The V is fixed to a flat marble base and on top of each segment of the V is attached a golf ball."

My thoughts were racing. "Was one golf ball a Titleist the other a Top Flight?" I enquired.

"Why, yes, I believe it was. But one thing that really mystified the Committee was that each ball was badly scorched. I would have thought with such a splendid trophy he could have afforded to fix new golf balls."

"He may have had a special reason for using those particular golf balls" I replied, especially as each arm of the trophy is about the length of a man's finger.

## *Fifteen*

# FALLING VALUES

George Driver's short and stocky figure rapped the door of Caravan 507. "Meat for money", he shouted, his eyes twinkling in anticipation. Meg Lee opened the door with a huge smile. "I've never paid for my meat yet, and I'm certainly not starting now."

He closed the door behind him. They embraced passionately. Meg removed her dressing gown. She was wearing the crimson underwear with matching thigh length stockings that turned George on so easily. The wall extending bed had already been lowered. They made full use of the springy upholstery.

George took a chair, watching Meg pour from the coffee thermos. How very much he owed to her, a dear companion, an exciting lover.

Together they gazed through the rear window with pride. Outside, their son, back bent over a wood-turning last, was busily absorbed in making garden gnomes to sell at the local fairgrounds.

* * * * *

Roddy was a sturdy, black-haired, swarthy youth of fifteen summers, not overly tall but with broad chunky shoulders and a cherubic cheeky face. Even when he was seriously minded it seemed he was smiling – the sort of countenance a travelling salesman would give his right arm for. His trousers were two inches too long, passed down from a friend in the next caravan. The open-necked bright red flannel shirt he perpetually wore meant it being washed weekly. Friends asked if he stayed in bed while it dried!

Meg looked at her lover. "I'd like to have him trained. Most gypsies can't read or write. Roddy can since you sent him to the primary school, but he needs training in a craft. He's picked up woodcraft naturally. With training he could become an expert. Do you think he'd be of any use to your friend, Charlie Nash?"

George thought a moment. "Charlie owes me a few favours."

Roddy started work at Charlie Nash's joinery yard at the beginning of the following month. He was a hard worker, keen to learn everything he was shown and quickly became the top apprentice. His progress far exceeded the other lads and a lot of Charlie's customers asked for Roddy when there was a specialist job to be done. Maples the furniture store, whose customers included Royal Houses, wanted exclusive rights for him to work solely on their products.

Roddy was paid a pittance, no more than his colleagues. However, at the end of his five year apprenticeship he would be in a position to negotiate the higher wages he was worth.

* * * * *

The end of his apprenticeship coincided with Charlie Nash dismissing him summarily from his employ. Roddy had formed a romantic liaison with the Nashs' daughter. Her mother caught them in an amorous embrace in the loft of the joinery works Eleanor's long legs completely enveloping Roddy's thighs, crushing him to her.

Mrs. Nash was aghast, there was no way she could accept a gypsy boy as a son-in-law. Roddy was despatched with instructions never to darken their doorstep again. Nor would Nash give a written reference for use with a future employer.

* * * * *

Mavis Driver was lamenting her thoughts. George had not slept in their marital bed for over two months, giving different excuses when she tackled him. For years she had control of the marriage, although knowing in her heart she was not giving good value from the loving side of their relationship. In the early days of their now eighteen year marriage, she had mingled with customers and helped George progress the firm. They did this with excellent results. George's aptitude at slaughtering cattle and processing fine cuts delighted customers. His prices were no more than his competitors but the quality of his meat far exceeded them. The business spiralled. George was able to edge up his selling prices without losing any turnover.

The bank manager smiled on the business. The meat processing firm of Charles Driver and Son Ltd. had become his best customer. Jack Mainwaring invited the Drivers out socially, George joined the Rotary Club. Mavis took to high social life as a duck to water. She soon became president of the Women's Institute, employing a variety of nannies to help with the upbringing of her two sons. This enabled her to continue voluntary work away from home.

George's inattentiveness was particularly worrying. Longer periods were taken between liaisons, mostly unsuccessful of penetration. Was there another outlet? Her two sons, already through formal education, were firmly entrenched in the family business. Mavis' conscience was troubling her. Noting from her diary for the previous twelve months, she had been absent from the family house on a hundred and eighty seven evenings – all for good charitable causes she consoled herself. With this record of devotion, she had reigned as president of the Women's Institute for twelve years.

The excellent meals that were part and parcel of her charitable duties had been instrumental in ravaging her erstwhile slim figure. Her sons affectionately nicknamed her 'Dumpty'. Over the period of the presidency from a young looking tall blonde with an hourglass figure she had filled out towards overflow. She now carried thirty five pounds more than when she walked down the aisle on George's arm. Nibbling between meals was a habit she must correct. The corset purchased only three months ago was fighting an increasingly losing battle.

* * * * *

The visit to the gypsy encampment near Hammerwich village was the third call George Driver made every Friday morning.

The approach through leafy paths was a one mile journey through the finest countryside in Staffordshire. It was the best part of George's delivery round. Weather permitting he walked the journey, carrying his cargo.

As he neared the encampment he could hear children playing noisily. Some were footing hopscotch. Rubber balls were flying and he had to dodge his way past the milling throng, nodding to several people he had become acquainted with over the years. None of them could afford George's prices. Meg was his only call in the cluster of caravans. One veteran of the Falklands War knew the usual time and had a begging bowl ready to prick George's conscience as he passed by. Invariably a pound coin changed hands. Visiting tradesmen were a rare event, usually gypsies acquired their victuals directly from the land or straying animals.

George arrived at Caravan 507 in full anticipation. Today her rimmed eyes showing deep distress, Meg blurted out "Charlie Nash's sacked Roddy and refused to give him a reference."

George nodded "He 'phoned me about it. Nash wouldn't listen to me, he said Eleanor's devastated. His wife can't do a thing with her. She's ranting and screaming Roddy's the only man she's ever cared for."

Meg vibrated with anger. "It's because we're gypsies – not good enough for them. They say the only trade we're good at is rearing whippets. It's us and them. Roddy's good enough for their daughter."

George tried to console her. "I'll do what I can." His arms clutched Meg to him. Her long black hair reached down the length of her unclad back, the strands touching the cleavage of her buttocks, all thoughts of Roddy's problems momentarily disappeared.

Before George could make his usual move forward there was a knock on the door, Roddy barged in. He had heard of a sawmill in nearby Chalk Hay which was for sale at a very reasonable price. Rather than look for employment, he would like to carry on as master of his own destiny. "Can you help me with capital, Dad?" It was a question George knew he would have to answer one day.

The following morning George went to see his friend Jack Mainwaring. They discussed Roddy's request for capital. Mainwaring asked,

"Are you throwing good money after bad, George?"

"Maybe, but everybody has to make a start. Roddy's the right age, he's certainly got the technical ability, it's whether he has a head for business. Obviously I'll advise him where I can and instruct my works accountant to guide him, but you know my son's headstrong. He's also inexperienced in pricing the services he's offering. When I started I worked for my father. It was several years before I put my toe in the water of managing the business. This way helps to alleviate mistakes, but father started the business with no management experience. Why shouldn't Roddy?"

Mainwaring nodded. "All right, how do you want it, an overdraft for Roddy which you'll guarantee personally?"

George said, "No, I have those shares in ICI, I'd like to sign those over to the bank. That should enable you to set up an overdraft for Roddy which will help him acquire the new business and give him adequate working capital. He has no money of his own. I know he'll try desperately hard, he's got this chip on his shoulder about being part gypsy. He intends to show non-gypsies like me how to conduct business affairs. You can't tell youth anything they know it all." Mainwaring nodded, thinking with a hundred and ten thousand pounds worth of ICI shares as security for an overdraft facility to Roddy of seventy-five thousand pounds, the bank's interest would be safeguarded.

Later that day Roddy called at the bank to complete formalities.

The Chalk Hay business was purchased two days later.

* * * * *

Eleanor went to live with Roddy in a caravan next to his mother's on the Hammerwich encampment.

Roddy's red blood and urging sex drive inherited from his father more than satisfied Eleanor's lusting loins. What a pair in bed, or anywhere when they were alone.

It was the environment that babies were made of. Surely it wouldn't be long before she was a grandmother thought Meg Lee.

In a few short weeks Eleanor became part of the entertainment scene. An old gypsy folk song was renamed after her. At night, as violins were played around a roaring campfire, she danced a wild, passionate and swirling jig. With full skirt billowing and her shimmering tambourine vibrating in rhythm to the music, Eleanor's shapely form brought back the exciting atmosphere the gypsies had loved so much when Meg Lee had danced for them.

* * * * *

Eleanor worked long hours alongside Roddy at the sawmill. They were slowly but surely recovering the trade which had deteriorated so badly under the previous ownership; the business quickly gained new customers and the firm's expertise and quality craftsmanship were becoming well known in the circles of high class furniture manufacturing. However, Roddy's business administrative skills didn't match his technical ability. He wasn't quick to chase debts and was much too lackadaisical, allowing customers to delay payment for many months longer than their agreed term. His other failing was a tendency to build up stocks that couldn't be sold quickly. There just wasn't enough cash circulating for an expanding business.

Jack Mainwaring was a constant worry to Roddy whose overdraft was always at full stretch and often exceeded. The timberyard was stacked with unsold stock and, Roddy told his bank manager, "If I could sell this I wouldn't have any overdraft and you wouldn't worry the life out of Eleanor. It's not so bad for me, I can take your constant badgering, but it's really upsetting her, she's not used to it. I just wish you'd keep out of my life." Mainwaring replied, "How can I? Your stock isn't sold, you don't collect overdue debts. My head office is always complaining about you exceeding your overdraft limit. You don't think I come here for the sake of my health. You should stop working the sawmill for a time and chase up some of the money people owe you. Lay off a few employees; at least pay money into the bank quicker than you've been doing in the past. You think once a fortnight's enough – it isn't. You'll need to get in your car and shake up those customers who owe you money. Be ruthless, not nice. Anyone whose payments are overdue must be pursued relentlessly, using all the legal angles available. There's little use in being the best quality producer in the business if you can't back it up with good finance."

Roddy said, "Great, you give me an umbrella when the sun's shining, now that it's raining you want to take it back."

Mainwaring looked at him. "Money makes the world go round. Without it, it will stop revolving for you."

* * * * *

In mid-October an amateur meteorologist telephoned the BBC and asked the weather bureau if there was to be a hurricane in the next few hours. The suggestion was laughed off. Within hours, southern England was being battered by winds gusting over 115 m.p.h., causing greater havoc than anything experienced this century. An entire woodland in Sussex containing many thousands of trees was razed to the ground. A 350 mile trail of destruction stretched from Cornwall to East Anglia, completely engulfing London where all the Royal Parks had been decimated. Everywhere trees had come crashing to the ground, seventeen people had been killed by them. Department stores in the West End had their shop fronts blown out; some buildings were reduced to rubble.

People residing north of a line through Rugby and Peterborough experienced no devastation whatsoever. They could only be thankful and wonder why they had been fortunate enough to be spared, living so near to the disastrous scenes shown on their television screens.

* * * * *

Coincidentally with the hurricane the world's financial markets had the greatest fall in value ever experienced. Fifty billion pounds was written off publicly quoted companies on the London Stock Market the day after the hurricane struck. A tidal wave of selling began as dealers rushed to their desks at 7 a.m. and worked non-stop throughout the day. Wall Street and Tokyo were panic stricken, both centres had falls matching the London Market. The crash on the American Market was twice as bad as the 1929 Great Crash. The financial markets had an unparalleled melt down.

* * * * *

Jack Mainwaring called on Roddy three days later; without any preamble, his opening words were. "Security for your overdraft is only a half what it was last week, what are you going to do about it?"

Roddy replied, "Surely other customers are in the same boat as I am. The bank will just have to support us until better times arrive and my father's ICI shares have recovered to their full amount."

Mainwaring countered, "A price is a price and the price of your father's ICI shares may never recover to what it was. When we gave you the overdraft facility we had a margin of safety. That margin has been eroded, shares may never recover."

Roddy countered, "Well that's not my fault?", although he was made to feel that it was and that he had personal control over the movements of the hurricane. Jack Mainwaring was a master of dealing with recalcitrant customers.

"My head office have instructed all branch managers to turn into cash any securities they hold. This means selling your father's shares and suing you for the balance."

"That would ruin me!" was the angry reply. Roddy continued. "I'm hoping I can get some raw materials at a very low price. London County Council are advertising trees that have been felled by the hurricane can be sold to the highest bidder. It's a type of auction and if I'm in at the beginning I'm sure a good deal can be obtained."

Mainwaring's face was grim. "That will expend further funds, don't look to the bank for any help. There's no more goodwill with your poor record with this bank. Not a penny more for you."

* * * * *

As the Range Rover passed Euston Square, not one tree remained standing in the parkland area fronting the railway station. The green lawns were covered with fallen timber and travellers moving into and out of the station were skirting round or stepping over uprooted trees. An elderly bystander remarked to his companion,

"Just like the Blitz this is." Further on the front windows of Madame Tussauds had been totally destroyed, the splintered glass strewn in every direction across Baker Street. The scenes of complete and utter devastation caused the pair from the Midlands to look at each other in bewilderment.

The part of Hyde Park known as Rotten Row was a scene of intense activity. Exercising the horses of the Royal Welsh Fusiliers was a major priority and workmen had cleared the one mile racing strip of the foliage and trees left in the wake of the hurricane. Four officers of the Horseguards on one side and four sergeants on the other were engaged in a full blooded race. Behind a railed fence the astonished pair jostled for a view among the throng of spectators as the contestants thundered past at full tilt. Crowds of tourists were loudly cheering the combatants in their full racing uniform; eight steeds at the charge, a free tourist attraction. It was an exciting time to visit the capital.

* * * * *

The young couple weren't the only ones inspecting the cheap timber. The telefax communication from the Forestry Manager had also been sent to their business competitors. Roddy greeted and nodded to buyers he recognised from sawmills throughout the United Kingdom; there were even representatives from mainland Europe.

The sight of his competitors lying on the grass probing trees caused Roddy to panic. He was desperate for a quick profit.

Roddy relied on his own expert judgment as he inspected the sample shown to him. Thankfully, he noted, several of his competitors disappeared without making bids. The Forestry Manager had agreed to accept the highest price offered before close of business that evening.

Roddy's bid was not only considerably higher than anticipated, it was also the only bid. At 5.00 o'clock that evening the offer was accepted.

The following day the Hyde Park Forestry Commission confirmed the order in writing. Payment was to be made within six weeks of the timber being delivered to Drivers Sawmills in Lichfield.

* * * * *

Roddy pulled off his old green working overalls and put on his best Savile Row suit. His major customers were those at the top end of the furniture manufacturing outlets and he was sure the quality timber purchased from Hyde Park would be an instant hit with them. He was still wondering why so many of his contemporaries hadn't bothered to compete. It was probably because of the downturn in the financial markets, he thought, maybe the effects of the hurricane depressing trading instincts. He had always been happier working with the raw timber than conducting the business side of his company, but for the business to be successful he had to take the rough with the smooth.

Roddy called on the buyer at Maples, a man expert at recognising quality grains of wood. Delighted with the samples he was shown he told Roddy, "This is some of the best timber I've ever seen. I'll place an order now and stockpile some for next year when we celebrate a hundred years in the trade; we're planning a whole new range of merchandise." It was the same reaction from all his main customers. Within four days the total consignment from Hyde Park had been sold at an average of six times the price Roddy had paid. "What a fantastic deal I've brought off", he boasted to Eleanor that evening. "I should think Jack Mainwaring could take me to lunch at the Conservative Club on the strength of this. Just imagine, a gypsy in the Conservative Club?" Roddy gave a huge laugh, hugging himself with obvious satisfaction. Eleanor merely acquiesced with a doubtful smile. "I hope it goes our way", she commented, "I have an unholy feeling that this deal has gone just a wee bit too smoothly." What also concerned her was the fact that her parents were still refusing to accept Roddy as their future son-in-law. Now that she was four months pregnant this continued obstinacy was really upsetting. Roddy wanted her to name the wedding day despite her parents' objections, but Eleanor could be just as stubborn, they must be brought to heel. "It's my life, not theirs. I did as they wanted until I was in my late teens but now I have a life to live of my own."

Roddy was exasperated. "You put all this silly trivia before our happiness. We're rich now, our financial problems have faded away."

Eleanor was quick to respond, "The money's not in the bank yet."

* * * * *

Four of Jack Galley's low loaders delivered the consignment in late October. Roddy signed the delivery note and initialled the Bill of Sale.

The following morning Roddy and Eleanor stayed in bed late. A lengthy session of passionate lovemaking, enhanced by the knowledge that Eleanor was now carrying their love child, was followed by a champagne breakfast to celebrate the end of their financial worries.

At 9.30 a.m. Roddy hurried into his office. He had barely sat down before the foreman crashed the door open.

"Where've you been, I've been trying to 'phone you since seven o'clock this morning." Roddy apologised, feeling guilty at having left the receiver off the hook.

"What's the problem?" he asked weakly. The foreman had in his hand a large silver coloured lump of metal. The jagged segment was over eighteen inches long with a diameter five inches wide at the zenith, made of sharp steel with a mass of prickly points. Roddy could see it was heavy, at least twenty five pounds he guessed. Gradually it slipped from the foreman's sweaty grip. "Damn!" he said, as it dropped on to the desk, leaving a series of heavy indents.

"What's that?" Roddy asked.

"I don't know" was the unhelpful reply.

"But this, and several lumps like it, have managed to ruin fourteen of our best chainsaws. Lumps like this were embedded in the timber brought from Hyde Park and when the saws hit them they just seized up."

"Ridiculous, there must be a reason. Why should there be steel inlaid in the trees?"

The foreman took Roddy back to the sawmill. In a barrel beside the ruined saws were a dozen pieces of the twisted steel in a variety of sizes. The two men looked at each other nonplussed.

* * * * *

Charlie Nash tapped the door. "Sorry to intrude," he said but I heard on the grapevine of your excellent piece of business and the way you outbid the rest of those timber buyers, even managed to score over those sharp Cockneys I hear. Eleanor's mother and I have been thinking, we'd like to forget the differences of the past Roddy, bury the hatchet so to speak. Guess we haven't been that kind to you and Eleanor recently, hope you can forgive us. Anyway, will you bring our daughter to lunch on Sunday?"

These words were music to Roddy's ears. Eleanor would be delighted.

* * * * *

Noticing the segment on the table, Charlie asked "What's that piece of steel on your desk?"

"Don't know, we're just trying to work it out, but there are plenty more round in the yard." the foreman responded.

Charlie Nash was taken to view the remaining pieces and shown the broken saws.

"Where did all this lot come from?" he asked. When he heard it was from the innards of the London trees felled in the hurricane, he screwed up his face in anguish. "For heavens sakes, they're pieces of shrapnel! During the war artillery guns were used to fire at the German bombers. Steel fragments were scattered goodness knows where as a result. London had the heaviest air raids, the capital was showered with exploding shells, fragments falling and lodging in all sorts of unusual places.

"My God," said Roddy "he's pulled a fast one on me." Grabbing the telephone he immediately rang the Head Forester at Hyde Park. "I'm not paying you a penny. This timber is absolutely useless for furniture making, all the trees were riddled with shrapnel. In fact I'll be suing you not only for misrepresentation but for the cost of transportation as well!"

The voice at the other end of the line was equally abrasive. "I presume you read the small print in the order you signed in Hyde Park?"

"No," said Roddy, "I trusted you that everything was above board."

The reply was "It's the signed written word that counts. I made no misrepresentations whatsoever. I left samples in my office and the fallen trees were there for all to examine. In contract law you haven't a leg to stand on. If we haven't been paid at the end of six weeks we'll be suing you, and bankrupt you if necessary to get our money. As for transport costs, you signed a delivery note when the goods were delivered by Jack Galley's transporters; it contained the phrase 'Caveat Emptor'."

"What does that mean?" Roddy demanded. The Forestry Manager replied,

"Mr. Driver, it means let the buyer beware."

* * * * *

Roddy made an appointment to see his solicitor, a man he knew well from their schooldays.

Whilst Alan Smithson was examining the contract of sale and the copy delivery note, Roddy gazed around the office. Volumes of shiny red leather bound Law books and Member Lists of firms going back to the turn of the century were crammed in the surrounding bookcases. Perhaps he should have worked harder at school; you rarely hear of a lawyer going bankrupt, he mused, safe occupation being a lawyer. A cartoon of Mr. Gladstone meeting Mr. Disraeli in the offices of the Law Society dated 5th July, 1888, took pride of place over the mantelshelf. His thoughts were rudely interrupted. "I'm afraid you'll have to pay" said Alan Smithson. Roddy answered, "But can't I force my customers to buy the timber they've ordered from me?"

"Have you a contract of sale?" asked the solicitor. "One that includes the words 'having examined and accepted the goods', the kind you signed in Hyde Park?" Roddy admitted he hadn't. Jack Mainwaring who had accompanied him was aghast. Roddy's overdraft was almost three times what the ICI shares were now worth. The bank would suffer, his own credibility would be brought into doubt at Head Office.

Roddy finally accepted the advice of his solicitor to file a bankruptcy petition. There was no alternative. He had agreed to honour the London County Council debt for £100,000. "It's now mid Friday afternoon," he said to Mainwaring "I'll attend to it first thing on Monday morning."

* * * * *

What didn't wait till Monday morning was the birth of twin girls shortly before midnight the same evening. The arrival was six weeks before they were due to make an appearance. Eleanor had been rushed into the Queen Elizabeth hospital in Edgbaston earlier that evening. The heavier baby appeared first, able to pull rank on account of her plumpness and greater strength compared to that of her sister's smaller and more fragile body. Only twenty minutes had passed before they were both breathing the air of new life.

* * * * *

Early Saturday morning Sarah and Charlie Nash crept into the side ward B at the maternity unit. Their daughter was propped up in bed sipping a cup of tea, looking pale and very tired. The babies lay sleeping peacefully in a cot alongside. Mother and daughter embraced, tears flowing. Both grandparents were overjoyed. Another world had opened. All thoughts of objecting to Roddy as a husband had crumbled.

They'd never met Roddy's side of the family. Meg Lee's smiling face peered round the door, her rosy cheeks were glowing and her brown eyes sparkled with sheer joy. "Can I come in?" Charlie Nash walked forward and greeted her fondly.

"You have to be the other grandmother?"

"Yes, and you must be Eleanor's Mum and Dad. I'm so pleased to meet you at last." Meg answered. "Are the babies healthy?" She received the answer she'd prayed for.

Each grandmother was cradling a twin girl in a state of ecstasy, gliding around the small room cooing and humming in turn.

Roddy walked in with the Ward Sister. Her hands flew up in horror at seeing the babies had been removed from their cots. Immediately the order was given to return them at once. Both grandmothers were given a stern lecture. Undaunted, Sarah Nash said "Doesn't the younger baby look like me, darling?"

A diplomatic husband nodded dutifully and added, "True, and I think the other little girl resembles the Lee side of the family don't you?"

Roddy added that he'd noticed that at the delivery. Eleanor glanced at Roddy. The visit of the grandparents had become wearing. Meg Lee asked what names the twins were to be given stating "A good old gypsy name is Ethel. It was my Mother's name. How about that for the older one?"

Sarah Nash flared up, "We can't have gypsy names. The name Ethel went out with the ark. No, something modern like Sharon."

Eleanor looked at Roddy desperately. He brought the meeting to an end by opening the door and unceremoniously pointing to the exit.

Now alone, Roddy commented. "At last something has gone right for me."

"Gone right for both of us" chided Eleanor, who continued "Now we're on a roll I'm sure the financial troubles will fall into the background." Roddy smiled, but with an ache in the pit of his stomach. The slings and arrows of outrageous fortune had matured him.

* * * * *

Later that afternoon Roddy was taking a welcome rest after a hectic match. Sitting at a table on the lawns which fronted the pavilion of Lichfield Hockey Club he was pondering on how fortunate members were to have such an idyllic environment. These superb lawns were a vestige of the long history of the club, they also played host to the Cricket Club in the summer months. In two years' time the club would be celebrating its centenary. Over all those years its lawns, shrubbery and playing areas had been kept in pristine condition by the sweat, toil and tender loving care of former members, mostly now long gone.

Gazing around him Roddy remarked to his companion that he could think of no grander place in the world to drink beer than on these beautifully manicured lawns. His companion agreed, "I don't know of any better place this side of heaven, and I hope it's a good long time before I discover whether there's a better place on the other side." Roddy smiled and nodded.

After two pints of best draft bitter tongues were loosening. Roddy let slip that in a few hours he would be filing a petition for bankruptcy. "Thank God I only rent my caravan, at least I'll be able to keep a roof over my new babies' heads. If I'd have owned the caravan, it would've gone straight to the Receiver."

Joe Kinton, who had played goalkeeper for the opposing side, gave him a thoughtful look. "Mmm, instead of filing a bankruptcy petition why not walk a further two hundred yards past the Receiver's office and call in and see me. I might be able to help you."

Roddy looked up expectantly, "Why, are you a magician?"

Kinton smiled "In the past some people have thought so. Actually it's my area of work, I'm an insolvency practitioner. My main business is to set up schemes for people in your situation. I negotiate a new arrangement with whoever they owe money to, in some cases merely asking for more time to pay off the debt, in others offering to pay less than what's owed immediately but in full and final settlement. Most creditors like this idea, at least they're getting something back. If formal bankruptcy proceedings are instigated, they usually end up with nothing at all."

Roddy asked hopefully, "Would you be prepared to negotiate with my bank manager, Jack Mainwaring?"

"Of course," Kinton answered. "I can't give any copper bottom guarantees but I've years of experience in arranging this type of deal."

By the third pint the world was becoming a rosier place. Roddy was imagining there may be light at the end of the tunnel after all. He was brought down to earth. "I must warn you there are always moral crusaders who won't have anything to do with people who can't or won't pay their debts, but that's a problem to be met if it arises."

Roddy replied, "But I haven't any money. I'm not in a position to pay you any fees."

"The first appointment is always free." he was told "If things work out as planned, the creditors usually pay me out of what I collect."

* * * * *

Eleanor remained in hospital over the weekend to make sure she and the babies were all doing well. Both the little girls were taking her milk naturally. Eleanor's breasts had swollen painfully to fulfil their new function.

The twins had been named Lisa and Joanne. "You can't please everyone so I'm having the names we chose" Eleanor told Roddy.

On Sunday afternoon he informed her of his impending visit to Joe Kinton. "What did I tell you?" Eleanor smiled.

The forbidding Sister appeared and told Roddy sternly it was time for the twins to "take milk" and then for his wife to rest.

* * * * *

Mavis Driver was reading the births column in the Sunday edition of the Lichfield Advertiser. The name 'Driver' didn't miss her attention. What pretty names she thought.

Her figure had lost some of its plumpness, she was trying desperately hard with her diet, worry also had a slimming effect. She was turning down some of the voluntary assignments and endeavouring to spend more time with her husband.

Rumours were rife in the Women's Institute. A whispering campaign had reached her ears even before reading the latest births' notice. Was it true her husband was playing away when he should have been at home? Deep inside she couldn't blame him if he was. An even greater effort was called for. She was in danger of losing everything she had worked and slaved for.

Mavis didn't have a great deal of capital. In recent years she and George had taken large cash sums out of the business so that they could enjoy a high standard of living and generally have a good time, there were no savings.

* * * * *

The following morning Mavis called at Lichfield's only private detective agency. It was opposite Cathedral Close, an office two flights up a circular rickety staircase. The name 'Bernard Ord, Private Investigator' was inscribed in flaking gold paint on the glass panelled door; dusty and well finger-marked, Mavis noted as she walked through.

The man sitting behind the dark mahogany desk was younger than Mavis had expected. She knew he had once been a member of the West Midlands Crime Squad but had retired early under dubious circumstances. Rising to his feet he stretched his hand forward to introduce himself. He towered above his client, six feet two inches in height and with a pleasing personality. Behind the genial smile hid a ruthless and dispassionate nature. If the price was right, the Agency would do it, stepping outside the law did not present a problem. Mavis poured out her anxieties, washing her troubled conscience as she did so. She needed evidence.

A report was promised within seven days.

* * * * *

Mavis Driver was scanning the report she had requested from Bernard Ord; attached was a copy of his bill and expenses. A full account of her husband's illicit affair with Meg Lee was confirmed and the existence of a half brother to her sons proved to be correct.

George walked into the breakfast room, she hastily dropped the report into her handbag. She asked "Have you always been happy in our married life dear?"

"Strange question over toast and marmalade" was the reply. "There have been a few doubts in the latter years I must admit. In the early days when we were pulling together everything was fine, but since the business has become more successful we've tended to go our separate ways."

Mavis said nothing. Breakfast continued and the conversation turned to how much the weather had improved in the wake of the hurricane.

* * * * *

The early Monday morning Stock Market report revealed yet another catastrophic fall in the London All Share Index.

Roddy called to see Joe Kinton as arranged. He recounted the whole story surrounding his financial troubles. Joe listened without comment for a full ten minutes. He then interrupted "Right, you need at least a six month respite from your creditors. Get them off your back for a while."

"That would be the answer to a maiden's prayer" said Roddy "But how do I manage that? I received a County Court Order against me this morning, delivered by hand at the office."

"Are all your records in there?" enquired Kinton looking at Roddy's leather holdall. Roddy answered "They're all there. The sales invoices, the amount I owe, and who owes money to me which is negligible."

Kinton replied "Fine, I'll have all your debts listed and a note taken of how long they've been outstanding. We'll get a letter in tonight's post to all creditors you owe money to, stating that a rescue package is underway. This office carries a great deal of credibility I'm proud to say. The major problems are with London County Council, Jack Galley's Transport, and the bank. You've got numerous smaller creditors to make up the remaining balance of your total debt."

Roddy answered emotionally "If I can only get a six months respite, I'm sure I'll be able to pay them all in full. I've got a large stock of garden gnomes standing in the timberyard. They've always been very popular with people and come the spring I'll have no trouble in selling them at fairs around the Midlands area. I'll get money that way and by then customers who owe me money will have paid. Some of the Hyde Park timber could be reclaimed and used for smaller pieces of furniture, there's still a ready outlet to the better class customers. I'm certain in six months everybody would have been paid. I could probably manage to pay you."

Kinton smiled. "I hope your creditors will be paying me, but you must show them that you are doing your utmost to discharge your debts, that way you'll get some goodwill going." Roddy gazed at the ceiling and gave a relaxed laugh. "Could it be that someone up there was smiling at him?"

"Come on let's walk round to the Head Office of your bank. I'm known there, we may be able to arrange something." said an optimistic Kinton.

They were lucky enough to meet the bank's Head of Lending, a short plump man with thick spectacles whose red face suggested a marked tendency to high blood pressure. He was aware of the name 'Roddy Driver' from the branch returns, and only that morning had seen how the day's large fall on the Stock Market had depleted Roddy's security even further. The bank was now unsecured for the greater part of the overdraft. They would have to take their chances with the unsecured creditors for most of their debt.

The banking hall contained several customers in similar circumstances, all trying desperately to re-finance bank loans. Agitated bank officials were running to any superior who would listen to them. Unlike the previous Thursday and Friday there hadn't been a suicide that day but it must have been a close run thing.

The Head of Lending was sympathetic through necessity. "If you are able to find the money to pay us in six months time, together with the interest owed, we'll go along with Mr. Kinton's proposal."

Roddy said "Great, fantastic. I'll make a supreme effort. You've been wonderful, thank you."

Joe Kinton stood on his foot beneath the desk. Afterwards, he explained "Never let people you owe money to think they're doing you a favour."

* * * * *

At mid-day Kinton took the dining car to Euston, then caught the underground to Kings Cross and walked along to the offices of London County Council's Forestry Department. It was a new office block of black marble and stained glass panelling. The quality of the interior was equally luxurious. Each member of staff had a highly polished mahogany desk on which was perched a personal computer. An open plan design, with a supervisor sitting on a raised dais at one end of the office, gave a visitor an impression of a disciplined working environment.

Joe Kinton met the Chief Treasurer over coffee, brought him up to date with the present position of the rescue plan he was drawing up. He added "It needs the support of the London County Council."

The Treasurer replied "A hundred thousand pounds is a lot of money. What happens if your client doesn't keep to his promises?"

Joe Kinton replied "You'll be in no worse position than you are now. If you bust him today the likelihood is that you will not get any money at all. With a six month breathing space you should receive at least half of what you are owed, but I'd guess it'll probably be much nearer the full amount."

Joe Kinton had inherited a little of the Irish blarney of a distant relative.

"Six months and no longer" said the Treasurer.

Working through the night Kinton produced an updated plan. This was forwarded in the following day's post to all persons that Roddy Driver owed money to. For it to succeed 75% of all debts added together would have to accept Kinton's suggestion. If this percentage was attained, the remaining twenty five per cent would be compelled by law to agree to the decision of the majority.

A meeting in three weeks' time was noted in the circular. Voting would take place at that point. Joe Kinton hoped to obtain the necessary acceptances before the meeting.

* * * * *

In the morning post Kinton received Galleys written rejection of the rescue plan. He had already applied to the High Court intimating he would succeed, but was now doubting his optimism.

He telephoned Jack Galley with a plea from the heart. "Look, you want your money, don't you?"

"Sure I do" was the reply, "But must I ignore commercial sense to save a person who's ignored financial boundaries? I'll be doing the business community a favour by taking this man out."

Joe Kinton interrupted. "Mr. Driver's had a tough time. He bought his timber at a high price and you know as well as I do it was full of embedded steel."

"I know that" replied Galley. "He should've given it a more thorough examination like his competitors did. He was obviously being reckless, not caring. A man like that doesn't deserve another chance. No. I'll not do it." The receiver slammed down.

Kinton, now desperate, left a plea for funds on the answerphone at George Driver's home. Without Galley's acceptance, Kinton was still twenty thousand pounds short of the amount needed for success. Could the smaller creditors be paid from elsewhere, he thought?

Joe Kinton called his client to his office. Roddy was told the bad news about Jack Galley's refusal.

"You need a white knight" said Kinton, "A friend, acquaintance, someone who'll give you a handout for nothing. Any ideas?"

Roddy shook his head. 'I've even tried a loan shark but the interest rate was extortionate, over five hundred per cent."

"No, no, for heaven's sake" said Kinton "that's no good. If you borrow money to pay off the smaller creditors, it looks as if you're preferring them to the transport company. Galleys would have you over a barrel when they read the Court documents. They would accuse you of fraudulent preference, a serious charge in bankruptcy law. No, it must definitely be gratuitous, a gift from someone who doesn't want any commitment to be repaid. I've even tried your father but he hasn't come back to me." Neither man knew anywhere else to go.

Kinton was deeply regretful. "It seems I'm going to let you down after all."

* * * * *

That night Eleanor and Roddy slept fitfully for differing reasons. Roddy was wrestling with his financial worries, dreams came and went but all had the same theme.

'Where do white knights come from?'

Eleanor was breastfeeding the twins at four hourly intervals. It was a cold winter, during the summer months the caravan was warm and snug but winter was an entirely different matter. Oh for central heating which she fondly remembered when she lived with her parents.

* * * * *

Birmingham's Jewellery Quarter was a major centre for the manufacture of high class jewellery from raw gemstones, in particular diamonds and rubies. A small area, only half a mile out of the city centre, it marketed and supplied the civilised world, and sometimes the uncivilised world, with expensive adornments. It brought a huge export monetary surplus to the United Kingdom and even included a financial market to provide dealers and customers with the funds to buy and sell. That morning, Birmingham's leading pawnbrokers, situated between a diamond merchant and a watchmaker, received their best customer for over a year.

* * * * *

Roddy picked up the telephone, noting it hadn't been cut off yet. He had received a final warning from British Telecom earlier in the week. He could hear Joe Kinton's voice gabbling excitedly, "Great news, the white knight's arrived on his charger!! I've a brown paper packet in front of me, neatly tied with bows of red ribbon, and it contains, wait for it, twenty one thousand in ten pound notes. There's a hand-written message on the back. 'A gift for Roddy and Eleanor Driver and their new family'.

"I don't believe it! Whoever can it be from?" Roddy shouted back.

"I've no idea", was the reply "but I'm not going to look a gift horse in the mouth. We now have seventy seven per cent acceptances of your overall debts. This'll force Jack Galley's hand. Bad luck to him, good luck to us."

Roddy couldn't bring himself to utter a word. He had to ring back to say 'Thank you'.

* * * * *

The following evening, the Meat Traders Annual Banquet was held at London Dorchester Hotel in the presence of royalty.

Members were being received by their President and his guests. The President's wife thought Mavis Driver looked five years younger as she approached the rostrum on her husband's arm. Surely she must be Weightwatchers' Slimmer of the Year? But where was her diamond tiara, the matching necklace and bracelets? When she curtsied, her fine array of gem encrusted rings was also absent. Mavis' hands were only adorned by her highly polished wedding ring.

*Sixteen*

# A LITTLE KNOWLEDGE

"You simply can't miss it. It's painted cream all over with red bits on the windows and over the door handle." These words were heard in the communal bath where Silhill had just had the better of Perry Grammar former pupils in a football match. Stanley Penn was talking to one of the younger players. "I will only charge you one hundred and eighty pounds for each week of your fortnight's stay." The younger man looked askance but nodded agreement. As an afterthought he asked "Aren't you using it yourself this summer, skipper?"

"No, we will be staying in the same area but at my wife's parents' new house. They love to see the grandchildren, really we are doing them a favour," was the reply.

The younger man was thoughtful, his wife of less than a year had given birth to a son six weeks ago. The Saturday before, he had been grateful to hear news of qualifying as a Solicitor. With the hard grind of intense studying whilst his wife had gone through a difficult pregnancy, a holiday break was necessary.

A new driver, L-plates discarded three weeks earlier, the hundred and forty mile journey would be the furthest the young couple had contemplated.

Gordon's mother's words of caution bothered the adventurous couple. "Don't take a newly born to stay in a tin hut on wheels. The condensation could stifle him." Skipper Stanley scoffed at this alarm.

"Pauline and I have had several holidays in the caravan since the eldest was five months old. Fresh air is a marvellous environment, sandy dunes and the briny only seventy yards away through a clump of bushes. You'll love it." The sales talk carried the day. The thought occurred to Gordon's father that the football skipper needed the rent money, but the new mother was enthusiastic for a break and pooh-poohed the sagacity of the older generation.

* * * * *

Their new car, purchased by the encashment of Gordon's mother's premium bonds, soared along the motorways of middle England. This is a good car, the two young marrieds chortled. The right turn to the North Wales coast was taken at Betws-y-Coed, the car checked to a 'smooth' pace, the right foot covered the brake as it passed a 'steep hill' sign: Third gear was taken in preparation for the expected sharp incline to come. "I'll push for a bit more speed to fly up the bill." His radiant near bride smiled nervously.

"Must be just around this sharp bend," he murmured. Baby Michael in the carrycot was sleeping soundly. Not a peep since the journey started three hours ago.

The holiday threesome were still moving at full speed, moving downhill but awaiting the steep incline to come. A particularly sharp bend was negotiated at speed. They were racing past a four foot high wall built of Welsh slate. The wall was the only division between the road and the mountainside which rolled down half a mile of foliage to the seashore below. The road's expected incline was still not in sight as the car slid into the slate-built wall at high speed, despite the clutch and footbrake being pushed to the floor. Gordon wrenched the steering wheel to the right. The left side of the car banged into the wall with a crunch that resounded through the countryside. The car spun and completed an opposite lock, now facing the way it had come.

Their seat-belts worked magnificently, husband and wife squeezed through the driver's door. The baby still slept. Badly shaken they hugged each other closely.

No bones broken, but severe pains in the arms used to protect the more sensitive parts of the body, and in the legs, foreboded heavy bruising. The car's body had not been so fortunate. The left side wing had soared over the slate wall and rolled down the mountainside and was now resting on the beach. Baby Michael had started crying. It was past the time for his evening feed.

Mother was able to comfort her baby and provide his supper from within herself. The back seat of the car had escaped the impact. Michael suckled contentedly.

The young husband surveyed the scene. He needed to change the passenger side front wheel. The metal hopelessly twisted and embedded into the rubber had ruined the tyre. The wheel was at a right angle to the direction it should travel. Gordon took in his bearings. A wonderful sea view but not a house in sight.

A novice at changing a wheel during daylight, at twilight he was glad of the lamp provided in the maker's kit. "Oh for the mobile phone left behind in the quest for more peace and quiet."

Baby Michael, now a picture of peace and contentment, was lying on the back seat, soundly asleep.

Carol was shakily holding the lamp while her husband was examining the Owner's Handbook. She thought but didn't say 'Surely a person who has passed his Solicitor's examinations at a high level should be able to change a wheel on a modest sized car'. The toolkit was assembled to an idiot's guide. "Just as well," remarked Carol "You're a desk man, not an engineer."

"Thank you for that unkind remark, you certainly know how to wound. You'll soon see I'm an all-rounder."

He applied his full vigour to the task, squinting in the now fading light.

"Where are the knights of the road, the people you hear about who arrive and whisk you out of trouble at the drop of a hat?" Carol asked.

"Well, we did start on a Thursday afternoon for a traffic-free journey," Gordon answered.

"That we did get, with a vengeance," was her reply.

The last wheel-nut was screwed into place, the engine roared into life. The car moved slowly forward with a very timid foot on the accelerator; the downhill slope helped. The busted headlights responded to the switch-on button. The sighs of relief were from deep down inside.

* * * * *

More for want of something to say, Carol queried, "Are you sure a steep hill sign means an uphill gradient, dear?"

"Of course it does, you silly woman," her husband snapped. "I have just passed my driving test, made an intense study of the Highway Code," he added.

This remark stung his wife, who replied, "When you were changing the wheel, with Michael asleep, I looked through the Highway Code booklet. According to that, but I'm sure it must be wrong," she added bitingly, "A steep hill sign means the road's gradient is descending." Gordon's fingers clenched on the steering wheel; he still hadn't found the steep incline he was anticipating. Also, the car had been descending for the last two miles.

"Sorry dear," he mumbled.

The car limped the remaining thirty miles of its journey.

* * * * *

The lamp in the owner's kit was again proving invaluable. Carol was caring for the baby with the car doors firmly closed. Even in August the midnight air was cold and damp. Gordon was shining his light at each caravan within fifty yards of the toilet block; he remembered an off-the-cuff remark from Stanley extolling this geographical advantage as a selling point. Nothing was discovered painted cream with red bits.

The open air toilets came in useful for washing the baby. The situation had now become more than an adventure, it was now a health hazard.

Carol suggested asking the guard in the administration block. The place was in darkness. "Evidently past his bedtime," said a dejected Gordon.

At least Gordon had a key to the cream and red edifice. He tried the key in the door of a number of caravans to no avail. One irate owner caught Gordon's wrist as he tried to fit the key in his door. Only when Carol and the baby were shown seated in the bent car did he withdraw the threat to call the police.

The irate owner became a guardian angel. "My brother's caravan is available for tonight. He's arriving tomorrow and I have a key." Carol thought grovelling on her knees would be appropriate but Gordon insisted on retaining a professional man's decorum. The newly arrived family's first experience of a night in a caravan proved educational.

Mother and son soon felt the warming glow of the central heating system, chilled limbs became supple. Peace reigned, the family slept till daylight. Gordon and Carol missed their usual morning alarm call as baby Michael slept through.

They were awakened by their new friend and neighbour who rapped the door. "It's 10 o'clock, my brother will be here in an hour."

Husband and wife cleaned the luxury caravan. "A very well furnished and spacious port in a storm," as Gordon gratefully described it.

"I hope Stanley's will be as nice," Carol added dubiously.

* * * * *

Their new mentor and his wife made them morning coffee and breakfast. The newly arrived couple now had the flavour of caravan life. The feeling was comforting.

"Do you use the nearby toilet block very much?" Gordon asked after using their luxurious bathroom.

"No, never," said his new companion. "They are only for the older caravans, like that blue and green monstrosity you can see through our rear window. It must be twenty years old. Modern caravans have the full facilities of a five star hotel."

"Do you let out the caravan when you are not using it yourselves?" a curious Carol asked.

"We do," replied their host, "But only to people we know. We never advertise. It's too precious for that."

"How much for a week at this time of year?" queried Gordon.

The host consulted his price list before answering, "£145 per week."

* * * * *

The now contented couple walked to their car wondering if it would complete the return journey to the Midlands in one piece, but perhaps they should wait awhile. The cold winds had given way to bright warm sunshine. "Life is better today," smiled Carol. Baby Michael was laughing and chuckling.

Gordon looked at an approaching car. "I'd know that car anywhere," he said. His soccer skipper's Porsche braked sharply and halted beside their battered heap.

"You found my caravan OK then?" directing his remark to Gordon.

"No, skipper. We had a bump in the car, arrived later than expected. If it hadn't been for a good Samaritan in the caravan over there, heaven knows what our plight would have been."

Stanley looked nonplussed. "But it's there," he said, pointing to the blue and green ancient heap immediately behind the five star structure they had spent the night in.

The day suddenly went dark. The sun floated behind rain clouds, the north wind blew coldly and baby Michael began to cry. "You said your caravan was painted cream with red bits over the door and windows."

"Yes, I know, but we arrived late ourselves at the weekend and then had problems with the dogs escaping. I didn't manage to paint the caravan. However, I have the red and cream paint in Pa-in-law's garage. As soon as you return home, I'll get the job done."

*Seventeen*

# GOLD CUP

Men kissing men has never been my forte, fifty years ago it would have resulted in a jail sentence. However in the winning enclosure at Cheltenham, the winning jockey planted a smacker on the winner trainer. The owner hugged and kissed his brother. The winning horse was not from a French stable, more understandable if it had have been.

The Gold Cup next race. The favourite very frisky, playfully nudges his owner in the neck, the man's large smile wiped away in one. Picking himself from the floor aimed a playful kick at Best Mate, being careful to miss. The horse showed no answer to the Brummie wrath thrown his way.

The celebrities are still on the Prize Presentation Stage from the previous race. Mostly men kissing men but at least the joint winners was a father and daughter combination.

Horse-coat number three leads the horses in the parade, no semblance of order. No 1, the punters favourite, at the rear of a line of twelve. Owners and hangers-on jostle in the paddock after the horses had gone top out. This is the place to be seen. Owning horses must be shown to have a semblance of status. Joe and Josephine Public press themselves forward and gasp for breath as they pile into the packed crush barriers. You must suffer to enjoy the Gold Cup. Persons see a lot more if they stay at home and switch on Channel Four.

"But the atmosphere", Ted gasped to Milly, "Nothing like this feeling unless you're here".

The favourite decked in Claret and Blue silks, "something to do with that football team from Aston" Ted muttered, leads the parade of horses in front of the tightly packed thousands of paying supporters in the main stand.

Most will only see a tiny part of the race "but the atmosphere" reiterated Ted. Some fans with mobiles jammed in their ears, phoning a friend at home for a running commentary. No such problem in the Royal box. The Queen looks contented and relaxed.

The horses now freed of parading are jockeyed forward to peer over the first fence at the deep chasm on the other side. Next time at full tilt they won't be so placid.

People crowd round the Bookies easels for improved odds. Some wait too long. "They're off". Best Mate moves swiftly to the lead, he's the one to beat. The handlers of Beef and Salmon think their horse can do it, but the horse with the appetising name fell at the first. A young horse can be frightened looking over the first fence before jumping it.

"You're a Goodun" is last, not such a goodun. Best Mate going along nicely. He can look forward to many a manly kiss if he wins and a kick up the arse if he doesn't. His owner is a much happier man today, even after being nudged to the floor, than five days earlier when the team his jockey colours were borrowed from suffered a severe defeat at the hands of local vindictive rivals in the blood bath of Villa Park. The owner had few "Best Mates" that night. His workers in the "wrong half" of the City saw to that. But he's 'Lucky Jim' today owning the best jump horse since Arkle, the all-time legend.

"M'dad brought me into racing and betting" replied a scouser accent to a question from Channel 4's Oxford-toned interviewer. "Although the nearest to him owning a horse was driving a milk float in the streets around Anfield".

Robbie Fowler and friends were giving a free interview in an adjoining field to the Racecourse. "Goals are scarce since moving to Manchester, like to repay City's faith in me by netting a few". He must miss the adulation, the ball hitting the back of the net used to be a weekly occurrence and oh those hugs and kisses. Men kissing men originated on football fields. In my day a pleasant handshake sufficed but nowadays at least six team-mates vie to the first with slobbering lips as soon as the ball crosses the goal line. Sickening to the older man, but nectar to players of Robbie's generation.

With a display of running and jumping that would have made Arkle proud to be termed better. Best Mate won the Gold Cup for the second successive year. Jim Lewis fell into the arms of the trainer's husband, whose wife and Mrs Lewis cried bucketfuls.

Every human in the Winner's enclosure kissed Best Mate, except the Queen, still very much on her dignity, but her smile showed what a happy Queen she is on this, her first visit to Cheltenham. Very different atmosphere to the recent televised meeting with Tony Blair, – no smiles by either – or kisses of course. Wonder who the Queen does kiss, never in public, must save herself for the Royal bedchamber.

Jim bows, Val curtsies, no kisses but the Queen is radiant. Villa colours ribbon the Gold Cup. Henrietta curtsies, the Queen takes her hand talking animatedly. Not every day the Queen has the opportunity to congratulate a lady trainer. Would the Queen proffer her hand for a kiss? No, protocol must persist. Maybe if the Queen had had a glass of bubbly earlier?

Picture time, ten in the group the Queen centre stage, such a nice smile. One for the grandkids and their grandkids.

Henrietta plants a big one on husband Terry, whose flowing tears of joy drenches his lady. At least it's the natural way the Lord meant it to be. Terry's replaced his battered trilby now Best Mate has won, couldn't he afford a new one in place of the crumpled misshapen chapeau now pulled down low over a disappeared forehead?

The joy on the Presentation Stand was not reflected in the betting ring, eight favourites had won in the three days so far and still six more races to go. The bookmakers will have to settle for Skegness this year. Bermuda will have to wait. Bookmakers' proceeds made one radiant lady say "yes" to her swain's proposal after a house deposit £4,000 win when Best Mate did the trick. They kissed urgently for the TV commentator who found the couple, remarking "men laugh for joy women cry". How true agreed the lady with a very damp handkerchief.

William Hill's sky balloon hovers over the racecourse. What are they looking for? There must be a devious reason, bookmakers don't go to the expense of acquiring an expensive piece of kit without a personal advantage. What can it be. Perhaps a sniper has been planted to shoot the next favourite leading the field in the run-in to the winning-post. They wouldn't shoot at Baptism, a beautiful grey horse, now running jockeyless to the stables. The race must start without him, going for a kiss and a cuddle back to the stables rather than face towering fences made of bracken and skin piercing twigs. Earthmover lived up to his name falling at the first fence.

Best Mate makes his first public appearance less than forty eight hours after winning the Gold Cup. Owner Jim Lewis grabbed the microphone outside the players dug out at Villa Park, shouting "Best Mate is a Villa supporter". The huge crowd rose as one, as Jim, holding the Gold Cup high, ran solo, to the twenty thousand fans in the Holte-End Stand continually bending then straightening his right arm emphasising the football club had won something. Even though it was a horse that accomplished it. How grown men can identify their innermost soul to a football club almost defies belief, but not quite, as I do it myself. The opposition has the easy task of scoring a goal. The England Captain playing for his club made it look, what it was, a very easy task. The kissing scrummage lasted a full sixty seconds. Surely two players were wearing make-up? By the opposition judiciously controlling the ball for the next hour our beloved team had lost for the fourth time in a row.

Five minutes from full time, a streaker wearing only his socks, suspenders and shoes ran on the field of play. His huge grin was the only superlative in his physical make-up. I noted to my companion a different person to the streakers that have appeared in previous matches. He replied "This is a hit-back to management of how the supporters had lost their self respect". The streaker, now gridlocked in a half-nelson by a policeman, represents the fans feelings, their emotions, their aspirations. When they return to work on Monday morning they want to hold their heads high. An occasional setback is to be expected but the last few weeks had been degradation. The players are controlled by the Manager who should direct and discipline their efforts. This can be recognised in visiting teams. The situation appears hopeless here relegation seems inevitable. Hence continual streaking has become the only way the supporters get public recognition. The suffragettes chained themselves to Government buildings – didn't they!

# *Eighteen*

# HAVE A NICE DAY

It began as a harrowing day but that Friday turned into a nightmare reality as it progressed to nightfall. I was playing golf at Marville Golf Club, a truly wonderful course, nipping out of the office my admiring gaze fell on my new luxury limousine, still in showroom gleam. I had put three miles on the clock since taking ownership. Today was to be its first journey of any distance, the 70 mile round trip journey from the office via Marville Golf Course back to my home later that evening. Travelling along the M59 motorway north, taking the Stourminster exit, journeying along the slip road to a large roundabout, stopping the gleaming apple of my eye, awaiting a space to slide into as half way round the island was the main 'A' road exit that eleven miles later would slow down and take a left turn into the Golf Club car park. Sadly before proceeding it took thirty minutes to travel the eighty yard journey from the slip road where I was halted. Whilst I was nosing my new limousine trying to identify a suitable space in the traffic I received an almighty bang in the middle of the rear guard rail, turning off the engine, throwing open the driver's door, dashed to the rear of the car to find one Cohn Greenhorse he was distraught, his ancient Ford Fiesta was enmeshed in the back of my stationary car. Full of apologies, "I thought you were going to move forward," he cried in anguish.

"I fail to see how you could know or even think that," I replied, looking at my beautiful limo now pranged and looking sorry for itself with a much cheaper and rustier car wrapped into the boot and rear guard rail.

Driving particulars were exchanged, as his car continued to emit water and oil that gushed into the roadway.

After this short and bloody encounter, driving my car forward, battered but unbowed, I found a space in the traffic to travel the eighty yards halfway around the island and travelled to the Golf Club car park. My severely shaken nervous system reverberated further, throwing my eyes to the heavens, I realised I had left my golf clubs and golfing clothes in the office. No golf shoes, shirt, golfing trousers, a left handed leather glove that golfers use for gripping the club properly, a cap with a large front peak to protect me from the blazing sun, but above all my golf clubs were absent. The professional shop owner who had never seen me before and probably neither of us would again encounter the other in our future lives, pound signs literally rang up in his eyes when I told him I needed every piece of golfing wearing apparel, his first words, "Have you your plastic credit card with you, sir?" I nodded meekly. "That's a good start, sir. Unfortunately I cannot give any movement in price because we have to pay bank charges on customers who use credit cards but I am sure we will be able to make you look a sartorially dressed golfer worthy enough to grace our wonderful golf course," he continued. This sounded expensive. My credit card limit was only three hundred pounds and the prices I noticed on the tags attached to the shirts and trousers were extortionately high. I realised somehow I would have to cut costs from this modern day Shylock. Shirt and trousers I had to pay his marked price. I told him I would wear the shoes that now adorned my feet. "But they are not golf shoes, have no grip on the soles and heels, you'll be falling all over the course, for a little over one hundred pounds you can have a wonderful pair of golf shoes that your friends will be delighted to see you in, and how about if it rains when you are out there, could do yourself an injury with non-grip shoes." I replied, "As it hasn't rained for three months and the weather forecast is more of this bloody clear blue sky and relentless sun, I am prepared to take my chances."

The Captain of the Society I was playing for entered the shop and frowned at me for arriving late. I took him on one side, told him of my plight after having a motor accident and forgetting my golf clubs and golf clothes. He said, "This will make a wonderful story in my after dinner speech tonight. When this afternoon's scores are announced to today's participants, there are thirty two of us playing today, the Accountants and the Bankers, you know how they all like a good laugh when they've had a few drinks." I smiled weakly. "Can you lend me a cap, a leather glove and do you have a spare set of clubs with you by any chance?"

"Sorry, old man, no spare set of clubs available, but I can let you have a hat and a glove. I thanked heaven for small mercies. The avaricious golf professional had joined us when he realised I was trying to curb is profit earning activities. When he heard my colleagues say he did not have a spare set of golf clubs to lend me, I am certain he doubled the price of the clubs he eventually loaned to me for the afternoon. I was receiving a severe lesson on the economies of running a golf shop and realising the benefit of him not having any competition for at least a twelve mile radius.

My partner and the two banking officials who were to be our opponents that afternoon waited with the patience of men who had never met each other, false smiles covered their impatience and ill temper at having lost the number two spot in the order of starting to the last position some three quarters of an hour later, wretched me. The match itself was played in scorching sun and took five hours to complete, my nervous system thoroughly shaken by the motor accident meant my performance with borrowed clubs bordered on reckless incompetency and except for my partner's ability at undercounting the strokes he actually took the match would have been over four holes earlier than it was, here was an ideal paradox, an accountant who could not count, I was thanking my lucky stars at an early finish as my shoes were pinching my swollen feat with a vengeance. The brisk shower after we had walked off the course was the best part of the day, so far. I thought the day can only get better from here on, little did I know.

I knew my alcohol intake would have to be severely restricted that evening, being thirty four miles from home was a long journey to travel through towns and villages of the West Midlands by someone who had not cared about the milligrams of alcohol in the drinks he consumed. Why is it that golfers play for a bottle of wine, which the losers pay for, and when that is finished the winners feel duty bound to reciprocate. They are then at that happy mellow point when they laugh and giggle at most inane remarks and when "one for the road" is suggested say "What a good idea, let's have a double." The thirty four miles back home through police speed traps, and the sight of blue flashing lights of overtaking police cars flashing a light that reads "pull into the kerb" no longer seems to have a detrimental effect, after a few drinks those things simply do not occur. Our four were the last to enter the dining room just as the captain of the bankers team stood up and said, "Joe Lineham, from Barclays of Shifnal achieved a hole in one at the fourteenth hole. This achievement is every golfer's dream, a mirage that so few ever achieve. "He is buying the wine" We could not let Joe down in his moment of glory, so two bottles of a fruity red from Bordeaux were placed between the four of us. The wine that evening was of a far higher quality than the food served from the kitchen, a low grade of beer was the main ingredient in a steak pie which did not digest well. It had now been eleven hours since breakfast, lunch being missed by my car being shunted in the back and the wheeler dealing with the avaricious golf professional taking more time to accomplish. In the alcohol stakes I was now a lost cause, I had reached the point of no return and when the Deputy Manager from Midland Bank, Shoreditch, suggested a large port to round the evening off, we all agreed what a good man he was.

Passing the rear of my car and momentarily glancing at the damaged rear guard protector, thinking that by moonlight it did not look as damaged as in bright sunlight of the early afternoon. Doubtless that was an illusion that would pass when the alcohol effects diminished on the following morning. I still had to negotiate thirty four miles to my home, the first seven of these through winding country roads were accomplished with the skill of a Formula One racing driver, the next part of the journey along the A road to the island where I had a nasty jolt earlier in the day. Reaching the turning to the roundabout, with a sharp left hand turn into the slip way a police car with blue flashing lights and a large sign which read "Pull into the kerb". The sign did not say they wanted me stop but I thought I would be pushing my luck if I did not. I realised I had stopped here once today already. "Hello, Sir," said a cheery Traffic Constable Nigel Seabrook as I jumped out of the car to meet him face to face. I did not want him pushing his head through the side window and smelling alcohol. He spoke. "I found it difficult following you, sir. This nice new car certainly can move a bit, but why haven't you got your rear lights on? You do realise faulty rear lights gives us the right to stop you and suggest you take a drink-drive breath test." My conscience pricked me. I had been drinking alcohol, of course, but I thought aggression the order of the day rather than acquiesce to some P.C. Plod's ridiculous sarcasm. "You are quite right, this is a new car, officer. I only picked it up from the garage the day before yesterday, the lights were working then so why not now?" It then hit me, the shunt this morning must have rendered them useless. "I'm sorry, officer, I had an almighty bang in the rear of the car, actually right on this spot, at 1 o'clock this afternoon, must have knocked the lights out." "A likely story, sir, you sound as if you've been drinking. Have you?" "Well, just had the odd glass of red wine heavily laced with fizzy water," I replied. "Well, if it's only the odd glass you should be well under the legal limit of 80 milligrams, perhaps you would step into the police car behind you and give us some of your breath, sir." My blood froze despite my protestations to my fellow golfers that we should moderate our drinking it had got a little out of hand. I was sure it did not impair my ability to drive safely but proving it at midnight to a policeman that I could drive equally safely drunk or sober was the difficulty of the year. "Sit on the back seat and my colleague, WPC Judy Porter, will instruct you on the procedures of taking a breathalyser test. He was making me feel hanging by the neck until dead was a far too good way out of my dilemma. With the tube in my mouth and giving it several lungfuls of my breath the arrow on the checkometer spun onto 79.8. "Sir, you are indeed a lucky man, you are legal within .1 of a milligram but I will have to book you for having no rear lights in working order." PC Seabrook continued with his solemn sermon, "I cannot let you drive with no rear lights, I will have to place my red safety lamp behind your motor and you come out in a taxi tomorrow morning as soon as it is daylight and retrieve your car." Now in a foul temper, alighting from the police car and passing the rear of my vehicle gave it an almighty kick which gave my right toe a painful stab, holding my foot I gave a hearty cheer – the blow from my foot had caused the rear lights on the car to burst into life. Turning to the constable I said, "How about that, can I drive home now?"

"Sir, I do not know how you did it visibly from here, your breath smells as if you have drunk far more alcohol than is good for you but our breathalysing instrument states you are marginally below the legal limit. You did not eat a meal recently of cheap steak by any chance, that is the only food I know that dehydrates alcohol?"

I lied, "No officer, I have not had a meal since breakfast this morning," as I turned on the ignition key to drive the last few miles and the safety of my bed.

*Nineteen*

# FIDDLERS THREE

*Chapter 1*

The third Sir George Jardine was sitting precariously on the rim of a maroon upholstered chair. The other person present was sipping coffee and seated at the centre of a boardroom table that stretched forever.

"Nearly a hundred and fifty thousand pounds. That's a large order we've taken from a new customer." Sir George queried.

"They're all right, George," his finance director replied. "They've delivered the bullion that we bought, gave me an invoice. It was only then that I gave them a cheque."

"Did we get it at a good price, Charlie?"

"Yes, they were anxious to open up a business connection. The price was very favourable." The accent on the word "very" rippled a smirk from the baronet.

"How about the documentation, invoices, VAT registration. Were they in order?"

"Oh, yes. As you know, when we're dealing with a new company I always obtain full documentary evidence as well as a bank reference."

Sir George replied, "Sometimes those bank references aren't worth the paper they're written on, full of commercial jargon protecting the bank, more than being a help to us."

"Well I did another check, George, I telephoned Customs and Excise at Wolverhampton to make sure the new customer was properly registered to charge us Value Added Tax in addition to the price I agreed with them. Then, as we had the metal in our vaults, I saw no reason to withhold payment."

George Jardine nodded. His Financial Director had done his usual good job. Also, as Chairman, he knew there would be no difficulty selling on the bullion at a healthy profit through their New York agent.

Sir George turned and sat at the end of the giant table, which was capable of seating thirty people in comfort. Placed unevenly around the table were the requisite number of maroon Victorian upholstered chairs, bought new when the old Queen ruled more than half the world. On each of the four walls hung an original impressionist masterpiece purchased by the astute agent of the original George Jardine in the late 1880's.

The boardroom had the atmosphere of old wealth; both men present liked the "feel". It gave them a sensation of superiority that few men experienced. Bullion dealing had been kind to George Jardine & Sons Ltd.

The company had been formed by Sir George's grandfather before the Second Boer War. At that time the map of the world showed predominantly red. If North America hadn't been allowed to escape as an independent a hundred or so years before, the greatness and invincibility of Great Britain could never have been challenged, as it was to be a mere fifteen years later.

Jardine's strode World War One like a colossus, financing ammunition and military arms manufacturing from the profits of buying and selling gold through their mining subsidiary company in South Africa.

It needed a stout heart and a deep pocket to finance the manufacture of the first battalion of tanks to come off the production line in 1917. The tanks were a great success in the field of action, heavily tipping the balance of the conflict. Jardine's made enormous profits from their government contracts.

The present chairman's father was knighted for services to his country. The promise of a knighthood by the then Prime Minister, David Lloyd George, helped to keep the price of the new weapon at a lower cost to the Government than it would otherwise have been.

The current Sir George reminded his colleague that the contract to finance the first hundred tanks used in 1917 had been signed on the boardroom table they were now sitting at, laying emphasis that such an honour did not come to everyone. The finance director had heard the tale many times since he commenced employment as a newly qualified chartered accountant three years before the Falklands conflict in 1982. He took the cue to remind the third Sir George that the first squadron of Chinook helicopters, so vital in the South Atlantic, had also been financed by loans from the company. Arms financing had the advantage of making enormous gains without having to dirty your hands.

* * * * *

Albert Newey took an early Monday morning call from his bank manager. With trepidation he whispered, "Good morning, John, to what do I owe this call on such a fine morning?"

"No need to feel apprehensive, I'm not going to lecture you, Albert. In fact, good news, the balance on your working account is in credit for the first time for three years. Congratulations, you must have pulled off some smart business deals." Albert couldn't remember any but was pleased his bank manager was happy.

"Yes, but not me, John. The younger chaps here are showing a great impression. Both Michael and Billy keep their noses to the grindstone working hard and their ears sharpened for an opportunity."

"I'm glad to hear it," was the reply. "You should make them directors before some other firm headhunts them. You have your weekly management meeting at midday, why not take the opportunity to make the appointments?"

Albert mumbled he would speak to his sister about it. The bank manager replied, "She'll definitely be in agreement, being the youngsters' mother. I'm asking my head office to take you off the risk list from today. You'll not need to consult me before cashing the wages cheque each Friday. Congratulations, old chap!"

As he replaced the telephone Albert breathed a huge sigh of relief. It had been a hard three years. This was the first good news he would report to the management meeting for many a day. He charged into his sister's office with a huge smile.

She said, "Why so happy on a Monday morning, Albert?" She was dressed in a formal black skirt and white blouse with a single string of shining white pearls lightly adorning her neck, her figure still as trim as the day Albert gave her away on her wedding day, twenty-two years ago.

"You look wonderful, Dorothy."

"Albert, have you gone crazy? The compliment's nice. I appreciate it, but what's the occasion, you haven't had an early morning drink or won the National Lottery have you?"

"No, dear, better than that, our pride's been restored. We're in credit at the bank. I can cash the wages cheque without asking. Two hundred jobs will be that much safer. As you know, I've always felt the moral responsibility for looking after the families of our employees. The wives and children would be devastated if we had to stop trading for lack of money."

Dorothy caught the infectious mood. "Perhaps we can pay Jardine's a cheque. We owe them a large amount, it's been worrying me for months."

Albert held his sister around the waist and kissed her for the first time since the peck on the cheek beneath the mistletoe last Christmas day. "You write out a cheque and I'll call on Sir George and make his morning," he told her.

* * * * *

Two months later a cheery voice at the end of a telephone answered, "Thompson Formations Limited."

The caller asked, "Do you form limited companies?"

"That's what we're here for, sir. Have you a name in mind?"

"Yes, I'd like a new company formed with the name of Precious Metals (1938) Limited."

"Don't you mean 1998 sir?" interjected the lady telephonist.

"No, no, it's as I said it," he answered. She again challenged the caller, said it gave the impression of a much older company. The caller snapped "Please do as you're instructed or I'm looking elsewhere!"

"Sorry sir, what trade shall we register for the company?"

"Precious metal dealers, buying and selling gold and silver."

"Yes sir, I suppose you'd need a large capital base for that?"

"No, on the contrary, I think a one hundred pound capital would be suitable."

"The Government have abolished stamp duty, from the 1st January this year. Why not make it ten thousand pounds?"

"Yes, all right, give a bit more credibility with the bank."

"What address would you like for the registered office, sir?"

The caller responded, "Mm, I understand you can provide a service where the registered office is at your address."

"We can but we don't like it, sir, we've had bad experiences in the past. If a company is forced into liquidation, we get the writs sent here and bailiffs with bowler hats call."

The caller replied, "I'm negotiating premises in the business area of Birmingham. When the lease is signed we could send a change of address form to the Registrar of Companies."

"Very well, sir, we'll do that," said the reluctant voice, "but we would like the address changed quickly for the reason I've just outlined."

"Oh yes, that's no problem. As soon as I receive the signed lease I'll call round and see you."

The operator asked, "Would you give me the names of the directors of the proposed company and who the company secretary will be."

"Do you need these immediately?" the client asked.

"No, after formation will be in order, immediately after you receive our package containing the company seal and the books that the law requires a company secretary to maintain. In the meantime my colleague and I will act as nominees."

"Good," said the client, "how long will it take to form?"

"About three days, but before we can commence the company formation we must have fees of three hundred and fifty pounds to cover our immediate costs. We will send a further bill when we issue the Certificate of Incorporation of the company, which I'm sure you know, sir, is the company's birth certificate and authority to commence trading."

"Do you add Value Added Tax on to your charges?" the client asked.

"No, sir, our turnover's not high enough for us to have to register. What do you estimate your turnover for the first year of trading will be?"

The caller mentioned a figure. The telephone operator let out an audible whistle.

"For that size of turnover you will certainly have to register for Value Added Tax."

"I understand," the voice replied.

"Will you be doing any trading before you are registered?"

"No, no, we won't."

"Very well, sir, as soon as the Certificate of Incorporation is issued you can take it to the Customs and Excise offices and they will give you a Value Added Tax number to print on all your stationery."

"Yes, that's what I need."

"How will you be paying us?" the receptionist asked quickly.

"You're only in the Colmore Row area, aren't you?"

"Yes sir."

"I'll call round and leave you an envelope of cash in your letterbox, it'll save time on a cheque clearing."

"Very well, sir, then we'll send the papers to the Registrar of Companies in Cardiff. You should be up and running in about a week."

"This is the Chancellor of the Exchequer," said Lee Farquharson, bowing slightly from the waist.

*Chapter 2*

Roger Long was instructed to report to the Government Treasury buildings in Whitehall. This was immediately prior to commencing his new job as the Senior Compliance Officer of Customs and Excises of the Midlands Area of the United Kingdom, based in Birmingham.

In the open plan reception area he was greeted by a smiling official wearing the 'official uniform'. Black suit, no trouser turnups, white shirt and an old Etonian tie. Highly polished black patent leather shoes completed the outfit. He had dark graying hair with a keen middle parting, no facial hair but cherubic cheeks and a fixed permanent smile without an eye twinkle. If he had not known differently, Roger Long thought the man could double as an undertaker. "Glad you could come, old man. Welcome to this old emporium. My name is Charles Lee-Farquharson." Roger Long had been recruited to Customs and Excise from an advertisement in the Times. His security screening had taken a terminally long time to process, though he assumed this to be usual for the senior rank the job carried. Without further words his escort said, "Come and meet the chief, old man."

The pair marched through the corridors of power, a labyrinth which seemed to take considerably longer than the few minutes it did. They eventually reached an oak door, after turning left into a tiny passageway. A uniformed police constable was seated outside. Lee-Farquharson knocked gently and entered the outer office. A male secretary looked up, and nodded acknowledgment. "Go straight through, Lee-Farquharson, the Chancellor's waiting." Roger Long followed his escort. The Chancellor's office had more splendour than any one person deserved. It had been oak panelled from floor to ceiling more than a century before. At a solitary desk, which seemed to have a surface of a quarter of an acre of red leather, sat a solitary figure. The man rose and proffered his hand. "This is the Chancellor of the Exchequer," said Lee Farquharson, bowing slightly from the waist.

Many years in politics of bowing and scraping and bending his mind to accept the instructions of superiors on his way through the ranks had given the Chancellor a weary, lined face. This, together snowy grey hair belied that he was still in his early fifties. He sported the same tie as the escort. "I assume you're wondering what this is all about, Mr Long?" "Yes, sir." The Chancellor continued. "Let me ease your suspense. The coffers of this country are being depleted by many millions of pounds each year by unscrupulous and clever fraudsters." There was a pause for the words to take effect. Lee-Farquharson always envied his principal's natural attribute of good timing. The Chancellor continued. "We have selected you to investigate the matter from the inside, so to speak. In the past our staff have suffered as they were recognisable by the criminal element. You have recently been recruited at a high level in the Treasury. You are not known to the criminal fringe." He again paused before continuing. "Our operatives in the field periodically visit the business premises of gold bullion dealers to check that they are complying with the Value Added Tax law and laid down procedures. It is relatively easy from Treasury returns to quantify the amount of money we are losing."

Roger Long waited expectantly. The Chancellor continued. "Gold bullion must be bought from abroad. Therefore we know the quantities coming into this country. Of that gold some is sold internally to banks, the National Mint for manufacturing gold coins, other dealers, and the numerous manufacturing jewellers for use in its products. However, the majority is re-sold abroad. The gold sold internally attracts Value Added Tax when it is sold. Gold sold abroad is zero rated. It does not attract a tax charge. From VAT returns from users, dealers and manufacturers, etc. we know the amount sold to customers within the United Kingdom, also that which is sold abroad. When we add the troy weight of internal sales to export sales this should be the same weight as the gold imported into the United Kingdom. However, it is not. There are always more sales of gold than gold imports into this country. The difference is gold smuggled into the United Kingdom. Roger Long looked doubtful. "I do not see the reasoning. Why should gold brought into the United Kingdom have to be the same as gold exported, plus internal sales?" The Chancellor smiled and said, "As a Chartered Accountant, I thought it would have been obvious to you. There are no gold mines in the United Kingdom. Therefore any gold bullion sold must have been imported into the United Kingdom before it can be re-sold. It is the weight of the commodity that must be the same. Money values differ, depending upon profits or losses made by the dealers, so we do not have monetary reasons but the weight difference tells the amount of smuggling done."

Roger Long reddened. "Yes, of course." The Chancellor continued. "You must ask questions, clear your mind of any doubts. Lee-Farquharson has been involved in this little caper for four years now. Have further meetings with him on any points you are not clear on. Dealing with experienced criminals can be costly if you haven't done your homework."

There was a long pause. "Is what I have outlined attractive to you? I do appreciate not everyone has the nose for the work I'm proposing." Before Roger Long could reply the Chancellor continued, "I have personally made a study of your CV and with the added benefit of anonymity, consider you're the man we need." Lee-Farquharson interrupted. "May I add a few words to your very concise explanation, Chancellor?" He received an acquiescent nod.

Looking directly at Roger Long, he said "The majority of commodity traders in the United Kingdom are as good as gold."

The Chancellor laughed out loud at this unintentional slice of humour. "Please continue, Lee-Farquharson, I'm sorry for the outburst."

His underling lowered his head, broadening his humourless smile, then continued, "It's the very few traders who are abusing the system whom we are looking for. We have political influence with the courts' sentencing policy, contrary to the Law Society's public image of what constitutes a fair sentencing arrangement. After all, it's up to Government to recommend peerages in the honours system. Judges appreciate this. The first bent bullion trader that's convicted will go to prison for a very long time. In addition the pecuniary punishment will be most severe. An example must be set." The Chancellor looked at Lee-Farquharson with mild surprise, thinking, 'I couldn't have put it more succinctly'.

The three men were now silent. Roger Long had been opportuned. He thought 'If I'm successful it is the fast track to high altitude promotion.' Also, the reference to who directed the honours system had not been lost on him.

The Chancellor broke the silence. "In the absence of any word to the contrary, may I assume you will take the assignment?" Roger Long nodded.

The Chancellor continued. "You will need a direct passage to myself: It's possible the police will not believe your story if you are arrested. I have no desire for them to interrogate you in depth. Lee-Farquharson will give you my mobile telephone number, I have the instrument with me twenty-four hours a day. Don't write down the number, it must be constrained to your memory. Only to be activated in exceptional circumstances." He again paused before continuing. "Unless you have any immediate thoughts I will close this particular meeting."

There was one question burning in Roger Long's mind. "I need a starting point, sir. Have you a lead I can latch on to?"

The Chancellor shook his head. "We do not have a clear path to follow. It is known that the gold bullion price in Spain is lower than most other European countries. There is not a government tax added to its cost. In several European countries there is a tax added to gold purchases, and the proceeds of this tax eventually ends up in the Government's treasure chest. The United Kingdom is an example. When gold is purchased by individuals or companies it attracts a seventeen and a half per cent addition to the basic cost. Therefore, Spain must be a most attractive European country for gold smugglers to purchase their wares. With the enormous number of British tourists entering and leaving Spanish resorts daily, it is also the easiest country from which to smuggle bullion into the United Kingdom. This is a calculated guess. It is imperative an agent visits Gran Canaria. We have agents in most Spanish colonies, but since our last man absconded to the arms and bed of a beautiful senorita, we have had no underground representation." The

Chancellor used his pause technique again. This time Roger Long was grateful, to give his mind a rest. There was considerable detail to absorb.

The Chancellor re-commenced. "A report from Customs and Excise at ports and airports of entry into the UK gave credence to the fact that smuggling into this country from Spanish islands is rife. Mostly hard drugs are coming in. If hard drugs, and wine by the shipload, are entering this country illegally, why not gold bullion? We feel Spain and its islands is the country of origin for wholesale smuggling, although not necessarily by Spanish nationals. Take your wife, have a holiday on the Treasury, all expenses paid. You will find such generosity rare, so make the most of it."

The formal meeting ended. The Chancellor was chatting during the second cup of coffee. "Lee-Farquharson, perhaps you would add a few words on the amount of loss the country is experiencing from this particular scam."

Lee-Farquharson smiled his importance at Roger Long. "My colleagues at the Treasury have calculated that gold to the value of two hundred million pounds has been smuggled into this country in the last six months. The officers of Customs and Excise have repaid to illegal dealers Value Added Tax of seventeen and a half per cent on this sum. My mental arithmetic shows this to be thirty-five million pounds. A vast sum that is haemorrhaging the Treasury coffers and getting worse as the villains grow in confidence. We have not been successful in prosecuting any of these people. If we could apprehend one operation and deal severely with the perpetrators it would send tremors of fear to their like-minded brethren."

The Chancellor stood, his time was limited.

* * * * *

Birmingham's newly constructed Symphony Hall, since its opening in 1994, had already attracted leading players from the world of serious music. Yehudi Menuhin had guest conducted the famous New York Symphony Orchestra, Kiri Te Kanawa had sung Verdi's arias and the unkemptly dressed Nigel Kennedy, whose recording of Mozart's 1st Violin Concerto had sold more classical discs than any other in the world of serious music, had given several concerts with the City of Birmingham's own Symphony Orchestra.

It was the resident conductor, a young aspiring Simon Rattle, to be honoured with a knighthood a mere four years later, who was the inspiring force to build the new concert hall.

"What's wrong with the old Town Hall?" asked the Lord Mayor of the day. The Opposition Leader in the Council Chamber replied "That edifice was built in 1837. It is completely outdated. If Birmingham desires to be a leading city in the European Union we must progress with the times. We have the National Exhibition Centre, which now houses more international shows than any single centre in London. We must push on to bigger operations."

The Lord Mayor, not to be outdone and in defence of the city where he was born and bred, replied, "I thought we could wait a few years before embarking on another major scheme, especially as we have only recently renewed the largest complex of canals in the world. Even Venice does not compare with our waterways."

The Opposition Leader, already prompted by the young Orchestra leader, responded, "Keep the impetus going, let's have a new Symphony Hall. The cost will look a pittance in a few years' time."

Those words dealt the deathknell to procrastination.

Considerable thought and design went into the construction of the new Hall. Visits to New York's Opera House and the Musikhaller in Vienna were made by the organizing committee. The idea of a honeycomb of rehearsal rooms for each section of the Orchestra had been derived from these visits.

* * * * *

In the rehearsal room marked 'Stringed Instruments', Dorothy Cornwell and her two sons were intently practising Mozart's Cello Concerto in B Minor. This was the main piece they were to present in the Concert Room of the King's Hotel in Gran Canaria later in the year.

Michael Cornwell had become increasingly exasperated during their frequent rehearsals. His mother's frown and pointing the baton in a two-prod action towards him, vigorously shaking her head in disapproval, had moved him beyond his normal composure. He had been the victim of this movement three times in the last ten bars. Michael slammed down his bow, retaliating by pointing his finger at her and shouting, "Mother, will you stop treating us as schoolboys. We know this piece of music as well as you do!"

Dolly grimaced. "Michael, you have become intolerable. You should be like Billy and appreciate what I'm teaching you."

Before Michael could respond, Billy interrupted with some temerity. "Mother, can I speak giving my own thoughts?" Without waiting for her permission he continued. "You and Michael argue as though I am invisible, my feelings are ignored. I'm a member of this trio and give as much to the ensemble as either of you. It's frustrating in rehearsals, with the two of you spending valuable time verbally insulting each other. Michael has a point, we are not in short trousers any more. Treat us as the adults we are and I am sure it will show in the maturity of our music. We deeply want to please the patrons of the King's Hotel, having created a good reputation both there and around the Midlands circuit. Please don't ruin it by constant bickering."

Michael laughed out loud. "Bravo, brother, I didn't think you had the spirit to speak to your mother with such vigour. We can improve this little trio if mother becomes part of a team instead of dominating our every movement."

Dolly was lost for words. She'd always had control of her younger son, now he was siding with Michael. The umbilical cord had been severed at a stroke.

Michael took the baton from her hand, symbolically broke it across his knee, and said, "Let's start anew. With our inbuilt family rhythm guiding us, we can only improve the quality of our performances."

Dolly was choked for words. She bottle-topped a feeling to cry out loud, gritted her teeth and slammed her music stand with the broken bow. Her two sons awaited a further reaction, but after a few minutes she recovered her equilibrium.

Slowly and deliberately she retrieved her spare bow from the leather cello case and rested it across her instrument. Without further ado, the three musicians recommenced playing Mozart's B Minor Concerto for three cellos.

With the restriction removed of not having to please their mother first, the quality of their performance improved immeasurably. The thunderous applause from two stage hands and father Jim, who had slipped into the rehearsal studio unnoticed, left no doubt that the quality of the music had moved into a higher gear.

The brothers looked at each other. Billy smiled. Michael put two thumbs in the air. Their mother broke into uncontrolled weeping. "I've been a silly woman in need of a sound spanking. I'm sorry boys, now we are a team with no dictator."

Michael poured oil on troubled water. "Mother, you will still tap the music stand to start our performances."

* * * * *

Parents and their two sons had adjourned to the coffee lounge. After the initial shock, they were enthusing about the new freedom and zest.

In an aside to his father, Michael said, "Mother will no longer have the added stress of concentrating on our pieces as well as her own. Now we are a team of three our improvement, which has been muted since we started playing as a group, will breathe fresh air."

Dolly heard the remark and gave a resigned smile. Looking directly at her husband, she said, "I guess I've had that coming. Now that it's occurred, I wish it had happened years ago. Anyhow, what brings you here on such a fine morning, dear?"

Jim answered, "I merely called in to take a few measurements for some carpentry alterations that need doing on the instruments. When the three of us had our last meeting it was accepted it would be necessary."

His wife nodded her head. "Yes, of course," she replied.

## *Chapter 3*

Marion Long had an aisle seat on the DC 10. Roger was ensconced between her and an amiable looking fellow sitting at the window seat.

"I shall be pleased when this journey's over," said their window seat companion. "Why my mother travels at half-term I don't know. I think we are the only tourists travelling without children."

Marion leaned across in the confined space. "No, you're not, Roger and I are on our own but I feel it will be an education for our future life."

The fellow passenger introduced himself as Billy Cornwell. He was a strong looking, stocky young man whose flashing smile disarmed Marion. She noted his blond wavy hair plastered down with more than a liberal application of gel. The aroma of Chanel aftershave made her warm to the newcomer and she whispered to Roger, "This hunk certainly takes a pride in his appearance."

Roger replied, "I'll wager he won't give me much time to read more than a few pages of my latest Jeffery Archer novel."

"Is this your first visit to Gran Canaria?" Billy Cornwell interrupted.

Marion had reached relaxation point before her husband. "Yes, it is. You sound a seasoned traveller."

Billy Cornwell replied, "I've been to the island several times, treat it as my second home, I love the place. The family always stay at the same hotel in Mogan. Its about five miles outside Puerto Rico, but you could be on another planet. Where are you staying?"

Roger replied, "I haven't booked anywhere yet. I thought I'd leave it till we arrived at the destination."

Billy Cornwell grimaced. "It is half-term week in the UK. It's likely the decent accommodation on the island has been taken. You really should have booked."

Marion looked apprehensive. "Why didn't you book, Roger?" she asked.

"The holiday was arranged in so much of a rush, dear. With a week available until my new job starts, it seemed an ideal opportunity. Apart from half-term, there would have been no problem with accommodation. It's usually obtaining flights that is the difficult part."

Billy Cornwell retorted, "Let's look on the bright side. Mother has some influence at the King's Hotel. As soon as the meal trolleys have vacated the aisle, I will take you to the front of the aircraft to meet my parents. They are travelling first class. My aunt's also with them, dad's sister."

After finishing their meals-in-a-tray, Billy retorted, "Only filled half the space available to it." The three passengers then sidled down the narrow passage to the more opulent area of the first class cabin.

Dorothy Cornwell shook her head when she heard their plight. "You could be terribly disappointed. You really should have booked, especially as it is half-term. I like travelling at half term. The schoolchildren liven up the journey. They make the hotel hum throughout the day."

Marion stiffened at these remarks. "I would have had second thoughts if I'd realised it was the half term holiday."

Dorothy gave the roomless people some hope. "Stay with us and I will see what can be done. Our family have some sway with the hierarchy at the hotel, as Billy here, his elder brother Michael, and myself, perform light classical concerts in their Palm Court."

"I would love to hear you," remarked Marion.

"Sorry to disappoint you once again, but on this visit we are not performing. Michael's not with us and we only perform as a trio."

"Please return to your seats and fasten your belts for landing," said a voice over the speaker system.

* * * * *

Billy Newey and Roger Long were the only standing passengers on the travel agency's courtesy coach which met the DC10 flight from Birmingham. The journey was in overbearing heat, the lack of an air conditioning unit stifling any thought of comfort. The journey twisted and turned through narrow streets designed for pony and trap not juggernaut autobuses carrying eighty people. Dolly was warming to her holiday, a five year old girl was sitting astride her legs. Dolly was telling her the gruesome tale of Red Riding Hood, not sparing any gory detail. The girl was terrified what would happen to nanny when she told the disguised wolf what a big mouth he had.

The first stop was to let off sixteen male golfers who had been singing rude rugby songs in loud voices. The airport duty free liquor shop in Birmingham was responsible for their lack of inhibitions. Roger remarked to the self imposed leader, "Seems a bit hot to play golf, old man."

He replied in a broad Welsh accent, "We carry our clubs as a blind to our womenfolk back home. We're the oldest swingers in town. You can join us if you like." Marion's sharp glance of disapproval left Roger in no doubt. "Thank you, but another time maybe," he replied.

Billy took the telephone number of the apartments the golfers were heading towards. "You never know," he commented.

The coach disgorged travellers at eight other stops before arriving at its terminus. Hotel porters at the King's Hotel were waiting to help the last six passengers on the coach. Jim made the newcomers welcome, buying them a drink in a lounge with two Union Jack flags placed on the bar counter. A smiling black moustached Spanish barman said, "For British guests only," ignoring the fact that the drinks he was mixing had been ordered in a guttural Germanic voice.

Dolly could be seen across a wide hallway gesticulating to the duty manager. His continued frown did not bode well.

Jim Cornwell interrupted Roger's thoughts. "A bit out of context a smart educated fellow like you not booking accommodation. Seems as though you could afford the best that money could buy."

Roger Long replied apologetically, "It was a quick arrangement. I obtained the air tickets easily, I felt confident that good accommodation would be just as easy to find." He wouldn't tell his new acquaintance he was on a 'fishing expedition' hoping to land at least one gold smuggler, especially as he hadn't mentioned the real reason for the visit to Marion. The Chancellor had insisted "Don't tell your wife what you are really up to. With little knowledge of our work she could easily mess it up."

Another man of the hotel's hierarchy joined Dolly and the duty manager. He wore a grey dress coat, high starched white collar complete with a grey cravat, his silk black trousers covering a portly waistline. His black boots laced over the ankles shone with a mirror effect. The deference the other staff paid him gave the unhappy couple the impression that the ultimate decision was imminent. The newcomer was a worried man, continually wiping his brow with a spotless white handkerchief, and shaking his head from side to side as if watching a tennis match whilst Dolly was talking and gesticulating.

Marion turned to Roger, gave a wry humourless smile. "Let's get a taxi, maybe we'll be luckier at the airport. Could be two vacant seats on the plane's return journey." Roger shook his head. Dolly was not taking 'no' for an answer. After what seemed an interminable age, the top official smiled and held open his arms and laughed the smile of a beaten man. Dolly's index finger beckoned the roomless couple who moved as quickly as decency would allow without it appearing they were running.

Dolly embraced Marion and said, "You've been allocated the bridal suite. It must be vacated for the last two nights of your stay, as a young virile bridegroom has prepaid a large fee, but it's yours until then." Roger and Marion expressed their sincere thanks and gratitude. Dolly smiled and said, "There's nothing wrong that a bottle of champagne won't put right." Marion giggled and whispered to Roger, "I'm looking forward to a performance to match the virile groom before we have to move rooms." Roger grinned, "I shan't let you down, darling."

At the end of an hour's relaxed occupation of the four-poster in the bridal suite, Marion whispered, "This holiday was such a good idea of mine, wasn't it, darling?"

Roger cringed. The perversity of women. A short time previously it was "Let's take a taxi to the airport". Now it had been turned in to "What a wonderful holiday we are having".

## *Chapter 4*

A table for six had been laid in a curtained annexe off the main dining room. Dolly's influence was apparent. The group had their own serving staff, its chief a short chubby waiter with an eternal chuckling laugh that melted the hearts of the ladies.

Dolly became "mother" and directed the charges to her seating plan. Roger was placed next to Dolly. Her sister-in-law, Ada, was on his right. Jim sat to Ada's left. Marion made up the 'Jim' sandwich with Billy on her left.

"There are worse places in the world," Roger murmured to Dolly.

"A lot, lot worse," she replied "and not many better."

After the wine had been poured Ada's curiosity had the better of her. "What do you do for a living, Roger?"

Roger had pre-empted the question. He considered it would be more diplomatic describing a previous job he had departed from some years ago, rather than his current position as a Customs and Excise officer.

"I'm an accountant, Ada, trying to save my clients a lot of their hard-earned money from the tax man. Obviously we stay within the law with the advice we give but we usually save the fee we charge clients with the less tax they pay. In many cases clients gain a considerable bonus." Jim grimaced and said with feeling, "I could have done with you when I was trading in Birmingham. It was nearly two years ago, but it was the bleeding tax man that brought me to my knees."

Dolly looked disapprovingly at her husband. "Let's leave the topic whilst we're on holiday, your problems stem from more than interest from the taxman."

Jim held his arms forward, palms spread upwards, an innocent look on his face as if he had been greatly maligned. "You remember when the tax man brought the bailiff round in a taxi, took my 'Roller' away without warning?"

"You shouldn't have left the key in the ignition," she replied. Marion opened her mouth to interject, but thought better of it.

Roger smiled at his wife, thinking how beautiful she looked. There was little doubt in his mind that the treatment she had received in the four-poster during the hour before attending dinner had given her a glow of serenity. Her strapless black velvet dress showed off her smooth white neck, which was adorned by a five-stone diamond necklace, the largest stone in the bottom centre placed half an inch higher than her most attractive cleavage. 'A beautiful woman will be more than welcome in any crowd of people,' he thought.

Marion, turning half left, said to Jim heatedly, "You musn't argue with your wife in company. In fact you shouldn't argue with your wife when you're not in company."

"That would be boring," said Ada. "Surely the benchmark of domestic bliss is a good old fashioned row."

Dolly replied tartly, "I don't know how you reach that conclusion, dear sister-in-law, since you are still a spinster."

"And I'll remain one if the arguments you and Jim have are the hallmark of wedded bliss."

* * * * *

The tomato and fennel soup was being served, the verbal contestants had ceased their battle, both were now smiling.

Billy Cornwell was into his second helping of the red soup. "This is wonderful, mother, almost as good as your home cooking," he said diplomatically. Dolly's eyes lit up.

Billy continued. "It's great to get away from filing gold strips; such intense concentration."

At the mention of gold, Roger's ears pricked. "Do you use much gold in your business? Seems an expensive commodity."

"Oh, it is very expensive, the art is to buy only as much as you are to use on a particular operation. Mother makes us search the floors for any small particles that we have filed and not used in the mount, and the contents of the vacuum cleaner are sifted."

"Waste not, want not," replied Dolly brusquely.

"Where do you buy your gold from? I hear it's cheaper to buy abroad, maybe in Spain?" Roger Long asked naively.

Dolly looked serious in her response. "We use only very small amounts. Gone are the days when we manufactured in a large way. We buy the commodity from a local dealer." Roger thought she seemed wary about using the word 'gold'. It was the second time in two minutes she'd used the word 'commodity'. He goaded the company.

"Are there many dealers in the Birmingham area?"

Billy replied, "Yes, for the size of the city it has more than its fair share. Many years ago, before my time, our firm did some dealing. I remember Uncle Albert talking about it, seemed to make more money selling gold stocks than from manufacturing jewellery." His mother took up the story.

"That would be in the mid-nineteen seventies when inflation rose by more than fifty per cent in a two year period. I know my building society savings, in real money terms, had halved over that period. However, the gold price increased considerably more than the inflation rate and we had been lucky enough to have bought a considerable amount of the commodity at very low prices two years before. Orders for jewellery had fallen alarmingly during those depressive days. Albert and myself had a meeting and made a conscious decision to turn all our commodity stocks into cash at the highest market prices there have ever been. Weren't we lucky?" she said, almost to herself, "We only buy minute amounts these days on a 'what we need now' basis. This paella is succulent," she continued.

Marion had been captivated, "How interesting to be involved in a commodity as fascinating as gold. If you ever hear of a vacancy from one of your bullion dealers I should be pleased to hear of it." Dolly gave her a non-committal smile.

"The paella does taste scrumptious, the chef deserves a drink," reiterated Ada.

"Charge it to the bridal suite," interjected Marion. Roger glanced at his wife, thinking the Treasury will pick up the tab. He must ask Marion to tone down his generosity.

The group were now into the second bottle of vintage Rioja. "Almost as good as the Vina Sol white," remarked Ada. "Isn't it marvellous to be on holiday? What makes it better is to have met you both, Marion looking so elegant and you, Roger, so suave."

"Have another glass of the Rioja, Ada, I like the way you talk. You've convinced me about my appearance."

Marion sniffed. "How easy it is to flatter a man," she whispered to Dolly.

Jim had recovered his second time around. "Let's finish off with coffee and a brandy." Then he re-opened his earlier topic of conversation. "You know, Roger, if I'd had someone as smart as you I wouldn't have lost my business or gone bust. I could do the clever work turning used waste paper into marketable recycled paper ready to use as new. The high percentage of profit was mind blowing. I had a staff of over 100 employees at my zenith, the majority of them collecting waste paper from designated roads in and around Birmingham and the black country."

Marion asked, "How did you go bankrupt if you didn't need to buy your raw materials? It's only waste paper and that's picked up for only the labour cost of collecting it?"

"Wagons are expensive to hire and you need trained drivers," Jim replied.

Dolly, steamed to boiling point, her blue Bol liqueur further freeing her abrasive tongue, said, "It's little to do with the high cost of hiring vehicles. It's the heavy expenditure he incurred in backing slow racehorses. Jim's known to all the leading bookmakers in Birmingham, in fact one of them paid a runner to chum him up and accompany him to take his wagers. Apart from the heavy cost of maintaining leading bookmakers in the style to which he has made them become accustomed, he's always looking for the easy way to make a fortune. He now knows from bitter experience there's no easy way to make it big."

Jim interrupted, "You and your bloody brother don't do too bad!" Dolly glanced at him with a wickedly fierce look but said nothing.

Roger Long whispered to his wife, "I wonder what that was all about?"

Marion replied quietly, "They've drunk too much of the products of the vine." Then changing the subject, she asked, "How are you earning your hundred grand a year now, Jim?"

Jim smiled before answering. "Firstly, I don't earn a hundred grand a year or anything like it but I think you were goading me, Marion?"

Marion gave a disarming smile. "Perhaps I was, but you seem an interesting man, a quick-decision maker."

Dolly intervened saying, "Oh, he is all of that, especially picking an obvious winner at Ascot, but I am told that is in the past now."

Jim gave a grimace, but he manfully struggled to tell his story. "It was almost a year ago to the day that I became a bankrupt. On that fateful day I had been berated and belittled by a pompous Official Receiver, a little man with a black moustache that made him look like Hitler. He even goose stepped around his office to impress me of his importance. He rubber-stamped the bankruptcy petition that had been brought against me by the Solicitor General acting on behalf of the Inland Revenue for unpaid Income Tax." Looking at Roger Long, Jim continued, "How I wished I'd known you at that time, Roger. I didn't know which way to turn. The Collector of Taxes said he would have the shirt off my back. He only left me with the tools of my trade, which was an out of date printing press that I had made obsolete years ago." Marion wondered whether she had done the right thing in priming Jim's story. She looked at him apologetically.

"I am sorry. I didn't know things were that bad, but by the fine quality of the clothes you're wearing, matters must have improved in the last few months? Certainly the fine quality shirt you're now sporting must be an improvement on the one the Official Receiver removed from your back?"

Jim nodded. "Sometimes fate smiles at you. As I was leaving the Official Receiver's office, head down, hands in my raincoat pockets, I literally bumped into a smartly dressed business man walking briskly through Piccadilly Arcade. With a big grin, he put his arm around my shoulder. 'Jim you old rascal, how are you?' he says. I immediately recognised John Turvey. We had been printer's apprentices at the same time, now over thirty years ago. In the Ink and Print Department of the old Evening Despatch, long since taken over by the Birmingham Post & Mail. John was now Chairman and Managing Director of the Post & Mail.

"It had been over two years since we last met at the Press Club's Ladies' evening. I was crestfallen having to inform a very successful businessman that I was now a bankrupt. Still with his arm clutched around my shoulder, he said, "Let's slip into the 'Fiddle and Pipe'. Things can't be as bad as you make out." We entered the warmth of the lounge bar, a roaring open coal fire greeted us. We sat as near to it as we could without singeing our knees. With a pint of best bitter, and a very agreeable companion, life had its brighter side."

Dolly interrupted Jim's story. "John Turvey is a fine man. After he and Jim passed their printing exams in the early sixties, the four of us socialised. I became great friends with his new wife, June. Our first babies were born within a few weeks of each other and for four years we were inseparable. Jim continued to work for the Evening Despatch but John, even in those early years, had ambitions of greatness and took a job as an assistant editor with the old News Chronicle in Fleet Street. They bought a house in Blackheath, his meteoric climb through the ranks is now history."

Jim was as equally enthusiastic about his friend's success. He continued from Dolly. "When the Daily Express took over the Chronicle, newspaper mergers were common at that period of time, John became City Editor. Dolly and I were avid readers of the share tips he gave. His financial writings were always worth following. I put our share gambles into Dolly's name, lucky for us that capital was immune from little Hitler."

Roger Long pontificated. "Lifelong friendships are a rare occurrence and should be nurtured."

Jim returned to the happenings on that fateful morning. "We were now on our second pint of best bitter, the fire had dwindled to embers. John's white starched collar glistened with perspiration. I noticed he was wearing his old Edwardian blue and green striped tie. He was now sporting a pencil thin black moustache. Indeed he looked what he was – a highly successful businessman. I felt I could have achieved the same dizzy heights."

Dolly gave a resigned smile. "You had the brains but not the disciplined character of John. You probably gave me a more exciting life than John gave to June but his strength lay in his firm resolve that he was right and nothing would shake him from it. Still, it wouldn't do for all of us to be hatched out of the same egg."

Jim took a long draught from his red wine glass before continuing. "John Turvey looked me in the eyes and remarked, 'Something must be done for you, Jim, we have known each other too many years for you to sink without trace.' His eyes glazed and he chuckled aloud as he reminisced. "Remember the time, must be thirty years ago now, when the chief sent me out to buy a bottle of rainbow ink? Jessie, the counter woman at Pope's the stationers, cottoned on to the old bugger's trick. She told me they had green, magenta; yellow and grey ink, but they had sold the last bottle of rainbow ink. The bosses laughed themselves silly when I told them. I'd only been working at the Despatch for two days, fresh from school."

Dolly laughed out loud and said, "That must have been about the same time they sent Jim to the shops for a bottle of Philadelphia. Stars haircream; no such thing, of course."

Jim added, "When I came back with a bottle of Missouri Moon ladies' hair lacquer they weren't so amused. Foreman Stan didn't like me spending his money on that. Then John looked at his watch and said, 'Gracious, we've been ranting on about the old days for over an hour. Let's get back on track. Is the Receiver taking your house to pay the debt?' I told him the house was in joint names with Dorothy here and so long as she paid the mortgage from her own earnings the roof over our heads was safe. However, my factory was closed down and the property impounded for the benefit of the Inland Revenue. The bastards just won't give a man a break. My friend became thoughtful. Silence reigned for a minute or two. 'Why not?' he said, more to himself than to me. 'Old Bob Miller is retiring at the end of next month. He's given a life's service to the industry. The Company will see he will be well looked after. His newsround needs pepping up, he's not the speedy Gonzales we used to know. I am sure you can put the zip into the journey from the city centre to Lichfield. It's a well rewarded job, £25,000 a year salary to the chief. You would have two assistants, they're each on a half of what you will receive. Your package would include an excellent pension scheme, not forgetting free newspapers, and private use of the vehicle.'

Jim continued, "This was music to my ears, after the treatment I'd just received from the Official Receiver – he also called me a pathetic grotesque man with no thoughts for anybody else but myself. I had to restrain from punching his face."

Dolly interjected. "That temper of yours will put you in prison if you are not careful. However, you seem to be over the worst of it and John's embargo on you to stop betting has done our finances a power of good. I can buy creamed milk instead of skimmed," she joked, before continuing in a serious vein. "Jim's health has improved since he has been delivering newspapers in bulk to retail outlets in Lichfield. He's had little time to call into public bars or smoke his usual forty a day. Both of us have a lot to thank John Turvey for."

It was turned midnight when the annex curtains were drawn back. Roger remarked, "We are the last diners, seems we have out-stayed our welcome. Tables have already been laid for morning breakfast."

As they left the dining room, Jim asked, "Did you like the meal?"

"Wonderful," the bridal suite occupants answered in unison.

Dolly had a sudden thought. "Jim's fifty in August. When we come back later in the year, perhaps you would return with us for the celebrations?" she queried.

"Thank you, we'll let you know nearer the time," Roger replied.

## *Chapter 5*

The happy couple spent the next two days acclimatising themselves to the delights of the hotel. They had certainly struck lucky. The Cornwells had been extremely kind. The sun shone, hours were spent by the Olympic size pool which ceased at the diving board end within a few feet from an idyllic beach, a walk of only fifty metres leading into the sparkling blue sea. Roger had to shake himself to concentrate on the real reason the British Civil Service was footing the bill for such luxury.

A half day trip brought the second-time-around honeymooners to the fishing village of Mogan, three kilometres from the hotel. They sat in beach deck chairs, hired for a few pesetas, feet resting on the harbour wall, watching the first wave of fishing boats returning with their catch. Mogan was famous for its shrimps, calamari, and Roger's favourite, sole. He said to Marion, "You have to be lucky to find a sole with deep soft texture that hits your taste buds with an exquisite feeling, leaving you in no doubt the fish was heaven sent. A glass of Andalusian white Rioja accompanying such a fish would be the meal I would choose immediately prior to the hangman saying 'Step forward, Roger Long'."

Marion retorted, "They don't do such barbaric acts nowadays, but I know what you mean. I think my last meal would be chunks cut from the hock bone of a newly boiled shoulder of ham, supplemented by a sauce boat filled with white parsley sauce. The glass, or even two, I would choose would be from the Chablis region of France. Thinking about it if I had to face the ordeal you are referring to, I think I would need two bottles of the stuff. Then I would be anaesthetised against pain where my necklace sparkles."

Roger retorted, "Hanging's too good for the people I am looking for."

"Oh, who's that?" His wife's curiosity was aroused.

"I was asked to keep the real reason for our 'free holiday' from you. My chief said the least you knew the least you could chatter about it. I now think otherwise. I am searching for gold smugglers."

Roger went on to recount the facts of his meeting at the British Treasury with the Chancellor of the Exchequer.

Marion replied, "That answers a lot of questions that have been worrying me, aspects of your behaviour have been strange indeed." There was silence for a couple of minutes whilst the two of them assimilated their new position, then Marion replied, "Now that I realise the significance of our visit, I want to help you, darling, and thank you for your trust in me."

It was approaching dinner time, leaving the couple little time to take the return walk to the hotel. The luxury of a taxi cost the British Exchequer a few more pesetas but it gave the happy couple time to make full use of the four-poster. Roger closed the curtains as Marion removed her bikini. "Let's enjoy our next few hours – I can smell trouble tomorrow."

As they were dressing for dinner, a radiant Marion questioned her husband, who was relaxing in a blue armchair with a yellow King's Hotel crest on the back rest. "If we're successful on this trip, darling, ask your new bosses for a bonus, to be spent on the purchase of a four-poster. I am getting to enjoy the feeling for them, I now know the buzz the ladies of the harem feel when the sheik closes the flap on their private marquee in the desert."

Roger raised his glass of scotch and soda and said, "Ill definitely drink to that."

* * * * *

By a coincidence Dolly Cornwall and the Longs asked the concierge to call a taxi within seconds of each other the following morning. Roger remarked, "Early birds catch the worm, where are you off to on such a fine morning?"

"I'm asking you the same question," Dolly replied defensively.

"Oh, we're off to sample the delights of the Palm Range Golf Course,' lied Marion.

"It's a game I've never taken to, it takes too much valuable time," Dolly answered.

"You probably spend as much time practising and performing your cello arrangements, surely it's what you do with your time that matters."

Dolly nodded, "Perhaps you're right, my two Sons are now involved with the golf bug, Michael especially. I'd like you to meet him, a real entrepreneur. He's destined to take his uncle's place as Chairman of Neweys. I'm a minority shareholder, brother Albert is the major shareholder, but has no children of his own."

Roger was interested in anyone who traded in gold and was showing an interest for her to continue her narrative, but Marion changed the subject.

"Jim's not with you, doesn't he accompany you on these little excursions?"

Dolly answered, "No, he's content being spoilt by his sister, she loves to do it and he's more than happy taking the local wine, lounging near the pool bar and being told what a wonderful man he is, rather than being harried by me on a shopping trip."

The taxi stopped in the harbour area of Puerto Rico. Roger jumped out and opened the door for Dolly, handing to her the attaché case. She gave them a smile and waved "Bon Dias!" The taxi continued to the British Embassy, a mile away, situated in a side street but protected from the fierce rays of the midday sun by the shade thrown out from the fifteenth century grand cathedral.

By appointment a Consul was waiting with morning tea and biscuits. "Very civilised to see you retain old British traditions," Marion said to the very tall slim aide who greeted them.

"Yes, wish we were as successful at pointing a finger in the direction of gold smugglers," he laughed. "I meet many criminals in the large hotels, all of whom have fled the old country. No extradition from here, of course. Often I am accosted by men whose crimes are well documented, seeking news from the United Kingdom."

"I understand you have a number of photographs and listed records that may help us?" Roger Long asked.

"Yes, we have a full rogues gallery," he replied. He then opened a blue-covered album bulging with photographs and typed data. "That's Charles Friend, he manufactured the early washing machines. A Jewish lad with a good idea, direct selling to the customer from the manufacturer, cutting out the retail shop. He cut the cost of the washing machine to the consumer by a considerable margin, and became the darling of the housewives. He brought their toil on washdays to a minimum. The large stores were deeply envious of his methods. They were very concerned if his methods were used for other commodities. Refrigerators and television sets were mentioned, it could ruin retail stores as we know them. Sadly he became greedy for quicker profits, cutting corners on the manufacturing of washing machines, couldn't fulfil orders quickly enough. Several machines short circuited, killing a woman in Leeds and a baby in Dover. The shares in his company which stood at over eight pounds each in their heyday went down to fifty pence in a three month period. He, of course, sold his own shares at the top of the market and absconded to Spain. He's boasted to me since I've been here that he's made several secretive visits to the UK, bringing back to Gran Canaria suitcases full of British currency, That was in the days of exchange control when transferring currency between foreign countries was restricted to one hundred pounds each visit. Charles Friend was charged in the United Kingdom with two unlawful killings and illegally transferring boodles of cash, but he's never stood trial."

"Are there many like that?" Marion gasped.

The Consul replied, "Just keep looking at the photographs and reading the information attached to them. You will soon become aware that Spain and its islands contain more serious villains than the population of all the gaols in Britain combined."

"What a terrible chain of events," replied Roger Long, "but what have you on gold smuggling? That's solely where our interests lie."

The lanky Consul spread his arms in bewilderment, looked up at a portrait of a young Queen Elizabeth riding side-saddle on a chestnut gelding at the Trooping of the Colour in 1963. "I have a particular album for them, but I hadn't been informed your brief was so specific." Opening a red-coloured album, be continued talking. "I thought when I began the second volume I would soon fill it up to match the bulk of the first volume, this one." He plumped his hand hard onto the page that Marion Long was avidly reading. "But no, only two pages contain information and no photographs. The difference between the two albums is that the villains who live permanently in the Spanish islands will not go back home, so they're careless in their utterances. In fact they are proud of their criminal conquests. Whereas gold smugglers keep their activities under wraps as they 'will o' the wisp' back and forth to the old country on the particular scam they are currently involved in."

"No, it's only gold that interests us," said Roger Long, seated comfortably in a brown upholstered chair, which the Consul confided was the same type ensconced in every British Embassy and consulate office throughout the globe. It was one of the few actions ordered by King Edward VIII during his short reign in 1936.

Roger commented, "This chair is most comfortable, must have a valuable antique value now. However, reverting to our problem, where do we start to look?"

The Consul, looking more doubtful as the interview progressed, said, "Have a walk round the harbour area, try the Victoria Hotel, ask the immigrant villains what they know about gold smugglers. Most of them are now upright citizens. The Spanish police have them constantly under surveillance. The Marina is a tourist attraction in itself Sheik Bageralti's yacht is worth looking at, sorry I can't be more specific."

Having left the consulate building, Marion remarked, "Didn't get much help there. Let's have morning coffee in the Victoria Hotel, seems exciting to be able to rub shoulders 'with real criminals."

* * * * *

The hotel was in extensive grounds, the buildings having been completed in white concrete stucco, the heavily watered lawns gaily bedecked in buntings attached to each sun parasol. Guests relaxed over morning coffee. In front of the hotel, the Paseo Maritimo had five lines of traffic, each line full of vehicles, nose to tail, edging slowly between numerous traffic signals. The Paseo Maritimo was the only division between the hotel grounds and the newest most splendid Marina in Europe, built regardless of cost and financed by funds provided by the European Community.

The international section of the Marina was cluttered with yachts and boats of all sizes, each flying its national identity emblem. The most expensive yacht yet built stood pride of place directly facing the Victoria Hotel's open air restaurant. The Consul had informed them heatedly that the cost of the yacht was paid for from oil revenue ceded to its owner, Sheik Bageralti. A man who had never paid any taxes in his life.

Marion said to Roger, "Here are we looking for pennies from gold smuggling and that man earns millions of pounds each day without turning his hand to physical work."

Roger answered, "It's not a few pennies we are looking for. We are trying to focus on many hundreds of millions of pounds that have depleted the Treasury coffers over the last few years."

In the shadow of the Saudi yacht was moored a Spanish vessel, flying a Barcelona identity flag.

* * * * *

The anxious couple sauntered hand in hand past the Saudi yacht, gazing curiously through the open porthole windows. The Sheik's four children were taking lessons from a European tutor who seemed exasperated by his task. Before Roger could comment, Marion gripped his arm tightly.

"Stop, look at the Spanish ship in the shadow of the Sheik's yacht."

Dolly Cornwell appeared at the top of the gangplank. She had lost her bandbox look of earlier in the day, her hair was straggled, lipstick smudged, but a wide smile brightened her face. She pushed her fingers through her brown locks as a tidy-up operation. She was followed to the top of the gangplank by a Spanish naval officer with three bands of gold braid on the epaulets of a steaming perspiring white shirt. Dolly still held the attaché case by her side, but had eyes only for her escort. At the foot of the gangplank a voice in hesitant English said, "I'll get a taxi for you."

"No, don't bother," was her reply. "I'll walk to the rank, it's only two hundred metres." They turned to each other, Dolly placed the attaché case on the promenade, pressed tightly between her ankles, they kissed passionately. Marion retorted, "That's a lot more than a perfunctory peck on the cheek, which is my usual farewell to a friend."

The Longs waited in the shadow of the Saudi yacht till the farewell greeting came to a conclusion. Roger then came out of the shadow and hailed Dolly. She was flustered, her face reddened with embarrassment at the sudden intrusion. With a supreme effort she recovered her formal status, "Why, Roger and Marion, how nice to see you again, so soon after our taxi journey. May I introduce you to Matteo Estartis, an old friend of many years acquaintance." She hesitated before continuing. "We first met when Matteo worked for the Thames Police at the Port of London. He was over from Madrid on a two year exchange visit." The sailor gave Roger a firm handshake and kissed Marion gently on both cheeks.

"That's more of a French greeting, but you Spaniards are certainly learning new arts since entering the Common Market," Marion said laughingly to the sea captain. She then suggested the four of them should take coffee in the Victoria.

Dolly was quick to interrupt. "No, I think we should return to the hotel in Mogan, otherwise Jim will begin to think I have another man," she said with a huge smile.

The Longs asked if they could share a taxi. An Oldsmobile appeared as if by magic. The rear seat enveloped the three travellers with room to spare. Roger's curiosity had been inflamed. "I didn't know you were so well connected in this part of the world?" he queried.

Dolly answered, "It's one of those coincidences that occasionally happen. It was long before I met Jim. We indulged ourselves in my favourite hobby. Matteo came to love it with the same deep feeling as myself"

Marion was curious. "What hobby was that, Dorothy?"

Dolly replied, "During the early 1930's, when the depression in the industrial Midlands was at its height, my Aunt Gertrude moved to London. She'd heard jobs were easier to come by. Within six months she had met and married a docker from East Ham. He never wore a tie in his life, not even at their wedding. He had a muffler round his neck that day. However, he was the Pearly King of Upton Park. In the mid-fifties as a little girl I used to visit Aunt Gert and Uncle Alfie and eventually became involved with their cult. I joined the Pearlies. It was really exciting.

"Matteo and myself almost married; being a Spanish Naval Officer, although very junior at the time, he needed the permission of the Admiralty in Madrid. This was refused. It appeared they didn't think my station in life was good enough. He was returned to Spain within a week of the application being rejected. During our time together Matteo shared my enthusiasm for all things Cockney and became the first Spanish Pearly King in history. I'm certain there hasn't been one since, either. My dear Matteo is unique in that respect." Having gathered her thoughts she continued, "Say nothing to Jim about what you have seen and heard today, the events were before his time and he does get very jealous."

Roger commented, "You do seem to have a varied life. You should write a book, written properly it could become a best seller."

The ten mile return journey had been completed. As the taxi pulled up at the foot of the stone stairs leading to the hotel reception, Dolly looked through the rear window. "Can't see any sign of Jim. I did forewarn him on my mobile."

Roger opened the taxi's rear door and said to Dorothy, "Let me take your case." The brown case, which first thing in the morning had been a light weight, now needed both of his hands to lift. He remarked, "What are you carrying in this case, Dorothy, gold bars?"

Dorothy's smile was almost enigmatic. "Don't strain yourself dear. It's a dozen bottles of vintage claret to help celebrate Jim's 50th later in the year."

Roger had covered only a few steps with the case clutched in both arms when Jim appeared from the direction of the swimming pool. "Didn't you get my mobile?" said a severe sounding wife.

"Sorry, dear, they only gave me your message a couple of minutes ago."

His wife replied, "It's your sister, she certainly spoils you. Treats you as a seven year old in short trousers. Had it not been for Roger here, I don't know what I would have done with the dozen bottles of claret. All for you, of course. I will speak to Ada later."

"Poor Jim," Marion whispered to Roger. "She'll let him have it when they're alone."

* * * * *

The holiday was four days old, Roger and Marion Long were no nearer discovering a gold smuggler. On the fifth morning, more in hope than expectation, they returned to the Victoria Hotel in Puerto Rico. The immigrant criminal element that had fled the United Kingdom to Gran Canaria had found a wonderful watering hole. Their unofficial club was on the second floor of the hotel. The management discouraged other visitors to the particular lounge bar where the prices were half as much again as those in other hotel bars. The immigrant bar had been decorated and created regardless of cost.

The lounge bar was decorated with four seven foot ironclad armoured knights standing at each corner of a squared Axminster carpet of black and white squares resembling a huge chessboard. A pianist with a bristling black moustache, a cream coloured double-breasted suit, blue handkerchief flapping from his breast pocket, was giving the keys a hard time. His lungs occasionally belted out a tune. 'My Way' was popular with the British criminal fraternity; the song was their signature tune. Most of them had done it 'their way', not caring if 'their way' had been legal or not. A crowd clustered around the art deco bar, a number of them waving large denomination peseta notes to the cocktail shaker impatient for his attention.

Roger Long brought two 'Bloody Marys' back to their table. Marion, who had been perusing the other customers, said, "There's Charles Friend at the table overlooking the marina, a beautiful woman with him don't you think?"

Roger directed a look. "Wouldn't have noticed her if you hadn't mentioned it, dear."

"Liar," she remarked coolly.

Roger made an attempt to converse with the occupants of the next table. This proved fruitless, their mother tongue was Russian. Looking past Marion he noticed Charles Friend walking from the cocktail bar. He followed him to the washroom. While the old villain was standing at a pissoir completely in oblivion, Roger placed a hand on his shoulder, saying, "Charles Arthur Friend I am arresting you for fraudulent conversion of currency." The ex-washing machine king turned suddenly, looked across the hand on his shoulder and in a dry, frightened voice said, "What the hell, who the hell are you?"

Roger Long replied, "I'd like to talk to you about the reasons you left the United Kingdom so suddenly in 1978." After zipping up, Friend replied "You can't nick me here! There's an extradition treaty, f**k off."

Roger laughed "Only a belated April fool's joke, wondered what reaction I'd get."

Charlie Friend shook the joker by his jacket lapels. "Don't do that again. If my hands had been free you would have received a right uppercut. You'd have known about it too, me being middleweight champion of the Navy for three years."

Roger Long apologised, but thought at least someone was talking to him. He could now appreciate the Spanish beauty at close quarters when he and Marion joined their table. Charlie blurted to Marion as soon as they were introduced, "Your man made me urinate over my hands!" Then he related an unabridged version, adding a few embellishments. Both women's eyes sparkled with amusement.

As an aside Roger asked, "Have you been back to London recently?"

Charlie Friend, in his broad Cockney accent, said, "No, I haven't been back in three years. It's not that I don't want to, I miss that crazy city something awful, I was born within the sound, if you know what I mean." Roger nodded his understanding.

Friend continued. "It's physically painful not going back, but the last time, I was observed near to Canary Wharf and lucky to reach the plane back here before Scotland Yard reacted. No, I'm incarcerated just as if I was in Dartmoor.

Marion replied, "I'm sure it's much more comfortable here than there."

Charlie nodded, keen to change the course of conversation. "Are you staying on the island for any length of time? We could socialise more. Help Paulo with her English."

Roger shook his head, "No, we're due back in the UK on Saturday. I'm here looking for villains who buy gold in Gran Canaria and then smuggle it into the UK. After a month or so they sell the gold to legitimate traders, then issue a sales invoice and add Value Added Tax. The villains get paid in full. Instead of paying over the tax element to the government, they close their bank account and their company disappears into the night. Know anyone who fits the bill?"

Charlie shook his head. "Wished I'd thought of that myself; people don't get hurt making boodles of cash typing out false documents. Besides, it's not criminal relieving the government of money."

Roger became annoyed, "The UK taxpayers are losing many millions of pounds to these smugglers. It's not funny."

Friend replied, "You're definitely edgy, you seem to be losing sleep over this. Sorry, there's no-one I can put the finger on. Today's villains don't want to know yesterday's crooks. We have nothing in common. The heat is still on them. We live in the cool of retirement. I'd appreciate something to get the adrenalin flowing again. Wish I could help. Can I?" he said with a sudden after-thought.

"Paulo and me sit at this table for at least a couple of hours a day over lunch. Sometimes another hour or so after the afternoon siesta."

Paulo interrupted Charlie's drift. "It's interesting to see the people entering and leaving the ships, the passionate kisses from some of the captains and sailors make me think the men must have been at sea a long time. They are earnest for the ladies to visit and the ladies always walk down the gangplanks with large smiles on their faces. Ooh la la!" She added a wicked wink to Marion. "Women know about these things."

Marion smiled her agreement, then queried, "Any particular activities in the last few days?"

Paulo thought before replying. "Yes, there's a woman who comes with a fair haired young man sometimes, but yesterday she came alone, I remember I was just finishing my morning coffee and brandy, Charlie had gone to the bar for another. In fact, I'm sure I saw the two of you greet her?

"That's correct," Marion answered. "You certainly have sharp eyes, but please continue."

Paulo carried on speaking. "She seems a great friend of the captain of the small boat nearest to the Sheikh's yacht. I wonder if they have some action going?"

Charles Friend interrupted his escort. "Don't say too much, I don't want to have to return home as a prosecution witness," he laughed.

The pianist was now playing 'Chicago', another popular song in the cocktail bar. Charlie was humming quietly.

Roger smiled, and flashed his eyes at Paulo. "The woman you're referring to is a friend of ours. There may be some activity with that Spanish sea captain but I think it's more immoral rather than illegal."

Marion interrupted. "Couldn't you offer Charlie immunity to return home? If he was a good boy, kept his eyes open for people who could interest us?"

Charlie replied, "Please don't continue with that line. Villains must stick together, unless the price is right, of course." He smiled knowingly. "In this case the price need not be money."

Roger nodded. "Help me and I'll help you."

Paulo was looking anxious at the turn of events. In her enchanting broken English, she asked, "You will take me with you, Charlie, won't you?"

He laughed. "It's unlikely we are going anywhere, dearest, but I still dream of my old mother pining for me. In the ancestral home, in a back-to-back house next to Battersea gasworks."

## *Chapter 6*

"All good things come to an end," murmured Marion to Jim as they were boarding the mini-coach that was to take the Longs and Cornwells to the airport.

Jim replied, "Another excellent holiday, the hotel up to its usual standard, food first class, and the best pint of British beer outside the 'Fiddle and Pipe' in Birmingham's city centre."

Roger replied, "I've never been, but wasn't that the pub bought by two former members of the Northern Symphony Orchestra, one a violinist, the other played the flute? Used their pension monies, if I remember correctly?"

Dolly answered, "That's correct. Birmingham's needed a pub that encourages live classical music. The Mellow Cellos' have played there several times, doing lunchtime performances of popular classics. Although, I don't like the heavy smokey atmosphere, gets on my chest."

Roger whispered, "A very shapely chest if I may be so bold, especially the bikini top that shows off your cleavage so admirably."

Dolly blushed, "Don't be so saucy, Roger, your wife will be jealous, but I do like your little quips. Makes a woman feel wanted."

The minicoach was only minutes from the airport. Manuel, who had driven for the hotel since it opened, asked if arrangements had been made for the luggage to be transported through the Customs. Jim shook his head and asked Manuel to do this with the heavy suitcases. They would manage their own hand luggage.

* * * * *

The recently opened new airport was a tourist delight in itself. Having once experienced its attractions many tourists arrived early for their homeward flight. The departure concourse contained an eighty metres square open area. Its flooring had a light brown background, with non-slip diagonal white stripes ingrained in the metre square slabs of marble. The surrounding shops, many with international names of repute, gave the area a village atmosphere. Strolling players and pierrots provided a free show; their hope of reward was obvious with the differing types of containers into which travellers were encouraged to throw currency of any denomination. 'Irono', the strong man, only the briefest pair of leopard skin trunks to hide his modesty, boasted on the hour, every hour during daylight, that be would lie on a two metre long bed of nails. The nails pointing upwards had very sharp points. The most heavily built lady spectator was invited to stand on his chest and do a little dance. At two o'clock that afternoon an eighteen stone blonde German woman of mature years did away with her modesty, removed her pointed stilettos and jigged on Irono's chest to the music of 'The Can-Can'. The crowd cheered the dancer as she raised the front of her skirt in a fast up and down motion to the quick beat of the music. A huge set of Germanic drawers were on view to the laughing crowd Irono's collectors were busy with their buckets.

A self employed pickpocket, dressed in Union Jack trousers and a tricolour shirt, was darting in between tourists plying his trade. When a tourist showed the pocket of his money for Irono's collectors, he attacked those pockets opportunely and without mercy. Currency was the main source of attention, but passports had a high monetary value with the right fence. Jewellery would disappear from a lady as if a magician were involved. The market in wrist-watches was active with the male tourists. It was possible to have a wrist-watch stolen whilst watching a show and buy it back from a Joseph further along the concourse. "Even free shows have a price," Manuel said to Roger Long, as they stood together now that the heavy luggage had been booked onto the Birmingham flight.

A large crowd of tourists were gathered in the open area some 15 metres from the 'Man of Nails' show. The sham golfers were among the crowds of spectators to see Adekin, a young black lady belly-dancer perform 'The Dance of the Seven Veils'.

"Would she remove all seven?" Billy asked the leader of the Welshmen, who replied, "According to that note written in French, if spectators give generously she will." The anticipation drew a large crowd. The Spanish police who controlled the concourse knew she would not. The limits of any exhibition had been made plain to the travelling group of Moroccan traders.

The male friends of the black lady performer were all very tall men. Breeding tall people in a village near Kabu on the North African coast seemed mandatory.

"Must be lack of rain that makes them grow tall," remarked Jim Cornwell.

"Surely it's the other way round," sister Ada argued. "I hear monsoons hit their village regularly which miss the rest of the North African coast."

The trade of the villagers was itinerant salesmen to the Canary Isles, a journey of thirty miles by sailing boat. Kabu was the nearest land point to the dumping spot, established over a thousand years by merchant ships travelling the silk route from the Orient to Europe. Unwanted merchandise had been thrown overboard in the same area since time immemorial. Nearly all of this found the sandy beachline in and around Kabu. The villagers had a system of sharing. Any surplus was ferried to the many islands comprising the Canaries.

Garments from the dumped bundles were sewn together, usually from different bundles. The itinerant salesmen, wearing sewn up coats of several colours, were given the nickname 'Josephs'.

The Josephs were the helpers of the dancer. They protected her from unwanted admirers. The sham golfers had already clocked this. Even the effects of draught lager didn't give them the courage to consider chancing their luck with the performer of the seven veils.

Whilst the crowd waited patiently, the Josephs intermingled, showing wrist-watches, all with international brands. Mostly the names were mis-spelt. Longines had two g's in the Josephs' interpretation, Cartier was spelt with a 'k' as its first letter and a double 't'. The bantering of the crowd, wheeling and dealing on price, gave the concourse an additional buzz. Adekin was not to perform until the head Joseph gave her the nod. Money had to be made.

Billy Cornwell had bought and suffered financially from the Josephs on past journeys but he was still susceptible to the sucker punch. He was asked for 60 American dollars for a 'Karttier' watch. Turning away, he offered 10 dollars as an insult. The Joseph grabbed his shoulder painfully, and cheerfully accepted. Billy was also given a 'money back' guarantee.

The mostly male orientated crowd were beginning to show their impatience with jeers and chants of "Why are we waiting?"

Adekin received the nod and two multi-coloured Josephs appeared with matching crimson red turbans. They carried snake charmer pipes. By sitting cross legged two metres apart, they formed a stage for the belly dancer.

The first veil was not long in falling slowly and gracefully to the marble squares.

The music of the pipes moaned incessantly, the dancer gyrating her hips to its rhythm. The little finger on her left hand, gently inserted into a looped hook that maintained the second veil in its place, was poised. After several swaying motions and a male voice from the crowd urging her "to give us a break", her right hand raised to replace a lock of hair. Simultaneously, both hands swept across her breasts. The second veil fell beside its companion. The pipes continued falteringly. The musicians were not as experienced as the dancer.

The Welsh contingent were becoming impatient for faster action. "Get 'em off girl" came a raucous Richard Burton soundalike. A further nod from the leading Joseph and two more veils fell in quick succession. The highly amused Spanish policemen knew the dancer's limits. Even with four veils disrobed, not one inch of her skin had been revealed. The Josephs tried another round with their collecting buckets, but the crowd wanted action from the dancer. One of the collecting buckets was wrenched from a Joseph. It took two veils in quick succession to join their companions on the floor to rekindle the interest. At this, the sham golfers raised their beer arms in one motion. "Bravo!" they shouted. Only the last all-covering veil remained, more pipe music – "keep them waiting" she thought. It was a matter of timing. The pipes continued to grind out. The black beauty was now fingering the waist hook on the last veil. She pirouetted three steps, simultaneously let the last veil fall to the floor. She stood as nature intended. A coquettish smile and the most submissive of curtsies brought tumultuous applause from the crowd. Whistles blew, the sound of running hobnailed boots created heavy echoes on the marble floors. The Spanish police were disgruntled. The Josephs had not kept their word, they were determined to make arrests. A coat of many colours was hurriedly draped over Adekin, and with gazelle like speed the bunch of Josephs moved as one towards an emergency exit. The leader was clutching the money bag. The police and their heavy boots were no match in the uneven race; the black people won by a distance.

* * * * *

The relaxed atmosphere didn't stop Dolly Cornwell fretting along with her husband. The party had been called to the departure lounge. Manuel had checked the large suitcases directly to the airplane hold in the rear of the Boeing 747. All had experienced the security camera checks.

It was the hand luggage that caused Dolly and Jim consternation. They walked to the doorway frame. A 'bleep!' sound detected metal on a particular passenger or a substance which activated the security mechanism. Jim placed his car keys and the hotel key he had inadvertently brought away with him, in a wooden tray, before going through the frame.

Billy was chatting to the leader of the sham golfers as they entered the security system. As a bunch they Indian-filed through the detection doorway frame, Jim Cornwell joined them. Marion Long had already passed through. Roger had also forgotten to return his room key to the hotel reception before the minicoach departed; this caused him momentary embarrassment at the doorframe check as he had to suffer the frisk procedure from a guard. Dolly hung back with a crowd of German tourists entering for a similarly timed flight to Berlin. She placed her brown attaché case on a side ledge near to the wooden tray, then walked confidently through the frame.

Jim joined the sham golfers. He shouted his opening remark which was loud enough for all of them to hear. "It's a good job your wives don't know what you've been up to on this holiday. Make their hair curl from what Billy said happened in the beachside brothel."

The leader of the pack turned sharply. "Billy should keep his mouth shut, his mother's only fifty yards away. He's certainly no angel using the upstairs room with the brothel owner's blonde daughter. He came downstairs with the largest smile I've seen since I saw the Ken Dodd Show."

"That's untrue!" shouted Jim. "His mother wouldn't believe such a crowd of liars as you lot."

The provocation was too strong, the leader of the golfers, fresh from four pints of strong lager, threw his first punch. The glancing blow made Jim shake his head with pain. Billy retaliated with a full fist to the chin of the assailant. In seconds, a melee was in full flow.

Marion and Roger Long walked rapidly through the departure lounge towards the coaches taking the passengers to the aircraft. Jim and Billy Cornwell were heavily outnumbered. The golfing pack, sensing blood, and with the high alcohol level encouraging them, were throwing punches and kicking indiscriminately at the Cornwells. The Spanish policemen drew their batons and waded into the fray, hitting out at the nearest available limb.

At the height of the riot, Dolly picked up her brown attaché case and walked away from the checkpoint. The police batons did their work effectively, three golfers lay on the tarmac. Billy's ear was bleeding profusely from a bob punch. His father's left eye had already discoloured and was still swelling.

The melee had taken only a few minutes. The Spanish policemen had taken full retribution. The participants were made to form a line; the remaining passengers were taken to the buses for embarkation on the returning Boeing 747.

* * * * *

A police captain, arrived from Puerto Rico, walked up and down the line of sullen faced combatants. In broken English he chided the group. "You have behaved as little children, but my guards have made you see the errors of your ways. Do not come back to Gran Canaria. I shall know you. Those of you my men did not berate are the lucky ones." At gunpoint the group was marched the three hundred metres to the Boeing 747 and escorted on board. The captain of the plane was doubtful whether he should take responsibility for the malefactors, but encouragement from the remaining passengers to speed up the take-off, as well as the Spanish police issuing dire threats, persuaded him.

A shamefaced Billy sat in a first class seat next to his mother. His aunt had exchanged her seat for a seat next to Roger and Marion Long in standard class. Jim sat on the other side of his wife and whispered, "I'm getting too old for this game, Dol."

She nodded in agreement, "So am I. We'll talk frankly with Michael when we return."

The plane's return journey was helped apace by the following hot Mistral winds over the Mediterranean. The captain's voice came through the sound system. "Our journey will be curtailed to four and a quarter hours, the return flight will be a saving of forty minutes, but we will still have enough time to serve an afternoon meal in comfort prior to landing at Birmingham."

Having cleared Passport Control, Roger and Marion joined the subdued party of Cornwells, The sham golfers were almost mute. Alcoholic drink had been refused them on the flight. The concourse at Birmingham airport was full of grim faced policemen.

Carousel number three disgorged the heavy luggage. The men in the party snatched the cases. Dolly was clutching her brown attaché case, Jim is an obvious target for Customs, she thought, he reddens at the sight of their uniform. She joined her younger son in the trolley march through the green channel. Billy's lip had now swollen to go in tandem with a purple coloured ear.

Roger had not bothered with the duty free shop in Gran Canaria. He shouted to Dolly, "Give me your case of claret, I have some influence with the men in the green channel," The march through Customs officials to the awaiting meeting point of passengers was a formality.

A fair-haired man in his mid-twenties hailed Billy Cornwell. "What's the other fellow like?"

Billy grimaced, his contorted features giving considerable pain. "Hello, Mike, thanks for coming. Dad and I were in a bit of a fight at the airport at Gran Canaria. I'll bore you with the details on the way home."

Michael moved forward, kissed his mother and whispered, "Was it a successful trip?"

Dolly nodded. "Only just, but will you take the claret from our new friend Roger Long?"

Michael Cornwell obliged and introduced himself to Roger, who in turn introduced Michael to Marion. Marion's eyes shone, the newcomer's bearing and appearance left no doubt he was Billy's brother, but he had that something extra. Who was the lucky woman who shared his life? she thought. They continued a formal conversation. Michael asked how Marion liked Gran Canaria and the King's Hotel in particular. She replied what a lovely holiday she and Roger had enjoyed. "Would you go again?" he asked.

"At the first available opportunity," was her enthusiastic reply. Marion worried momentarily about the contents of his mother's attaché case. Michael's eyes lost their sparkle. He braced himself before asking, "What's the cause of your concern?"

Marion replied "I know something of foreign wines, some people think I have an expert's knowledge, and although I wouldn't make such a claim I do know that many vintages do not travel very well. There could be considerable disappointment when a bottle is opened."

Michael's smile and eye sparkle returned. "Oh, don't concern yourself. I'm sure the contents of mother's case will have travelled exceedingly well."

## *Chapter 7*

The busman's holiday paid for by the state had been the forerunner to starting work in earnest.

The largest building in Birmingham's commercial centre was housed entirely by government offices. The Inland Revenue section dealing with personal and company taxation took the top four floors of the sixteen-storey building. They had been Roger Long's employers until his recent application to Customs and Excise, who were located on floors three through to five.

Long's new office had wall to wall carpeting, a sure sign of his promoted status. When he received the executive toilet key, he had really arrived in the high echelons of the civil service. A senior secretary and a junior typist, who also acted as filing clerk, completed his personal staff.

Immediately on arrival at 8.30 am, an interview with the regional civil service controller left him in no doubt as to the priority of his work.

"The brief you received in London will be your only work until a breakthrough has been achieved. The highest ranking civil servants in this office and our colleagues in the Inland Revenue on the top floors have been instructed to give every co-operation. All you need to do is ask."

* * * * *

Roger Long sat in his office, sipping tea in real china cups and nibbling biscuits provided by the Queen's grocer in Piccadilly. He thought, "I must come up with the right result." He and Marion had talked long into the night, had they any successes? Roger thought he could use Charles Friend as an agent. The thought he could not remove from his mind was when a ghost company was repaid the tax on bullion it sold, it simply disappeared into thin air. All that remained was a file in the offices of the Registrar of Companies at the Board of Trade in Cardiff with either fictitious directors or directors supplied by formation agents who had no trading connection.

Long made his first telephone call in his new job. The female voice answering was her usual cheery self "Thompson Company Formations, good morning."

"Customs and Excise here, agent Roger Long speaking. I'd like to make an appointment to visit your offices, please."

"Why would you want to do that?" she answered.

Roger added severity to his tone. "To ascertain that you're complying with Value Added Tax rules and regulations"

"But we don't have anything to do with you," said the cheerful voice. "We're here to form companies."

"Who's your principal?"

"I work for myself," she said.

"Are you registered for Value Added Tax?"

"No, no need to," was the reply. "Our turnover's below the registerable limit."

Long answered, "You seem to know your way about the value added system."

"Oh, I'm commercially trained," retorted Sandra Poole.

"I'd still like to call at your offices."

"Well, if we don't need to register for the value added system I can't see what our records have to do with you."

"I could take out an Order under Regulation 734B to enforce entry and remove your books and records. I'd rather do it the easy way, but if you force me..."

The cheerful voice became sullen. "All right then, when do you want to come?"

A date was agreed.

Roger Long then made two further telephone calls of a similar nature to other formation agencies working from Birmingham's commercial zone.

* * * * *

Birmingham was being spearheaded because of its unique jewellery quarter, which was situated at the edge of the city on the east side. Most gold bullion dealers had started commercial life as manufacturing jewellers. They bought gemstones and bullion as necessary ingredients in a piece of finished jewellery, the larger manufacturers buying gemstones and jewellery in bulk and re-selling in smaller quantities to the one man bands at an enhanced price.

The larger wholesalers purchased diamonds, and gold in particular, directly from South Africa. Over a period of years, some, like Jardine's, had no need to manufacture and converted to buying and selling bullion. This led, in time, to forming their own merchant banking operation. They had discovered a niche market; from the profits of bullion dealing they loaned money to arms manufacturers to finance operations throughout the world, especially 'Third World' countries whose constant civil wars or wars with neighbouring countries to preserve national pride made Jardine's super wealthy.

Roger Long also remembered the Chancellor's words at their London meeting.

"As a gambling man, Birmingham is the favourite starting point in your quest. Most conventional bullion dealers are in that city so it is odds on there is a smuggling arm attached somewhere."

* * * * *

Long called his senior secretary to his office, a kindly soul in her late forties. Alice Cattell had worked for Customs long before her marble smooth cheeks had attracted a few wrinkles and her flaming auburn hair had become tinged with strands of grey. Her experience could prove invaluable.

"Please stop me from going up blind alleys," her chief asked.

Alice nodded, then advised "Start your compliance inspections at the largest printers in the Jewellery Quarter. Printers know earlier than other outlets when a new business is about to start operations. They have the initial order to provide stationery, letterheads, sales invoices and other sundry items. You can tell, by checking the copy letters on the printing office files, the categorisation of the type of trade their customers carry on. If a new business has authority to buy and sell bullion, make a compliance visit to their premises as quickly as possible."

Roger Long replied, "Yes, that's sound common sense. I'll follow that line."

His secretary then asked a favour. "Incidentally sir, all my time with the Service has been confined to this office, I would like to see some action as your assistant on a compliance visit if you could see your way clear?"

Roger Long replied, "Let's play it by ear, Alice. I will if I can." He changed the subject abruptly. "My first call must be to our new Registrations Department at Albany House in Wolverhampton."

Alice intervened. "I agree with that, you check your findings of new clients at the printers with the new registrations at Albany House. We know that bullion smugglers must register for Value Added Tax and enter the system so that they can complete quarterly returns and claim Value Added Tax on the gold they sell."

The couple covered other aspects that either of them considered would help in their quest. Roger concluded the discussion. "My first visit will be to see some familiar faces at Neweys, and immediately after that my second visit will be to K. J. Thomas."

*Chapter 8*

Albert Newey of Newey (Manufacturing) Jewellers Limited, greeted Roger Long warmly. Albert's limp handshake contrasted to that of the man from Customs. But Albert's eye twinkle and cherubic smile made Roger think 'This man is a born salesman'.

"You must meet my sister Dorothy. She keeps all the account books and will answer your queries. We have had these compliance visits before, so we know your usual line of questions." Albert's sister's office was a throwback to the early reign of George VI. She sat on a high stool at a long, dark brown mahogany desk, writing in a massive steel bound ledger. She was dressed very differently from the last time they met. White herring-bone pattern blouse, buttoned to the neck, a one-string set of dark grey pearls tightly fitting around her neck. A black full length skirt, side buttoned and tightly fitting at the waist.

"There's no need to introduce us, Albert. We met in Gran Canaria two months ago." Turning to Roger she turned her right cheek, which he dutifully kissed.

"You are much more formally dressed than on holiday. Do you remember, Dolly?"

Her eyes sparkled. "I do, Roger. You remarked about my neckline, If I remember correctly. However, we now meet under very different circumstances. What books, records and documents would you like to see?"

Albert Newey made a quick departure. "Books are not my line. Dorothy will call for some coffee and biscuits. If you do want me, my office is the second door on the left. It's more modern than this relic of the past, but Dorothy won't change it, says it reminds her of the days she first joined father's business as a slip of a girl."

Roger asked for the purchase invoices that related to goods that Newey Limited had transacted with Jardines and K. J. Thomas, the printing company standing in grounds directly opposite Newey's factory. Dorothy Cornwell brought in the tea and biscuits together with three thick files of purchase invoices. "All the goods we have bought and services we have required, like printing and petrol bills, are contained in these three files. They cover a period of twelve months. You will have to sift through yourself. I don't have the time to pull out the specific items you have asked for."

Roger Long smiled and accepted the files with thanks. He could now inspect every purchase invoice, not just a selected few. He knew from his days as a professional auditor that from examinations of apparent trivia, large frauds had been uncovered. After purchased merchandise had been followed through to the point of manufacture it sometimes showed that not all of the merchandise had been used; this suggested fraud or severe neglect. The same reasoning occurred when expenses were considered. Long remembered one salesman claiming enough petrol to have circumnavigated the world at least fourteen times in a six month period. The man received a one year gaol sentence for forgery.

When examining the purchase invoices, Long noted that gold was bought in small quantities from George Jardine & Sons Ltd. He examined the invoices carefully. On average there were three purchases each month of a few ounces of the precious metal. He asked Dorothy to show him how the gold was used.

She took him to a small workshop that still had the grime and dirt embedded in the walls of a hundred years of manufacturing. Coal had been firing the furnaces in those days, but the foundry had been redundant for the last twenty five years. During the time the furnaces had been in operation black smoke had coloured the skies of Birmingham and the surrounding districts. With numerous businesses adopting the same industrial method, it was apparent where the term 'Black Country' originated.

Michael Cornwell, seated behind a lathe, was turning a half inch section of an alloyed metal bar into the shape of a chain link. This to be joined by nine identical pieces to form a high quality bracelet. He had a single telescopic lens entrenched in his right eye, looking over and directly into the link. A diamond stone, held securely in the claws of a pair of tweezers, was about to be dropped into the linked cup. This accomplished, he tightly closed the metal claws with tiny pliers to keep the stone entrenched in the cup attached to the bracelet. He had already completed eight of the nine cups. Michael's concentration was disturbed. Both men recognised each other from their brief meeting at the airport. They shook hands.

"Quite an eye testing operation you're working on," Long remarked. "The concentration must make it a younger man's trade."

Michael continued. "Older men can do it, but the more mature you are the slower you become. I'm okay at present but in another ten years I will be working at half the speed I am now. We need young apprentices to train but the metal schools simply can't find the right quality. However, that's our problem. How can I help you?"

Roger Long acknowledged his cue. "I'm following the trail of the gold you bought on the 18th July from Jardines to its source in a piece of jewellery."

"Quite easy – we are manufacturing six gold and diamond necklaces with matching earrings for an order from Asprey's for their Christmas trade. We always buy gold for a specific job. It is too expensive a metal to carry in stock in any great quantity. When criminals know of gold stocks the information passes like wildfire. Our burglary insurance only covers us for six ounces of gold in stock at any time."

Roger nodded. "So all the gold in this invoice was used in the order from Asprey's?"

"Yes, sir," replied Michael Cornwell.

His mother became haughty. It seemed her son's word was being questioned. "I will show you the signed order from Asprey's for the bracelets and earrings," she said.

Roger Long diffused the situation, "Thank you, that's kind of you."

Michael Cornwell paused for a tea break. He asked Roger Long why he seemed so engrossed in following small ounces of gold from purchase by his company to the point of disposal.

Roger Long outlined the Government's problems of losing millions of pounds to gold smugglers.

Michael mused, drawing the palm of his left hand across his chin. "Ah well, with the very small amount we use it doesn't seem we can be of any assistance to you and I am sure mother keeps the books in apple pie order."

Roger Long was quick to agree and said how sorry he was to have caused a break in production.

The bills from the printing company were equally well filed and documented. The printing in the previous month was for letterheads in the two most popular sizes, A4 and foolscap. The unused stationery stock, still held in hand, was examined. A sample examination of documentation of goods purchased from other suppliers was made.

After two days of hard and intense work covering his audit, Roger Long spoke to both directors at the end of his review. "I must congratulate you on the quality of your books and records. However, there are two points you must remedy." He paused before continuing, "The first is quite serious. I will refer to it in a letter you will receive from the Customs and Excise Controller for Central England. You have claimed five thousand pounds relating to special car tax from a new Jaguar that was bought four months ago. This special car tax is not reclaimable, but you reduced what you owe us in Value Added Tax by five thousand pounds."

Dolly looked horrified. "But the salesman at Kempton's Cars said if we are a business user it would be alright."

Roger Long shook his head. "Some salesmen will say anything to achieve a sale."

"What's the second error?" queried Dolly. "You're looking solemn, it's really worrying."

Roger grinned. "I will excuse you the Value Added Tax on five chocolate bars that I noticed on your petrol bill."

Dorothy was quick to reply. "Oh, those were for five schoolchildren who came on visiting day. Kids of employees, they were. Thought you wouldn't mind us doing that."

"That's the end of my visit. I will leave you with one final thought. If you ever come across a gold smuggler, please give me a ring."

"Oh, we will," they answered in unison.

*Chapter 9*

Alice Cattell had badgered her principal to take her on a compliance visit. She was full of nervous energy as their Rover saloon drove into the large car park of K. J. Thomas (Printers) Ltd. Had she overstepped her capabilities? It was one thing pontificating on a taxpayer's affairs from the comfort of her own office but quite another when confronting taxpayers on their premises. A cool head and a pre-determined argument was needed to keep in charge of the situation. The agent must retain the whiphand in any discussion concerning doubtful claims and interpretation of VAT law. The traders' view invariably meant a lesser amount of tax to pay. These thoughts flooded her mind as they were shown to an office, roomy and comfortable with its own drinks dispensing machine, but it was in a building forty metres from the main administrative building, where the day-to-day action occurred. Roger Long retorted, "This is usual – keep the Vatman isolated. He won't see things that will cause him to ask additional questions." Alice Cattell merely nodded, bowing to his experience.

The two Customs officers had utilised the five days since finishing Newey's inspection to review the printing company's files. In particular, the sales invoices Newey's had received from the printers. Roger Long had also photocopied sales and purchase invoices from three compliance visits he had made to other traders in the jewellery quarter in recent weeks.

Colleagues from other VAT districts had been asked to retain copies of correspondence, sales and purchase invoices, when on compliance visits to companies who had reciprocal trading with K. J. Thomas (Printers) Ltd. These had been forwarded by internal mail to Inspector Long's office. His own specific visit to Thompson's Formation Agency made him realise that the agency has the first inkling of when a client intends to commence trading. The Formation Agency's account with the printers was very active. "We are one of their best customers," remarked Sandra Poole in her finishing interview with Roger Long, "Any new company we incorporate, who have not a printer's service, we recommend to Thomas's. They should give me a commission, maybe one day I'll suggest it. Still they do take hubby and myself to their Christmas party. Have a wonderful time, they're very generous then. The champagne really flows." Roger Long made a mental note.

* * * * *

It was usual for a trading company to treat a visit from Customs and Excise very seriously. Severe consequences could ensue for defaulters. The cavalier attitude of registered traders had disappeared since the early days of the inauguration of the new tax in 1973, when visiting inspectors had no real effective powers and were made to feel as interlopers. The extensive powers now enjoyed by them, which were enacted in successive Finance Acts in the early 1990s, now gave finance directors nervous palpitations at the mere prospect of a compliance visit. Penalty provisions now carry a £5,000 fine, or two years gaol, or both, even on the first occasion a trader has been reckless in the claims he had made.

Roger Long had already made use of the penalty provisions against a Farming Partnership. In a three man organisation, the partners had deducted, against tax owed by the firm, a substantial amount of VAT they had paid on items of jewellery mounted in gold bought for their joint mistress. She was shown on farm records as a milkmaid. The lead into this operation had been provided on the Inspector's compliance visit to Newey's, 'where he took details, then checked them when on a compliance visit to the Farming Partnership. VAT Compliance Inspectors were now taken very seriously.

"They are a throw back to Nazi Germany," one disgruntled trader was heard to remark as he was marched down the courtroom stairs to the cells below.

* * * * *

The first file examined was checked to ascertain that the information taken from Newey's inspection was duplicated in the records of the printers, merely in reverse. A sale in the printer's books was a purchase by Newey's. Apart from trivial differences the records matched. "Seems this account is okay," remarked Alice, following with "Let's look at the records of Precision Metals (1937) Ltd." Roger asked for the file from the elderly accountant employed by the firm since he left the Armed Forces in 1946, after serving with the two directors, who were the founding fathers of the firm.

The ledger sheet relating to Precision Metals (1937) Ltd, contained one item of the purchase of printed letter heads at a cost of £73.47. This sum had been paid in cash the day the goods were collected at the reception counter. The order had been received by telephone. On the printed letterhead was an address Roger Long immediately recognised as that of Thompson's Company Formations. He asked Alice, "Why does a firm start business, register for Value Added Tax, then disappear into the night?"

She replied, "I think we both know the reason, it's proving it and finding the perpetrators that's the difficulty."

Roger nodded acquiescence, then said, "I do consider the Formation Agency has been reckless, not giving the care and attention to their statutory duty that company law requires. Their main thought is always to do the business and get paid. The more doubtful their client, the higher their charges."

The two Inspectors made a nuisance of themselves for a further three days at the printer's offices, and then requested a final meeting with the two controlling directors and their internal accountant.

Cracks had begun to appear in the veneer of the bonhomie of the three people. A person can 'keep up appearances' for so long. The Chairman of the directors lost control of his feelings when asked why he had reclaimed Value Added Tax on six bottles of vintage champagne. “Why do you pillory innocent traders as you do? It looks as if you enjoy giving us a hard time.”

His colleague continued “We do everything in our power to make the system work, send our VAT returns in on time, together with a large cheque for the proceeds we have collected from our customers on your behalf and you still treat us as common criminals. If we had fiddled you, I could have understood it, but we haven’t. It would be easy to do, but we are honest traders wanting to do the best for our customers, and to be able to sleep at nights.”

The accountant intervened. “Couldn’t you disrupt someone else’s business? It shouldn’t be difficult to find traders who are manipulating the system in a big way. The champagne bill is for the staff party at Christmas, very small beer I may add.”

Alice burst out laughing.

* * * * *

Driving from the printer’s offices for the last time on the current visit, Roger Long remarked to Alice, “I like it when people we interview become heated in their arguments, the more heated they are the better pleased I am. It’s a sure sign of honesty. The people who need watching are those who nod and say “Yes, sir” to your every remark, however rude it may be.”

* * * * *

My new job in charge of precious metal investigations was proving most interesting. Many thousands of pounds could be made with little effort if the bullion scam was properly set up. Looking through records of newly formed companies at Companies House, I hoped would give me a lead. Ostensibly I visited these new traders on behalf of my new employers, Customs and Excise, advising them how to record the Value Added Tax regulations in their accounts books. Secretly I was looking for a lead into a vastly fraudulent sector that was costing the government many millions of pounds every year.

Printing companies came across new businesses before they were known to the general public when the first stationery was ordered. Birmingham’s jewellery quarter contained a large firm of printers. ‘Maybe,’ I thought, ‘I’ll pay them a visit.’

“Who’s this firm Precious Metals 1937 Limited? I haven’t met them before.”

“They’re a new company recently started up, they collect their printing and stationery supplies and pay us cash on collection.” remarked the Manager.

I remarked, “Their head office seems to be an address of convenience, just a formation agent, I’ve come across it in other cases.”

“Well, I don’t know about that, all we require is that they pay us good money.” retorted the Manager.

* * * * *

Gold bullion dealing grew up as a subsidiary trade to manufacturing precious mountings into which cut diamonds, rubies and emeralds were inserted. It was cheaper to buy gold in bulk and strip off pieces when needed to supplement the gems in a mount of fine jewellery. Due to gold prices rocketing in the early nineteen-eighties, manufacturing jewellers found it more profitable to sell their gold stocks. Then they would only buy tiny quantities for a specific gem setting.

Mike and Billy Cornwall were both expert at cutting and setting gems in new mounts, but due to the slump in the financial markets and redundancies being progressed throughout the United Kingdom in the early nineteen nineties, the profit was razor thin.

Their Uncle Albert, who had taken over the reins from his father in 1948, was a very worried man. He had had a nervous breakdown three years ago. Mike said to his mother, "There must be an easier way of making a living than trying to scratch out a few pennies on each mounting. We don't even make enough to pay the workers a decent wage. Something must give, mother, or this firm will go bust sooner than later. You remember the heartbreaks when Dad's business folded. I just can't take that again."

* * * * *

Back home, Mike and Gina cracked open a bottle of Spanish champagne and let the liquid flow down their throats without the formality of flute glasses. He had saved the financial stability of his uncle's company, he thought. They hadn't reached the bedroom before Mike caught up with Gina; she noticed a large present sticking out of his trouser pocket. He still loved her, he hadn't been led astray in Gran Canaria. She gave him the reward he deserved.

The telephone rang in the offices of Thompson Formations Limited. Sandra Hyams put down the Cosmopolitan magazine she had been reading, irritated at losing the theme of how men satisfy themselves on a Friday night.

"Thompson Formations Limited."

A male voice said, "This is Customs and Excise for the Midlands, Roger Long speaking. I'd like to make an appointment to visit your offices, please, to see if you're complying with the Value Added Tax rules and regulations."

"But we don't have anything to do with you," said the cheerful voice, "we're here to form companies."

"Who's your boss?"

"I work for myself" she said.

"Are you registered for value added tax?"

"No, no need to," was the reply, "our turnover's below the limit."

The official said, "You seem to know a lot about the value added system."

"Oh, I'm commercially trained." retorted Sandra.

"I'd still like to call at your offices."

"Well, if we don't need to register for the value added system, I can't see what our records have got to do with you."

"I could take out an Order under Regulation 734B to enforce entry to your premises. I'd rather do it the easy way, but if you force me..." The inference was obvious.

The cheerful voice became sullen. "All right then, when do you want to come?"

A date was agreed, the telephone replaced.

The pressures of life had become easier for Mike Cornwall. His recreational time had lengthened and love life with Gina had had time to blossom. He had a golf appointment with his brother Billy for that afternoon, the first working time they had taken together since joining their uncle's company over seven years ago. Dolly knocked the door and asked Mike when they were next off to Gran Canaria.

"Not for a couple of months yet," was the reply. "I feel we should have a consolidation period. The firm seems to be doing well. With our new financial freedom we can ask higher prices for the jewellery we manufacture. If we lose business on price it's not the end of the world and the business we do get is lucrative." Billy nodded. Mike was a big asset to the firm. His fair hair, blue piercing eyes and endless smiling face endeared him more than his younger brother to his mother. She realised she couldn't trust him but mothers rarely accept faults in their sons readily; especially when they have left home and are managed by another woman.

Roger Long called on Sandra Hyams on the agreed day. He asked for the file of Precious Metals 1937 Limited and used the firm's photocopying machine. The meeting lasted fifteen minutes.

"Roger, won't you at least stay and have a cup of coffee?" asked Sandra.

"That's kind of you, but I've a full day's appointments elsewhere."

"I've not even found time to ask if you're married, a girl must never miss an opportunity!"

Roger smiled wryly and said, "Yes, I'm happily married with two children, but thank you for the thought."

* * * * *

Roger Long and Mike Cornwall were on a collision path. The art of being anonymous was one that Mike had not perfected due to inexperience of the game he was playing. He knew of others who had done it and greed alone had brought about their downfall. It was easy money, the system was in place, just one last go. With the new financial freedom at the bank it could be the big one. A new Porsche for him, a diamond bracelet for his mother.

"Are you having another holiday?" his uncle asked. "Why do you take so many of the family with you?"

"Oh, it's nice and jolly," Mike answered. 'We're known at the King's Hotel in Moyan, one big happy family, besides, there are only four of us this time."

* * * * *

Jim Cornwall loaded the three cellos into his white transit van, it was covered in bold black lettering advertising the latest news features of the Midlands Evening Mail. His wife and two sons were thrilled at the prospect of playing before a captive audience of at least two hundred holidaymakers. The holiday luggage was also in the van.

Mike assumed command of the expedition, the party being made up of his wife, Gina, his mother, and brother Billy. They took a Boeing 737 from Birmingham International for a seven day sojourn, Mike's third that year. Also on the plane was a swarthy, dark-haired traveller sporting a full moustache. He was just short of six feet, of unexciting countenance, dressed casually in black denim jeans, a McDougall tartan shirt buttoned to the neck, and white canvas shoes.

The hotel transit coaches met the Birmingham flight. Mike Cornwall's troupe entered their allotted coach. It was an operation they were well used to, on Christian name terms with the coach driver, Manuel, who commented, "You must like our wonderful island. Is it the sun and the pretty Senoritas?" he asked.

Gina turned sharply. "He's brought his pretty Senorita with him this time!"

Manuel grinned broadly. "A very wise choice." Gina returned a relaxed smile.

As the doors were about to close the swarthy stranger stepped onto the coach. He slipped a one thousand peseta note into Manuel's hand and sat down in an empty seat.

* * * * *

Dolly commented, "The restaurant here is one of the finest I've ever had the pleasure of eating in."

Billy nodded his agreement. "I wish you'd take me on these trips a bit more often." Mike and Gina joined them. She had heard Billy's remark.

"Yes, you and me both, brother. It's how I imagine a honeymoon would be," she said. Then, gazing intently at Mike, added as an afterthought, "If I was ever invited to share one."

The dark, curly-haired man who had joined the party at the last minute seemed to know his way about the restaurant and took a seat three tables away from the holidaymakers from the Midlands.

* * * * *

The following morning Dolly and Mike, each carrying an attaché case, took the 8 am courtesy coach to Puerto Rico and then walked the last half-mile to the downtown dock area. The tugboat 'S.S. Queen Sofia' had arrived the previous day from Barcelona. The Spanish captain hailed them. He shook hands warmly with Mike and gave Dolly a passionate kiss. "It's nice to meet old friends." he said.

"Not so much of the old," said Dolly, "but you kiss very well for a Spaniard."

The captain smiled. "That's not all I could do for a fine English lady like yourself Dolly blushed and said, "Not in front of the children, please. Down to business."

"Do you have the supplies?" Mike asked the captain, who nodded.

"Do you have the money?" It was Mike's turn to nod.

"What do you carry that's so very heavy for a small cargo?" the captain queried.

"What you don't know you can't talk about." Mike retorted.

"I'm always curious as a cargo carrying ship to know what I'm carrying. It could be toxic. I bar drugs, but this was delivered from the Bank of Andalusia by three grey suited officials; I was given a signed receipt on their notepaper that the trip was authorised and legal."

Mike nodded. "Nothing illegal, you needn't have any doubts on that score." At this the captain pushed a bell. Within seconds there was a knock on the door and a grey-suited bank official entered and joined the meeting. The captain bowed and withdrew from the party saying to Dolly on his way out, "Perhaps we could have a glass of sangria before you return?"

She replied, "Oh, I'd like that, thank you." Mike asked if he was included in the invitation but was not surprised when the answer was 'no'.

* * * * *

Mike opened his attaché case and Dolly hers. The contents bristled with American dollars of one thousand note denomination. "Two million dollars for your cargo, where is it?" Mike asked.

"It's in the security hold next door." The bank official walked through, spun the lock and wheeled out a metal container. The cargo was divided equally into two parts and placed into the attaché cases. Mike obtained a receipt for the cash but refused to reciprocate when the official of the Bank of Andalusia requested one for himself.

"Money talks in my country, not written paper." the fair-haired Briton replied. Mike told his mother she hadn't got time to daily in the captain's cabin, a taxi was hailed. A brawny Spanish sailor helped with the cargo.

"So far, so good, mother." Mike remarked after the hotel porters had moved the attaché cases to the vaults behind the porter's desk.

* * * * *

Gina and Billy in bathing gear were beside the pool drinking white rum and coke. The swarthy English tourist had joined them. He had a surfeit of dubious jokes which Gina found tremendously amusing. When Dolly and Mike appeared, now relaxed and smiling, the stranger made his apologies.

"It's time for my tennis lesson. Thank you for the drink," he said, and departed.

"These holidays go all too quickly," said Gina. "You could soon get attached to this place. The sun, sand, evening music, night walks across the beach. This really is my idea of heaven."

* * * * *

On Sunday evening it was time for the 'Mellow Cellos' to repay their debt for free accommodation. Michael and Billy were each sporting a white tuxedo, white shirt and black bow tie, matching black trousers with a shiny navy blue stripe down the side of each leg, complemented by lightweight soft leather black shoes. They accompanied their mother, also dressed with white top and black skirt and shoes, to the auditorium.

The audience were already agog. It was a free concert for the guests of the King's Hotel. Most of them were dressed in holiday gear: jeans, T-shirts and casual flip-flops. The main party of the hotel directors and their guests were dressed formally and occupied the three front rows of the auditorium. The ladies, wearing formal long dresses, each had a pink gardenia in her hair. Their perfume made a more pleasant odour than the perspiring holidaymakers. The main party's menfolk all wore black dinner suits with matching ties. There was not a spare seat in the auditorium. A few of the hotel staff literally hung from the rafters.

Dolly Cornwall tapped her music stand. Her sons were alerted, a further tap and they led into 'The Swan' by Saint Saens. The poignancy of the piece enthralled the audience who, in the main, were not geared for classical music. The breathless hush which continued for the fifteen minute duration of the piece gave Dolly some indication of the audience's concentration. No murmuring, coughing, babies crying. "Good," she thought. Both her sons were sliding their bows smoothly across the strings to the famous children's classic, popular with all who heard it. Before the second piece Dolly noticed the hotel's managing director nodding and smiling to his companion. There was a buzz between the main parties, as well as the holiday audience; it seemed that the concert was going well. The second piece of music was an equally restrained largo based on an old Spanish folk song which the Latin element in the audience recognised and to which they quietly sang an accompaniment. The end of the first half was received rapturously. There was to be a half-hour interval. The bar prices had been doubled for the occasion. The bars were teeming with holidaymakers clamouring for drinks.

In their private room, the Mellow Cellos' were resting. It had been a nerve racking situation. Dolly wiped Michael's brow, he was perspiring profusely. There was an inner excitement between the three of them. Although they were proficient they were not yet professional enough to book the larger concert halls. This was an exhilarating experience.

The second half of the programme consisted of an arrangement of themes from Elgar's Cello Concerto and included a part for piano played by the resident pianist. For the forty-five minutes of the performance a pin could be heard to drop. Halfway through the second piece Billy missed two notes which caused his mother to shudder and grimace but she carried on, only the experts in the audience could have noticed this. The formal concert ended but due to the loud and continued cheering, two encores, both by Albeniz, known to the Spanish element as their most famous composer, enthralled the audience. They did not want the 'Mellow Cellos' to leave and the 'Mellow Cellos' would probably have stayed all night. The audience was rapturous in their applause, but there was a party afterwards to which they were committed. The directors and their party stood. Dolly realised they must terminate the concert.

* * * * *

The director of the hotel group shook hands with the boys and kissed Dolly warmly.

"What a terrific concert you put on." he said. "You might even get your next holiday free." His eyes twinkled. "We had record takings in the bar and all our selling points are still full of the audience who really appreciated your efforts." Billy was surprised to see his mother and brother in animated conversation with a group of naval officers. He joined them and was introduced to the captain of 'S.S. Queen Sofia' and his fellow officers. After two drinks Dolly whispered to the captain that she had a bottle of his special sangria in her room, how thirsty was he? The captain nodded and said he was very thirsty.

* * * * *

The hotel bus was full of tourists returning to the United Kingdom. Mike's party were sprawled across the back seat. Seconds prior to the driver turning the ignition key, the swarthy stranger appeared and took a seat next to the driver, who removed the 'Reservado' sign.

* * * * *

Dolly, fully experienced, marched with her small party through to the departure lounges their hand luggage going through the security camera check on the way and the cellos being carted to a separate gate to be loaded with golf clubs belonging to fellow travellers.

The flight to Birmingham was uneventful; Billy and Gina drank more white rum and coke than was good for them. Dolly and Mike kept a clear head.

As a close group the party sauntered casually towards the Green channel, the cellos in their protective cases being pushed on one trolley by Mike whilst Billy's trolley carried the remainder of their holiday luggage. The four of them walked through, Gina smiling enticingly at the customs officer as she passed. He nodded in return, Dolly was fraught with anxiety. There was no challenge.

* * * * *

Jim met them at 'Arrivals'. Occupying one area of the vehicle were the evening edition deliveries for the Lichfield newsagents. Tightly packed with luggage and instruments they sped away, closely followed by an unmarked Ford Corsa driven by a balding man with a woman dressed in jeans and t-shirt in the passenger seat.

Jim snaked his vehicle through the traffic with expertise; delivering newspapers in great haste had its advantages, he took no prisoners in the traffic. Each delivery driver assumed that with the painted inscription 'Midlands Evening Post' on the side of their delivery van, the rest of the traffic would move over. They usually did without argument.

They arrived at Newey's Works, Warstone Lane, in the jewellery quarter. Jim drove the van to the back of the building into the factory parking lot. Mike was soon out of the vehicle. Billy picked up his cello. "My God, Mike, this weighs a ton!"

His brother answered, "Only a dozen bottles of claret we're bringing back for Dad."

"Oh, you didn't mention this to me?"

"Oh, didn't I? I meant to," said Mike, adding, "leave the instruments in the van. Dad'll look after them."

After Billy departed to the office, Mike shook his cello and noted that his father had done an extremely good carpentry job; the cargo had fitted in the instruments like a hand in a glove.

* * * * *

Dolly took Michael to one side and whispered, "That's the last time this is happening. I can't take any more of it. Going through that green channel Customs line was harrowing, it gets worse each time."

To pacify his mother he replied, "Okay, Mum, it could be the last time. When we've got rid of the present load to Jardines, we'll lay low. If business picks up on the jewellery side, maybe we'll never re-start in this line."

* * * * *

Dolly slipped into the passenger seat of her husband's van. He was to drop her at home for a soothing cup of tea.

In his own office, Michael slid two wooden partitions out of the wall, walked through and replaced them. He climbed three flights of stairs.

Tyres screeched. Three cars came to a sudden halt. Roger Long jumped out of one and crashed through the door marked 'Alfred Newey Limited – Registered Office', closely followed by a police inspector in charge of his constables. The only person present was Billy Cornwell.

"What's all this, Roger?" he asked. "You haven't rung the enquiry bell, are you gatecrashing our premises?"

Roger Long replied, "We've a search warrant, signed ten minutes ago by a magistrate. These are two colleagues of mine from the VAT section of Customs and Excise and half a dozen policemen to make sure no one prevents us from doing our duty."

"Sounds very alarming," said Billy, "but what's happening what are we supposed to have done to warrant this activity?"

"You smuggled a large amount of gold bullion through Birmingham airport this afternoon."

"You're going over the top, old chap," scoffed Billy, "if there was any smuggling it was a dozen bottles of claret as a present for my father."

Roger Long retorted, "I can't stand here talking."

Inspector Bloomsbury instructed his squad to make a thorough search of the premises, from the underground cellars to the attics three storeys high. The house was formerly the residence of a leading Birmingham industrial family when it was first built in late Victorian times. Like most of the Jewellery Quarter, these splendid old residences had been gradually converted into workshops, offices and retail shops in a warren of alleyways jutting off four main roads which enclosed the 'Quarter'.

Long said to the police inspector, "Organise your men." The outhouses, old stables and brewhouses were allocated to three constables. Bloomsbury and two more constables moved around the first floor. Long asked Billy, "Where's Michael's office?"

"It's on the first floor."

"Come with me, will you".

They both went upstairs to Michael's empty office.

"I'll give you a hand if you like," said Billy, "I want to keep my brother's office as tidy as I can." Both of them searched through desks and cupboards and examined floorboards which were firmly fixed.

"It doesn't look as though there are any floorboards recently disturbed." Long said to Billy Cornwall.

"I shouldn't think so. You're really playing the detective, aren't you? I'll leave you to it." Roger tapped the wooden slats which comprised the wall. After a time he discovered one that moved at his touch. Quickly sliding out the partition, he went through and tiptoed carefully upstairs. There were two doors. He listened carefully at the first one and heard the whirring sound of a computer printer. He put his shoulder to the door: it was locked from the inside. Michael's voice shouted, "Who's that?"

Roger Long said, "Mike, open the door. Roger Long from Customs and Excise here!" A fluster of activity came from inside. The sound of paper being moved quickly could be heard. It took the Customs man a full five minutes to force the door. He rushed to the open window, saw Michael's lithe figure moving across the rooftops at as fast a speed as he could, carrying a bulging attaché case. Long followed him through the window. After both contestants leapt over two chasms from one building to another, Michael reached a dead end wall. The two men were within two metres of each other.

"Where are you going with that suitcase?"

"It's no concern of yours." was the reply.

"It's very much my concern. I have a search warrant. There are eight policemen downstairs. I want to see inside that case."

Michael turned and continued his run across the rooftop. Putting out a hand against a large Victorian chimney to steady himself; he withdrew it sharply, giving an involuntary shout. "Damn it!" The brickwork was burning hot.

"My God, that burned me!" He was over the 'Jewel in the Crown' public house. They advertised their authentic Edwardian Room widely; this included a roaring fire constantly at full blast. Many a man had stood with his back to the fire, airing his knowledge. Without a second thought Michael threw his suitcase up and into the wide chimney cavity. "Good." he thought. Then, descending the fire escape to the street below, he walked the final hundred and fifty metres back to his office and sat down.

On the ground floor Inspector Bloomsbury greeted Roger Long. "We've found what looks like an underground safe buried in a floor in an outside old stable. We can't open it but it seems recently built." The policeman asked Michael to open it.

"I don't know what you're talking about. New safes in old buildings, I'm not with you, officer", chided Michael Cornwall.

"Sir, it would be best if it was opened with the correct combination number rather than us blasting it out with dynamite." Michael moved to the safe, spun the combination clock five times, covering the numbers with his free hand.

Pulling the buried safe door with both hands, then pressing the interior light button, he moved away from the twelve inch gaping aperture. Roger Long fished out a wad of old betting slips that made up the entire contents of the safe.

"They're my father's. Keeps them away from my mother's eagle eye!"

* * * * *

The headlines of the Midlands Evening Post read 'Gold Bullion Fraud – Birmingham family firm raided.' The narrative continued, 'Late yesterday evening the police and a number of Customs and Excise officers raided the offices of Newey Limited, a firm of jewellery manufacturers. However, after a thorough search of the premises, which included a rooftop chase, neither the Customs officers nor the police discovered the contraband gold bullion bars they had expected to find on the premises. Mr. Roger Long, the Customs Officer in charge of the investigation, said he could not offer a full statement at present but was disappointed in the result of the search. Their inquiries were continuing.'

* * * * *

Steelhouse Lane police station was its usual hive of activity. It was Birmingham's central police headquarters attached to the Victorian Law Courts, which only meant a short underground walk for remand prisoners when their case came before the Law Lords. The Criminal Investigation Department had its offices on the first floor of the police station overlooking Birmingham's General Hospital, a building erected in mid-Victorian times. It had seen the advance of medicine from limbs being amputated without anaesthetic, to present day heart transplants. The medical profession worked hand in glove with the police. Inspector Bloomsbury and Roger Long were looking at the scene without appreciating it was there. Long posed a question, "I'm certain the gold was smuggled through. I didn't see it in the Canaries but the circumstantial evidence was overwhelming."

The police inspector answered, "That Michael Cornwall's a cool one. He knew what he was doing when he spun the combination lock, and the grin on his face when he showed us the betting slips was mischievous. He enjoyed that."

"Yes, but why did he go on the roof? I followed him up. It was dusk. The light had almost faded but I'm certain I saw him carrying a brown Gladstone-type bag. I only followed him a few steps across the indent in the slate roof. He had an advantage over me: as a child he lived in the premises before they were converted into the family's manufacturing unit. I climbed down the stairs and saw him walking up Warstone Lane to his office. He was carrying nothing at that point."

The inspector answered, "Well, my men made a thorough search of the surrounding streets, didn't find anything."

Long answered, "Without the gold, and I feel in my bones the Gladstone bag as well, we are losing out here."

The inspector interjected, "What part do you think Michael's father has in this, if any?"

"Jim's a nice man in a bar," Roger Long replied, "but I wouldn't trust him. He seems one of life's losers. I think that's because he won't put his back into any work for a sustained period. He's more of a hump man or a baggage carrier. He certainly handled those cellos carefully, wouldn't let anyone move them off the trolleys. He did the whole operation himself Michael kept Billy and the airport operators away, said the instruments were far too valuable to take chances with. I was watching Jim place them so carefully and meticulously."

"How good were the family at making music?"

"Oh, they were excellent, almost professional standard." Long replied. "They certainly slapped and handled the instruments like masters, especially Dolly. She shook and rattled the cello, swung her bow at it vigorously, really let off steam." Roger Long thought, and said out loud, "If she treated the cello like that, why wouldn't they let Billy help with the handling? It could have saved them fifteen minutes outside the airport."

The inspector said, "The cello's a big instrument, you could get a lot of contraband inside one of those."

"Of course!" exclaimed Long. "Have I had mud in my eyes!" The two men ran out of the office and down the main stone staircase. The duty sergeant raised an eyebrow. He was used to sudden bursts of activity from the younger constables, but the portly Bloomsbury was not known for his athleticism.

Commandeering the first police vehicle in sight, Bloomsbury jumped into the driver's seat and Long rode front passenger.

The mile journey took twenty minutes. The early afternoon traffic was intense.

"We could've walked quicker." Bloomsbury remarked.

The general enquiry officer at Symphony Hall informed the pair that the stringed instruments safe depository was locked. He was not looking for a key unless he received instructions from the Musical Director.

"That's ridiculous!" shouted Long. "You're perverting the course of justice!"

"Don't be absurd!" said the man. "It's my job not to let possible impostors have their way with the instruments in the stringed section. They're worth up to a million pounds in total."

"Probably more than that." muttered Long dismally.

Michael Cornwall and his father entered Symphony Hall through the artists' entrance. It had now been four days since they had returned from the Spanish island. They made their way down the two flights of stairs, over the plush red carpet, tapped in the security number and walked directly to the three cellos.

Michael said, "You did well, Dad, to bring these directly here. What a piece of good fortune." They each took a cello to a wheeled carrying trolley, then pushed it to the ramp that led to the car park, making the forty yard walk in quick time. Jim Cornwall's van, complete with its advertisements for the 'Midlands Evening Post', stood waiting. It took both men to place each cello in a secure spot at the back of the vehicle.

It took a further ten minutes for Roger Long and the policeman to receive authority from the Musical Director who had accompanied them to the strong depositories.

"Where do the 'Mellow Cellos' keep their instruments?" Long asked.

"That's strange, there's only one of them there now. I'm sure there was a full complement earlier this morning." was the reply.

Long looked at Bloomsbury, then at the Musical Director. "Where are the other two?" he asked.

"Superintendent, there's no rule which says that artists must leave their instruments here. Most musicians do unless they're playing an engagement away from Symphony Hall. For practice purposes the instruments are usually kept in this secure room."

Bloomsbury said, "We need a break. All the luck has gone in their favour." They examined the remaining cello carefully. Long placed it across his knee, looking at front and back, examining the front belly and 'f' holes. The weight was about right, he thought. The Musical Director broke his train of thought.

"I'm sure there were three cellos there first thing this morning," he reiterated.

"How long would you think they've been a complete set?" Bloomsbury asked.

"Oh, since they came back from their last gig in Gran Canaria" the Musical Director replied. "Seeing them absent is a bit like looking at a mouth without two front teeth, you always expect them to be there." Long and Bloomsbury made their excuses.

"I hope we get back to the station more quickly than the journey here." remarked Long. The traffic along Broad Street was intense, black taxi cabs proliferated. The roads were crowded with lunchtime travellers taking the break. Most of the work in Birmingham's financial and commercial offices which covered the west part of the city centre was done prior to lunch, along with the decisions when minds were fresh. Bloomsbury, still waiting for the traffic to clear before leaving the car park, cast a glance at the rear mirror. He saw a white newspaper van immediately behind him but thought nothing of it. A lull enabled him to turn left on the first stage of the return journey to the police station. The white van moved immediately after him but turned right. Roger Long exclaimed, "God, that's Jim Cornwall's van!"

"Oh? It's been standing there for three or four minutes immediately behind me." Bloomsbury replied.

"Can you turn?" Long immediately asked.

They reached the Hall of Memory, circumnavigated the island at three hundred and sixty degrees and immediately retraced their steps along Broad Street. The newspaper van was a further fifteen vehicles in front, but stopped at a red light. Bloomsbury blared his siren. Within the next half mile fourteen vehicles moved over and let the blaring sirened police car through. Jim Cornwall didn't follow suit. He came to the underpass at Five Ways as fast as he could go. The last intervening driver moved sharply to his left away from danger. Cornwall's experience at quick delivery of newspapers came in very useful. The police car was blaring its siren at a continuous blast. The van, now only a hundred yards in front, didn't use its brakes. Bloomsbury edged closer, his Ford Jaguar more powerful in engine size, was approaching the rear of the white van.

Bloomsbury used his hailer. "Stop or we'll ram you!"

Roger Long was discomforted. He was an office man. The chase continued through Edgbaston. Jim Cornwall used every piece of available traffic to his advantage. He caught a green light at Monument Lane. The light turned red and traffic moved across to Bearwood Road forcing the police car to stop. Bloomsbury was fuming, waving his arms for the traffic to move out of the way, his siren blaring continually, but the white van had travelled a further quarter mile away before he could move forward. Continuing along the main Hagley Road out of Birmingham city centre, the Jaguar was travelling at full speed again. The police hailer was threatening, imploring, cajoling the white van to stop. Both vehicles went over the lights at Mucklow Hill on the red light with only ten yards between them. Bloomsbury started to overtake the white van and edged it to the left. Long's eyes had been closed for five minutes. He should have altered his Will, he thought, brought in a new nephew and niece, twins that had been born to his sister. Would he ever see his own wife and children again?

Bloomsbury swung a hard left, half a car's length past the white van, racing down the steepest hill in the Midlands at high speed. Jim Cornwall jerked the steering wheel hard right. Both vehicles locked; they were travelling at over seventy miles an hour down the incline. The police vehicle had again moved its horn into permanent sound. They travelled like this for a quarter of a mile before the van veered left. Both vehicles crashed through a wooden fence into a cornfield, continuing several hundred yards before they came to a halt.

Inspector Bloomsbury radioed through to headquarters of his plight and position.

"Get help!" he said. The white van had rolled on to its side. The occupants of the van weren't going anywhere. Michael Cornwall was unconscious, his head slumped against the windscreen. The windscreen had cracked, along with Michael's head which spurted blood. His father was more fortunate with only a leg wound. Jim was greatly concerned about his son's plight and, when Long and Bloomsbury appeared, dishevelled but with only abrasions, he gave no resistance. In a few minutes four police cars and an ambulance had arrived at the scene. Father and son were transferred for the return journey. The police car sirens and hailers were again at full tilt on the way back to Birmingham General Hospital. The police made a search and found two cellos, one smashed to pieces with the back torn off; the belly of the second one had been completely removed. Inside each one were six bars of gold bullion.

* * * * *

The Jaguar that Bloomsbury and Long had used in the chase limped the six miles back to Steelhouse Lane. On their way past the long reception counter, the same duty sergeant stopped the dishevelled policemen and said, "Sir, you've had three urgent phone calls from Warstone Lane police station."

"Bugger them," said Bloomsbury "we've had one hell of a morning!"

"Sir, I think you should return the call, it's to do with the case you're on." Long's head jerked. He was so far into this case every lead must be followed. He asked the duty sergeant to return the call and he would speak. After he had been sitting in Bloomsbury's office for a few minutes, the telephone rang. It was the duty sergeant. He said, "Sir, there's a police constable outside direct from Warstone Lane. They thought it was important. Would you see him?"

"Of course, straight away, bring him in." The fresh-faced constable was carrying a bound and tattered Gladstone bag.

"Sir, this has been handed in at Warstone Lane nick. The gaffer at the 'Jewel in the Crown' brought this relic in this morning. Thought it would have some relevance. It refers to company records and things that are way above our station's thinking."

"Where did he get it from?"

"Well you know the 'Jewel in the Crown' has this Edwardian room?"

"I had a drink there after last week's raid," replied Long.

"It was time for the chimney to be swept and this has to be done at both the bottom and the top. When the chimney operative had been lowered into the aperture, he discovered this case between one of the three ledges that were built into chimneys in Victorian times. Sootboys could then climb inside when they were cleaning the chimney. They only do it once a year."

'Perhaps that's the break I've been looking for.' thought Long. "Thank you very much, constable, I'll certainly bring this piece of initiative to the attention of Inspector Bloomsbury." The constable smiled and left the room.

* * * * *

In the lounge at Jim and Dolly Cornwall's semi-detached in Perry Barr village, an agitated Gina was drinking a soothing cup of tea with Jim and Dolly.

"I'm sure Michael's much better than he's letting on." she said. "He might as well recover quickly and let the case continue. We have the county's leading defence barrister acting for us. He rarely seems to lose a case, even those heavily loaded against his client. He'll charge a hefty fee but we're talking about the liberty of the three of you. I don't want Michael to go down for twenty years. You only live once and a wait of that length would finish me as much as him. Let's get the thing moving."

Dolly retorted, "We can't make a positive move whilst Michael insists he's too ill to be questioned. The police have a permanent guard outside his ward and are only letting us in for short visits."

"Well, how can we see whether he's shamming or not?" Jim said. Dolly looked knowingly at Gina and said, "It's up to you, dear. Jim, isn't it time to deliver the Lichfield papers? They must be overdue now."

"Yes," he confirmed "I must dash."

After Jim had left, the two women went into animated conversation, Dolly mostly talking, Gina listening intently, often nodding her acceptance of a point made. "It's the only way I can think of to discover how fit he really is." Dolly said in conclusion.

* * * * *

Michael was an in-house patient, his private medical insurance paying for five star treatment in a luxury ward. With visitors he maintained the part of a very slow recovery. Nina had begun to recognise the sham and thought she would put him to the test.

Dressed in a deep claret top with matching mini skirt, the hem finishing six inches above her knees, a light blue open-necked blouse, the two top buttons unfastened to show an alluring cleavage between her forty inch cups, colour matching three inch heels, she arrived earlier than Michael had expected.

"How are you today, dear?" she asked.

Michael put on his rehearsed act. "No better. I think 'stable' is the word." She thought a compliment on her dress would not have been out of place.

"What do you think of my new outfit?" she asked, doing a full swirl, lingering on the back turn.

"Very nice, dear, but remember I'm a sick man."

Nina smiled, "I believe you, but I want to make sure." She leaned forward, her cleavage a mere three inches away from his lusting eyes. She slid her hand under the sheet and untied the cord of his pyjama trousers, leaving her perfumed hand inside, adding mischievously, "A really sick man could not respond, could he?" The swift action caught Michael unawares.

"Don't. Remember, there's a policeman sitting outside the ward!"

"Oh, I shan't touch him," Nina answered, continuing with, "I do think you're fitter than you tell. What a big boy you are becoming." Michael found his recovery was stronger than he realised. A little more vigorous friction had him gasping. With her free hand Nina unfastened the waistband of her mini skirt which fell in a crumpled heap at her feet. Withdrawing the hand that had caused Michael's increased blood pressure, she turned back the sheet. The sight that met her left no doubt that Michael had been shamming his recovery. Kneeling astride him she had little difficulty in guiding him into her love channel Michael sat up, throwing his arms around her waist, and thrust eagerly at her entry point. Nina's thighs retreated six inches backwards and came crashing forwards to coincide with his upward thrust. Michael had been deprived since the accident. The speed of his coming surprised her, usually he had control until minutes later. His recovery was complete.

They were embracing each other. She said, "You must leave hospital and face the music like a man. I've spoken to a top barrister. He gives hope for a shorter spell in stir than I thought possible."

"I'll miss you, dearest," Michael answered "but I shall fight every inch of the way."

Leaving the ward, the seated policeman asked her how Michael was progressing. Nina smiled sweetly and said he was looking far better than yesterday when she visited. "I'm sure it will only be a few days before you can return to your normal duties. I'm not a doctor, you understand, but I have the feeling this visit has given him the medicine he appreciates."

* * * * *

The duty sergeant at Steelhouse Lane police station sat behind the reception counter surveying the hive of human activity. Seated on a long wooden bench adjacent to the entrance to No.1 charge room were the usual type of vagrants picked up the previous night in the centre of the city. The seated element were hard-core cases long since having used up their allocation of police warnings to be law abiding citizens in future. There were beggars who used threats to engender gifts from the weak and the elderly. Two youngsters, still not yet sixteen, caught by a police car which attained speeds their stolen Skoda could not compete with. It was the fifteenth time they were to be charged in the space of six months.

The duty sergeant reflected to his WPC assistant, "My father's belt would have done them far more good than the lectures we give them. They sneer at us each time we catch them. With their unpaid fine record and thousands like them across the country, income tax could be lowered by two pence on the standard rate if a method could be found to make them pay."

"No, a belted backside would make them think twice before stealing another car."

The dregs of society on that bench included two hardened women with more soliciting convictions than the youngsters had for car thieving.

"Won't they ever learn?" said the duty sergeant.

"Learn what, sarge?" queried the WPC. "How not to get caught and learn the error of their ways?"

"Either." was the response. "Whichever it was would cause us less grief and filling in forms."

It was no coincidence that the Law Courts and Birmingham's General Hospital were built in the close vicinity of police headquarters. The bodies of hanged criminals were only a short carrying distance to the hospital to await the last journey to their final resting place at the Hodge Hill cemetery.

The historical connections of the buildings were lost on the nine to be accused, sitting on the second wooden bench immediately behind that containing the usual suspects. There was a distinct difference on the second bench. The two men at the head of the seated line were clearly strangers to the surroundings they now found themselves in. Both dressed in formal lounge suits with satin collars and wearing their golf club ties, they were waiting to be called for interview. George Jardine and his finance director, Alfred Cornwall sat stone faced, each wearing bracelet handcuffs.

"This is degrading. Having to share a dock with paid thieves and prostitutes is bad enough, but being shackled with these bloody handcuffs is the utmost in humiliation," Jardine said to Cornwall, who replied, "I still can't understand what's happening. Carrying out our normal business operation as we have been doing for many years and suddenly to be told we're aiding and abetting a massive fraud, leaves me speechless. Perhaps that VAT man, Long, will explain."

The next five in line on the same wooden bench were the members of the Cornwall family. Michael, immersed in an excess of sympathy bandages, sat next to Albert Cornwall, his mother and father immediately next to him, with his brother seated furthest away. Billie ran across and asked Albert Cornwall why they were all in attendance.

"Your guess is as good as mine, Billie, but a gold bullion smuggling operation has been mentioned. I'm anxious to know, as none of us have done anything to be ashamed of, when we'll be rid of these damned handcuffs and be let out to carry on our normal business activities." Billie passed this message on to his two aunts who were seated adjacent to him.

"I dunno about this, where there's smoke there's fire, but I'm still mystified," replied Ada Cornwall whilst her sister nodded in agreement. Last on the bench was Albert Newey, sitting rigidly upright, staring in front, oblivious to all around him.

"Why have I been brought here?" His thoughts did not give a satisfactory answer.

* * * * *

Behind the door of the Charge Room Roger Long was talking animatedly to Chief Inspector Bloomsbury. Although only two metres away from the nine to be accused, they were separated by a stout wooden door that had stood the test of past batterings from prisoners shocked at the unfairness of charges made against them.

Roger Long, the investigating Customs and Excise officer, was talking to Chief Inspector Bloomsbury who had co-ordinated the previous evening's raid.

"I think we've taken a huge hammer to crack a nut, by charging everyone who's been involved in the financial arrangements and travelling on the trips to Gran Canaria. Most of them are totally innocent. I think there's little doubt that the co-ordinator of the fraud was Michael Cornwall, but proving it is another matter. He's a very cool customer indeed."

The police chief nodded, "I think a joint interview session with all the accused might serve a useful purpose."

Interview office number six had the necessary space for the numerous people involved in the mass interview. In addition to the accused, there were Roger Long and his number one at Customs and Excise, plus Inspector Bloomsbury and two junior officers. Two armed police constables were also in attendance.

The accused were instructed by Inspector Bloomsbury that this was part of the official interviewing time the police had as their legal right, prior to defence solicitors being allowed to accompany their clients.

Ada immediately recognised the face and interjected, "Seems funny to see you here Roger, always thought you were one of us. We had such a good time in Gran Canaria."

"Yes, I told you I was starting a new job the last time we met. It's the position I now occupy." responded Long. He then turned to Billy, "I certainly enjoyed our drink by the pool on that last holiday." Billy mused for a while and Gina looked up. She was still handcuffed but her face showed recognition.

"Yes, you do have the same eyes and smile as that hilarious chap we met by the pool, but you've certainly got a lot less hair and no moustache or beard."

"Yes, I rather fancied you in your bikini, envied Mike somewhat. I confess I was the stranger who joked with you and your brother-in-law by the pool. Your husband and his mother were to be followed when they next travelled to Gran Canaria. I felt certain I knew the hotel they would stay at. My office booked a late flight and accommodation there. It was the first time I'd ever worn a disguise."

"Well, you did a pretty good job," Dolly interrupted, "I'd never have recognised you."

"He's certainly lost quite a bit of hair since we first met at the hotel. Gives him a head start to wear a wig." said Ada. Her remark brought about the only laughter in the interview.

Inspector Bloomsbury opened the session. "I don't know too much about the legal intricacies of this case, but as I have a chief investigating officer of the Midlands Customs and Excise in attendance, Mr. Roger Long, he will chair the interview.

"It was the weight of the twelve bottles of claret that started a suspicion. I had been appointed to investigate the huge amount of revenue that was being lost in bullion scams across the British Isles."

"What's a bullion scam?" asked Ada.

Inspector Bloomsbury interjected, "It's what you've been charged with."

"I don't even know what it means" Ada replied.

"It's where a dealer in gold goes abroad and buys gold bullion bars quite legitimately. There is no tax when you buy gold in Spain and of course Gran Canaria is a Spanish island. When that gold bullion is brought into the United Kingdom it should be declared to the Customs at the airport of entry and duty of seventeen and a half per cent paid on it before the bullion is allowed into the United Kingdom. Usually these arrangements are made before the air travellers arrive here. They then proceed to the Red Channel and make the necessary arrangements to pay the duty. The scam is that the smugglers walk through the Green Channel and do not pay the duty. In this case we noted them but didn't apprehend at that point. I felt they would have excused themselves, saying 'Oh, sorry, it was a mistake we should have gone through the Red Channel', and turned tail. We wanted to see them outside the airport and through Customs. Then they wouldn't have the excuse of any smuggling being a mistake."

Ada said, "Well, it's still a bit hazy, I still don't see how we've gained any money or how we've gained benefit."

Roger Long continued, "After the gold bullion was carefully hidden away, Michael would then have instructed his mother, as he had done at least three times before, maybe more, to type out an invoice to Jardines selling gold for two million pounds, plus three hundred and fifty thousand pounds Value Added Tax. Jardines would make enquiries as to whether the new customer was legitimate. When they came to the conclusion that it was, they would then send a cheque for two million three hundred and fifty thousand pounds to the new company who would then pay the amount into the Halifax building society in Cheltenham, which is near to where Michael lives, and where he had opened an account some months ago in readiness. Jardines sold the same gold to their New York agents and, as they had paid three hundred and fifty thousand pounds extra for their purchase, on their monthly Value Added Tax return they asked the Customs to repay the sum to them which is quite legitimate and above board."

He paused. "You may not realise Customs not only charge duty on goods coming into and out of the United Kingdom, but they also manage and administer the Value Added Tax system in the United Kingdom. In the normal course of events the computer of the Value Added Tax authorities would send a cheque for Neweys for the amount deducted, i.e., three hundred and fifty thousand pounds. We find that the trail ends there. The company's registered office is a formation agency and the directors are the staff of the formation agents, who, of course, deny everything. The net effect is that Customs and Excise have been cheated out of three hundred and fifty thousand pounds. This is not the first time that these particular defendants have pulled off this trick. They use a different firm of formation agents for each new company they start, but the last one is by far the largest scam they have ever attempted. It was a bit of luck when my gentleman's act of handing Dolly's case to her on our first journey from Puerto Rico made me think her explanation of twelve bottles of claret didn't add up. I had already been alerted by my new employers that unusual things were happening in Gran Canaria concerning gold bullion that made me ponder."

Lily interjected, "What's all this about Precious Metals 1937 Limited?"

Roger Long replied, "Precious Metals 1937 Limited is a shell company. Its administration has been conducted from the top floor of Newey Limited's premises in the Jewellery Quarter."

Lily said, "But that's an old unused attic that we don't even use for storage. Nobody's been up there for years."

"Somebody has." Long replied. "When we raided last night, there was a personal computer, printer, photocopier, all the trappings of a business office. It was even on Internet and had an electronic mail connection."

"I wonder who that could've been?" Billy asked.

"There'd been an attempt to destroy the stationery cabinet and the files."

Albert Newey shook his head in disbelief. "There was no need for anything like this to happen. The firm was prospering. We'd seen off the bank overdraft and the Manager had begun to ask me out to lunch again. The good times were back so why the need for this smuggling business, which frankly I disbelieve and, when it's all over, I'll certainly be suing you personally, Mr Long."

"'You'll have to prove malicious intent, Mr. Newey. I have complete and full powers in all aspects of this investigation. Traditionally, going back in time over a thousand years, a Customs officer has more powers than the police when it comes to entering premises and seizing goods."

"Yes," sighed Bloomsbury, "I envy them. We have to tread very warily on a raid, they enter in gay abandon."

"How are we connected with the firm Precious Metals 1937 Limited?" asked Albert. "That's what I want to know."

Roger Long continued, "I had to make a compliance visit to Mathesons and saw they had bought a large amount of bullion from Precious Metals 1937 Limited. I then looked at the file of the latter company at Companies House in Cardiff. I found they had been recently formed and their registered office was a firm of company formation agents. The directors were also employees of the agency. There was nothing to connect the new company with any other firm. I visited the formation agency, again ostensibly on a compliance visit."

"You certainly get around!" interjected Ada.

Long smiled at her and continued, "I noted the costs of forming the company had been paid in cash; there was nothing to tie up the new company with any person outside the agency who had been naive in agreeing to their client's instructions. They only wanted the fee. The owner of the formation agency had asked the caller to her office to complete forms during the next four weeks so that the directors could resign and have the registered office changed to a location where the new company would trade from. This was never done. She described the person who called to pick up the new company documents as fair-haired and blue eyed, in his late twenties and with a charming personality."

"Sounds like our Mike." said Ada.

"I think it was your Mike." retorted Long.

Mike looked up and smiled. "Very flattering, but I don't know what you're talking about."

Long continued, "When we looked at the printed stationery in the attic, it had come from the printing firm just around the corner from Neweys, a firm I had recently visited."

"On another compliance visit, I suppose?" Dolly Cornwall asked sarcastically.

"Indeed yes, madam."

"You certainly get around!" she replied.

"You have to move your butt when you're dealing with a gigantic fraud on this scale."

"Are you accusing us?" Mike Cornwall demanded.

"Well sir, you've been charged." was the reply.

Mike said, "I'm saying nothing until I have legal representation. Again, I understand it's obligatory to have all interviews on video. Is this being done?"

Inspector Bloomsbury nodded, "Yes, it's on video. I'm sorry, I should have made that clear at the outset."

"On the compliance visit to the printing works," continued Roger Long, "I noticed an invoice had been sent to a new company, Precious Metals 1937 Limited, for printing their stationery. I look for new companies recently formed in any way attached to gold and jewellery companies and this stationery stated the trade to be bullion dealers. The trail was warming up. I now had an address in Warstone Lane in the jewellery quarter but there was no sign of offices. When I telephoned Albert Newey he stated he had never heard of the firm. Indeed, I believed him."

"Well, why am I being charged then?" Newey asked.

"Call it a protective charge whilst inquiries continue." Long answered.

"And why are the two of us being charged?" asked George Jardine.

"For the same reason as Albert Newey."

"So the charge may be dropped at any minute?"

"Depending on our further inquiries, yes, but don't take it for granted."

Long directed another question at Jardine, "Why did you pay such a huge amount of money to Precious Metals Ltd. for Value Added Tax?"

Jardine replied, "When we buy gold bullion and a new customer is involved, before opening an account we inspect the Certificate of Incorporation which, as you know, is equivalent to a birth certificate of a new company to show that it is in existence. Also we insist on perusing and photocopying the VAT Registration Certificate which you lot issue. This was done by our office manager."

"I still feel greatly aggrieved to be in this position with handcuffs when we've done everything asked of us. You issued Precious Metals with authority to trade as bullion dealers and gave them a number to place on their stationery to deal with any commercial enterprise, surely you're as much to blame as anyone that they were able to recover vast sums of money from my firm?"

Roger Long replied, "That's the clever part of the scam."

"Who was it who called to show you the documentation you've just described? My office manager can't remember."

Ada shouted, "I went down there with some stuff Mike gave me. I've no idea what it was!"

Mike grimaced and said,"That was only giving advanced sight of Newey's annual report."

"Why would they want to see that?" Long asked.

"There's a strong relationship between the firms and it gave increased credibility to our credit rating." Mike replied.

Matheson nodded and said, "Yes, we do have that relationship with Neweys but I don't particularly remember seeing a recent report, but there again my office manager doesn't refer every detail to me. He does have some degree of authority to act on his own initiative." The trend of the interview was complicated for a simple policeman. "I'm glad you're investigating this, Mr. Long," said Inspector Bloomsbury, "it's far too highbrow for me. If Jardines paid out to this new company a large amount of money, how do they recover this tax? Surely they can't pay out such large amounts and not claim it back?"

"But they do recover it," Long replied, "every month we send them a cheque."

Jardine interrupted, "That's because we export all our gold bullion to North America. We can't charge Value Added Tax on export orders so in the case of amounts we pay to firms like Precious Metals 1937 Limited, Customs and Excise send us a cheque. We're only collection agents for Customs and Excise."

The policeman answered, "Oh, I see now, when gold is brought into the country Value Added Tax should be paid when it comes in, in this case at Birmingham Airport, and when it goes out of the country that amount of tax is repaid to the person sending it to the States and Canada, in this case Jardines.

"Precisely so," Long affirmed, "and if it is smuggled through Customs from abroad, like I am contending in this case from Grand Canaria, my controlling body is losing huge amounts of revenue." Mike Cornwall was squirming in his seat. He could not take the rest of his family with him; he had tried desperately to save his uncle's firm from bankruptcy. He could not let his family go to jail. He looked at his mother, she nodded. Michael Cornwall then addressed Inspector Bloomsbury, "Could my mother and myself have a separate meeting with you?" Accompanied by Roger Long, they walked into a vacant room. The video machine was switched on. Michael Cornwall confessed the scam was wholly his idea and his mother had acquiesced and helped with the arrangement.

Roger Long answered, 'I'm glad you're adopting this attitude, Michael it'll save a lot of bother in the long run as the evidence I have from the suitcase I took from you two days ago completed the whole jigsaw. The four new companies you started with different formation agents were recorded, indeed the company birth certificates were there. I see you used a new company for each visit to Gran Canaria. When you'd received a cheque from my head office, the company was allowed to lie dormant, never to be used again. I've a file on Jardines and the other gold bullion dealers that you conducted business with. It'll pay you to plead guilty and throw yourself on the mercy of the court. At least this is your first offence, and your mother's. I'll give evidence in mitigating circumstances that I know you as a friendly acquaintance. Against this, of course, is that in tax fraud cases the court sentences are heavy as a deterrent to others, but hopefully a guilty plea will bring a lighter sentence than dragging everyone through the courts by pleading not guilty."

Michael and Dolly Cornwall were the only ones charged except for Dolly's husband, Jim, who was the courier.

* * * * *

The crime reporter of the Midlands Evening Post followed the gold bullion scam case very carefully and in detail. He noted the spirited and well thought out defence by George Careless, the barrister in charge of the defendants. A 'Not Guilty' plea was made by all three defendants who refused the Customs and Excise offer to mitigate for a lenient sentence for a 'Guilty' plea. Customs and Excise also offered the lesser charge of conspiring to defraud, instead of recklessly knowing and not caring that their actions were fraudulent and deliberate. Prosecuting Counsel laid heavily on the fact that the six bars of gold bullion had entered the country illegally, with a deliberate attempt to evade paying customs duty of three hundred and fifty thousand pounds. The gold bars had been impounded at the scene of the crash and extricated from the cellos where they had been carefully concealed. Jim Cornwall had done an expert carpentry job on the interior of the cellos.

Whilst defending Dorothy Cornwall, George Careless claimed she had been inveigled into the operation by her son, Michael, who had not informed her that they intended to go through the Green Channel. She was astonished when, this happened. Dorothy had instructed her brief along these lines with a story invented by Michael, who was desperate to keep his mother from jail.

Now fully recovered from his injuries, Michael Cornwall was in the witness stand four hours, during which time he said he had read of the gold bullion scam being perpetrated in various parts of the United Kingdom by organised crime syndicates based in London's city financial district. The operation was done by small time criminals acting on instructions, the official transfers of currency being done through a careful money laundering operation. If Customs and Excise investigators discovered the bullion moving through to the United Kingdom from tax free countries, there was nothing to connect the masterminds with the people doing the smuggling operation. The small time criminals were punished with the full rigours of the law and the gold impounded, but the masterminds escaped detection. It was this idea that gave Michael Cornwall to think that if the masterminds and the actual perpetrators were one and the same, proceeds would be enormous.

Roger Long gave a full account of his part in the detection of the scam and felt he and Michael Cornwall had been on a collision path unknowingly since he joined the service.

After a four day hearing the three defendants were found guilty. The defending Counsel gave the mitigating circumstances that the firm Newey Limited, an old-established jewellery manufacturer, was financially strapped. It was a matter of a short amount of time before their creditors would place them in liquidation and their directors made bankrupt. This included the son of the founder, Albert Newey, who knew nothing of the scam but whose nephew, Michael Cornwall, one of the defendants, was determined the firm would succeed. He wished to protect the family name and maintain the high lifestyle which he had been used to. Dorothy Cornwall, Michael's mother, was influenced by her eldest son and acted as administrator and secretary, typing out the fraudulent paperwork necessary to dupe the authorities and the companies the gold bullion had been sold to. Roger Long stated the scam had been perpetrated four times in the previous two years by the Cornwall family. His evidence concluded the case for the prosecution.

The Judge's summing up leaned heavily towards the evidence given by Customs and Excise officers, which he accepted as thorough and truthful. He thought Defence Counsel had given a case which was very close to the borderline between truth and fiction and admonished George Careless. The jury seemed heavily influenced by the summing up and took only thirty minutes to bring in 'Guilty' verdicts on all counts. Notwithstanding, Roger Long spoke well of the defendants and commented that it was circumstances of being involved in buying and selling gold bullion for the manufacture of their products that had brought temptation which proved irresistible to the younger Cornwall.

Michael Cornwall was sentenced to three years imprisonment, his mother to two years. James Cornwell, who had acted as courier in this country, received a two year suspended sentence and was ordered to do one hundred and eighty days community service.

* * * * *

Albert Newey was interviewed by a reporter when leaving the Law Courts. He was in abject misery over the fact that his sister and her eldest son had received such long custodial sentences. Asked if his firm would survive the scandal that had occurred, he answered that the firm was in a stronger financial position now than it had been since the mid-1970's.

"But won't you be repaying the half a million pounds that is owed to Customs and Excise?"

"Oh no," Albert Newey had replied, "it isn't my firm that owes the money, it's Precious Metals 1937 Limited and they went into liquidation six months ago."